WATER FALL

BY
KEIR FARRELL

Published by
Celeste Books
57 Jacklins Approach
Bottesford
Notts
DN16 3GB

Cover and design by Celeste Books

Cover photograph by Etienne Marais (etiennemarais.com) via pexels.com, Creative Commons Zero Licence (CC0)

.

Typeface: Georgia 10pt

Printed by Createspace

ISBN-10   0-9565741-6-5
ISBN-13   978-0-9565741-6-9
GTIN-14   0 97 80956 57416 9

ACKNOWLEDGEMENTS

Flintstone, Ian Melville, Boecopter, Paul Sengupta, Charles Hunt, Mercianmarcus, Dave W, Gertie, Reptile Smile, TheFarmer, Foxmoth, Talkdownman, MercianMarcus, Davef77, Derryn, Backpacker, Neilmurg, JoeC, Chevron: the aircraft choices and aerial scenes were done under the critical gaze of these guys from the community on the flyer.co.uk forums, and if I got anything wrong, it's entirely down to me!

Genuine encouragement is a scarce resource, and Pete Casey and Mike Downing came through when I needed it most. Pete, on his own journey of discovery (see *ascentoftheamazon.com*), is also a source of much inspiration. Go Pete!

Great thanks to Caleb Foale, Geoff Hope-Terry, and Martin Shead for 'giving a damn', and for providing invaluable ideas and critique at various stages of the book.

Finally, great thanks to Rabea Garari, Dawn Rocca and Garry Yule for their amazing support in dark hours. You see what you've done now...?

For Naice and Aaron

PREFACE

Thirty years ago, the port of Marseille moved 45,000 cubic metres of water via converted oil tankers to drought-stricken areas in Spain and Italy (eppm.com) A long-term contract between the Indian city of Sitka and Alaska for the supply of Alaskan freshwater by Ultra-Large Crude Container (ULCC) vessels has been in place since 2008 (KCAW Raven Radio).

In December 2011, Peru's Limón Dam project was completed. Constructed by a Brazilian company, the project's tunnel diverts two million cubic metres of water per annum from the Amazon Basin to the western side of the Andes. It is just one of seven irrigation projects planned for the region. (RPP Notícias)

In March 2014, the USA's leading agricultural producer, the state of California, signed drought emergency relief legislation valued at US$687m (CNN). It is argued that California's ongoing struggle with drought and wildfires calls into question its ability to continue to provide food for North America into the future.

In the years to 2016, China's "South-to-North" water pipeline transferred 10 billion cubic metres of water 2,700 miles across China. (Reuters)

As of 2016, more than 275 hydroelectric projects are planned for the Amazon basin, the majority of which could be constructed in the Andes, whose rivers supply over 90 percent of the basin's sediments and over half its nutrients (Mongabay, September 2017).

The Amazon River system, containing a fifth of the planet's freshwater, recently fell to its lowest level in recorded history.

Peru is the second largest cocaine producer in the world, while the USA is the largest cocaine consumer. The value of the international drugs trade is estimated to be more than half a trillion dollars per year. (talkingdrugs.org)

In 2016 the American president assured supporters that climate change is "a hoax", and promised to 'make America great again', 'whatever it takes'. After withdrawing from multilateral trade agreements, the USA is looking for new partners to do business with...

1

Wet to the bone though he was, and weighed down by a hundred pounds of gear in his rucksack, Jack McCrae still cut an imposing figure. In the gloom of the bruise-dark sky and torrential rain, each flash of lightning lit up his streaming wet, military poncho and made his six-foot frame appear even broader than it was. His movements were confident; his pace measured. Even the water that drummed and crashed as it fell, and that cascaded from his bush hat when he bent his head to watch the treacherous track, did not slow the young man down.

He strode purposefully along the trail, resigned to the discomfort, paying close attention to his footing, and deliberating the best way to keep dry in the rainforest. Since transitioning from the cold, dry, brightness of the Peruvian altiplano to the warm and humid forested slopes of the Andes, this was the worst tropical thunderstorm he had experienced. Not only that, but in earlier downpours he had been able to find some shelter, whereas now he was on an exposed ledge that curved crazily around the hills and valleys stretched out before him. The barren track of stone and mud was about the width of a donkey cart, with a sheer cliff face extending above it on one side, and an impossibly steep ravine clawing at it on the other. Cut through the fringes of the largest forest on earth, the path afforded not a single tree for shelter. So he just walked on, deep in thought.

The poncho had worked well for the first five minutes of the storm, but the rain came down so hard it simply bounced off the ground and soaked everything underneath. With the heat generated under the waterproof fabric, he soon found himself sweating, and everything he wore was quickly saturated with either precipitation or perspiration. Ponchos, he decided, were not a serious piece of kit.

"Still, only another three thousand miles to the Atlantic," he said aloud, summoning a mental map of his planned route along the

Amazon. He smiled at the thought, revelling in the idea of the hardships to be endured and the extreme physical and mental demands that would be placed on him in the months ahead. This was the right place for him. He felt the deafening solitude wrap itself around him and knew that here, alone, his life was measured only by the simple decisions he made for survival. He depended on no-one, and no-one depended on him. Success meant another day, or another step; failure meant death. His smile faded, and his jaw muscles tightened against a sudden flash of anger that blazed in his eyes. *His death, and his death alone.*

He blinked away the distracting thoughts, and decided that this would be a good time to make sure his GPS worked in these extreme conditions. He reached up, pulled the little unit off his shoulder strap, and brought it out from under the poncho. As he pressed the button to wake the screen, he felt a tiny buzz of vibration. For an instant he thought it was the GPS, but then he felt it again, more strongly. He stopped walking and stared down through the rain at the path. Another pulse of movement. A longer one. Two more. Then the whole mountain seemed to shake.

He felt himself losing balance on ground that was suddenly moving, lurching, cracking. It was like trying to balance on a trampoline with someone else bouncing on it. He staggered closer to the cliff face and pressed himself against it, but the shaking was getting worse. It was so bad now that he could hardly stand. A large crack opened beneath his feet. He jumped to the left and watched as the crack widened in a fraction of a second, and tore up the trail to his right. A huge section of it slid away, breaking apart and tumbling down the ravine.

He moved further left, to get as far as possible from the gap, but just as he thought he had reached a safer point, a boulder the size of a fridge crashed down onto the path, and more cracks appeared under his feet. They radiated out in an instant, left and right, and the ground began to disintegrate. He felt the trail collapse beneath him, and then he was falling. A lightning flash gave him a momentary glimpse of the whole abyss opening up below him, and then he hit something hard. He was spinning around, being carried down the ravine. Now he was face down, and he felt himself being smothered in a deluge of mud and water. He tried to turn, struggling to breathe. He sucked in a great lungful of air, and then something smacked into the side of his head and he felt the world slipping away. The noise and the shaking and the lightning faded.

Peace. Quiet. Darkness.

KEIR FARRELL

2

"Excellent! Excellent shot! I cannot compete with this, Mister Adam." The use of a title plus a first name was the usual way of being respectfully friendly, and the Peruvian Presidential Adviser smiled broadly at the American. His even, arctic-white teeth caught the sun perfectly, and his painstakingly stubbled face shone with confidence and regular over-indulgence.

The lush, crisp, eighth green of the well-manicured *Los Incas* golf course stood out clearly against the shimmering backdrop of the parched, grey-brown Andean foothills, but Adam Torres still had to shade his eyes and squint to follow the ball as it arced down, took a slightly lucky bounce and rolled to within six feet of the hole.

"*Gracias. Eras muy amable,*" he finally replied. "*Usted–*"

The Adviser held up a deprecating finger and waggled it at Torres. "English only, please. I want to practise my English, remember?"

"Of course, *señor,*" Torres agreed, sticking safely to the more respectful title alone. "But I can't let my guard down when your short game is so good," he added, relaxing and leaning on his club.

The Adviser walked to his own ball, just a few yards away. He lifted his Oakley sunglasses briefly to scan the edges of the fairway where an audience of security personnel stood in stony-faced contemplation, then concentrated on his shot. "Well, we'll see, we'll see," he said. He addressed the ball carefully and swung as smoothly as his belly allowed.

They stood together, watching as the ball flew low, fading slightly. Of the two men, the Peruvian was the taller, but Torres had the more athletic build, and the relaxed, alert stance of someone who is physically fit. The ball bounced twice and spun into a green-side bunker.

The Adviser shook his head. "You see?" He shrugged nonchalantly. "I believe it is the pressure, you know."

They walked back to the gleaming Garia electric golf buggy they were sharing, and swung themselves into the tan leather seats via polished titanium supports. As it took off with a slight lurch, the Adviser steered it onto the cart path and glanced across at his guest.

"Look, Mister Adam, I am a simple man, you know? Competition and confrontation – these are not for me. I like everything honest, simple, easy. No competition; no confrontation. Me, I like everyone to be happy and relaxed, you know?"

Torres nodded. "Certainly. It is the same with me, señor." He paused for a second as the Adviser manoeuvred the cart clumsily around an inconvenient bush. "But as they say, you can't keep everyone happy all the time."

"Ah, no indeed." The Adviser shook his head. "It is difficult. Very difficult."

Torres' facial muscles barely moved, except for the slight twitch of an eyebrow and a colder set to the habitually narrowed brown eyes. His short black hair was combed straight back from a pronounced widow's peak, and he was dressed with expensive, understated precision. A strong, oval face and olive skin gave him his playboy Latino looks, but the Roman nose and pronounced jaw line were strangely at odds with everything else, and the permanent frown and piercing eyes promised all the fun and warmth of liquid nitrogen. He stared ahead.

"There is a lot of pressure on us at the moment, over this question of drug seizures," he began. "It's alarming how information gets out. There are so many sources. I received a copy of a report this week complaining about what the authors said was 'a substantial increase' in Peruvian cocaine production, and a 'significant' lack of drugs seizures. You know how it is, I'm sure. And of course they demand action – results – a clamping down, and all the rest of it." He finished the sentence but continued to stare straight ahead.

"Hmm. I can see how that could be an embarrassment for you," said the Adviser, noncommittally.

"Frankly sir, yes it is. Particularly given our close relationship now with your administration, when people are expecting us all to be working together—"

"And we *are*, Mister Adam, we *are!*" the Adviser cut in emphatically.

Torres nodded, and put on a well-practised, mechanical smile. "Yes indeed. I know we are. I believe that everyone is pleased with the level of cooperation, and I know my President is satisfied with the level of financial commitment we have made. Including the transfer of yesterday, of course." He paused and smiled again.

A look of something approaching irritation flashed in the Adviser's eyes before he too nodded and smiled. "Certainly."

Torres continued. "The joint development businesses are also adequately funded, and income from, um, *domestic activities*," he placed some emphasis on the phrase, "are increasing satisfactorily."

"*Sin ninguna duda.*" The Adviser's face brightened again and became more animated as he nodded enthusiastically and steered the cart to scatter a group of inquisitive Black-necked Stilts that had wandered onto the fairway. "Hah! Damned things," he cawed happily, as the birds flapped strenuously into the air. He steered back towards the green. "And we are getting close to the date for the first consignment, are we not, Mister Adam?"

"We are, señor, although there is still one station to power up, and that will give us only one complete line so far."

"Only one line! Ha ha!" The Adviser brought the cart to a sudden stop, threw back his head and laughed. "But just that one line is amazing, don't you think?"

Torres nodded again. "Certainly," he said without much emotion.

The Adviser looked across at him, mock concern on his face. "But seriously, my friend. It is what you Americans would call a 'game changer', is it not? Unthinkable - unimaginable - four years ago, and now it is a reality! Anyone would agree it is a wonderful thing. The USA gets what it so desperately needs, and we sell more of our traditional products."

"It is an incredible feat of engineering, for sure," said Torres, "Although I'm not sure everyone would see it as 'wonderful'."

The Adviser's smile faded, and he started the cart off again. He looked thoughtful for a few moments. "Ah, no doubt you mean the Brazilians, no?"

Torres said nothing.

"But they are *burros* - they know nothing. They do not even know what day of the week it is. I mean, one of their companies is helping us build it. Ha!"

"Yes. But we must keep some of the old supply lines open for those *traditional* products of yours. We must keep some going in their direction. We have stressed the importance of this many times, señor."

"Yes, yes. Of course, Mister Adam. It is agreed. We don't want any angry Brazilians on our doorstep."

"No."

"Although, with your help, I'm sure we could - how would you say it? - I'm sure we could *see them up*, if we needed to."

Torres nodded. "Off."

"See them *off*. Yes - that's it - thank you! I'm sure we could see them all off, isn't that right, Mister Adam?"

"With all due respect, Señor *Consejería*, that is not on the cards. Never was; never will be." Torres used the Adviser's title and spoke with a clipped formality that could not be mistaken.

The Adviser gave him a sharp look, but said nothing.

"So, as I was saying," Torres continued smoothly, "we have all these people looking for results, and my superiors feel that we must give them something soon, if we are to avoid any, um - let's say, any *complications*. In fact, I am directed to provide a progress report in the next twenty four hours reassuring my superiors that plans are well in hand to produce a result."

The Adviser stopped the cart gently by the green, and as they selected their clubs, he leaned over and placed his hand somewhat heavily on Torres' shoulder.

"My friend, do not look so serious. Do not worry so much. Enjoy your golf." He turned his head away for a moment, as if checking for something, and then looked back, staring straight into Torres' eyes. "I – personally – assure you that we are doing everything in our power to work together on this, and you can tell your people that we will have some good news – some *significant* news – very soon, with respect to the seizures. Very soon indeed."

Torres nodded, his poker face unmoved. "Well, my government will be very pleased to hear that, señor. And of course good results from our joint operations will help secure the ongoing funding we all need."

"Exactly, exactly." The Adviser's teeth showed again in a half smile. "None of us really wants any 'complications', do we? That would be most regrettable – for *all* of us – don't you think?"

They looked intently at each other for a second before the Adviser squeezed Torres' shoulder and abruptly released his grip, throwing his head back and laughing.

Torres nodded gravely. "You are absolutely right, as always, señor. I'm sure my people can be persuaded to be patient for another few days."

"*Maravilloso*," said the Adviser. "Persuade them, my friend, persuade them." He motioned to the green with his left hand. "Now, let us see if I can rescue this hole, shall we...?" he asked, turning and leading the way towards the green.

3

A slim, middle-aged man with thinning, fair hair looked up to one of the screens in his office, and reached for a remote control. He turned up the sound and studied the screen.

"...so I think there's every chance he'll pull it off," a man was saying on a CNN current affairs panel. He leaned forward and tapped the table. "And a sad day for US democracy, it will be."

"Oh come *on*, John," said one of the other participants, and the camera cut to a grey-haired, immaculately coiffured woman. "Even *you* would have to admit he's been the best President the US has had in a hundred years?"

"Damned right," breathed the man in the office. His eyes briefly followed the scrolling banner on the screen that displayed the news item they were debating – SENATOR CALLS VOTE ON THIRD TERM UNCONSTITUTIONAL – and then he turned the volume down again and discarded the remote.

In his left hand he was holding a copy of Adam Torres' latest faxed report, headed 'PERGEN Update', and after skimming it again, he fed it carefully through a large shredder that stood next to his desk. He abruptly stood up, snatched his jacket from the back of his chair, and walked quickly out of the office and down the corridor.

After negotiating three security checks and two elevators, and descending a long, spotlessly clean escalator, he finally reached the White House metro system. It was warm in the lower levels of the complex, and beads of sweat were forming on his brow as he sat down. The ride gave him a few minutes to compose himself before another brisk walk and a final security check brought him to the briefing room. He pressed the buzzer and waited for the electronic bolts to withdraw, then he opened the door and entered. As the door swung closed again, he walked briskly across the room and sat down at a large conference table to join four other men.

"Thanks for coming, Mr Jensen," the man at the head of the table said flatly. His heavy jowls wobbled as he shifted his portly, middle-aged body to make himself more comfortable. His careworn, pockmarked face creased in concentration, and his massive bald head shone in the harsh glare of the over-bright lighting. "There are a few things on the agenda, but we all know the most urgent at this time is the DUMAR project." He paused for a brief murmur of assent, and then turned to Jensen. "So, Robert, what do you have for us?"

The highly polished table was absent of the usual paraphernalia of business meetings. There were no pens, no papers, no diaries scattered around, and Jensen did not add any now. Instead, his eyes narrowed slightly and his gaze shifted momentarily, in concentrated recall.

"Everything is under control. The final installation on line A will be finished soon and the whole line will go live next month. The first shipment is scheduled to depart shortly after that. Facilities Stateside are complete and have been handed over to the military."

"Okay, good. Anything we need to action on our side?"

"No...," said Jensen, drawing the word out slightly. "Not at this point, no."

The bald man looked at him doubtfully before continuing. "And what about U-PED?" he asked. The US-Peruvian Eradication of Drugs Treaty had been in force ever since the Mexican border wall had been completed. It was one of the key hard-line treaties the administration had negotiated in Latin America, and was held up as a shining illustration of the success of the President's tough stance on drugs and immigration.

"We have the reassurances we wanted, and we can expect a major operation very soon, with credit shared between Peru, Brazil and the DEA.

"Can't come soon enough, Robert."

"I understand that, and I'm satisfied they'll deliver something within a few weeks. Advisory information should start coming through normal channels in the next couple of days."

"Fair enough. What about security?"

"Good. I'm satisfied that all the work done since our last meeting is unattributable. As it stands now, the only person – apart from us – with any significant overview is our man in-country."

The tall, thin man sitting immediately opposite Jensen sat forward. "What?" he said sharply. "Are you talking about PERGEN? I thought he was out already. We agreed it was an unacceptable vulnerability. If the shit hit the fan over there—"

"*If,*" Jensen cut in. "It's a very slim chance, and it wouldn't make a damned bit of difference," he went on, his voice hardening slightly. "We still have complete deniability, whatever angle you come at it from. There are no records linking the projects – no paper, and nothing electronic. We're clean. Sure, someone might moralise about the agency's close relations with this group or that group, but it's normal – the usual bullshit that hits the streets every day."

The thin man shook his head. "Dammit Robert, we agreed months back – this is too big to leave anything to chance. You were to remove PERGEN, and get him the hell back here where we can look after him. What's he still doing, anyway? The work is complete, and all the commercial stuff will be handled by the companies now. We don't need that level of oversight any more. It's too high a risk."

Jensen nodded. "That's what was originally agreed, I know, but the reality is that juggling the interests of the military, the politicians and the Sendero at the same time, needs someone *in situ* –"

"Aw come on, Robert," the thin man interrupted. "That's all being done at arm's length now. The only people still supposed to be there are the mopping up team."

Jensen sighed heavily and held up his hands. "Look, it was my decision; my responsibility, okay?" He lowered his hands and placed them carefully on the table. "And, might I add, I communicated it to you all at the time, and no objections were raised."

"I never agreed to it."

It was Jensen's turn to lean forward. "Look, why are we arguing about this now? As I said, it was my decision. The fact is that dealing with terrorists—"

"Freedom fighters," the bald man corrected, without much conviction.

"Freedom fighters, then. Whatever you call them, we're dealing with an organisation with no proper command structure, operating as a bunch of squabbling factions scattered across the country. It's impossible to organise anything unless we have someone on the ground. It's as simple as that. I mean, how do you think the bust was organised?"

The fourth man at the table thrust his head forward a little. He was the only one in military uniform, and its precision-pressed lines, four stars and chest candy contrasted markedly with the sombre suits around him. "Sure. I can see that," he said. "And I agreed with the delay in removing the last link. But that was back in May, Robert."

"I understand that. But it's still complicated. In my opinion, we need someone there until the bust goes through, and maybe a month beyond. He's our guarantee that everything's in place for the go-live, and that we have an asset that can handle any dissent."

"*Dissent*?" said the General, his voice strained in disbelief. "Did I mis-hear you a few minutes go? Didn't you just say that everything was good, or did I dream that bit?"

"It *is* good, General, precisely because we still have someone there – and that's why I believe he should stay for the moment."

"Well it gives me the cold sweats, I don't mind telling you." said the thin man. "He knows too much and he's vulnerable. And if *he's* vulnerable, *we're* vulnerable."

Jensen shook his head. "I don't think so. He doesn't know any of us at this end. All he has is a codename for me as his handler."

"That may be, Robert," said the General, "But he knows the operation, which means he knows *of* us. And that's enough." His lips narrowed as he sucked in a breath. "Shit, I seem to spend most of these meetings reminding everyone what it has cost us in time and money – and people – to keep this confined to the four of us."

"Five," the thin man broke in. "The *five* of us, right?" It seemed to have the effect of stunning everyone for a second or two.

"We're all aware of that," the General snapped. "It doesn't need to be stated."

"With all due respect, General," the thin man continued, "I think it *does* need to be stated. This is a POTUS project." He punctuated the last two words by tapping his finger on the table, and stared at everyone in turn, as he continued. "Personally, I like to remember that we're not alone in all this. It also helps keep me on my toes." He finished with his eyes locked with the General's.

The General's face coloured slightly and he glowered across the table. The bald man cleared his throat loudly and lifted his hand a little from the table. "Okay, point taken." He turned to Jensen. "It *is* risky, Robert, for sure. And the longer PERGEN's in place, the riskier it is." He raised his hand again when Jensen opened his mouth to respond. "I know there's no provable link, but if *any* connection – however tenuous – emerged between us and the activities of the, uh, freedom fighters and their merchandise, the mud could stick. It's a prospect that doesn't bear thinking about." He looked at Jensen, as heads nodded in the short silence.

"So," he asked calmly, "in your opinion, Robert, what's the very earliest we can get him out?"

Jensen replied without hesitation. "As soon as the first shipment leaves port and everything is tidied up."

"Explain?" the bald man prompted.

"It's simple. At that point, everyone in the game has too much invested and, by definition, every part of the jigsaw has been put in place. Any prying eyes would see only a few commercial interests with international contracts, and two governments carrying on a legitimate trade in commodities."

The bald man frowned. "And that's a month from now, correct?"

Jensen nodded. "That's the best-case estimate. However, if we're deciding on a final date for extraction, I'd strongly suggest we allow two months, to cover commissioning, testing and any issues that might arise."

The General's eyebrows shot up. "Oh, don't let's have any issues, for God's sake, Robert," he intoned.

Jensen smiled thinly. "I don't expect any. I'm just being prudent."

The General thought for a second, then sighed. "I suggest six weeks, then."

"It's not leaving much margin for error," said Jensen, frustration clear in his voice.

The bald man's hand rose again. "I understand Robert, but I think it's enough time." He paused. "And I think we could all agree to it," he added, speaking slowly and clearly, as he looked around the table.

The thin man nodded gravely. "Very well. On one condition. If there is the slightest *sniff* of PERGEN being compromised – I mean the merest *hint* – we terminate his contract immediately."

All heads nodded their consent.

"Yes sir," Jensen acknowledged.

"That's agreed, then," the bald man said. "Anything else? What about our illustrious allies?"

"Nothing to report," said Jensen, "We'll have our bust, and the players are all delivering what they promised. There's just the usual whining about resource allocations and what they like to call *bonuses*."

"Bonuses for *what*, for God's sake?" the General cried.

"Just about anything. Every time they do something they think advances our interests, they want to dip their hand in the cookie jar. You know that – you've seen the figures."

The General grunted. "Yeah. But it still sticks in my craw. They're like a pack of dogs."

"Well at least they're *our* dogs," the bald man said, and suddenly smiled. "It doesn't matter, anyway. Once deliveries start, we're in the final phase, and they won't need any more of our money – it'll all come from their own operations. And there'll be plenty of it, too."

The General thought for a moment and then sighed. "What the hell," he said resignedly. "Yeah, I guess you're right." He pushed himself back in his chair and nodded.

"Well then, gentlemen," said the bald man, "It looks as though we may have a success on our hands."

"Five years on," the thin man said, dryly.

Jensen nodded. "More like eight, if you count the original project plan."

"Yes, yes, yes. But a success at last," the bald man said emphatically, leaning forward again, his head bent low as he spoke softly. "All the resource we can handle, and control of half a continent. Right under everyone's nose, and without a shot being fired. By any standard, it's a hell of an outcome, isn't it?"

"Amen to that," said Jensen quietly, as smiles began to crack around the table.

4

A few people among the group sitting at the table on the small dais had the decency to look down, but most of them just sat there, staring at her.

"Well what do you expect, Carla?" said one of them, finally. "It's not our fault. There'll always be extremists in any organisation. How can we stop them?"

Carla da Silva had a physical presence that belied her average height and slim build. While she was clearly doing her best to remain composed, her emotions showed plainly enough and her handsome, angular Indian face was now almost ablaze with passion. Her hazel eyes narrowed and her normally full lips stretched thinly in anger, while her chin pointed out slightly in defiance and a flush appeared across her high cheekbones. "They're nothing but criminals!" she cried. "You saw the footage of them looting the shops and breaking windows, didn't you? We should speak out against them. Disown them. Tell them they're not welcome. Tell the police about them—"

"Pah!" came a cry from the back of the room, among the crowd that had come to take part in the third official meeting of the nascent anti-corruption movement *Grupo Contra Corrupção*. "The police are as bad as the rest of them!"

"Yes, well if you want to go down *that* route," Carla continued, "everyone in the country's corrupt! So why are we bothering at all?"

She raised her voice again to make herself heard above the jeering that ensued at this last statement. "There's good and bad in the police force, just like everywhere else. You know it and I know it!"

The room grew quieter as she went on.

"We need to appeal to the *good*, that's all. Let's face it, if we talked more to the police, we could have even more of an impact than we've already had. Do you really think they *like* these idiot politicians? With all the corruption and the stupid bureaucracy? You think they don't want decent hospitals and a proper education for their kids?"

At this, everyone started talking at once, the noise levels increased, and within a few moments the meeting descended into a shouting match.

"Listen everyone! Listen!" cried a tall, well-dressed man with glasses, getting up from his seat near Carla and raising his hands. "Listen for a moment *please!*" He spoke with a polished, educated São Paulo accent, and his voice cut easily through the clamour.

He waited patiently as everyone who had packed into the little meeting room slowly calmed down.

"Look," he continued, "I think Carla has a good point–" The groans from the crowd made him pause and hold up his hands again. "But I also think that if we don't keep going – if we don't keep the initiative – we'll get nothing at all."

"Damned right!" came a shout from the middle of the room, followed by a general buzz of agreement.

Carla started to get to her feet, but the man motioned her to sit.

"We know that Carla is one of our best campaigners. Look at her work here. Look what she achieved in Rio – in São Paulo. A lot of you wouldn't be at this meeting now, if it weren't for her, right?"

There were lots of nods of approval, some more enthusiastic than others.

"I think we owe it to her and to ourselves to take some time to think about how we can – eventually – get rid of the extremists. After all, we're not terrorists, are we?" He paused for breath and then went on quickly, before anyone had a chance to interrupt him. "No! Of course we aren't!"

"No!" came a significant chorus.

"Okay, then. Now, I think we should ask Carla to carry on doing what she does best – recruiting and organising for us in her own brilliant way – and in the meantime, we will get our heads together here to work out a solution to our problem."

Carla knew she was being out–manoeuvred, but although she was seething inside, she also knew this was not the time to be creating division. So she sat and did her best to summon a bit of grace.

"We should be asking her to go up north," the man continued. "To go and help our colleagues up there mobilise. With Carla organising things, I *know* they can be more effective."

"Well they couldn't be *less* effective, could they?" came a cry, followed by some laughter.

"Yeah. Let her sort it out!" came another.

"Get them organised, Carla!" came a few more.

The man held up his hand for quiet again. "Only when our network – our movement – is truly national, will the politicians sit up and take notice as they should. Look what we've achieved up to now – and think what we'll achieve as a national force!"

The argument was over. Carla accepted stoically the pats on the shoulder and the shouted accolades about her earlier work. She made the right noises for the rest of the meeting and was one of the last to make her way out of the building. As she reached the door, the tall man with glasses was waiting to speak to her.

"*E aí?*" he asked, smiling at her as he held the door. *So...?*

"So what?" Carla replied, shrugging. "I was railroaded," she added matter–of–factly as she walked through the door.

"No you weren't. You could have refused."

She stopped and turned round.

"Look, Marcus, I don't mind trailing half-way round Brazil garnering support. I agree the more the movement is nationalised and expanded, the better. But you'd better make quite sure you take care of the extremists, or pretty soon you're going to have blood on your hands. Is that what you want?"

Marcus held up his hands. "Of course it's not what I want. But I also don't want the whole thing to just dry up and wither away. This movement is the first real chance Brazil has had in forty years to change things – to finally sweep away all the crap and get the country on its feet. This is our chance to make a difference and I won't see it slip away just because of a few lunatics on the periphery."

Carla stepped nearer and looked up into his face. "You, my friend, are playing with fire," she said slowly and deliberately. "It's a dangerous game, Marcus. Mark my words."

"Maybe, Carla. Maybe. But I know what I'm doing. I'll take care of it. By the time you come back, it will all be sorted out. You'll see." He smiled.

She looked at him for a second and then sighed. "I hope you're right. I really do."

They exchanged a brief, stiff embrace and the customary kiss on both cheeks, then Carla pulled back. "Good luck Marcus," she said, turning quickly and walking away.

5

Tied to a makeshift A–frame stretcher and blindfolded, Jack had no way of knowing exactly where he was. Dragged for countless hours along some jarring trail, barely conscious, he had precious little to go on. The pungent scent of growth and decay might be from any part of any rainforest in the world. The river he heard rushing by, could be any one of a thousand nameless streams and rivers that twisted through the tangled jungle vegetation and bounced over the sharp boulders exposed along the forest floor.

A satellite traversing the upper slopes of the Andes would not pick out one in a hundred of these rivers. Originating pure and clear, high in the mountains, they criss–crossed and cascaded down the mountains, joining, dividing and joining again, before eventually uniting to form the greatest river on the planet. His plan had been to walk nearly three thousand miles to the point where they collectively poured fifty million gallons per second of sediment-laden fresh water into the Atlantic Ocean. The plan had been contingent on not falling down a ravine and being kidnapped.

He had spent days hoping and praying for rescue. He had a contact in Cuzco and an extraction plan in case of emergency, and he imagined a dedicated, competent, army of people applying themselves and their technology to tracking him down. But the plan would not kick in for three weeks, and he knew that in any case satellites were blind to the paths he was travelling, and that even an observer in a low–flying aircraft would see only an undulating carpet of green, stretching unbroken to the distant horizon. If anyone were looking for him or his captors, they would find no trace. They were off the radar. Invisible.

In lucid moments, he tried to reconstruct their journey in his mind, starting from his last-known point of reference – the precarious ledge that had collapsed in the torrential rain of the thunderstorm, dumping him and half a ton of mud at the bottom of a ravine – but there were too many variables. How long ago was the fall? What direction had they taken? How quickly had they been moving? The pain from his injured leg, the convulsive shivering, the crazy hallucinations and dark dreams from his fever: all had left him with only the vaguest notion of time or place.

Of his captors, all he could tell so far was that there were at least three people in the group, although he thought he could feel the presence of more. When they stopped, always in the dark, they sometimes took his blindfold off, but never untied his hands. They propped him against a tree and fed him some sort of cold, watery pap, but even with his eyes so sensitive to the slightest amount of light now, he saw little beyond the occasional flicker of a torch light. When he could manage it, they let him stand for his toilet, although his clothes were already rancid with the smell of stale urine, faeces and vomit.

Although he had no way of knowing for certain, he had long since decided that these people were narco-terrorists – Peru's equivalent of the FARC guerrillas in Colombia. Why else would they be holding him? No doubt they would eventually issue some ridiculous ransom demand, and keep moving him around until either he died or they got what they wanted. Or both. In any case, Jack was not at all sure who would want him back badly enough to pay for the privilege, and the opportunity to contemplate his lack of family and friends had been as welcome as a kick in the teeth.

But today, for the first time, he felt less utterly forlorn than on previous days. Today he was able to keep his mind just that little bit clearer; to flex and feel his limbs and joints occasionally. Someone had bandaged his right leg, but he had not been able to examine it, and could not tell how badly damaged it had been in the fall. The level of background pain had certainly diminished, so maybe the enforced period of lying on his back had at least been good for something. Now, his thoughts contemplated his immediate survival. More than this, his heart beat strongly on a faint but rising hope of getting through this ordeal and out the other side.

He kept his new-found sensibility to himself for the moment, feigning unconsciousness or febrile convulsions throughout the day, while he concentrated on building a better picture of his surroundings and his predicament. Now, even under the blindfold, he knew the day was drawing to a close. The edge had gone from the tropical heat, making it past three in the afternoon. Within two hours, the sun would disappear behind the mountains to the west, and an hour or so later, night would descend.

As he lay wondering what new trials tonight's camp might bring, a conversation started. He listened intently to try to catch the words. His Spanish was not fluent, and these people seemed to chop and change from Spanish to another language – Quechuan, he supposed – but some of the words and phrases were clear enough. If he could just concentrate more...but the damned pain that shot through his body with every stone or rock or channel or rut they hit, made it almost impossible.

Then suddenly they came to a halt. Jack heard raised voices up ahead. He stiffened instinctively, eyes wide open under the blindfold. He held his breath, straining to understand the voices. Something was different; the atmosphere more tense. Someone was shouting now. He heard some muttering behind him. A voice cut through – hissing, as if its owner did not want others to hear, although the word *estúpido* was absurdly clear, and hung strangely in the air. Movement. Another raised voice. Someone running. The sound of something heavy hitting wood. His stretcher fell to the ground, knocking the breath out of him. Adrenaline flooded his system. More running. Footsteps passing him. He struggled wildly with the ropes that bound him. No one tried to stop him. A confusion of voices; someone screaming and cursing. A thump; crashing undergrowth. He struggled free of the ropes, and as he tore at his blindfold he heard shots ring out – one, two, a burst, two more single shots – deafeningly loud in the heavy humidity of the forest. Screams. A choking, rasping sound. Another shot. He launched himself awkwardly from the stretcher and made a hobbling, painful run for it – away from the trail, down the steep riverbank. He waded in to the startlingly cold water, fell, picked himself up, and stumbled across. He emerged sodden wet, but with every nerve in his body on fire, and he scrambled rapidly up the banks and flung himself into the tree line on the other side, gasping and cursing his weakness.

He waited for the inevitable sound of people calling out, chasing after him, splashing across the river. He concentrated on getting into a position from which he could defend himself, and then he stopped, his ear cocked. Beyond the fading echoes of the last gunshot, there was no noise. Nothing but an edgy silence, as if the birds, animals and insects had caught their collective breath and were waiting for something. The harshness of his own breathing surprised him. He could not understand what had happened, but at that moment, he really did not care: he was alive, and he was free – and he meant to stay that way. So he waited, lying quietly, watching a thin sliver of smoke drift slowly up through the trees.

6

He tried to count the seconds off, but his mind played tricks on him. How much time had passed now – a minute? Ten? Twenty? It was hard to tell. He automatically glanced down at his wrist, but his watch had long since been lost or stolen. Damn. The light was fading for sure, but perhaps it was a growing storm, rather than approaching nightfall. It was still very quiet, and his breathing seemed disproportionately loud, although some of the normal forest sounds were cautiously starting up again. As if to make the point, the raucous cries of some macaws suddenly shattered the silence and startled him.

He stared up to the canopy. His first instincts had been right – the valley was in deepening shadow, and probably in another hour visibility would be reduced to almost nothing. If he stayed where he was, he might be safe for a while, but he would be stuck here all night, just waiting for someone to come and put a gun to his head in the morning. To hell with that – it was time to move.

He peered round the tree and looked across towards the trail. He could see three – no, four – bodies lying motionless. He felt his throat grow dry with a mixture of hope and fear, and he spent another minute carefully scanning the area. He found he was holding his breath again. Suddenly he coughed; almost laughed. Was he dreaming, or was he in some sort of shock? Had his captors just shot themselves to bits? All of them? He closed his eyes for a moment. It was so ludicrous; so sublime.

He unwrapped the over-tight, filthy bandage from his leg and inspected the wound, wincing as blood pulsed anew around a livid, three-inch scar down the calf of his right leg. He poked it gingerly and found that the wound was quite closed, although there was a thumb-sized, puckered gouge out of the calf muscle. He got to his feet and limped gingerly down the bank and through the water, climbing up the other side and back onto the trail. He was shivering now – from either the descending cold or the shock.

Probably both, he thought.

He stopped and shook his hands and arms vigorously. Better. Then he cautiously approached the first two bodies, about ten yards beyond the abandoned stretcher. They lay only a few feet from one another. One was face up, eyes staring wide – completely lifeless, although no blood was evident. He studied the second one, face down in a large pool of congealing blood that was already surrounded by hundreds of black ants. He looked for some signs of life, but there were none.

There were two guns by the side of the bodies – a battered old revolver, and an AK47. He picked up the revolver. It was heavy, and felt good in his hand. He bent over and prodded the second body with the gun. Nothing. He turned and walked down to a third body – face up, with a neat black hole in his head and his tongue protruding through his teeth. Flies were buzzing around his head and crawling over his face. A huge bull of a man, probably the owner of the deep voice he had heard from time to time. Another one quite dead. Amazing. He removed a machete and a black pistol from the ground beside the man, and moved on to the next body. Face down. No sign of life. He leaned over, and was about to poke it, when it moved.

"Shit," he cried, staggering back unsteadily. He flung the machete and the pistol to one side and pointed the revolver with both hands, lifting the gun so it was aimed at the head. All he had to do was pull the trigger and he was free of the whole pack of them. His lips drew back in a snarl as his finger tightened on the trigger.

Do it.

The body twitched again, and the head moved. Jack jerked the gun to the right just as he pulled the trigger. The bullet kicked up mud a few yards away, and the noise of the single shot seemed thunderous, so that he found himself backing away and quickly checking for movement among the other bodies before he returned his attention to the survivor. He stood with the gun pointed off to the side, watching the man crawl a few feet then turn over to face him. Jack braced himself again and aimed the gun carefully, but as he did so, he realised that the person staring at him with the expression of a cornered cat was not the pockmarked bandit scum he had expected, but a woman.

Her short black hair was matted with blood, which had also run down the side of her face, and there was a long slash down her shirt, from shoulder to waist, dark with blood. He backed off further, still pointing the gun at her, while he decided what to do. She sat up slowly, shaking her head. She tried to get up, but her eyes glazed over, flickered slightly, and she fell forward. Instinctively, Jack went to her, dropping the gun to one side. She did not resist as he supported her, then turned her slightly and laid her on her back. He pulled her legs around so she was lying straight, and as he started to stand up, she lifted her arm.

"*Las otras*," she croaked.

"What?" asked Jack.

"*Las otras*," she repeated, more urgently. She was clearly disorientated and probably in some pain. Her pale, dry lips were drawn back and her dark eyes stared weakly at him through drooping lids. He bent down to her again and she grabbed his arm. "*Cuanto las otras?*" she asked. What about the others? She released his arm, and Jack stood up.

"Dead. *Muerto*," he said with grim satisfaction, assuming she was concerned for her friends. He drew his thumb across his neck with some relish, to make sure she understood. "And I don't see why I shouldn't kill you, you son of a bitch. Who the hell *are* you? Where are we? What the *fuck* is going on?" He picked up the gun again and pointed it at her, and she obviously recognised the danger in his anger and frustration. She raised her hand, palm towards him. "No! Pare! Lo siento. Lo siento. Sorry. Not me – not my decision, okay? Okay?"

Jack stood over her, his face a mask of rage, the gun still pointed at her head.

"Okay?" she repeated, almost shouting at him now

Jack blinked, breathed deeply, and allowed the gun to drop to his side.

"Yeah, right. Whatever," he said with disgust. He knew damned well who this shower were anyway – narcos, by whatever name. He might hate her, but he knew he could not just kill her in cold blood. Right now, he needed to concentrate on getting away from this place.

"*Cuantas?*" the woman asked again.

"What?" said Jack, vaguely.

"*Cuantas personas? Cuantas muertas?*"

"Uh, three – *trés*," he said, holding up three fingers and shaking them at her.

She shook her head emphatically. "*No, no. Cinco!*"

"Five? What are you talking about?" he said, before the significance of what she was saying got through to him. The hairs stood up on the back of his neck, and he backed further away, looking around anxiously. He raised the gun again and pointed it at her. "Stay here," he said, cocking the trigger to make his point.

He kicked the other weapons down the bank towards the river, then made his way back up the trail. As he passed the bodies, he uncocked the trigger of the revolver and stuffed it in his waistband. He picked up the AK47 and examined it. It looked like an old AKM, with a badly chipped wooden stock and a body worn shiny with use. Like just about every soldier or ex–soldier in the world, Jack was familiar with it, and after a cursory glance to confirm that the safety was off and the bolt charged, he moved on. Grimacing from the dull pain in his leg, he walked a good hundred yards beyond the first two bodies before turning and retracing his steps, watching carefully for any signs of life.

On his way back, he collected two small backpacks and dropped them beside the woman, who lay still now, her eyes closed. He wondered vaguely whether she might have conveniently died, as he walked ahead to explore another hundred yards or so in front of their position.

When he was quite satisfied there was no one out there, he made his way back and sat down near the woman. He put the rifle to one side and pulled the packs across to rummage through them. The noise brought her round.

"*E allí?*" she mumbled. "*Cuantas?*"

Jack held up his three fingers again, and she tried to raise herself up, failed, and fell back heavily. He ignored her now in favour of organising his getaway. He found a small, dirty first-aid bag in one of the packs, with a few bits of lint and a couple of plastic bottles of iodine. He pulled one out and placed it on the ground next to the woman. He stood and made his way over to the big corpse, where he found and removed a hunting knife attached to a webbed belt. He tried to roll the body over, but it was wedged between a rock and some saplings and was too big to move. Instead, he used the knife to slit the back of the shirt from top to bottom and cut off various strips of material. He searched the other bodies too, removing a shirt, trousers and an aluminium water bottle from one. He even found that one of them had Jack's good trekking boots and even his socks. He pulled them off with maniacal glee, took everything back to where the woman was, and placed it in a little heap. She had managed to sit up, but still looked groggy and dazed. Picking up the pieces of material he had stripped from the big guy, Jack went down to the river with the water bottle. After drinking as much as he needed, he filled it again, soaked the material, and returned.

He held the bottle for her as she drank, and then took it back. He pointed to the iodine and placed the strips of material next to it. She looked at him uncomprehendingly.

"Oh for God's sake," he muttered, suddenly feeling angry with himself for not being able to just shoot her. He knelt down, and she offered no resistance as he bent her forward and poured the rest of the water on her head to wash the scalp wound. It had already stopped bleeding, and he decided it had looked worse than it really was. Afterwards, he flushed it with iodine, ignoring the woman's yelps, and bent to look more closely at the body wound. He started to clean out the top of the wound at the shoulder, but this produced fresh blood, and he could see bits of cloth still stuck in what was quite an ugly gash. He gave up and sat down again, suddenly feeling exhausted.

The woman shook her head, picked up a piece of cloth and dabbed gingerly at the wound for a few moments. Then she stopped, drew a long breath and turned an angry face to him.

"*Corra, gringo!*" she said. Run!

Surprised at first, Jack looked at her in irritation and pointed to his injured leg. "*Corra* my ass."

She raised her eyebrows and stared at him.

"*Cinco!*" she said again, holding up her fingers to emphasise the point.

He nodded. "Yes, yes, I know. So you said." Bloody woman. He sat back and looked around, considering his options. Maybe she was right. Maybe he should just run – leave the woman and make use of whatever daylight remained to get as far away as possible. His head placed this option at the top of the list, but his heart was interfering as usual.

She reached out and poked his arm.

"More – come – back," she said finally. "More come back."

Her touch and her insistence interrupted his thinking and brought a fresh surge of anger to the surface. "Yes. I get it, for Christ's sake!" He almost shouted. He stared at her coldly. "And no doubt if I go, and leave you here, you'll just lead them straight to me, won't you, you little bitch." He scowled at her.

She looked puzzled.

"Your *amigos* – your *compañeros*, huh?" he said, gesturing along the trail with his arm, and making as if to spit on the ground.

"No." She shook her head. "No! *Not* friends. I will run also." She looked at him and pointed over his shoulder to the forest beyond. She pointed to him and then to herself. "You run – I run."

Jack stared at her in disbelief. She wanted to go with him? Why? Could he trust her? Or would he be better off alone? He wiped the sweat off his face with one of the wet rags, and stared down at his injured leg while he thought.

He had a backpack, some first–aid kit, some clothes and his boots, guns, a decent knife and a few other useful bits and pieces. But he didn't have a map, a compass, or any food to speak of – or very much strength or stamina. If she were being honest about wanting to get away from these people, she would know the area and how to avoid anyone on their trail. They could also divide the weight of the few things they had, and she would know better how to find and prepare food. If she survived her wounds, of course.

He knew he needed to make his mind up fast, and finally he nodded. "Okay," he said. "You and me. We run, right?"

She nodded.

He pointed at her body wound. "But you need to clean that, first." He pointed again. "Clean first," he said. "*Lavar. Limpar?*"

Nodding her understanding, she started to get up. She was clearly still shaky, but with his help she stood and walked down to the river with some rags, the bottle of iodine and the shirt he had taken from one of the bodies. She walked straight into the river and stripped her own shirt off, ducking down and cleaning out her wounds with the rags. Jack stood at the riverbank and watched for a moment, transfixed by the bizarre picture of this bare-breasted woman – young woman – girl – casually bathing a twelve inch knife wound in the river, with hardly so much as a grimace, then he walked up to the trail again.

Working on the body he had left relatively undisturbed, he was able to peel off the shirt. It was covered in blood and ants, but was still a lot better than his own. Picking up his socks on the way, he walked down to the river and washed both shirt and socks. As he was wringing them out, he saw the girl dry her wound, apply the iodine, and finally pull on the new shirt.

Jack helped her back up to the trail, but when she reached down for the pair of trousers Jack had left there, he quickly grabbed them, scowling at her and pointing to his own filthy rags. She shrugged and walked off.

After Jack had pulled his old boots on, they went quickly round the bodies once more, collecting a few other things including food, another machete, some ammunition and a thin nylon tarpaulin, then they loaded up the two backpacks Jack had retrieved. He also found the pistol he had kicked aside earlier, and when the girl shouldered her pack and looked at him expectantly, he knew instinctively what she wanted. He refused to give her a gun, handing her a machete instead. He wrapped the guns in the clothes he had taken, after deciding he would wait until tomorrow and the heat of the day to change into them. He shouldered the AK47 and the pack, and kept the other machete in his hand. She looked at him contemptuously, turned, strode straight into the river, and began walking purposefully downstream. Jack limped after her, finding the weight of the guns a real burden, and hardly believing that he was having trouble keeping up with a girl who had looked like she was about to die just ten minutes earlier.

Less than an hour after the gunfight, they were half a mile away in the middle of the forest, dug in for the night.

7

"What a god-damned crazy place to be working," one of the men complained. "Ten thousand feet up the side of a mountain. The most barren landscape this side of the moon, and no beer or smokes."

"Aw, quit moaning, will you?" said another.

"Yeah. As soon as this baby's on line, we get two weeks in Chimbote and a free ticket home," said a third.

"And you'll never have to work with the locals again."

"Yeah yeah. That's *if* they get their part of the job finished. Some of them couldn't find their ass in the dark."

"Sure they'll finish. All they gotta do is connect up."

One of the workers, a serious-looking young man, stopped what he was doing and put down his wrench. "Say, Ed, how many of these damned stations have we put together now?"

"This is number fifteen for me. But then I've been here since the beginning. You're just a junior." Ed smiled.

"Junior my ass, I got here a week after you, you clown."

"I've still been here the longest. I am the man, my amigo. I am the *man*."

"Bullshit. Tell that to our glorious leader. If anyone's the man, he's the man."

"The Black Widow? Hah – I ain't scared of him."

"Crap. *Everyone's* scared of him. I dunno where they got him from, and I dunno that he knows shit about pumping, but *everyone's* scared of him. And that includes you, Ed."

"Bull," said Ed. He smiled again. "Hey, did I tell you about the time I asked him what this is all about?" He laughed. "'Irrigation', he says, with that dumb frown on his face. Hah – irrigation my ass."

"Yeah. You only told me like a dozen times."

Ed put his tools down. "Yeah, well you usually need telling

everything twelve times, right Junior?" He laughed loudly and the sound echoed strangely around the room, bouncing sharply off the mass of steel pipes and girders they were working on. "Hey, tell you what," he suddenly announced, "I'm going outside for a smoke, okay?"

"Thought you said you didn't have any."

Ed shrugged. "So I lied, right?" He stood up. "You want one or what, Junior?"

"You'll kill yourselves with that shit, man," the third man mumbled with a piece of cable held in his teeth.

"Yeah yeah," said Ed. "We'll be back in a minute, okay?"

"Sure. But don't be too long – we're just about ready to put this mother on line, and I don't want to spend another night up here if I don't have to."

Ed gave him a thumbs-up as the two smokers walked past the control panel, onto the gantry that crossed the gleaming pipes and machinery, and up the steel steps to the heavy external door.

Outside, the cold afternoon sun lashed the parched, dusty, brown terrain. A few stunted cacti grew up through the stones and rocks to a height of a foot or two, and a black vulture, drawn by the team's presence, perched on one of them and spread its wings for a few moments.

They walked round to the side of the building, which afforded some protection from the sun and the dust borne by gusts of wind that blew uphill from the west. Behind them, the mountains ranged for miles; in front, they sloped gradually down to a distant blue haze that marked the Pacific Ocean. Ed drew two cigarettes from his pack and gave one to Junior.

After they lit up, Ed leaned over and patted the brick-and-steel building. "Another neat job, man," he said.

"Yeah. Lot of work, mind you, digging them in like this – nothing much visible on the surface."

"I know. Everyone just the same too, I reckon – not just the ones we've worked on." He took a long drag, and the blue smoke streamed from his nose and mouth as he continued talking. "Once we've gone, and the site's been cleared, it'll just be one harmless little building with a fence round it. You can't even see the pipelines."

"Yeah. Amazing. Protection, probably."

"Or camouflage, right? Although hiding from who or what, I dunno." He took another draw on his cigarette and shook his head. "Asked him about that, too, you know – the Black Widow. He just walked off."

Junior swore softly. "You shouldn't piss him off, Ed. What's the point?"

"Aw, I can't help it. It's all too secretive. Anyways, I'm just being curious, right?"

"Yeah, well I'm not one bit curious. I just want my money and I'm outta here. They can do whatever the hell they like after I'm gone, and good luck to them."

They walked to the end of the building and turned the corner.

"Holy shit!" said Ed. "I didn't even hear that arrive, did you?"

They were staring at a military helicopter parked at the far end of the site. Judging from the stationary rotors and the soldiers milling around it, it had been there for some time. As they watched, they saw some frantic activity develop on the other side of the aircraft, but it was hard to make out exactly what was going on, with the wind whipping up the sand and dust. Then one of the soldiers suddenly pointed in their direction, and it was clear that the two Americans had been spotted. Three people started walking towards the station.

"Jesus, is that who I think it is?" said Junior.

When the wind dropped a little, Adam Torres was easily identifiable as the man in the middle of the small group. He was flanked by two soldiers with automatic rifles in their hands.

"Yep, I reckon so," said Ed.

"Right, that's it, then – I'm off."

"Aw calm down, Junior. He doesn't scare me. Finish your smoke. What's he gonna do – fire you the day before your contract ends?"

"Well, I suppose... say, where are the Peruvian guys?" Junior said. "What happened to them? They were working over there where the chopper is, weren't they?"

Ed shrugged, taking a long draw on his cigarette. He dropped it in the dirt and slowly ground it out with his foot, watching the approaching soldiers raise their guns.

"I dunno, pal, but I don't think I like the look of this at all."

8

Jack and the girl had crossed the river and camped further into the forest. Apart from arranging their single tarpaulin as a cover and clearing the ground a little, there was nothing else they could do to prepare for the night. They ate the same pap that Jack had been fed every day, and which he now found was made from the local staple *farine*, and washed it down with river water and iodine.

He sat propped against a rock, staring unseeingly into the obsidian darkness in the direction he believed his companion lay. He did not trust her, and he had placed the revolver by his side. He touched it every now and again to feel the reassuring coldness, and tried to stay awake as long as he could. His body protested at the slightest movement, and the relief he felt at being free was at odds with a sense of foreboding that kept starting him awake when his eyes began to close. He listened intently to try to catch the sound of the girl's breathing, or the occasional rustle of clothing, but in vain. He thought about calling out a question, and was still working on what it should be, when relief won out over worry, and he succumbed to a deep and dreamless sleep.

He awoke cold, with the pre-dawn mist condensing in his nose. In this steep-sided valley, they would not see the sun until it was well up in the tropical sky, and instead the day began with a gradual infusion of dim, grey-green light. He was vaguely aware that the sound of something falling through the trees had woken him: a nutshell, twigs or leaves discarded by an animal far above them. He looked up and saw a large bird hopping clumsily from one branch to another, sending down a new shower of detritus. The girl was already awake, and was dividing up some more farine. She proffered it with an expressionless face and a faraway look in her eyes.

"*Toma*," she said in such a low voice it hardly carried to his ears.

She pointed to a battered tin with water in it, resting on the ground.

He opened his mouth to say something, but she put her finger to her lips. He stopped himself, and merely breathed out heavily. The noise of it in the heavy silence startled him, and the girl frowned. He simply nodded and concentrated on his farine and water. Questions could wait.

By mute mutual agreement, they collected their things, tidied away any trace of their presence, and made off in a line angled away from the river and climbing gently up the valley side, Jack following about twenty yards behind the girl.

When they had been moving steadily for over an hour, she suddenly stopped. She crouched down, and Jack followed suit, then she pointed down to the river. Jack could not hear or see anything, but he waited in place for several minutes while she squatted on the ground, intensely focused on the direction from which they had come. Finally, motioning with her hands for them to stay low, she started to climb more directly up the steep slope.

It was painful, creeping, progress for Jack. There was no way now that he could avoid placing weight on his injured leg, and in trying to favour it, he was putting an increasing strain on his good one. They worked their way slowly up the valley side, and in spite of regular stops to look and listen behind them, an hour later Jack was reaching his limits. The sun was spilling into the valley now, and even under the canopy, the air was noticeably hotter and more humid. The sweat poured from them, while the thorns on the spindly, tangled stalks and leaves of the scrubby vegetation tore at their clothes and their skin, leaving myriad long, painful welts all over their legs and arms. Jack's breathing became more ragged, and after their last stop, he was struggling badly to get back into any sort of rhythm. He was grateful when they breasted a ridge to find themselves almost at the very tip of an outcrop of rock.

Their vantage point allowed them to look down at the distant curving river, along an unbroken arc extending as far back as last night's camp and around the corner to a point that Jack estimated might be as much as a mile downstream. As he studied the scene, following this thin line, he caught a movement. Then another. Something was disturbing the vegetation down there, and he tapped the girl on the shoulder and pointed. After a second she nodded, and they both instinctively lowered themselves even closer to the ground.

So now what? thought Jack. Maybe they should head upstream instead of downstream, or maybe perhaps they should abandon the valley altogether and try to cut across the hills and valleys. He grimaced at the thought – he had barely made it to the top of the ridge. Maybe Little Miss Terrorist would have some idea, although exactly where she was leading him or what she was running from or to, was still a mystery. He looked at her, squatting down a few feet from him, her sweat-covered face a picture of concentration, and her whole form tense: poised like an animal. She was quite small, like most Peruvian women, but slim, unlike many. In profile, her features were a mixture of native Indian – not Quechuan – and Hispanic, with markedly high, broad cheekbones. Beyond the cheekbones, he could see the tip of her small Greek nose and he realised abstractly that underneath all the blood and dirt and sweat she would probably be considered attractive. His expression darkened and the incipient thought was smothered by his anger when he remembered who she was and the scumbags she represented. He kicked her with his foot, and looked at her questioningly. The irritation on her face gratified him strangely.

"*Vamos seguirlos,*" she said flatly.

"Follow them? Are you mad? *Loco?*" he said with his eyebrows scrunched into a scathing peak.

"No. Not mad. We follow, but we stay two hours back. They will not know."

Jack shook his head, balking at the idea of trailing a bunch of murdering thugs through the jungle.

"*Mira – al próximo rio, vamo al norte. Eles van al este,*" she whispered, as if reading his mind. She picked up a stick, and moved closer to him. Kneeling down, she talked urgently in Spanish, in a low voice, and as she talked, drew intersecting lines in the barren earth. Pointing to one, she switched to speaking slowly in English. "We are here. *Rio Taksamayu.*"

Jack kneeled over the drawing too, and nodded his understanding. She made the other line bigger with her stick. "This is the *Rio Iniru.*" She extended it beyond the intersection, so that there were effectively two segments to the new river – an upstream segment on the right, and a downstream segment on the left. She pointed towards the search party below and then to the upstream segment of the second line. Then she pointed to Jack and to herself in turn, and afterwards to the downstream segment.

Okay, Jack thought. *We go one way, they go another. But how does she know which way? And what if they split up?*

"How do you know? *Como sabe?*" he asked.

"Pah," she said dismissively, with a flap of her hand. "I know."

As they watched the group below them get further downstream, they both relaxed a little, and the girl eventually explained in her odd mixture of Spanish and English that she believed her leaders – her erstwhile leaders, she was keen to emphasise – undoubtedly would think the two of them had headed upstream, not downstream. This was why the group they could see disappearing in the distance was so small – maybe six people in total.

"They arrive in new river without to find me, they go home – east."

"Without finding *me*," Jack murmured, as he nodded, took the pack off his shoulder, and set it on the ground. He sat down and took a drink from the water bottle. He offered the bottle to her, but when her hand grasped it, he held on to it and stared into her face.

"So, just who the hell are you, anyway?" he said quietly. "You and your asshole friends? Huh?"

The girl first tried to wrest the water bottle from his hand, and then let go, drawing her hand back and sitting down.

"I mean, what's your name, for a start?" Jack continued. "*Como se llamas?*"

The girl sighed, staring down at the ground for a second, and then finally looked up.

"Elena," she said simply.

Jack nodded. "Okay Elena, and what exactly are you then? Some sort of narco-terrorist or something?" When she said nothing he continued. "*Sendero Luminoso?*" he tried, and then "*Tupac Amaru?*" he said, naming the two Peruvian terrorist groups he had heard of. They might once have been considered freedom fighters, but whatever moral authority either group had ever possessed, he knew they were generally regarded now simply as criminals who earned a living through extortion, drug dealing and arms trafficking – and any other illegal activity that suited their purpose.

She shrugged. "You gringos say *Sendero Luminoso*, but we are *el*

Partido Comunista del Perú."

"Well whatever you call yourselves, you're blood-thirsty murdering scum, is what you are."

"I not understand."

"You are bad – evil – *muy mal.*"

Her face clouded. "No! It is *you!* You are imperialist rapers of our country!" she shot back, glaring at him. "You kill us, you take our land, you tell us how to live. *You* are *muy mal.*"

"Not *me. I* do not do this," cried Jack, up on his knees again, looking down at her with a snarl on his face, and prodding his finger in his own chest. "Why you attack *me*? I innocent!"

"You not innocent! Just *estúpido!*" spat Elena. "*Not* innocent."

"Bullshit!" Jack cried. Some spittle escaped his mouth and he felt it drip from his lips onto his chin. "It's pointless talking to people like you. Fanatics. Bastards! You should all be–" He stopped dead, suddenly shaking with emotion. The tension of the days and nights of fear and pain threatened to overwhelm him, and he turned away from her and bent over, pounding a fist into the ground. Finally he sat back on his heels again, still looking away from the girl. They remained like this, each in their own little world, for what seemed to Jack like an eternity.

"*Vamanos,*" he heard the girl say from a long way off, and without any further words they got up, slung their packs and made their way slowly back down towards the winding river.

Progress was slow but relatively easy, the vegetation near the rock-strewn river being mainly ferns and a few other more or less benign species. It took them nearly four hours of unhurried progress to reach the mouth of the Rio Taksamayo, and once they were satisfied that the other group had really turned upstream, Elena led Jack in the opposite direction on the Iniru.

Although they stopped a couple of times – once to eat, and once to bathe and rest – their slow march continued uneventfully. Jack's spirits had been lifted hugely when he had finally had time to wash properly and put on the clothes he had taken from the dead men. He had also carefully examined his leg and found it to be in pretty good shape. It ached badly, but he figured this was as much from lack of use as anything else. Elena had bathed too, and had asked him to look at her head wound. Like the gash down her chest, there was very little fresh bleeding, and the greater danger was probably from infection. He applied more iodine and ignored her sharp intakes of breath as he worked.

They continued in a more positive mood than before, and made good progress. The canopy above had opened a few times along the new river, giving them their first view of the clear blue sky, and this too was uplifting for Jack. He was feeling pretty good about things right up until Elena stopped without warning and pointed to the opposite bank of the river.

"We must go there," she said simply.

"Why?" asked Jack, who was content with the comfortable progress they were making, and who did not want to throw it all away by taking the time to cross the river. Not only had it been gathering speed and depth, but it would no doubt be very wet, and damned cold.

"People," Elena said, pointing up ahead.

"People? What people?"

"People. Bad for me. Bad for you."

"Bad for both of us? Sendero, you mean? If you knew that, why did we come this way, for God's sake?"

"No. Not Sendero." Elena shook her head, opened her mouth as if to say something, then turned and walked down to the river.

Jack watched her for a few seconds and then followed her. "What is it, Elena? What are you scared of? Is it Indians – *Índios*?" Who?"

She was standing with her hands on her hips, studying the river. When she replied, she spoke quietly, without looking at him, and he had to strain to hear what she said.

"*Lo ejército.*"

"What? The *army*?" cried Jack. "And just how is that bad for me, Elena?"

"All army is bad."

"Sure – when you're a *terrorist*. But I'm not, remember? I'm just a tourist. It's spelled differently. I just want to get the hell out of this god-forsaken place."

Elena nodded slowly. "OK. You go then. I run." She looked up at him, half defiantly, half fearfully. "But you tell them about me..." Her voice trailed off.

Jack looked at her, wanting to be angry, but finding that the hatred he had been nursing had somehow burned itself out along the trail. He shook his head. "I won't say anything. Go ahead – knock yourself out." He waved her away, and they stood facing each other for a few moments, Elena with a puzzled expression on her face and Jack avoiding eye contact. When no one made a move, Jack finally shook his head again. "Look, just go, for god's sake. I say nothing. *Yo no hablo nada!* Go on – bugger off, will you!"

He saw the lingering suspicion in the girl's eyes, and knew she did not believe a word. She would probably be happier if he were dead, he decided, although he wondered what exactly she was going to do if she was now being hunted by the army on the one hand and the terrorists on the other. Well, it was not his problem. Live by the sword; die by the sword. He unslung his rifle and handed it to her, then he shrugged, turned and walked off, feeling her eyes burning into his back all the time it took him to walk up into the tree line and finally reach the bend in the river. He looked back just before he turned the corner, but she was gone. The jungle had swallowed every trace of her – and just for a split second, every trace of what had happened.

9

An hour after splitting up, Jack had descended to the river again and could see the army outpost in the distance, looking more or less like any other riverside village in the Peruvian interior, with a few wooden huts on stilts. The only thing that set it apart was a large Peruvian flag hanging limply from a makeshift flagpole, with white-washed stones placed around its base, and a couple of speedboats painted in camouflage colours, pulled half out of the water along the river bank.

He could see no sign of activity as he approached slowly, which worried him a little. He knew that a tall, fair-haired, blue-eyed gringo appearing suddenly out of the forest would be enough to spook most Peruvians. He slowed down even more, keeping himself clearly visible, wading noisily in the margins of the river with his empty hands by his side, hoping that he looked non-threatening. He had already removed the guns and buried them, along with the knives and even the machete: he did not need them anymore, and he did not want any misunderstandings before he could explain what had happened to him.

As he walked, he thought about what he would do when he got back to Lima. No doubt the Army and the Police would want to know everything that had happened, but once he had sorted out the paperwork, he would have to go and see his contact in Cuzco. He had left a spare set of gear there, and some money. From Cuzco, he could decide whether to have another crack at the expedition or return to the UK with his tail between his legs. It would be a difficult decision: on the one hand, he hated the thought of quitting; on the other, the original appeal of spending more than a year in the jungle – however impressive the cause – had diminished considerably, if not disappeared altogether.

He was still more than a hundred yards from the base when he heard a harsh voice to his left.

"*Alto! Pare!*"

He stopped and raised his hands, waiting. He heard a movement behind him and a split second later a sharp kick at his legs brought him to his knees. Someone ripped the pack from his shoulder and another soldier appeared with a gun trained on him. He felt another gun prodding his back.

"*Ayuda!*" Jack said, looking up. "*Ayuda. Soy Inglês.*"

"*Marcha!*" was the only reply.

He got unsteadily to his feet and walked slowly, being prodded occasionally by the guy behind him, and always covered by the one to his left, until they reached the little outpost. Another two soldiers unslung their guns and pointed them at him.

They were suddenly all talking at once, and Jack's Spanish was not good enough for him to understand one word in ten. He moved again when he felt the gun in his back, and two of the soldiers in front waved him towards a small wooden hut on stilts. He walked up the steps and someone opened the door. He was pushed inside and three of the soldiers entered after him. They threw him against the wall and pushed and pulled him until he was in the classic spread eagle search position.

"What the hell...?" he shouted angrily, but the only response he got was a hefty crack on the head.

They patted him down and then turned him, and a second later another soldier strode through the open door. On his shoulder were epaulets with three bars, which Jack reckoned probably made him a captain, and he walked straight up to Jack and started shouting loudly at him.

Definitely an officer, thought Jack.

He peered into Jack's face, and kept throwing questions out that Jack could not understand.

"What's going on?" cried Jack. "*No entiendo. Soy Inglés.*"

"*Espía,*" muttered one of the other soldiers.

The officer seemed to like the concept.

"*Espía?* Spy?" he said, pointing his finger at Jack.

"What? No! No spy. Tourist! What the hell would I be spying on out here?" cried Jack in exasperation.

The officer stood looking at Jack, menace in his eyes.

"*Turista?*" he asked quietly, with as much venom as it seemed possible to inject into one innocent word.

Jack nodded. "Yes. Just a tourist. Yes."

The officer turned to the table, where the meagre contents of Jack's pack had been dumped by one of the other soldiers. He opened the first aid kid and poked through it without much interest.

"*Passaporte?*" he asked.

"Stolen. Taken. *Robado,*" said Jack.

"Okay," the officer said, nodding thoughtfully. "Okay." He gestured to one of the other soldiers, and spoke curtly to him. The soldier opened the door and shouted something. The officer turned and paced, with his hands behind his back, until a few moments later everyone looked towards the door and the sound of approaching footsteps. When the door opened wide and another soldier appeared, Jack's heart sank. The soldier walked across the room to a small table and began to lay out the guns and knives that Jack had carefully buried along the riverbank.

Jack shook his head vigorously. "Not mine. They're not mine."

The officer just nodded and smiled. He opened his mouth to say something, but was interrupted by the sound of a scream of anger or pain and a long stream of breathless cursing and shouting from a woman somewhere outside.

"*Sus cornudos!*" came the clear, female voice before it ended abruptly in a guttural cry.

Elena. Jack was lost for words for a few seconds, and the officer looked at him smugly.

"Ah. *És su compañera, mi amigo.* Your friend, no?" he said. He walked slowly to the table and spun the revolver round, then turned to Jack again and smiled. "*Turista,* hah?" The smile abruptly vanished "*Turista* bullshit!" He nodded to the other soldiers, and walked out of the room, closing the door behind him.

WATERFALL

10

From the air, the only thing visible was what looked like a small community of palm-thatched houses dotted along a narrow metalled road. From the ground, an observer would see nothing unless they were an invited guest – and if they were uninvited, they would be dead before they got within two miles. The three men who had been bused in from an agreed pick-up point, were VIP guests for the morning.

The mud-caked yellow school bus stopped in a covered garage that linked two of the simple houses, and the group was escorted to the side of one of the buildings, where they descended in a series of tiers to a machine shop complete with pumps, generators, tools, and welding equipment. Beyond this lay an extensive series of pools, all covered with camouflage netting. After being shown this, their tour took them back up the tiers one by one.

There were gasps of amazement at various points along the way, until they emerged at the top level in another covered park where five army trucks were being loaded with the finished product they were here to talk about.

"Where the hell is it all going?" one of the group mumbled as they walked past the trucks.

Finally, they were escorted into a small, dusty office in one of the houses. A man behind a desk rose as the group was ushered in.

"Gentlemen," he said, shaking hands with them as they came forward. "Thank you for coming. Please, have a seat." He indicated the half-dozen chairs dotted around the room. "Water, anyone? Whisky?"

Once everyone was comfortable, with a drink in his hand, the man behind the desk smiled.

"This facility is as good as anything the Colombians have," he said, simply.

The men nodded enthusiastically. "Never seen anything like it in Peru," said one of them.

"A hundred percent pure, Señor Fernando?" asked one of the other three men seated in the small room.

"One hundred percent."

Fernando jerked his thumb over his shoulder towards the window. "And it's all totally safe. As long as we keep it camouflaged, we're guaranteed not to have any unwelcome guests."

"It's incredible, Señor Fernando."

"Thank you. And as you've seen, you can bring your produce in whatever form you want. We can output both base and cocaine. We can even do paste, if anyone wants it."

A thin man with a large purple burn mark down one side of his face was shaking his head. "It's a whole fucking factory, man."

"It is, Paquito," Fernando agreed. "And now you don't have to go to anyone else, right?"

The three men nodded. "Of course not," one of them said.

"But Señor Fernando," said Paquito, "With all due respect, that depends on the price, does it not?"

"Ah. Yes, of course. Forgive me – I should have told you." He rose, picked up some papers, and walked round the desk. "Here, gentlemen. My offer – your price list." He handed them each a copy.

They studied the papers, and there was a low whistle from someone.

"Señor Fernando, these are very good prices. What's the catch?"

Fernando sat on the edge of his desk and laughed. "Ah, José, my friend – how long have you known me? You think I am trying to cheat you now?"

"No, Señor, no! Of course not. But..."

"Okay, José. I know. Don't worry – I would have asked the same question." He stood, walked round to his chair again, and sat down. "Here's the deal." His expression became serious, and he looked at each of them in turn, as he spoke. "I guarantee those prices, *and* I will guarantee your safety and the safety of your operation. However, I can only accept a certain quantity each month."

"No problem," said Paquito. "What quantity?"

"It will change from month to month, depending on demand–"

Paquito interrupted. "That's fine by me, Fernando. I will sell all I can to you, and when you can't take any more, I'll send the rest north as usual."

Fernando tutted and shook his head. "Ah, well, that is the 'catch' as José put it. You see, you must agree not to supply anyone else. It is my only condition."

There was a sudden silence in the room, and the men exchanged bemused looks.

"So what *is* the quantity, exactly?" someone finally ventured.

Fernando wrote a single figure down on a piece of paper and held it up. "Base. Or base equivalent."

The men stared at the figure with worried expressions.

Fernando put the sheet of paper down again and raised his hands. "My friends, think about it. You'll sell a little less, perhaps–"

"A *little*...?" said Paquito.

"A little. But you'll get a better price on what you do sell, and halve your costs at the same time. You'll have no security problems. A guaranteed price. Fewer people to pay. None of the usual logistics issues. You can just sit back and rake in your money. What's the problem?"

After a few seconds, two of the men began to nod.

The third still looked doubtful. "But where are you sending all this production?" he blurted. "I mean, it's fine by me that I don't have to worry about logistics, but as I see it, unless you've some magical way of putting this up the consumers' noses, you have the same problems as we all do now."

Fernando nodded. "Hmm. Well, as I see it, that's my business, gentlemen. But let's just say that the size of my operation opens up certain, um, new possibilities, okay?"

"But surely the size is exactly the problem, isn't it?" José asked. "It's hard to keep something this big, quiet. And what if you *do* have problems with the operation? I mean what if–"

"What if someone comes after me?" Fernando smiled. "They won't, José. You weren't listening to me. I said the safety of the operation is *guaranteed.*"

As the implications of the words sank in, it was José's turn to whistle, and he stared at Fernando for a couple of seconds before smiling broadly. "Okay, Señor Fernando," he said, nodding happily, "I don't know how you managed it, but I agree it's none of our business. I've known you nearly fifteen years, and I think it's a good offer. More than good." He stood up, crossed to the desk, and extended his hand.

Fernando stood up too.

"I'm in," said José.

They shook hands firmly – fiercely, almost – each looking unwaveringly into the eyes of the other. Then the other two men rose and came forward.

"I'm in," said the next man, and repeated the same handshake.

"I too am in," said Paquito, but he looked down momentarily as he was shaking hands, and Fernando's eyes narrowed for a second as he watched him return to his seat.

"Chaska!" Fernando called. "Bring some more whisky for my guests. We have something to celebrate!"

11

"For the thousandth time," Jack mumbled, "I'm just a tourist." He could barely speak, he was so tired. How many times had they woken him to ask the same questions? He could not remember. Who was he spying for, why did he have the guns, what was he doing with the *Sendero*. The same stuff, over and over again. He was still in the little hut, where they had left him without any food or water. He sat on the single wooden chair to begin with, listening to the screams of abuse between Elena and these people. Sometimes there was the noise of a smack or a thud, and a cry of pain, and then silence for a while before the whole thing started again. He tried to get some sleep by lying on the floor, but soon discovered he was being watched: as soon as he lay down, they came in and dragged him to his feet again. He protested his innocence as best he could with his inadequate Spanish. Why were they treating him like this? He was a British citizen. He had done nothing wrong. But the officer and his soldiers either ignored him or became even more choleric.

After another round of stupid questions, he was having difficulty thinking straight. He mumbled a few words, but he was beyond making much sense in English, never mind in Spanish, and the soldiers realised it. They left the room, and Jack sank to the floor in the darkness, his eyes seeking out the tiny slits of light that penetrated the wooden wall in front of him. His leg ached – no great surprise after the physical effort of the past 48 hours – and he was desperately thirsty. He wondered how long the nightmare would continue before they let him go; before he could get the hell away from this place. At least they had not started beating him yet, like they were clearly doing to Elena.

Elena. She could get all this stopped, god damn her. All she had to do was tell them what had happened. But what was the likelihood of that? He could hardly expect her to own up to having kidnapped him. He did not know exactly what the military did to terrorists in Peru, but he figured there was a pretty good possibility she would either just be shot, or – if she was senior enough, he guessed – hauled off and incarcerated until she could be dragged through the courts and put on show. One way or another, confessions would hardly be part of her plans just now.

As he sat there trying to collect his thoughts, he heard the faintest of sounds in the distance. One moment it was there; the next it faded. An unnatural, rhythmical sound. He concentrated, and finally recognised it as the sound of a helicopter. The noise grew, and soon became almost deafening. Bright light flickered crazily through the cracks in the walls, the little wooden cabin shook, and the tin roof above him rattled as bits of dirt and debris fell on it. There was some shouting, and the helicopter descended in a cacophony of scything blades and shrieking engines.

Two soldiers rushed in and dragged Jack to his feet, bundling him quickly out of the cabin with one of his arms pinned behind his back. He had no strength left to protest, as he was pushed outside. In any case, he reasoned, this had to be progress: if they were going back to civilisation, then surely it was getting him closer to his release.

They manhandled him into the cargo bay of the big helicopter, and pushed him into an uncomfortable, rear-facing seat. The camp's officer sat to his left, and Jack saw that another seat on the opposite side of the bay was occupied by an Elena who had clearly suffered more than he had. In the harsh lights that swept erratically across the bay, he could see the matted hair and the blood-streaked face, while her clothes were torn almost to ribbons. Although he was not about to forgive her and her compatriots, he could not help feeling some sympathy – empathy, perhaps – for her.

The internal lights were switched off, and the engine note rose in pitch to almost intolerable levels. His tired mind spiralled downward towards a numb semi-conscious state into which confused thoughts of fairness, revenge, irony and freedom crept unbidden. As the slow, screaming, upward motion of the helicopter resolved itself into a growling, inclined, forward movement, his thoughts became less and less clear, until finally he succumbed to a fitful sleep.

He was stunned to consciousness by a blow to the side of his head. He was pushed forward out of his seat and then hauled from the helicopter. Hands grabbed him roughly and kept him on his feet, and he was hurried away. It was still dark, but he could see a long row of lights stretching away into the distance to his right, while in front and to his left were what looked like portable works buildings variously stacked around. He also noticed a jeep, and behind it a row of diggers and bulldozers. Beyond them was a tall wire fence that ran behind the buildings. On the other side of it lay what looked like thick, impenetrable, scrubby forest. His hopes of being nearer civilisation were dashed. The whole place had the atmosphere of a busy, dirty construction site, although at the moment at least, the noise was subdued. The other thing that struck him as he was marched into one of the portable cabins was a vague, low, rumbling vibration under his feet. His escort pushed him roughly through the door and then withdrew, closing and locking it.

The interior was lit by a flickering strip-light, and looked like a typical works office – small, grey, dusty, littered with paper. There was mud all over the springy wooden floor, and to one side was a partition with a row of pegs hung with dirty overalls, and a collection of muddy boots beneath them. A few battered plastic hard hats sat on top of a cupboard. There was a desk with a chair and a filing cabinet behind it, and three other plastic chairs in front of it. He noticed a water fountain to the side of the desk, and he grabbed a cup and drank greedily, refilling it several times until eventually he took a full cup and sat down on one of the plastic chairs.

A minute or so later, the door opened and a tall military officer stepped in, flanked by two soldiers. He stood looking down at Jack for a second and then motioned to the other men to leave.

The officer's face might have been considered good-looking, except for the reptilian eyes that stared out from it. Jack managed to produce a faint smile, but it was not returned.

"Choo are *espy*," the man said matter-of-factly, in a voice and an accent that immediately reminded Jack of every stereotypical Spanglish accent he had heard. This time the genuine smile that spread across his face clearly irritated the officer. "I *know* choo are *espy*."

Jack shook his head. "I'm *not* a spy," he said. "I was attacked.

Kidnapped. I escaped. I just want to go home. That's all."

"Bullshit. Choo are espy. Make trouble for everyone."

"No–" Jack started.

"Son of a bitch gringo. Choo lie. Choo are here to observe everything. Whatchoo know about *los narcos*? Why choo have guns? Pah - of course choo are *espy*."

Jack stood up suddenly, and the officer stepped back and drew his pistol. He pointed it straight at Jack's head, and looked like he would be quite happy to use it.

"Sit," he said.

"You people are un-fucking-believable," Jack spat, backing off and sitting down again. "Why won't you believe me, for Christ's sake? I was kidnapped. Ask the woman. Elena. She knows!"

The officer lowered his gun slightly, but kept it pointed at Jack. "Choo think I am *estúpido*? The woman is Maria Fernandez - a dangerous Sendero bitch. Why I would believe anything she say?"

Jack was not sure what to say to this. He was not much surprised that Elena – Maria – would give him a false name, since as far as he could see every aspect of Peruvian society seemed to be based on mutual mistrust, but further thoughts were interrupted when the door opened. The officer spun round to see who it was, and a man in smart blue overalls entered and closed the door. He smiled at no-one in particular and then looked at Jack.

"You must be the guy they found, right?"

Jack nodded.

"Hi. I'm Charles." He stuck out his hand, and Jack shook it tentatively.

"You're American?" asked Jack.

"Sure. I'm the site manager here."

"Well thank God for that. What the hell is going on here? I'm just a tourist, you know. First I get kidnapped by terrorists, and then when I finally escape, the army treats me like I'm some sort of enemy of the State. I don't know what this guy's on about – I haven't done anything wrong – and I just need some help to get out of here." Jack looked expectantly at the American, but it was the officer who jumped in first.

"*Estás mintiendo*," he said, with a scowl. He's lying.

"*Espere*," said the site manager, firmly; coldly.

"No. Es un espía. Voy—"

"No va nada, Major..." The man spoke with some authority, but clearly not quite enough to satisfy the officer. A heated argument ensued in which Jack could only pick up some of the words and meanings, but there was obviously no love lost between the two of them.

"Tu va a arrepentir," spat the Major after a minute or so, then he spun round, opened the door and left the room. Jack could see two armed soldiers standing just outside.

"Hmm. Look, excuse me a moment, will you?" said the site manager distractedly. He walked towards the door and then turned to Jack again. "You look pretty dreadful, you know," he said, and smiled in a strained sort of way. "There's a small shower room there behind the partition, and you can help yourself to a pair of overalls, if you like."

"I don't want a shower, dammit. I just want to get the hell out of here. Where am I, exactly? And what are the Americans doing here? Why am I being treated like this?" He stood up. "I think it's about time I got some bloody answers, mate."

The man held up his hands as Jack advanced. "Sorry. I understand your frustration, but don't worry, okay? I'm sure we can resolve the whole thing for you. However, for the moment, you'll need to wait here. This is a restricted area in the middle of nowhere, so you see..." He trailed off.

"Yes?" Jack pushed.

"So, um, we'll need to fly you out again, won't we? In the meantime, I'm afraid they're not going to just let you wander round, okay? No offence, or anything, right?"

Jack shook his head in frustration, but realised there was some logic in what the guy said. He sighed. "Yeah, right. Sure."

"I'll be back in a few minutes and we can sort out all the details." The man turned again and left the room, closing the door behind him.

Jack heard the lock, and sat staring at the door for a few seconds in thought. Then he looked down at his muddy, sweat-soaked clothes and sighed. A shower would not do any harm at all.

The low-pressure dribble of water was cold and refreshing, and when he had finished, he dried himself on a thin, smelly towel and pulled on a pair of the blue overalls, noticing it had the word "Consbras" embroidered on the left breast. He also found an almost-clean, dry pair of socks that felt wonderful on his aching feet. By the time he had finished dressing, he was feeling much better.

He emerged from the shower cubicle and walked over to a little window behind the desk, thoughts of escape suddenly filling his head: so far, he had no reason to trust the American any more than the Peruvian military. The window was far too small to climb out of, but it gave him a good view of the site, which he saw now was on a huge scale. The arc lights showed him a massive excavation operation within the confines of a valley, and in the distance he could see what looked like a huge cave or gallery cut into the valley wall. He wondered vaguely what it was all for. A lake? A dam, perhaps? He stared out for a few more seconds and then turned his attention to the inside of the cabin.

He looked for anything that might help him escape, but there was nothing much except for a considerable amount of paperwork strewn all over the place. A series of technical drawings lay in a pile on the small, blue desk, and a portion of a map underneath them caught his eye. He pushed the drawings aside to get a better look. It was a 1:50,000 scale map, presumably of the local area. It was clearly mountainous terrain, and as he scanned the topography, his eyes widened as he saw the full extent of the works marked on it. A drawing that had been rolled up within the map showed what looked like groundworks for some sort of reservoir. It was labelled simply 'Obra AE'. Works AE.

He heard approaching footsteps and just had time to rearrange the papers and sit down again before the door opened.

12

The site manager entered the room, smiled at Jack, and walked across to the desk. He looked at the drawings on the top, glanced quizzically at Jack, and then started rolling them up together. Placing them to one side, he sat down behind the desk.

"You look a little more human now, at least," he said, nodding at Jack's overalls.

"Yes. I'm feeling okay, thanks," said Jack.

"Sure. Well look, I'm sorry about the business with the Major earlier. He's just a little stressed at the moment. Hardly knows what he's saying." He paused for a moment. "Right, so let's see if we can sort all this out."

Jack looked at the man without saying anything. As the seconds ticked by, it seemed to unnerve him, and Jack watched him shift slightly in his chair.

"You're British aren't you, Mr, um...?"

"Look," said Jack, "I just want to go home, okay? Can someone help me get to Lima? I can pay, you know."

"Ah. Of course. Forgive me, but I kind of assumed... I mean, by the looks of it, you don't have much money or anything. You know – no bags, no wallet? Do you have a wallet...?"

Jack shook his head. "I lost my stuff, that's all. When I get to Lima I can sort everything out."

The man nodded. "Sure. I understand."

Yes – so...? Jack said to himself, struggling to keep calm.

"You must have had a rough time, of course," said the man.

The implied question hung in the air and Jack decided to ignore it.

"So what is this place, anyway?" Jack asked. "Eh, Charles? It is Charles, isn't it...?"

The man nodded.

"Hmm. So, why did they bring us here? What's happened to the girl? Why am I being treated like a criminal? What the *hell* is going on, exactly?" Jack's voice had risen steadily, and his last words came out as an angry shout.

The man held up his hand. "Wow. One thing at a time, my friend; one thing at a time. I'd just like to get some more details from you and then we can straighten it all out, okay?"

Jack said nothing.

"Look," said the man. "We can certainly help. Just give me your details. I'll phone your embassy, and then we'll arrange to get you to them, okay?"

"Ah - you have a phone?" Jack exclaimed. "Well, if you could just let me borrow it, then I could call the embassy, or m–" He had been about to mention his contact in Cuzco, but thought better of it. "Problem solved. How about that?"

The man frowned. "Well, when I say *phone*, I mean a *radio* phone. We have a radio for contacting base. So I'm afraid you couldn't actually phone your embassy directly."

"Oh. I see," said Jack. The man was lying, and doing a bad job of it.

"So, just your details and embassy..."

Jack sighed. "Look I'm sorry, Charles, but with what I've just been through, you'll forgive me being a bit paranoid. If you could just get me to Lima, I'll sort myself out, okay?"

The man thought for a few seconds and finally nodded.

"Very well. I understand. Just wait here please and I'll see what I can do." He rose from his chair and left the room.

With the click of the lock, thoughts crowded in on Jack. He had already been kidnapped by a bunch of terrorist psychos, and held at gunpoint and interrogated by an army that seemed little better. Every fibre in his body told him that the last thing these people were going to do was just drop him off at a hotel in Lima and walk away. If he wanted to get home, he was going to have to do things the hard way.

He got up and started going through the maps and drawings again. He also rifled through the desk drawers, looking for more information and anything small that he thought might be useful. All he needed was the slightest opportunity and he would willingly throw himself back on the mercy of the jungle.

The footsteps returned and Jack sat down again. The American walked in, his face set hard, although it was not difficult to see that he was upset in some way. He looked at Jack and tried to smile, but what came across was a sort of grimace.

"It's all fixed," he said, his eyes failing conspicuously to lock with Jack's. "We're flying you to our base in Lima and from there we can give you a lift in to the city."

He opened the door and two soldiers walked in.

"Shall we?" he asked Jack, and motioned for him to leave.

Jack forced himself to smile. "Okay. That's great news. Thanks."

As they left the building, Jack looked around frantically, considering the possibility of making a run for it, but he was closely guarded by the two soldiers, and the three of them were in turn escorted by a small group of onlookers. They all marched over to the only substantial-looking building Jack could see. It was made of brick, two storeys tall, and there was a metal staircase built onto the outside wall. Their footsteps clanged loudly as they went up.

At the top, a sheet-metal door was unbolted and Jack was invited to step in. The door was quickly pulled to and he heard the bolt slam home. There was no light inside the room, save for what little filtered in from a broad expanse of glass along one wall. He stood there for a few seconds, allowing his eyes to grow accustomed to the gloom. He was trying to make his mind up what the place was exactly, when he heard a shuffling noise.

"*Olá* Jack," came a thin, weak voice.

He looked round and saw Elena sitting on the floor, her back to the wall. He walked over and bent down to see her better.

"Jesus you look rough, Elena. Or Maria, or whatever your name is."

"Elena," she said. "Maria is my Sendero name. I gave you my real name."

"Hmm. I'm honoured. Well, Elena-is-my-real-name, you look like shit. Are you okay?"

She nodded. "*Sí*. I am okay."

She sounded drained, somehow lifeless, compared to how she had been earlier.

"We go to Lima, no?" suggested Jack, in an effort to be positive.

"Ha ha. No. We not go to Lima," said Elena flatly, shaking her head.

"No?"

"I think you already know."

"But they told me..." Jack began to protest, but his heart was not really in it. He just nodded.

He could see Elena smiling at him.

"*Si*. Yeah. You know."

"Dammit," Jack said, getting up. He looked round at the room again. They had probably been thrown in here because it was the only brick-built building the site had. He paced round, vainly tapping the solid walls, peering up at the steel and aluminium of the roof, feeling the cold metal of the bolted door, until he worked his way back to the long window. It was made of heavy plate glass, and there was a control panel placed in front of it. Jack looked at it curiously, and then a slight grin spread across his face as recognition suddenly dawned. He cupped his hands to the glass and peered through it to confirm his suspicions, and then got down on his knees and started to poke around at the back of the unit. It was roughly the same control panel he had seen a hundred times in his youth. When his father had left the army, he had taken a job managing concrete plants in the North of England, and as Jack had grown older, he had often been dragged around the quarries where these plants were usually sited, sometimes being roped in to help move, fix or adjust things in the cabins.

He pulled at the whole unit and found he could just about move it away from the wall. Behind it, he found what he was hoping for – a flimsy knock-out for the cables and connections between the control panel and the machinery on the other side of the window. It was the same as he had seen in most of the batching cabins the length and breadth of North Yorkshire, and with a bit of effort he was certain he could make a space big enough to get through. He almost laughed with delight.

"Elena!" he whispered urgently. "*Vamanos!*"

It was time to clear out.

13

Adam Torres paced round the bedroom of his apartment with the phone to his ear. In his capacity as a U.S. Public Diplomacy Officer in Peru, he was accustomed to being disturbed by work at odd hours. Usually it would be a colleague on the management side bleating about something, or someone advising him of the arrival of one so-called opinion former or another. Often, it meant he would have to drop everything to go and 'make friends'; sometimes he would have to drive to the embassy for a meeting at some unsocial hour. It was all part of his very respectable but largely unremarkable job. This call was different, and had come in on a different phone. Torres' habitual frown had deepened slightly, but this was the only evidence that he was concerned in any way. He bent down and picked up a small holdall as he carried on a terse conversation. He placed the bag on the bed and started to collect a few things, throwing them onto the bed.

"They don't know," the voice said, in answer to one of Torres' questions. "One gringo. English-speaker. One Sendero: Maria Fernandez. That's all we got."

"Who else knows?" asked Torres.

"No one. Just the army guys and the site manager."

"The *site manager*?" He stopped pacing and stood still.

"Yep. Apparently he and the army don't see eye to eye on the way to deal with the situation."

"Jesus Christ. Okay. Well, let's keep a lid on it."

"Yes sir."

Torres hung up and dialled another number.

"*Buenos noches*," he said. "Torres. *Obra A ponto E*," he finished, using the Spanish for 'site' and 'point'.

"*Si Señor. Cuando?*"

"*Dentro de una hora.*" Torres' Spanish was perfect. A local might know he was not from Peru, but his accent, looks and manners could convincingly place him as a native of just about any Spanish-speaking country between Mexico and Chile.

"*Convenido*," came the reply.

At this time of the evening, the six-mile drive to the obscure southern entrance of the airport was painfully slow, but once they were through the security gate, the driver was able to go straight to the helipad, so that Torres was airborne less than an hour after the call had come in.

This was no military helicopter, but a luxuriously appointed Eurocopter EC135 Hermès, and Torres sat on his own on the comfortable leather seats at the back. He had already exchanged the minimum pleasantries with the pilot, and now stared out at the lights of Lima while he reviewed the problem and considered his options.

The Peruvian Presidential Adviser had been as good as his word, and it had surely been worth losing another game of golf. Torres had already received the necessary details of the proposed anti-drugs operation, and all the pieces were in place for a major show involving the US DEA, the Peruvian Anti-Drugs Police DIRANDRO, and the Brazilian *Policía Federal*, in less than three weeks time. The DEA would be billed as acting in an advisory capacity, while the Peruvian forces would be responsible for the actual bust. The Brazilians were just in on it to keep them sweet. That was all anyone on the US diplomatic team really knew or cared about it, although of course Torres was aware of the location, timing and size of the operation. He also knew it was a complete fabrication, and that a few of his old 'friends' were to be sacrificed at the altar of good PR. He felt no qualms about that.

It was all timed to coincide with a new tranche of funding for Latin American projects, led by Peruvian Operations, which had received unprecedented levels of U.S. financial and non-financial support over the last years. They needed this bust badly if they were to continue to get the funding they needed. *He* needed this bust badly. In just a few short months he would retire early to realise his 'investments' in Peru. He already had the perfect injury planned, Purple Heart and all, and afterwards he would quietly fade into the background. He would keep an address in the U.S., and no one would even notice his move to the original home of his grandparents just north of the

Nicaragua-Costa Rica border. Whether America's grand imperialist project succeeded or not in the end, was not something he particularly cared about – just as long as no one found out what was going down on his watch.

His grandfather had instilled in him a cold hatred of America and the Americans. He had shown Adam by example how it was possible to keep secret and yet nurture a deep disgust and loathing while taking advantage of America's soft gullibility. He showed him how to plan calmly for revenge for the wrongs done to his family in Nicaragua before they had fled across the border to Costa Rica and eventually been dragged to the USA by Adam's father.

His father had betrayed the family and become one of *them* – married a Yank when his first wife had died in an accident, and even joined the U.S. Coastguard. But Adam was different. He had been all but abandoned to his grandparents, and had watched his father's desperate pursuit of the new ladylove and an American job. The great American dream. He remembered the pain of being ignored – deserted – as if it were yesterday. But in the end even that had worked to his advantage, since no one ever questioned his own allegiance to Uncle Sam – not when he had a father with a long-service medal in the oh-so-wonderful U.S. Coastguard.

The CIA had welcomed him with open arms, and since then, he had worked hard to get where he was right now – just as he and his grandfather had planned it. It had devastated him that his grandparents had both died before he could put the plan into action, and his father and stepmother were more or less confined to a pleasant, sterile, retirement home in Florida. But the plan was intact. And he would see it through. In fact, the Americans' latest crazy scheme - no doubt dreamed up by the dick-wad at the very top – had been an absolute gift to Torres, providing him with the perfect cover for his own schemes and a brief that made him laugh every time he thought about it.

As it climbed steadily up the sides of the Andes, the helicopter was buffeted by the thermals. A light flashed in the cabin and Torres put on his headset.

"Storm out there," came the pilot's voice. "I think we can avoid it, but best buckle up."

"OK," said Torres.

He smiled grimly as he heard the pitch of the engine increase. He was ready for any storm. He would make it up to his grandparents, and restore the family's fortunes. He would allow no one – the holier-than-thou Americans, the grasping Peruvians, the idiot Brazilians, or anyone else – to get in his way now. He would deal with the current unfortunate complication efficiently, effectively and economically – just as he had dealt already with wayward construction workers, smart-ass narcos and anyone else dumb enough to cause trouble. He would do his tongue-in-cheek bit to 'help make America great again', but only he knew that this was *his* moment.

The helicopter bucked and skidded a little for ten minutes or so before conditions stabilised and they descended relatively smoothly towards the forested eastern slopes, finally touching down gently at ten to nine.

Torres stepped from the helicopter and crouched to run across to the operations room fifty metres away. There, he was greeted by the site's senior Peruvian military commander.

"Okay, fill me in," snapped Torres in Spanish.

"A gringo and a wayward narco. Won't talk; no ID," said the military man casually. "The gringo has some dumb story about being kidnapped."

"I see. And how did you catch them? What were they doing?" asked Torres.

"It wasn't us, actually, sir. It was a detachment stationed in the interior."

"I thought they were caught here." Torres voice remained unchanged, but his eyes narrowed and he tilted his head somewhat as he stared hard at the officer.

"No," the officer repeated, somewhat uncertainly. "It was on the *Rio Iniru*."

Torres looked coldly at him and spoke very quietly.

"So let me get this straight – you plucked some foreigner from whatever innocent and wholly irrelevant nature ramble he was on, and flew him over three hundred kilometres to a carefully-concealed, restricted site. Am I correct so far, er...*Major*?" he finished, glancing at the man's insignia.

"Sir."

"*And* you brought a rogue narco along with him."

At first, there was silence from the officer, who merely nodded grimly. "But sir," he finally managed, "he was *not* on a 'nature ramble', as you say. He is a spy."

"A spy? You are fucking kidding me aren't you? Who said he was a spy? What would he be spying on, on the Rio Iniru?"

The Major began trying to convince Torres of the spying claims – after all, he said, they had drugs operations all over the area – while Torres turned and walked over to the large cement-dust covered desk that was the centrepiece of the manager's cabin. He sat down in the swivel chair and remained almost motionless, elbows on the desk and chin on steepled fingers. The only evidence of a furiously working brain was the look of concentration in the cold brown eyes.

When the Major had finished, Torres sighed heavily.

"Sometimes I wonder whose side you lot are on. You realise this jerk is probably nobody of any importance whatever, don't you?"

The Major stared past Torres at the wall.

Torres paused for a moment, deep in thought again, and then shook his head.

"Shit. Why can you people not *think* before you act?"

The Major tensed and shifted slightly.

"And this Maria what's-her-name,"

"Fernandez."

"Fernandez. Hmm. Name rings a bell."

The Major nodded and seemed happy to be firmer ground. "Yes. She was part of the surviving Sendero Luminoso group of course."

Torres nodded. "Our people."

"Yes of course. And absolutely no threat, until she went out on her own with her Huallaga Valley cronies. She's been a thorn in our sides this last year and more."

"The New Sendero. Okay, well you know what to do with *her*, then, at least."

"Sir."

"Okay. And the gringo. Where is he now?"

"We've locked them both in the batching tower. Over there," said the officer, nodding in the direction.

"You put them both together?"

"It's the only secure building there is – brick built on a steel frame."

Torres shook his head and sighed. "Right, well, remove her and get rid of her. Let me know when the guy is on his own, and I'll speak to him. And listen – I don't want anyone talking to him at all – about anything. Clear?"

"Sir."

"Okay." He sighed. "And you'd better get me the site manager."

A slit of a smile cracked across the Major's face. "Yes sir."

Torres waved his hand dismissively, pushed his chair back and put his feet up on the desk as he watched the Major walk towards the door. The gringo would either have to be persuaded that he had imagined the whole thing and that everything was sweetness and light, or he would have to be got rid of. Whichever way it turned out was okay with Torres, just so long as this operation – and his own retirement plan – was safe.

A few minutes later, there was the sound of raised voices outside, a rush of footsteps and the door was suddenly flung open. In walked a tall, young, fair-haired man in mud-splattered overalls and a hard hat perched on his head. He was breathing heavily and wore an indignant expression on his face.

"Ah," said Torres, smiling thinly. "You must be the site manager. Come in, please. Have a seat."

14

With the control panel levered away from the wall, access to the knock-out was simple. It was made of thin fibreboard, damp from the ambient humidity, and when Jack pushed it with his hand, it flexed. He sat on the floor with his feet against it and his back to the panel. Pushing with all his weight, he made it bend and finally buckle with a dull cracking noise. He tensed for a few seconds, waiting for someone to come. When no-one did, he repositioned his feet and pushed again. This time the board gave almost immediately, and suddenly there was a gaping hole in the wall.

Elena joined him in removing the rest of the bits of board, and as she squeezed herself through the hole, Jack got up and looked quickly around the room again. There was a flimsy, locked cupboard beneath the control panel desk, which he forced open by pulling hard on the handle. From the jumble of tools he found inside, he took some art knives and a length of wire. From the top drawer of a desk by the far wall he helped himself to a box of matches and an empty mineral water bottle. The other drawers were empty, but as he pushed and pulled them carefully in and out, a piece of torn paper fell to the floor. It seemed to be part of a memo or report, and in the bottom margin was an illegible signature, the word 'DUMAR', and the references '*T.AE, HEP 01-11, 15m*' to the right. He stuffed it into his pocket. Then he noticed, stuck to the wall, a map with lengths of cotton pinned to it, forming a series of convergent lines. There were lettered points on it, too. On impulse, he pulled out the pins, removed the map from the wall, folded it up as tightly as he could, and stuck it inside his overalls. As an afterthought, he grabbed some of the pins and put them in the matchbox. After another quick look around, he got down and crawled through the hole to where Elena was waiting on the other side.

It was absurdly familiar to him, even in the dark. He could see the huge hopper, with feeds coming into it from different directions, positioned in the middle of a steel lattice support tower. Although there was some sort of flooring mesh laid down, a cement truck parked underneath was visible. The ground was a good twelve or fourteen feet down, but the top of the cement truck's loading chute was only a couple of feet below them, and next to that, welded onto the side of the truck, was a metal ladder. If they could squeeze past the mouth of the chute, it would be child's play to get down to the ground, and if they could avoid being spotted, he was certain they could make it past the perimeter fencing which he knew was just a short distance away.

The hopper, designed to move or vibrate, was relatively easy to squeeze past. Their clothes caught on the sharp edges a few times, but they were through and hanging on to the truck's chute in less than a minute. They worked their way round to the ladder and quickly climbed down. As soon as they reached the ground, they ducked under the truck and lay in the mud, looking out. The arc lamps cast huge pools of light in the grey murk, and diesel generators clattered and droned away in the background. The rear of the next building along was in almost total darkness, and Jack pointed to it. Elena nodded, and after another look around, they made a dash for it.

Catching his breath and scanning the area for the best path to the perimeter, Jack saw what he was looking for – the cluster of trucks he had noticed earlier, parked no more than twenty yards from the fence – and pointed them out to Elena. Then, just as they were poised to make their run, Jack held his hand up. He could hear snatches of a conversation in English coming from inside the building, and he motioned to Elena to wait.

He heard a well-spoken American voice, slow, deliberate, mocking.

"This isn't some sort of game. You can't just go back home to Happysville and forget this all happened. No-one forced you to take the job. You made a choice, my friend. You're taking the company's money, so you play by the company's rules."

"Sure. I know that," came another American voice, higher, younger, tight with emotion. "But we're not actually doing anything wrong here, are we? I mean, so what if word gets out, right?" Jack immediately identified this second speaker as the man he had met earlier, Charles. "They'd just fly us home and brush it all under the carpet." It was a statement, but came out more like a question.

There was loud sigh. "Look, you're clearly a guy with a conscience. Good for you. But you just need to concentrate on your job and let me worry about the big picture. Fact is, there's more to this than you need or want to know. That girl out there is Sendero, for example, right?" A pause. "Right. And there are plenty of people out there – however innocent they might look, from whatever part of the planet – who would like to bring us down. People who would like to bring down the whole American government and take us back to the bad old days."

"Sure. Right, but—"

"So trust me. These are the bad guys. Really. The very worst guys."

"They don't seem so bad to me – and anyway, they deserve to be treated fairly. I'm not just going to stand by and watch them be delivered into the hands of the Peruvian military. Jesus, their lives won't be worth shit."

"They're not being delivered into the hands of the military. We're just using their transport. We're hitching a ride to somewhere where they can be properly de-briefed. Then it'll be my problem, and I can assure you you'll not hear any more about it, okay?"

"But what assurances do I have—"

The cold voice broke in sharply. There was an edge to it now that Jack was familiar with from long years of experience. It was the voice of the powerful, growing tired from the effort of being needlessly pleasant to the weak.

"Excuse me? What *assurances* do you have? You have no assurances about squat. It's nothing to do with you. I mean, who the fuck are *you*, anyway, right?"

After a second of silence, the same cold voice again.

"Look, Johnson - it is Johnson, isn't it?" Back to the smooth tones of a man well-versed in faking sincerity.

"Charles."

"Charles. Look, Charles, all you have to do is carry on with your job here and let me do mine. Forget all about this little incident. I'm sure you're being very well rewarded for being the big boss man here, so you just let me handle this distraction, and I'll have the pair of them out of your hair in an hour."

There was a slight pause. "Hmm. I guess." Another pause. "But–"

"Excellent," the cold voice interrupted.

"But when you say you'll have them 'out of here', I want to know exactly what that means." An unconvincing last stand by the site manager.

"No, you don't."

"Pardon me?"

"I said no, you don't want to know – and no, I'm not going to tell you," snapped the other man, real irritation in his voice now. "All you have to do is do *your* job and let me do *mine*, right? They will just disappear from here, that's all. My problem; my responsibility."

"But..."

Jack had heard enough. It was perfectly clear who was in charge here, and equally clear that the safest place for Jack and Elena at the moment, was in the middle of some nice piranha-infested part of the jungle a million miles away. Between the Peruvian army, the narco-terrorists and this American operation, their lives were not worth a damn just now, and his original notion of just hopping over a fence and making it to the nearest high street was out of the question.

He pointed to the group of trucks again and this time when Elena nodded, they made a run for it. From there, it was an easy limping sprint to the fence, and they were through. A few seconds later, their fragile forms simply vanished in the stygian darkness beyond the lighted perimeter.

15

The priority was to put as much distance as possible between themselves and the site, and together they began to march downhill away from the lights. Jack let Elena take the lead, for there was little doubt in his mind that this was her element. He did not know exactly what would be going through her head right now, but he was sure her immediate priority would be the same as his. He stopped worrying about it and just concentrated on keeping up with her, following the sound of her movements and her breathing in the dark. He was surprised to find that he was able to match her measured, relentless pace, and that his leg was steadier than before. His mind turned to figuring out exactly where they might be, and where the hell they were going.

The map he had looked at, and which was now tucked into his overalls, was the wrong scale to be of much use – especially in the dark. He had hoped it might be possible to use it to help them head west, beyond the rainforest, in search of more populous areas, but he knew now that it was out of the question. Neither of them was in great shape, and the climb would quickly tell on them. Even if they made it out of the forest, there was still the unhappy prospect of walking across the barren, exposed uplands with just about everyone in the region looking for them. And even if they succeeded in crossing it, where would they go?

Their only option was to pick up the direction he had been going when he first set out on his mad odyssey. A descent of the rivers into Brazil or Colombia was potentially easier and more plausible, crazy as it seemed: a small matter of five hundred miles due northeast - or northeast-*ish*.

Once they were through the secondary growth near the site, the forest floor vegetation was mercifully thin at ground level. This, the hallmark of primary forest, meant they were almost certainly on the eastern slopes of the Andes. Unfortunately, that was about all he could tell, without some other point of reference. He went over events again, searching for clues, but without success. Quite apart from the uncertainty of what had happened before he reached the army base, he had no way of telling for how long or in what direction they had flown in the helicopter. It seemed colder here, so he guessed they were now further up the mountains, but beyond that, he calculated they could be anywhere along a four hundred mile southwest/northeast line, the midpoint of which might lie around eighty to a hundred miles northwest of his original position. So although it *felt* to him like he was northeast of his last known position, and while his *instinct* put him around two hundred miles along that line, a potential error of four hundred miles made further speculation meaningless.

He did know that by continuing down this gentle slope, they must eventually come to a river – the downstream course of which would be the easiest option for them to take. However, it would also be the most predictable choice for their pursuers. So no matter where they were right now, they would have to try to cut across the valleys. Hard, hard going, but it was a lot better than strolling back into the arms of his captors.

As they penetrated further into the jungle, they left the lights from the site far behind them. Jack could see virtually nothing, and was following Elena more or less blindly. She would be using her instincts to avoid the worst of the obstacles in the dark, a trick he himself had picked up only after having to walk in the darkness for several hours one night to get to a village. For now, he had to trust Elena's senses, and no doubt they were a good deal better than his own.

They had been walking for half an hour or more when sharp shadows suddenly swept across the forest ahead of them. The origin was a light source far behind, and they both stopped as the shadows passed back and forth for a few seconds and disappeared. A little later, he heard the sound of a helicopter approaching. He could hardly believe they would send a chopper to look for someone in the dark in the rainforest. What were they thinking of? He nudged Elena, and they started moving again.

"Dumb bastards," he whispered to himself.

The helicopter came and went, and he saw a few brief flashes from its searchlight away ahead in front. He could see that the beam barely penetrated the canopy. It was no threat at this distance, and he scoffed silently at the idiocy of sending the thing out at all.

The terrain was sloping more steeply now, and the effort needed to maintain his balance was making his leg ache again. The slope would end soon: either gently, at the banks of a stream or river; or abruptly, at the edge of a cliff or ravine. Soon he heard the faint gurgle and plop of flowing water, and as the noise grew, Jack relaxed a little. The sounds were more consistent with those of a gentle, slow-moving stream than with the violent, echoing shudders of the rock-strewn torrents he had seen so often in the upper valleys.

He glimpsed a clearing in the distance. Or was it his imagination? He strained to see it, and was concentrating so much that he almost walked into Elena, who had stopped, breathing heavily. She was also focusing hard on something. The sound of the river was louder now, the clearing around it faintly visible only because of the indistinct, spectral light from a cloud-covered sky. He was about to reach out to Elena, when he heard something else – something that did not belong. A click, or a snap. He listened again: nothing. Elena crouched down, very slowly, and Jack followed suit. He focused all his attention forward, and when the shadows from the distant light source appeared again and wavered ahead of him, he could see water in the clearing. He felt himself drawn to it, almost as if with a sudden rush forward he could cross the river and be free. He closed the thought out and remained frozen for another few seconds, and then he heard it again – another click. Not a snap, but a muffled metallic click. There was something – someone – between them and the river.

The noise was a good distance away – Jack estimated it at well over a hundred yards and slightly to their left – and he was focusing so hard on the spot that he almost failed to notice Elena moving off – slowly, smoothly, noiselessly, out towards the right and away from the source of the sound. Jack was riveted for a second by how she just seemed to melt away before his eyes, with scarcely a sound. With his sore leg and his ragged breathing, how could he hope to emulate that? He took a deep breath: he had done this stuff before, and he could do it again.

He began to move. He could barely see Elena's outline, but he could feel her presence just a yard or so in front. His eyes were focused dead ahead, but he was intensely alert to the area he estimated the sound had come from. As they approached the river, he heard something behind and to his left, and out of the corner of his eyes he finally saw a head in silhouette. A soldier. He realised the helicopter must have been dropping men by the river.

Never underestimate your enemy.

They moved on steadily, and when they reached the riverbank, they picked a spot with plenty of vegetation nearby, got down on their stomachs, and crawled slowly into the water.

It took less than two minutes to cross the shallow river, and they slowly crept up the banks and into the vegetation on the other side. They heard the helicopter return, and stopped when its searchlight swept briefly down the river, but they were beyond the tree line by now and when Jack turned to look behind him, towards the opposite bank, he realised how ridiculously hard it was to see more than a couple of feet into the forest from the river.

Once the searchlight disappeared, they got slowly to a crouch and made their escape. The potential folly of descending the first river they came to had been clearly demonstrated, and Jack now promised himself that no matter how tempting it might be to head downstream at the next river, they must cut straight across again.

16

"**N**o news, Major?" demanded Torres as he entered the room, still drying his face with a hand towel. It had been a long night for him; longer still for those operating under his withering gaze and terse questions and comments.

The Major removed his headset and dropped it on the desk by the side of the radio operator. He shook his head wearily. "Nothing," he said.

Torres nodded and waved his hand dismissively. They had been hunting their quarry for four straight hours with no sign of them at all. No-one had even been able to identify where they had got through the wire or in what direction they had headed. It was frustrating, but there was little to be gained at this point by tearing strips off the Major. Besides, it was getting light now, which would help the hunters more than the hunted. He reasoned that four hours in the dark, blundering around in the jungle, was not likely to have taken the two fugitives very far, and with everyone in the state on alert, they would be unlikely to remain undetected for long.

He looked at the map spread out on the nearby table and considered the possibilities again. Two people in rags – untrained, tired and injured. Where would they go? Uphill would be madness – cold, little water, little shelter, hard going. If they were foolish enough to try it, they would be easily spotted wherever they emerged. Going across country would be the choice of someone with a map, who knew the terrain and had time to figure things out. Someone with the right preparation, the right gear and the right support. More likely, they would head downhill, looking for a river to follow: the obvious thing to do. Still, although he knew little about the American, the woman had a reputation as a hard-case guerrilla. Not incompetent by any means.

Unlike some of the idiots pursuing them.

He studied the terrain again, tracing the intricate patterns of the streams and rivers as they ran east down the valleys and slowly came together. He shook his head. He was not going to leave anything to chance.

"Major," he said, beckoning with his left hand while he jabbed at the map with the index finger of his right.

The Major walked over to the table.

"I want your men to concentrate the search in this area here," he said, circling a point at the junction of two rivers. "Equip a team and insert them there before noon today. If our friends follow any of these streams, they must still come out here, probably within the next 24 hours. I want a good team, well hidden, dispersed between here, here and here." He indicated a triangle covering the area just downstream of the 'V' formed by the rivers. "And do you have people you can rely on at any of the towns along the Huallaga?"

"Yes. A few sir," said the Major.

"Good. Instruct them to monitor the river between Tinga Maria, San Martin and Tarapoto closely, until further notice."

"Yes sir. But they're hardly likely to make it *that* far."

"They've already escaped from you once, haven't they?" Torres growled.

"Sir," was the quiet response.

Torres sat back in his chair and stared at the map again, reminding himself that provided he stopped them getting out of Peru, they were really no threat. Anywhere they chose to go from here was likely to kill them, and if they did survive, they would be picked up and Torres would finish the job. Thinking of finishing the job, he remembered there was another problem to resolve.

"Major?"

"Yes sir?"

"You said this gringo had a partner somewhere. Is that right?"

"We think so, yes. From what we've put together, it appears that two men started off on an expedition to walk to Iquitos. They split up, though, and one of them remained in Cuzco. The other is the one we're chasing. We don't have names yet, but they should come through in the next few hours, although we probably won't know which one is which."

"Right." Torres nodded. "I need an address for the one in Cuzco. I'll be back in Lima by midday, and I'll need it by the time I get there."

"Yes sir." said the Major.

Torres got to his feet, nodded, and left the room.

WATERFALL

17

Jack stopped walking for a second and stared ahead. His eyes stung from the sweat that had trickled into them, and he had to blink several times to make certain of the creeping infusion of the pale grey, pre-dawn light. As the forest slowly began to take form around him, he felt his weariness lift a little. Enough to get his legs moving again on the gentle upslope.

A few minutes later, they came to a fallen tree, and Elena stopped and leaned against it. Jack glanced around: it was as good a place as any to rest, and they were both exhausted. He started pulling out everything he had taken earlier from the cabin, laying it on the ground in front of them. Elena looked on without saying anything.

"I'm going to wash," said Jack, when he had finished.

Elena nodded.

He walked slowly back down to the river they had just crossed, stripped off and bathed in the cold water. The simple act of removing the wet clothes was wonderful, and washing the sweat and grit out of the cuts and scratches on his hands and arms was invigorating enough to make him gasp. Finally, he rinsed his pants and overalls in the river and wrung them out. Dressing again, he made his way back to find Elena lying draped along the tree trunk. She looked like a cross between a wet tee-shirt model and a drowned rat.

He saw her watching him as he walked over and sat on the trunk near her feet and started to inspect the larger of his cuts and bruises. He massaged his leg, and the ache that had been bothering him throughout the walk seemed to abate.

"Do you know where we are?" he said in his broken Spanish.

"No," was Elena's flat reply. "Peru?" she added a second later, and when he looked at her, he saw the trace of a smile on her face.

He smiled back and nodded. "Ha ha."

She looked at him for a second and then abruptly sat up. "I wash too," she said, sliding off the trunk.

Jack turned his attention to the folded map on the ground. He had protected it as best he could, but where it had been folded, the ink had been completely rubbed off. He was still able to unfold it successfully by peeling the thin, wet sheets of paper apart very carefully.

He spread it on the ground and studied it in the growing light. He saw now that it was a composite of more than one individual map, judging by the white blocks around some of the joins. All the information that would have been useful – scale, grid references, key – had been lost in creating what was obviously a simple overview map for someone already familiar with what they were looking at. It was based on topographical charts that he reckoned were probably to a scale of one to two hundred and fifty thousand. He had used a few of them early in his expedition, but in this case, what was left of the original maps, after being hacked about to make the composite, was poor quality.

He scowled, holding the map up to the grey light to look at the holes where the pins had been, and studying the adjacent lettering. Letter groups like 'AE' and 'CO' meant nothing to him, and although there were a few names on the map, they were all but illegible. There certainly were no large towns or settlements or named rivers. He had little doubt that they had just come from one of the pin-hole positions - 'Works AE', presumably, or 'Terminal AE' maybe, based on the piece of paper and the larger-scale map he had seen earlier. He sighed. It was academic – the damned thing was no use for navigation. He was tempted to throw it away, or bury it, but in the end, he spread it out to dry and turned to the other items.

The matches were useless as they were, but everything else was fine: knives, wire and pins for traps and hooks, and the water bottle for transporting at least a little water. He was sure the two of them together could improvise shelter, and while fire was not an option now, if he could dry out the matches, they would be able to get something going in no time. It was a lot better than nothing.

He was concentrating so hard that he was startled by Elena's returning footsteps. She looked a lot healthier after her wash. Like him, she had hundreds of tiny cuts all over her arms and face, as well as some bruising and a larger cut across her cheek. Her left eye was half closed from a blow she had taken, and the surrounding skin was puffy and discoloured. They would have to try to keep cuts as clean as possible and otherwise trust to luck that no infection set in.

Together, they looked over their meagre supply of tools and equipment again, and then Elena sat down and allowed Jack to examine the body wound she had originally sustained in the fight with the other Sendero. It seemed to be healing now, and the scalp wound was definitely much better.

"Bloodied but unbowed," he said to her, after checking her head.

"What?"

"Expression in English. It's okay – it's *good*," he added, when she looked at him suspiciously. He gave her a thumbs-up and a smile as she sat down on the tree trunk and looked at him. She was pretty beaten up, but she still looked lean, fit and eminently capable. "Could you have a look at the map? See if it means anything?" he asked her.

She did as he asked, coming over and squatting down to get a better look.

"No. This does not help," she said, after a few minutes.

Now that there was no immediate danger, no distractions, no angry emotion, Jack found her accent and her mixture of Spanish and English fairly easy to understand. He wondered how easily she understood him.

"Even knowing we started from point 'AE', it makes no difference. There is nothing I recognise," she said.

"Damn," said Jack.

"But I would guess we are probably somewhere in San Martin."

This was one of the *Departamentos* – states, or counties – that Jack had originally considered travelling through, and he tried to picture its layout in his head.

"How do you know?"

"Well, first, the helicopter was flying on a course of 330 degrees almost all the time."

Jack looked at her in surprise.

"What, you think because we live in the jungle we can't read a compass? *Que sesgo, gringo,*" she said, with a disdainful look.

"No. But in the helicopter, I thought you were unconscious or something. You were pretty banged up."

She touched the side of her head, as if remembering the blows she had received.

"That was nothing. I've had worse. I was watching the pilots' panel."

"Okay. So you do know where we are, roughly?"

"Not really, no. I don't know San Martin much."

"Really?"

"Of course not. I operate – operated – in Ayacucho and the VRAE. Before that, I lived in Lima. I have never been anywhere in San Martin."

Jack knew 'VRAE' was a reference to the river valleys of the Apurimac, Ene and Mantaro rivers, an area synonymous with the drugs business and in times past a law unto itself. San Martin and the Huallaga Valley were probably not much better, and the narcos were known to have a strong presence throughout the Upper Huallaga.

"Great."

They sat in silence for a few seconds.

"We have to continue downstream," Jack finally said.

Elena nodded absently. "But they will be waiting somewhere."

"Yes." Jack tapped the map. "If it were me, I'd be waiting at one of the river mouths further down. All this water – here, back there –" he indicated with his thumb, "the streams we crossed – all this will come out on some bigger river somewhere. That's where I'd be waiting."

"Yes. We must be careful," said Elena earnestly.

Jack smiled at this, and Elena suddenly looked angry.

"Why are you laughing, gringo?"

"'We need to be careful' – understatement of the year, Elena."

"But it's *true*."

"Yes, but – oh, never mind." He shook his head, still smiling. "Look," he said, leaning forward, "if I remember correctly, all the rivers as far west as this – assuming you're right about where we are – flow into the Huallaga, right?"

"Of course."

"So that's probably the river we're going to end up on, and where they will be waiting."

"Almost certainly, yes."

"So," said Jack thoughtfully.

"So what?"

"So we should go down the Ucayali instead.

"What?" cried Elena. You are *loco*?" We don't even know where it is. It must be hundreds of kilometres away!"

Jack looked at her, and his expression slowly changed from thoughtful hesitancy to grim determination.

"Listen Elena, I don't know about you, but I'd rather face an extra hundred kilometres in the jungle than any more soldiers – or terrorists, or Americans, for that matter."

"Okay," she nodded, after a moment. "I understand. But the Ucayali? You are really mad. I will not go with you."

He stood up. "I'm not mad, Elena – I'm angry." As he spoke, the emotion was clear in his face. "I am going to get out of this. I don't know how, but I *will* get out of it."

He stared at Elena. "And when I do, I'm going to get every one of the bastards that did this to me."

Elena looked at him. "Does that include me, gringo?"

"No. Yes. I don't know. Your little terrorist friends, anyway."

"They were *not* my friends."

Jack snatched the map from the ground and started folding it up again. Elena sat with her eyes closed.

"It was not my idea to kidnap you, gringo," she said.

"That's nice to know," said Jack, dismissively. "You went along with it, though, didn't you?"

Elena shrugged. "We were desperate for money."

Jack ignored her and continued. "And if you went along with it, then you were one of them, weren't you? Who gives a shit whose idea it was?"

Elena's eyes flashed, a look of anger growing in her face. "But I did *not* agree. That was why we fought."

"Hah - yes, that was pretty spectacular. A brilliant bit of organisation, there. You're all the same, you people – criminals and no-hopers with your eyes on the main chance. So go on, tell me – why were you killing each other?"

Elena scoffed. "You would not understand."

"Try me."

She thought for a moment. "We – our organisation – we have our differences. Many members want to make agreement with the government. I do not. Our group is one of few that fights for freedom, not money. The rest are already in the pockets of the politicos."

"So...?"

"So, the ones I was with, they wanted to take you to the other Sendero – to the government. They wanted to betray us."

"Why didn't you just leave, then?"

"Because they would betray all of us who still believe in our cause."

"So you disagreed, and your solution was to kill each other?" Jack mocked.

"No. Of course not." The anger in her face was obvious, but she blew out a long breath and her black expression cleared. "It doesn't matter what you think. It doesn't matter now."

When it was clear she was not going to continue, Jack started picking up the other things from the ground. "Well," he said, "if you're not coming with me, what are you going to do?" he asked.

Elena said nothing.

"Back to the Sendero?" he prompted.

"No. They will kill me now."

"So...?"

She shrugged. "I can look after myself."

Jack stood up straight, putting all his bits and pieces back in place. He looked at Elena, then sighed.

"I know how to get to the Ucayali," he said.

"Okay."

"Roughly, anyway."

"*Si.*"

"I could use some help..."

Elena glared at him, her anger erupting again. "I do not need your sympathy, gringo."

"My *sympathy*? Ha! Not in a million years. Listen, I can find my way to the Ucayali, but–"

"So go, then! I am not stopping you, am I?"

"*But,*" Jack repeated, with attitude. "Someone who knows – who understands – the locals and the local way of life, could make the difference between being discovered or not. That's all." He looked around, checking he had everything. "Sympathy, my ass," he muttered.

"And if you get to the Ucayali?" Elena asked, as he prepared to walk away. "What then? How will you escape?"

"I'll keep going down river, until I get to Brazil. Simple."

Elena shook her head. "It is mad. It is thousands of kilometres."

"It is *not* thousands of kilometres, Elena. It was part of my original plan, and it's all up here." He tapped his forehead. "Anyway, do you have any other suggestions?"

"Ha ha. Funny man," she said. "I have no plan. The Sendero will kill me. The Police will kill me. The Army will kill me." She looked at him thoughtfully.

"What?" asked Jack.

"Okay, I will help you. When we get to the Ucayali, I will leave you."

Jack nodded. "Okay then. No problem."

They stood there for a few seconds, looking at each other, and then Jack stuck out his hand.

Elena looked down at it, before slowly extending her own. They shook firmly.

"You are a funny man, gringo."

"Sure. 'Hilarious' is my middle name." Jack stopped shaking her hand, but continued to grip it. "Just one other thing."

Elena looked at him suspiciously.

"The name is Jack, okay?"

"Okay, Mister Jack."

"Ha ha – no, not 'Mister Jack' please," he burst out. "It makes me feel like an old man. Just 'Jack'."

"Jack."

"Right."

They shook again.

"Let's go then?"

18

J ack's instinct was to head due east – preferably slightly north of east – in order to avoid the potential risk of paralleling the Ucayali, and getting even deeper into Peru. Fortunately, navigation this close to the equator was straightforward: all he needed was to be able to see the sun in the morning or the evening.

Their first hours were easy going, in spite of having to traverse some shallow valleys and wade two small rivers. At one point, Elena stopped him and pointed out some plants, which after a good deal of digging and scraping yielded small edible roots like emaciated turnips. To these she added some broad leaves she had scavenged, and when they were washed down with the little water they were able to carry, they tasted marvellous to Jack's hungry stomach. He knew they would need more than a handful of roots every now and then if they were to keep going for any length of time, but for now, they were trading food for distance and safety – and when he felt tired and hungry, Jack was spurred on by encouraging thoughts of the Peruvian army swarming all over the rivers well to their north or west. He was also thinking positively about his contact in Cuzco, Greg, and how long it would be before he raised the alarm.

Greg was an Australian who had accompanied Jack some of the way to Cuzco, but decided to remain in the ancient city to pursue his own agenda. He had a long-stay visa and was happy to be Jack's link man for the rest of the Peru stage of the expedition. One of his responsibilities would be to trigger a search after a pre-defined period, and Jack had found the timing of this to be a difficult decision, partly for technical reasons and partly because of his dread of a false alarm that might kill off the expedition prematurely. After a good deal of discussion, they had come up with twenty-one days as the agreed period.

Neither he nor Elena had an accurate fix on the current date, but after she had told him how many days he had been held captive by the Sendero, Jack was pretty sure the last time the satellite messenger he had been carrying would have sent its automated signal was at most twelve days ago. He decided that even if Greg started an alert nine days from now, it would probably need another day for anyone to take it seriously and one more day to mobilise any sort of effort. Then of course they would be looking for him hundreds of miles in the wrong direction. This black thought was tempered by the idea that if he could get to the Ucayali River, he would be back on his planned route to Iquitos. It would mean that either he would be able to contact Greg at one of the larger towns, or he would at least be in the right area if someone were searching for him.

So, all they had to do was keep going east and stay out of trouble. He tried to picture the topography, and was still thinking it through when they came upon the largest river they had encountered so far. The opening formed by the meeting of the rivers gave them a rare glimpse of the terrain well beyond and to the east, and it looked dauntingly high.

"This must be the Huallaga," said Elena, as they lay hidden on the west bank, checking the river margins for any signs of life.

"Yes," agreed Jack. "So we have that lot over there to climb." He pointed to the ridges in the distance. "But at least we should be well to the south of where anyone would be looking."

"*Quizás*," said Elena. "Perhaps." When Jack looked at her, she continued. "You forget about the local people. Our army friends and the Sendero – your *Americanos*, too – will spread the word and scare people into informing on us."

"But so soon?"

"Radio," said Elena, putting her hand to her ear and miming a phone. "*Muy eficiente* in remote areas – radios, boats, aircraft..."

They spent almost five minutes lying in the baked mud making absolutely sure there was no-one around. Here by the banks the heat from the noon-day sun was intense, even though they were still within the shade of the tree line. Jack studied the river and watched a broken branch float past. The river looked placid enough, but the swirling eddies that seemed to boil up and spread out, constantly renewed and energised, gave the lie to its depth and speed. The branch swung round crazily as it sped past them and finally disappeared downstream. Jack was not looking forward to the crossing.

As if reading his thoughts, Elena touched him on the shoulder and pointed upstream, to a wider section of the river. She made a walking motion with her fingers. Jack nodded, and they got to their feet. He followed her as she led the way, until eventually she stopped and pointed across the river. He could immediately see why she had picked this spot: on their side was a rock shelf that extended several yards into the river, while on the other side, maybe eighty or so yards back downstream, there was a pooled backwater behind some exposed rock. In the middle, the water looked mercifully untroubled, although he knew it was still travelling at a good brisk walking pace at least. He sighed and nodded.

"You are afraid, gringo?"

"Jack," he said.

"You are afraid, Jack?"

"Crap."

Elena laughed. "Come on, then. *Vamanos*! See you on the other side."

By the time they were knee deep in the cold river, at the end of the rock shelf, the force of the water was evident. Jack's adrenaline was flowing too, but he concentrated on the thought that even if he got swept away, he was unlikely to die provided he kept his head above water and struck out for the far bank.

Elena gave him an enquiring glance. He nodded, and she surged ahead, wading a few yards and then dropping into the water and starting a strong, confident crawl. Jack hesitated only a second before following.

Almost immediately, the water pulled at him and he could feel it trying to turn him round – first one way, then another. He had to fight hard to maintain his direction. The river carried him downstream shockingly quickly, and he put all his energy into his swimming stroke, seeing with alarm the rate at which he was descending. Then suddenly he was in the middle of the river, in the gentlest of currents, making steady progress across to the other side. He started to look for Elena, but could not see her. He was getting closer to the opposite bank, still well upstream of the backwater. His progress was strong and steady, and he was starting to feel confident when the current grabbed him again, this time spinning him round a hundred and eighty degrees and dragging him under.

Disorientated, he struggled to get his head above the water. Another frighteningly strong pull, and another. He saw Elena briefly. Saw her encouraging him. Saw the backwater just a few yards across the river, approaching rapidly. He struck out, using every ounce of energy he had left. He felt the pull of the water around his legs. He was not going to make it, dammit! Then his leg touched something, twisting him around. He saw a smooth boulder not a foot from him and clutched at it. He got a tenuous grasp on it, but could not hold it. His fingers were slipping. He felt hands grabbing his arm, pulling – helping – and suddenly he was out of the turmoil, clinging to the rock, the calm water almost unmoving, a line of froth bobbing gently against the rock. He got a footing, pushed himself up, and sat down heavily by the riverside.

"God almighty," he said at last, still breathing hard.

"He helped, I am certain," said Elena.

Later, when they had climbed away from the river, Jack reminded himself that the biggest challenge was not dealing with the rivers and the forest, but avoiding human contact. The jungle was a harsh environment, certainly, but it was not going to put a bullet in his head. He could get by in the rainforest, but he was much less certain about how he would deal with a full-on confrontation with narcos, the army, the police or the Americans. When he thought about it at all, his thoughts quickly became unfocused – slower somehow – his mind refusing to deal with the problem of a possible violent encounter.

When he had been taken by the Sendero, he had been unconscious; unable to resist. Later, he had given himself up – almost joyously, he remembered bitterly – to the army. But in a straight confrontation, how would he deal with it? He felt his stomach tightening and his heart pounding. His mind dragged him unwillingly back to his home town. To a cold, damp, winter's night, leaving Duffy's bar with some friends, laughing and joking, and arguing over the next port of call. He could almost taste the salt-laden air and smell the seaweed left on the rocks at low tide.

They walked down the hill from Duffy's and turned the corner onto the Seafront, where the wind drove needles of icy rain into their faces. Looking across to the car park, they saw a small gang of youths beating a man up. Jack's friends ran straight over to help the man, but Jack remained rooted to the spot. Even now, six thousand miles and twelve years distant, he remembered the cold sweat and the feeling of numbness spreading through his body.

It had probably been only a few moments, but it seemed an eternity to him at the time. His heart rate soared, his breathing becoming more rapid. His neck muscles twitched and his whole head seemed to quiver. His mouth became dry, while his eyes, which had seemed almost to flicker, started watering. All he could do was watch, transfixed, as his friends crashed on top of the gang. It stopped the fight in an instant, and the two sides drew back, mouthing, pointing, staring.

Finally, Jack felt himself move – slowly, trance like. He walked over to the group, his muscles tense and awkward. He looked down at the victim, lying in his own vomit, his face a bloody pulp, his legs pulled up to his stomach. He was moaning, rocking from side to side, unable or unwilling to get up. The two groups stood over him, glaring at each other, spellbound. He saw their lips move, but did not hear a word. His eyes flicked from the victim to the biggest, most aggressive member of the gang, who stood to the front of the others, his face a mask of hate. He watched as the guy raised a forefinger and pointed it at one of Jack's friends. He had a big, pudgy hand with a tattoo on each finger. Jack noticed a capital 'E' on the index finger, in faded black, with a small dot underneath it, and he watched as a bit of spittle bubbled at the corner of the guy's mouth. He saw the pudgy hand draw back, balling into a fist – watched as the left foot slid forward and the body started to twist subtly... and then Jack smashed his forehead into the side of the guy's face, with every ounce of strength he possessed. When it happened, it felt just like he was heading a heavy, wet, leather football. He felt a twinge of pain, and watched as the guy staggered and went down on one knee. Jack's friends advanced slightly, and the others ran off. The guy got to his feet, reeling, and wobbled off towards his mates, who had now stopped running and were shouting obscenities from a safe distance. The whole incident was probably over in less than a minute, and as they stood there together, looking at the victim lying on the ground, he heard the sound of a police siren.

His senses, which seemed to have withdrawn for a while, suddenly snapped back like a piece of elastic, and he turned, walked a few yards to sit heavily on the edge of the sea wall, and vomited onto the beach. Afterwards he felt that cold sweatiness again, and when the police asked him what had happened, he found he could barely speak; could not remember the details. The brief interview felt worse than the incident, but an hour later the police were satisfied, the victim had been taken to hospital, and the group of friends were back in the bar having a drink. Jack found he was being hailed as the hero of the moment.

"If Jack hadn't taken out the big shit-head, we'd have been in real trouble."

"Yeah. Good call, mate. That stopped the bastards dead."

"Our hero – here, get him another drink!"

Hero my ass. He had had no control over his actions at all. Had not known what was going on, or what he was doing. He'd been plain terrified from first sight of the gang to the interview with the police.

Twice more in Jack's life, he had had the same experience – that numbing fear, a feeling of being detached from reality – and twice he had reacted violently and unpredictably. Both occasions had been in his short army career: once in the barracks, and once on a tour. In the barracks, it had done him no harm – quite the contrary – but the last time, he considered that it had cost the lives of several of his own squad. What made it worse was that the whole shitty situation had been caused by having to follow the asinine orders of a superior officer. The physical and mental trauma had affected him badly, as the enormity of it all slowly sank in. He should have had the courage to refuse the damned order in the first place. As usual, the thought made him angry, and the explosive minutes of the ambush came back, with the slow-motion replay of those first, critical moments when he had felt himself lock up. His sweat turned cold. Four of his men died in the first hail of bullets, and a fifth was badly wounded before Jack had been able to get them to safety. He had carried the wounded man out himself, but the man – little more than a kid, really – died three weeks later in hospital. The fact that Jack was later awarded a medal for the action was a bitter irony that fuelled bouts of drunken introspection and self-recrimination in unguarded moments. After that, he spent every waking hour figuring out how to make sure he would never be placed in the same situation again, and planning how to get out of the army in the shortest space of time without putting anyone else's life in danger. Six months later he was out, and the first thing he did was get blind drunk and toss his medal into the Liffey.

That had been three years ago, and he thought he was free of all that crap – until now. In the last few days he had twice been caught – or at least, allowed himself to be taken. In both cases, there was not the remotest possibility of taking action, but what if the outcome depended on his response? What if he had to take a stand or make a decision in the heat of a confrontation?

Lost in his thoughts, he stumbled and went down on his bad leg. The sharp pain made him grunt, and drove the dark thoughts from his mind. He had to concentrate. The solution was to avoid any confrontation – and the best way of doing that was to get out of here as quickly and quietly as possible. Forget any thoughts of revenge. Forget trying to figure out why all of this was happening. Just get out.

He picked himself up and limped on, the dull pain focusing his mind on the task at hand.

Just get the hell out.

19

Their progress was good on the first day. The ground was reasonably clear, although rising steadily now, and they had picked up two stout sticks to use for clearing the way, testing things they had to walk over, and checking for bugs and snakes. These had only bothered them twice: once when Jack's stick had been attacked by an absurdly aggressive spider, and once – somewhat more worryingly – when they narrowly avoided disturbing a pit viper sleeping among the branches of a fallen tree. They only crossed two small streams, stopping each time to wash and to fill the little plastic water bottle. There was no sign of any human activity, or of much animal life, and so it continued for the remainder of the day. Late in the afternoon they picked a spot, made a rough shelter from palm leaves, and prepared for nightfall. They bathed in the nearby stream, drank some water, and sat on their beds of sticks and leaves as darkness enveloped them. They still did not want to risk a fire, so the only food they had was some more of Elena's roots and leaves, but they felt safe enough to spend some time talking before they put their heads down.

Elena was eager to know why Jack had come to Peru, and could not believe his plan to walk the entire length of the Amazon.

"But why?" she kept asking, a question which none of his explanations seemed to answer to her satisfaction. "Did no-one tell you we are at war here?"

"You are not at war," said Jack. "You have an elected government – it's a democracy. How are you 'at war'?"

"Hah! You are like the others – you do not understand. This government was not elected. It was *impuesto*."

"Imposed? But you had elections. Verified elections. What's imposed about that?"

"The votes were not counted. The result was invented. The people who are supposed to *verificar*, were bought. You Americans helped."

"I'm not American."

"Well, you are all the same. You live in little shells, isolated from reality. Reality is not pleasant. Life is hard. You know nothing; understand nothing." She snorted. "If you did, you would not come here."

"It's still wrong to take the law into your own hands. It doesn't solve any problems."

"It does when it is the difference between life and death."

"Uh-huh?" said Jack, disbelief clear in his voice.

"*Yes* 'uh-huh'! You think I am lying, gringo?" Her sudden anger seemed to come from nowhere. "Let me tell you something, *cínico*. Let me tell you how it really is in Peru." She paused, her head bowed for a couple of seconds, before she continued. "My father..." She faltered, but recovered. "My father was a good man. An honest man. When he was a boy, the family had nothing to eat. They used to take a – a *catapulta*, and walk around the village looking for lizards and little birds for food. But he survived. He survived and he succeeded. He built his business from nothing. He kept us and fed us and clothed us, and built our house with his own hands." Her angry look evaporated for a moment. "I remember when we got our first car – an old Volkswagen with no windows and just one seat. We thought we had reached the very top when we got that car."

Jack could feel the smile in her voice, and found himself smiling too. "Sounds good."

She looked at him, and her angry expression returned. "What would you know? It *was* good. And he sacrificed everything to do the best for us. He got us into private schools – me and my brothers – and he slowly built his business – his *comercio* – starting with a market stall, then a shop, then two shops. He bought a small farm from a man who owed him some money, and by the time I left school he was a respected local businessman." She paused, drew a long breath and sighed heavily.

"So what happened?"

"The usual *mierda*. Anyone who has success here will tell you you cannot make everybody happy. He had enemies." She shrugged. "There were local elections, and one of those enemies got elected Mayor. He destroyed my father's businesses. He used public money to *sobornar* people – to make them to not buy from us. He pressed charges against our farm and it was taken away from us."

"What? But surely he couldn't do that. I mean, your father could have done something – you know, complained about him or something, right?"

A cry of derision escaped her lips. "Maybe that works in your country, but not here. Here, the only thing that matters is who has the more money. Of course we tried to complain, but it made no difference. We lost everything."

"Well, I'm sorry Elena. That's pretty tough, but–"

"And when they murdered my family, I became Sendero."

"You what? They *murdered* your family?" asked Jack, not quite sure he had heard correctly.

"Yes. My father was not without friends. They started to put pressure on the Mayor and his *bandidos*, and they had some success. Too much, I think. So they came to the house one day and shot my father, my mother and my two brothers."

"Jesus Christ. And what about you?"

"I was in Lima, studying to be a Doctor."

"You're a *doctor*?"

"I said I was *studying* to be a doctor. I never finished. I was in my final year when I heard the news, and I rushed back. I never even got to my parents' house. The taxi I was in was ambushed. The driver was killed, and when the car went off the road I was thrown clear before it exploded. I got to my feet and ran. *Jesús* did I run." She paused for a second. "I found the Sendero; now I am Sendero."

Jack was lost for words. He mumbled something about condolences, and found he was grateful they could no longer see each other now that the blackness of the night was complete. They sat unseeing together for a while, each lost in their own thoughts, before Jack lay down and drifted into an uneasy sleep.

He awoke to the sound of a couple of jungle chickens squawking to each other in the canopy. The usual grey pre-dawn light showed him that Elena was already up, and he could hear her moving around down by the stream. He thought about her story. If it were true, did it make what she was doing right? Was it possible that Peru could be so corrupt in this day and age? That there really was no rule of law at all? What if it had been him? What would he have done? He had been in the army; been overseas for a while. He had fought in someone else's country for a cause he had accepted as being right and just, but he was no idealistic fool.

He sat up and prodded his bad leg. Not so bad any longer, and the pain of yesterday had already gone. He looked up when he heard a noise.

"You're a freedom fighter then," he announced as Elena walked up the slope towards him.

"Sorry?"

"Nothing. Just thinking, really." He regretted the comment and did not want to carry on the conversation right now. Maybe he could be persuaded to reclassify his erstwhile captors to some degree, but in his book nothing excused kidnapping innocent civilians.

"I went up ahead and climbed a tree," Elena said brightly. "I saw a valley, just north of our line. It could save us much time."

"The valley runs north?"

"No, east. *Codo con codo* – sorry, parallel – to where we are going, but a little more north of here."

"Sounds good," Jack said, his hopes rising. "Any problems?"

She shrugged. "More people, perhaps."

Jack considered. Was it worth the increased risk of detection? Climbing up and down even these lower *cordilleras* would be tough, slow progress, and cutting through the valleys could save days.

"If you think you can keep us away from everyone, I say we go for the valley."

"It should not be too difficult. It's very remote up here."

They continued to make good headway that morning, dropping down gradually from the slopes and finding the going becoming easier as they journeyed east. The only concern was that all the streams they encountered still appeared to be flowing west, probably back to the Huallaga, and Jack was growing uncomfortable with this until they breasted a small ridge and got a glimpse of the promised valley. Narrow here where they were entering it, it widened dramatically, quickly becoming a shallow-sided basin, miles wide, surrounded by ragged mountains the highest of which rose in the southeast to tower over everything else. The whole – even the highest of the peaks – was covered in unbroken forest, and a stream meandered into the distance to the east, where a nick in the surrounding ridges showed its course and what promised to be their immediate destination. It was unusual to get such a clear view over more than a few hundred yards, and Jack stood and gazed across it. It looked bizarrely like the Boyne Valley back home, albeit without the castles and with a lot more trees. He felt inspired by the thought that this was their escape route to the east: to the Ucayali, and to rescue.

"Beautiful, isn't it?" said Elena, and Jack turned to see her looking at him with some amusement on her face.

Jack shrugged. "Especially if it gets us out of here."

"It will. I am sure. If you are right about the geography..."

"I *am* right about the geography, Elena. Trust me."

"So, it must come out on the Ucayali. All we need to do is follow it."

"Easy," said Jack.

"Easy," she agreed.

They sat and rested first, eating some more roots and leaves. Jack's stomach was in knots, and he had been feeling the lack of carbohydrate slowly sapping his energy with every hour of walking. He really needed some proper food. Elena looked okay, but it was difficult to tell from her expression how she was feeling. Sometimes, as he followed her, he was reminded of the battery advertisements he had grown up with – little pink rabbits drumming on and on and on... He smiled at the thought.

Once they had eaten, they headed off, Jack taking the lead. They descended to the water's edge and covered enough ground that by nightfall they were within striking distance of the narrower part of the valley to the east where the stream looked like it squeezed between the mountains.

When they stopped, they ate roots and leaves once again, this time from the little stock they were carrying with them, and once again Jack drifted into an uneasy sleep. In their perpetually damp clothes, they found it natural to huddle together for warmth, but even this left backs or fronts exposed, and led to twisting and turning which woke first one person and then the other. It was something of a relief when he could lever himself up to greet the dawn; and although the first rays of light invigorated him a little, there was no escaping how badly affected he was by the lack of food.

They were back on the trail again by seven o'clock, and had covered a lot of ground by midday. Elena was leading now, and she suddenly held up her hand and pointed ahead. There was a stand of banana trees and coconut palms, quite out of place amongst the native trees, and a clear indication of civilisation. They redoubled the care they were taking to remain out of sight, and when they eventually came to a small clearing with cultivated plants, they had to decide whether to try to avoid it completely by working around it, or go through it carefully and perhaps gather any food they could find on the way. A couple of minutes later the sight of a bunch of ripe bananas hanging from a distant banana tree was all they needed to make up their minds. Besides, there was still no sign of any habitation, and Jack hoped that with it being soon after lunchtime, most people would be having a siesta.

They picked their way carefully through the ponderous secondary growth in the plantation. It was full of biting insects and a host of lizards, and they disturbed two thin green snakes that shot out of their way as they approached. It was slow progress until they came to a narrow dirt path, and when they got to the first *bananera*, Jack used one of the craft knives to cut out the ripest bunch of bananas on the tree. After several seconds of cutting, it dropped noisily to the ground, disturbing a couple of large birds, which flew off shrieking.

Jack and Elena plucked as many bananas as they could from the heavy bunch and hurried away, but not quickly enough to avoid being seen by a small boy. The boy turned and ran, with Jack in pursuit and Elena hissing fiercely at him to stop. After less than a minute, Jack and the boy emerged at one end of the plantation where stood a wooden house built high off the ground on thin stilts. The boy charged up the steps, shouting, and a woman came to the door, peering out at Jack, who stopped at the edge of the clearing.

He had been stupid to follow the boy. If they had just disappeared, perhaps no-one would have believed the kid's story; now, there would be no doubts. He had to think quickly. He decided there were probably no men around, or they would have been the first to show themselves at the door. Probably away hunting or fishing. That gave Elena and himself time to disappear. He made a feint towards the house, prompting the woman and the boy to retreat inside and shut the door. He then turned southwest, more or less back the way they had come, and disappeared into the tree line. As soon as he was hidden from view, Elena appeared at his side. She said nothing, and when he moved off again she followed as he circled round the house, keeping out of sight, and they continued their way downstream. With luck, the woman and child would believe they were heading west, not east.

"What do you think they'll do?" asked Jack.

"Nothing," said Elena. "At least not until the men come back. Then they might decide to go to the nearest community to tell someone, or maybe they'll do nothing at all. It is difficult to say."

"But we have to assume they'll tell someone." It was more a statement than a question.

Elena nodded.

When they had doubled back to the river, they saw a tree on the river bank with a few boards laid on the muddy bank next to it. By the water's edge was a larger board with a scrubbing brush and a plastic washing-up tub sitting next to it, and alongside were two small canoes, each with its own paddle. He looked enquiringly at Elena.

"Can you paddle?" he asked.

"*El Papa es católico?*" she shot back.

Jack hesitated for a moment. He felt uncomfortable with the idea of stealing the canoes. How much did they mean to the family? How would they get new ones? And how would the act be regarded – perhaps it was like horse stealing in the American West. But it was clear to him that the theft could make all the difference – it would double or triple the amount of ground they could cover with each hour, and it might delay the alarm if these were the family's only canoes. Tomorrow they could abandon the canoes, hide them somewhere, and disappear into the jungle again. He felt there was little choice. The family would survive, and so must he. He grabbed one of the canoes, baled it out and pushed it into the water. Elena followed suit with the other canoe. He stepped in carefully, and although it took a few moments to find his balance, they were both on their way in less than a minute.

Paddling as smoothly as he could, he found the small amounts of water that spilled into the canoe could be easily bailed out with the cut-down plastic bottle left for the purpose. Even paddling easily, the speed of the current meant they were achieving a likely ground speed of three or more times their earlier walking pace. If they kept going overnight, they could conceivably cover forty or fifty miles before having to abandon the canoes. They could be confident of avoiding detection in the dark, which only left the remainder of the daylight hours to worry about. It was definitely a risk worth taking, and he fixed his eyes firmly on the narrowing valley ahead.

20

E ven from the balcony of the exclusive tenth-floor apartment on Malccón Cisneros, it was an uninspiring, grey morning in Lima, and the mist-shrouded ocean looked cold and forbidding. Adam Torres did not mind in the slightest. He was feeling more relaxed today, after getting the information he needed on the gringo in Cuzco. He also felt confident about running the other gringo and the girl down sooner rather than later. It was one of the reasons for this meeting today. Besides, he was enjoying the opulence of the rented apartment's furnishings, as well as the beautiful decor and all the little electronic gadgets. One of these gadgets was the security console that allowed him to simultaneously monitor four internal and eight external HD security cameras.

He saw a white Toyota hatchback with a rental sticker on the back window park on the street opposite the building. A man emerged from the passenger side, looked quickly around, and walked towards the apartment block. He was expensively dressed, in a dark suit, white shirt and red tie. He looked to be well groomed, too, which was perhaps surprising in someone who was more used to living in a hammock in the middle of the jungle. On the other hand he was short, stocky, and unmistakably Peruvian, and because of this, Torres knew the security guard would grill him well before letting him through. After all, Peru was still run mainly by European descendants who discriminated relentlessly against the indigenous low-lifes. As he considered the fact, his mouth twitched into a shape that was half smile and half sneer.

He watched as the man was finally admitted, the guard having no doubt thoroughly checked his false ID, and he saw him stand by the elevator, staring into the sparklingly clean mirror along the wall. He was not doing it out of vanity, Torres was sure, but because the mirror gave an excellent view back to the security doors and the outside of the building. When you had a million-*Sol* price on your head, you tended to be careful. It also gave Torres the opportunity to study the heavy face and dark eyes of his visitor. The broad, sloping forehead and the distinct brow ridge which even carefully trimmed eyebrows and beard could not make light of, marked him out as someone who would be shunned by the Peruvian social elite. Perhaps it was this that had turned the man into the violent, criminal sociopath he was reputed to be. Or perhaps it was just greed. No matter.

The elevator arrived and the man stepped inside. Torres saw him emerge on the tenth floor a few moments later. His eyes also glanced across the views from the other cameras. The driver outside had turned the Toyota around so that it was facing into the road. A sensible precaution. He had a newspaper held up in front of him now, although no doubt he was watching the building carefully. All pretty much as Torres expected, so that he was quite content to release the electronic security bolts in the apartment door when the man arrived and pressed the buzzer.

Once he was inside, they embraced.

"Hey, my frien'," the Peruvian said. "How's things?" In spite of the occasional dropped 'd', his English was good, spoken with a strong American twang probably picked up from several years laundering money in Miami.

"Good. And you? All going smoothly?"

"Can't complain. Can't complain at all."

Torres ushered him into the living quarters and offered him a seat and a glass of water.

"What, have you run out of whisky?" the man asked, and laughed.

Torres laughed with him. "Of course not. Irish, Scotch or American?"

Once they had their drinks in hand, they sat down across the polished chrome and marble coffee table.

"Sorry to bring you here, my good friend," Torres oozed politely, "but I needed to talk to you about our operations."

"I see. Well, they are all going well. Nothing to report, really."

"What about the problems in the east?"

The man waved his hand dismissively. "We ha' some issues with that break-away group, but they have been disbanded."

"The Real Sendero?"

"Real Sendero, Nuevo Sendero – whatever. *Si.* Disbanded or dead."

"Would it interest you to know that the army had Elena Lopez in custody two days ago?"

A blank look.

"You might know her better as Maria Fernandez."

"What? That treacherous bitch? I thought we ha' nailed them all. "

Torres shook his head. "Not quite."

"Shit, man," he paused. "Well, surely the army can be trusted to take care of that, at least."

"I'm afraid not."

A quizzical look.

"She escaped."

The man almost choked on his whisky. He put the glass down heavily and raised his hands in exasperation. "Man, it was easier when the army was the fucking *enemy*!" He shook his head and picked up his drink again, studying the glass with narrowed eyes. "No matter," he said, finally. "We'll fin' her. You can be sure of that."

Torres took a sip from his glass and sat forward. "My friend, people have been promising me this for the last year, but no one has managed to do it yet. And now things have become more complicated.

"More complicated how?"

"Well, it seems this Lopez – Fernandez, if you prefer – picked up some gringo somewhere, and they've both had a nice tour of one of the bore sites."

"A tour? What? What the hell does that mean? How–"

"The army."

"Jesús, they really are a useless bunch of clowns."

"I know. But it's a cross we have to bear. The important thing is that the threat she and her companion represent must be removed."

"Damn' right. And we will see to it."

"I hope so – although we are also on their trail now. Frankly, I don't really care who gets to them first: if you find them, either eliminate them yourself, or give us a location and we'll do it. There has to be confirmation on this one."

"Of course."

Torres stood. "Another one?" he asked, pointing at the man's glass.

"Sure."

Torres took the glass and walked over to the drinks cabinet.

"And there is another small problem in the northwest..."

"What? What problem? I know nothing about any 'problem'."

Torres filled the man's glass and returned to stand in front of him. "Apparently not," he said.

The man's face flushed with anger for a moment, and he hesitated to take the proffered drink, but he took a breath, accepted the glass and sank back in his chair. He shrugged and sighed. "Well, after all, you are intelligence, my frien' – we are just operations."

"Yes indeed." Torres sat down in his armchair again. "Now, I know you've done a good job at, um, *aligning* all the operators."

The man smiled and nodded.

"And I am content to leave it up to you how you do it." Torres continued. "However, we've had word of a grower who may not be with us a hundred percent." He reached into his pocket and pulled out a piece of paper. "Here. It is centred on this village, and that's the name we've been given."

The man looked at the few words on the paper, his eyes narrowing. "Who the hell is Paquito? Never heard of him. This village is part of Fernando's territory. He has not said anything to me. How confident are you of the information?"

"Very confident. I believe Fernando is a good man, and he has most of the producers signed up, but my source tells me these people have been trying to make contact directly with the Valle cartel."

"Medellín," the man observed matter-of-factly.

"Medellín," Torres agreed. "Fernando needs – *you* need – to make an example. It's your affair what you do, but afterwards blame Tupac or leave a Sendero calling card – it hardly matters which – and make sure it is impressed upon everyone that no one operates outside the system."

"It will be done."

"Excellent." Torres got up from his chair and paced to the window. "You know, it's really down to you and me to keep this thing on the rails," he said, as he looked out at the sea.

"True enough. True enough."

They were silent for a few seconds, then the man took a drink from his glass and spoke conversationally. "I, uh... I read about the tragedy at one of Brascon's sites."

Torres turned, a perfectly blank expression on his face.

"The workers that die...?" the man prompted.

"Ah, yes," said Torres. He shook his head sadly. "A terrible business. We have asked for a full report from the company, of course."

"Of course."

"Yes. In cases like this, the company clearly bears the responsibility."

"Right." The man looked thoughtful. "Can't be many Americans left working for them now, I guess." The statement hung there for a second or two.

Okay, I get it. You're not as dumb as you look. Torres tilted his head non-committally.

The man took a breath and sipped some of his whisky. "And now," he continued, "can I ask *you* something?"

Torres nodded thoughtfully. "Go ahead."

"I received details of the raid."

"Ah yes. It is all confirmed now by our partners."

"Sure, but do they realise how many people we're going to have to sacrifice? It will put operations back some time."

"Yes. Everyone is aware that there may be some production and delivery problems for a few months. No one is going to get excited about it. Besides, it has to be done. We need to offer the world a morsel."

"I understan' that, but there are going to be a lot of really pissed people out there."

"Well, just remind them how the prices will go up. They'll sell less, but charge more for a while." He shrugged. "What's the big deal?"

The man levered himself out of his chair. "You do not know the people I have to deal with. They will all have to be brought into line. I'm going to have to dig deep into my pockets."

There it is.

"I know them better than you think, my friend."

"Hmm. But perhaps you don't have to deal with them on a daily basis." His expression suddenly changed to one of irritation. "Remember, it's my ass hanging on the line out there, right?"

"I'm well aware of that." Torres turned to stare out the window again. He raised his glass and drank the remaining whisky, and then turned back, his eyes locking unwaveringly with those of the man. "But then, that's why you get the cut you get, isn't it?"

"My frien'..." the man began, drawing himself up and sucking in air. He seemed on the verge of saying something, and then thought better of it. He looked at his glass instead, drained the last of his whisky, and suddenly smiled. "You're absolutely right." He held the empty glass out. "Now, you got any Glenfiddich, man?"

21

As the plane banked for its final descent into the sprawling jungle city of Manaus, Carla looked down upon the ebony-black waters of the Rio Negro, still bordered by lush tropical vegetation along both banks. It was over ten years since she had left Manaus to take up a place at college in Brasilia, and she had been expecting everything within a fifty-mile radius of the city to have been deforested and covered in the usual untenably thin layer of tarmac. But as the plane levelled out and they skimmed over the little river Tarumã to the northwest of the city, she was surprised at the amount of forest still intact. A few moments later, the plane touched down at the recently refurbished *Aeroporto Internacional Eduardo Gomes.*

There were no real checks for domestic flights at the airport, and she was able to walk unchallenged straight from the arrivals lounge to the wall of heat and humidity outside the air-conditioned terminal building. No-one was there to meet her, nor did she expect anyone. Most of her work for the Grupo Contra Corrupção was low key, and as far away from the government's gaze as possible, even though the movement itself was anything but low key. The name GCC – uttered with delight or anger depending on which side of the political divide you called your own – was now an established part of the national political debate.

After ten years in Brasilia her body was used to a drier climate, and she found herself beginning to sweat in the short space of time it took to hail a taxi and throw herself and her small bag in the back seat.

"*Tá quente, né?*" said the driver, noting her look of discomfort and turning on the air-con in the car with a flourish. "I can take you somewhere where we can cool off, if you like. A little swim, maybe, somewhere nice and quiet?"

Carla sighed, fighting the urge to tell him what he could do with his nice quiet swim. It was something else she had got used to in Brasilia – not being constantly hit on and pawed at, everywhere she went. It still happened occasionally, of course – any half-decent looking 29 year-old woman was fair game to the average Brazilian male – but in the capital city a vague notion of political correctness had long ago been imported from the U.S. and filtered down to the streets.

"Another time, maybe," she said, in the conciliatory tone she reserved for simpletons. "Right now I really need to get to this place." She proffered the business card she had been given with the address of a logistics company on it, and the driver looked at it and shrugged.

"Sim Senhora."

They pulled out from the kerb and nudged past the confusion of taxis and other cars cluttering up the terminal building pick-up area. Carla settled into the sweat-stained, nylon-covered seat and patiently fended off a few more clumsy advances before the driver finally gave up and left her to her own thoughts.

It was a slow crawl down the main road into the city centre, and Carla vaguely registered the predictable changes - new supermarkets and car dealerships, apartment blocks and apart-hotels, a refurbished hospital, and an explosion in the amount of traffic. As they passed DETRAN, the driver and vehicle licensing authority, she automatically reached into the depths of her bag and fingered the fake driving licences she had brought with her. She pulled them out and selected one after a quick scan, nodding to herself. It went with an ID – a *CPF* number – she would use in Manaus and would need to learn, so she spent a minute or so memorising it.

She was not overly concerned about her personal security, but neither was she under any illusions about what could happen if she did not take a reasonable amount of care. Under cover of Brazil's relatively recent democratic lustre, the old vested interests still infested large parts of the economic, financial, legal and commercial systems. Their influence extended directly through to the police and the military via a labyrinthine network of official and unofficial contacts, and they would stop at very little to maintain the status quo. To her, they were a choking influence on her country that she and the GCC were actively working to sideline, and ultimately disenfranchise, by lobbying effectively for a broad range of constitutional and legal reforms. She knew that the more successful she and her compatriots became, the more likely they would be to have their lives deliberately and comprehensively screwed up or, in the worst case, terminated.

Just thinking about it made her anxious, but she slipped the licence back again and reminded herself that she had already done enough to be safe. She had used two false IDs to get to Manaus, and using a third one while she was here was probably somewhat extravagant, even if the cost of a fake was only a hundred *Reais*. She shrugged inwardly. The cloak-and-dagger stuff was a minor inconvenience, cost very little, and probably had already thrown anyone interested in her, off the scent.

She tensed when a police SUV passed the taxi and pulled in front of them, but moments later it shifted lanes again and disappeared. She smiled, remembering a colleague's favourite admonishment that *just because you're paranoid, doesn't mean they're not all out to get you.* When she saw the taxi driver looking at her in the mirror she put on her serious face again.

Further thoughts on paranoia were interrupted when the taxi stopped at the lights next to the pink facade of the city's theatre. She stared up at its brightly-coloured dome, and considered how little the country had changed since those days. At the turn of the nineteenth century, Manaus had been awash with money from a short-lived rubber boom. In the Victorian world, the city had sparkled briefly as *the* chic place to be, attracting the rich and famous from across the globe, who came to see its tram system and wonderful electric lighting, She smiled at the idea. Meanwhile, the rubber barons became the super-rich of the day, thinking nothing of sending laundry off to be cleaned in Europe, rather than risk their finery in the inky waters of the local river where the poor scraped a meagre living. Their power extended across Brazil and beyond, and although a few of the names might have since changed, the same old families still controlled the country.

The lights turned green and they inched forward past the Praça do Congresso, finally turning right off the main road. The taxi stopped outside a bright yellow, well-maintained, colonial building bearing a plaque proudly proclaiming the name of its corporate owners.

Subtle, thought Carla, closing her eyes and shaking her head slightly. She paid the driver, grabbed her bag, and made her way into the tiny reception area at the front of the building. She was redirected to another room on the first floor, and as soon as she opened it she recognised her contact, if only from his sheer bulk.

"Ah - *Senhorita* Carla!" exclaimed the tall, obese man. His forehead and upper lip glistened: he was clearly sweating profusely in his expensive but hopelessly ill-fitting suit, and as he bent to kiss Carla on the cheek, she could smell a vague undercurrent of B.O. beneath copious quantities of expensive eau de cologne.

"I hope you had a good flight, *Senhorita*? How is Marcus? I was disappointed he was unable to come." He smiled at her condescendingly, and indicated a small chair behind his desk. "Please, sit down."

Carla watched him as he turned, shuffled back behind the huge desk and sat down heavily in an enormous fake-leather executive chair. He was leader of one of the many trade unions in Manaus, but not a major player. He was, however, the GCC's link to the other unions and the State trade's union council, and this was enough for her to put on her well-practised plastic smile.

"Thank you," she said, as demurely as she could.

"Would you like some coffee or water?" the man asked, picking up his phone.

Carla nodded. "Water please," she said.

He ordered, and put down the phone. As he leaned back in his chair, Carla noticed that his arms were too short to rest comfortably across his huge stomach, and she watched as he clasped his pudgy hands together to keep them from sliding off.

"You know," he began, in an overly loud voice, "there are a lot of people who believe that all these demonstrations and strikes of yours do more harm than good."

"That's an interesting position for a trade union leader to adopt," replied Carla.

He shrugged, and his jowls wobbled. "Well, I believe that working in harmony is the right way to go."

Yes, working in harmony with the rich tossers who are paying your bribes, you fat twat.

She leaned forward a little and smiled. "You are right, of course. And we also believe in working in harmony. I am not here to upset anyone at all."

She could see a flash of something like relief pass across the man's face.

"Our only request," she continued, knowing even as she did so that her mouth was already hostage to her irritation and disgust, "is that people do their jobs honestly."

His little piggy eyes flickered slightly and he looked uncomfortable for a moment, before he managed to construct a smile.

"Ah, but if only things were that simple," he said.

Carla nodded in agreement. "I know," she said, pausing for a second. "But they will be, soon enough." *You slimy, fat pig.* "When we achieve our aims - and we *will* achieve our aims, I can assure you – everything will be very simple indeed." She shrugged and smiled again. "Either people will do their jobs honestly, or they'll be swept into the gutter along with all the rest of the lying, cheating, stealing vermin who are running the country at the moment."

The man's face coloured, but he recovered creditably quickly.

"Hmm. Yes, well, our meeting will be held next door, in our conference room. The others will be here at five thirty, I believe." He looked at his big gold wristwatch. "But it will be another, what, half an hour or so...?"

Carla was happy to take the hint. "Yes indeed," she said. "Perhaps if I could take a seat now in the conference room, and prepare my notes?"

"But of course. Be my guest." He pointed the way with a wave of his hand, and relief writ large on his face. "I'll have your water sent through."

Seated in the conference room a few minutes later, still riled after her brief conversation with the fat man, she cursed herself under her breath. She remembered the arguments she had often had with Marcus, and his description of her as an 'over-emotional idealist'. There was no doubt in her mind that Marcus was the better politician – the wheeler-dealer. He was the one who could make things happen, while she just could not control her anger and resentment over the useless slime that permeated every level of responsibility throughout the country.

She still remembered the day her family had been tossed out in the streets by henchmen working for a local politician. The politician had decided he wanted to acquire all the houses in the little cul-de-sac they lived in, and a four-year legal battle had killed her father, cost them all their money, and changed nothing – the legal title they held to their property proved worthless. Every family in that street had been sacrificed to the greed of one *político* – and his entourage, of course. Worse still, the same man was now a rich and powerful senior Brazilian statesman marketing himself as the whiter-than-white, eco-friendly, political representative of an adoring, underprivileged public.

Filth, like the all the rest of them.

She stared down at her computer, willing herself calm, and trying to ordering her thoughts again, but the noise of the first people to arrive disturbed her. The banging of doors and the clump of footsteps left her unable to concentrate on anything. She sighed, closed her notebook, put on her best 'meeting' face, and turned to greet the newcomers.

In the doorway stood two armed police officers.

22

"This is not an arrest, *senhorita*," the police lieutenant said. Carla was sitting in the back of a beaten-up old car bumping its way through the backstreets of Manaus. The two policemen who had escorted her from the building were sitting in the front. At her request, they had shown her their police ID, and the wreck of a car they were driving was standard for the *Polícia Civil*. But there was something strange about the whole thing.

"Well what the hell is it, then?" she demanded.

The driver pulled the car over and they stopped in the shade of a huge mango tree whose roots were slowly breaking up one side of the road. The young lieutenant in the passenger seat turned towards her.

"Let's call it friendly advice."

"Great. So I can just leave, can I?" Carla made a move for the door.

"Sure you can."

She pulled on the door lever but nothing happened.

"Oh – sorry – automatic locks," the driver said, looking at her in his rear-view mirror as he released the locks.

She pulled the handle again and the door clicked opened. She started to turn her body, ready to get out.

"But..." began the lieutenant in a voice loud enough to get her attention. "But," he repeated more quietly, once she was looking at him "You've really nothing to lose by just listening to us for a minute, have you?" He shrugged. "If you don't like what we have to say, I promise you're free to go."

She hesitated. The whole setup was weird, but something told her the guy was genuine. She decided to trust her instinct, and turned towards the front, still holding the door in position.

"Okay – one minute then," she said.

"Thanks. First of all, we represent the good guys. The people you were about to meet are the bad guys. Well, some of them are, anyway."

"I don't know what you're talking about. I'm just here for a business meeting."

"Of course you are. Carla da Silva from the GCC, up in Manaus for a simple business meeting. What, you're placing an order for fish or something, are you?"

She looked at the man sharply when he mentioned her real name and the movement's name in the same breath, and he nodded in response.

"Miss da Silva, some people here are very interested in you and your group, you know. You should be more careful about how you get around and who you talk to."

"Hmm," was all she conceded. "Go on."

"Okay, well, to begin with, that guy you just met? That fat slob's sister is married to the nephew of the Police Chief of the State of Amazonas. He and his parasite family rake off millions every year in bribes and their share of drugs and arms deals, at the same time as they're creaming off government funds for anti-crime initiatives."

"Sure," agreed Carla. "So what's new? It's the same in all twenty-six states."

"It gets worse. All the time they're doing this, they're also protecting their cronies who are selling huge civil contracts, running massive over-billing scams and grabbing every available plot of commercial land the length and breadth of the state."

"Still within the norms of Brazilian society. So?"

"So, if you think they're just going to stand by while your movement threatens their wonderful set-up here, you're out of your mind."

"The tip-off is appreciated, thanks, but we've plenty of assholes down south, too, you know – the country is knee deep in them, right?"

The Lieutenant raised an eyebrow and cocked his head in acknowledgement of the fact.

"*You*, on the other hand, are...what?" Carla added.

"Ah. Well, we, on the other hand, would be very supportive of the Movement. If you're looking for new recruits, we can deliver them. Here and across the whole of the State. Probably the whole of the north of Brazil, in fact."

" 'We', being exactly *who*?" Carla pressed.

"Well let's just say we are a fairly disparate group," began the Lieutenant.

Carla shook her head. "Oh come on. Don't give me that crap, *please*."

The man hesitated for second, and Carla started pushing the door open again.

"You're right," he said finally. "I'm sorry. We are part of a growing network of people from all walks of life, perhaps mostly military–"

"Ah."

"No, no!" He shook his head emphatically. "Not *just* military. That's where we started from, but it's much bigger than that now."

"So why do you need us then, if you're that big?"

"Because, as you know very well, if we are going to achieve anything, it's going to be from a national – not a local or regional – movement."

"I see. And what is it you want to achieve, exactly?"

"Change. Just like you. Out with the old, in with the new."

She shook her head again. "We want change. But we want progressive, ordered, democratic change. That doesn't mean kicking everyone out. We're not looking for a revolution, and we're not the Black Bloc, FIP, FIST or any other so-called revolutionary movement." She paused and the lieutenant jumped in.

"No – of course." He shook his head. "No-one is looking for a bloody revolution. But you'll never get those who are running the place to voluntarily curb their own power. You'll never get the thieves to police themselves."

"I disagree. You can do it if you gradually bring in legislation that adds the right system of checks and balances. Eventually, that will squeeze them all out."

It was the Lieutenant's turn to shake his head.

"That could take years. Decades. Generations. We don't believe such a wait is either workable or desirable."

"Which means you *do* want a revolution. A coup. Back to a military dictatorship? Is that it?"

She watched as the two policemen made eye contact, and saw the mild discomfort on the Lieutenant's face. She homed in.

"You're not even policemen, of course. If you were, you could have pulled me anytime – without making a song and dance about it in the city centre. And wasn't that a bit dumb, by the way? I mean, what happens when someone makes enquiries?"

The lieutenant looked somewhat diffident. "Actually, pulling you from a private building was the most subtle way of doing things. If anyone there does ask, they'll be met with a wall of silence. No-one will be able to tell them anything about it." He smiled awkwardly. "But it *is* true that the authorities are watching you. A few fake IDs are not going to protect you from that, you know."

Carla chose to ignore the reference. "Okay. Well, for the sake of argument, let's say we might be interested in exploring ways we could work together – and I'm specifically *not* saying the Movement would accept any form of radicalisation–"

The man sighed. "We're pretty sure it would, Senhorita Carla – and we know Marcus would have no problem with it."

She held up her hand. "Marcus represents one side of the argument, that's all. But in any case, I concede the point about the need for a broader, national movement."

"Okay then."

"So – what's the deal? What's on the table?"

The lieutenant leaned forward with sudden enthusiasm. "Well, first of all, we can place considerable funds at your disposal. Funds you can use for staffing, IT, communication, printing, equipment and so forth. All untraceable, naturally."

"Naturally."

"And we can offer our considerable network across the North for bringing you all the new members you need."

"And from us, you want...?"

"Just your backing and those of your members, when – if – any direct action is required."

"And what about the bad guys?"

"Don't worry about them – we can take care of them."

The car suddenly seemed stiflingly hot as Carla considered the meaning of this.

"No," she said emphatically. "Just hold it right there. I will not–"

"No, no. Of course not," said the driver quickly. "It's just an expression. A bad choice of words – sorry."

Another moment of silence.

"Look," began Carla, "this is something we would need to think about very carefully. Our movement comprises members who are decent, law-abiding citizens who simply want to lobby for political change. We are not radicals or revolutionaries. We do not condone violence and we certainly don't believe that two wrongs will ever make a right."

"Senhorita, I'm sure a lot of your members fit that description. But everyone has also seen that there are violent radicals in the Movement too."

"That's bullshit. The people splashed all over the media have nothing to do with the GCC. They're just criminals hijacking our peaceful demonstrations."

"You really believe that?"

"Yes I really believe that." She was suddenly getting angry and not doing a very good job of controlling it.

"You don't think some of your members are just desperate enough to behave like that, with the right encouragement?"

"No, I do not."

"And you don't think the violence could have been organised by those who want to discredit the GCC?"

"No, I don't, dammit." She could feel her face flush slightly and she knew she did not want to continue this conversation right here and now. "Look, whatever the reality of the situation, there is no way I can commit to any sort of agreement or partnership without knowing a lot more about your movement, or organisation, or whatever it is. I need to meet those involved and have a full and frank discussion with them."

The Lieutenant nodded.

"That's exactly why we would like to invite you to a regional meeting where you can get to know the key people and listen to what they have to say. After that, you can take the message back to the Movement and make your decision. Does that sound reasonable?"

She thought for a moment.

"Exactly where and when is this meeting? If what you've been telling me is true, I'm not altogether comfortable hanging around here for too long."

"We hold our meetings outside Manaus, on friendlier territory. The next one is ten days from now. We can get you there safely – it's a day's journey from here – and we can also help you get back to

Brasilia afterwards without any hassle. No problem."

"A day's journey? Where the hell is it, France?" She held up her hands before they could say anything. "Just kidding – I don't want to know." She thought for a second or two. "It's a deal. I'll be out of Manaus from tomorrow, but I'll be back again in time for your meeting. Just one thing, though – I have an arrangement with my colleagues in Brasilia that I make regular contact with them. So even if we are going under the radar, they will still need to hear from me."

"That's fine. We can organise that. We'll get a secure phone to them. You're talking about Marcus, I presume?"

"He would do, yes."

"In that case I can get something to him at the right time. And we will make available a phone you can use from the meeting place. Is that satisfactory?"

"Yes. But I make no guarantees one way or the other about what the GCC may or may not do, right?"

"Agreed." The Lieutenant said. "Now we'll give you a little tour of the backstreets of Manaus and then get you a taxi to wherever it is you want to go, Okay?"

Carla nodded. "I need to get back to my meeting with the fat slob and the others. They'll be a little spooked about me being lifted like this."

"I doubt it. We told them it was just routine, and you won't be away long enough for anyone to fret too much. Besides, the bad guys will be happy to know you're being monitored – they'll think it's their friends in high places – and it can only enhance your reputation with the good guys, I would have thought."

She gave the man a disparaging look. "I wish it was that easy, my friend, I really do."

"Well, I think you'll find it was worth it." He reached into his shirt pocket and pulled out a business card. "Just one other thing. When you come back to Manaus after your canvassing, please stay at this hotel." The man passed the card across. "We'll contact you there."

She looked at the card. She knew the place. Nothing special, but perfectly acceptable. "Fine."

The lieutenant turned to the driver. "Let's go?"

The driver nodded, starting the car up. "Perhaps you could close your door now, Senhorita?"

23

"Where is Paquito?" the man with the gun asked.

He was clearly the leader of the group that had arrived at the village five minutes earlier in a jeep and two SUVs. He was thin and wiry, wore simple green army fatigues, and he was separated from the rest of the villagers by an armed guard of six men. Four other men stood guarding the dirt track entrance to the village.

They looked like the usual Sendero Luminoso rabble, dressed with black or green tops - some with blue trousers, some with black. A few had floppy camo hats, but most wore baseball caps. Standard Sendero fare, except that instead of the usual collection of old revolvers, rifles, and broken RPGs, these people all had brand new, shiny black Heckler and Koch MP5 machine guns. The thin man also had a Beretta 92FS Inox pistol, which he was now pressing against the sixty-two year old community leader's head.

"Last chance. Where is Paquito?" he asked.

"I don't know–" began the old man.

The noise of the pistol was followed a moment later by a wail from a woman in the small crowd held back by the guards. She fell to her knees and two other women hurried to comfort her.

"*Madre de Dios!*" she cried. "My Jorge! My poor Jorge! He never hurt anyone. He never hurt anyone. Oh my god, my god..."

Jorge lay quite dead at the feet of the man with the Beretta.

"You," said the man, pointing at a tall villager with a pronounced Adam's apple and a mop of greying curly hair. "You. Come here."

"No! My god, you animal!" another woman screamed, rushing forward and hurling herself at the guards. "No one knows where he is. Leave us alone, you *hijo de puta!*"

The leader nodded at the others to allow her through, and as she approached, he raised his gun and without blinking shot her in the face as she ran towards him. She dropped like a puppet with the strings cut, and bits of scarlet-coloured blood and viscera splattered the Sendero men.

There were more cries from the villagers, and the woman's husband threw himself at the wall of men. He was clubbed with vicious blows from the guns, and fell to the ground unconscious.

"Stop!" cried a tall woman from the back of the crowd. "I will take you to him, if you leave us alone."

"Ah, some sense at last." The man smiled. "But do not *bargain* with me, senhora." He stepped past his victims' crumpled bodies and looked at the crowd. "You do not bargain with the Sendero. You just do as you are told." He nodded to his guards. "You and you – take her to the jeep."

He placed his pistol in its shiny new leather holster, and put his hands on his hips. "The rest of my men will stay here until we have talked to Paquito. You will feed them and give them whatever they need." He turned his head and nodded towards the dead bodies. "And you will bury this lot before I return."

An hour later, as the villagers were distributing food to the Sendero, a huge explosion shook the ground, and everyone watched as a fireball rose hundreds of feet in the air beyond the trees to the west of the village.

Fifteen minutes later, the jeep returned. A body was tied across the bonnet, and the little man cut the ropes and let it slide off onto the ground. It lay there in the dust, the purple burn mark that Paquito had had since childhood, visible to everyone. This time, the villagers just looked on.

"Paquito did not want to talk," he said. He nodded at the tall woman who had gone with them, and she descended from the jeep and walked back to the other villagers. "Now, my friends. I am sorry we had to do this. It is very tiresome for us all, isn't it?" He walked towards the group, who flinched.

"And the others, sir..." began one of the old men, braver than the rest.

"What?" snapped the thin man, turning on him. Then he suddenly smiled. "Oh, don't worry – they're all fine. A few burns here and there, perhaps, but they're all okay." He suddenly laughed. "What do you think I am – a monster?" He paused, and looked round at the people. "They'll be a bit late back, however, as they'll have to walk." He walked across to one of his men and spoke briefly with him, then turned back.

"Now. Just so there is no misunderstanding, your next crop will be delivered to the processing facility at Fernando's place. If you have too little, well, tough. If you have too much, you can do whatever you like with it – except sell it. Is that clearly understood?"

No one moved or said anything.

"I said, is that clearly understood?"

There was a mumbled chorus of 'yes' and 'okay'.

"Excellent. Now, the fire that is burning in your fields–"

A stifled cry made him pause again.

"The fire that is burning in your fields will soon die out, and it will leave the soil well fertilised for the next season. So I'm sure it will be a great success. We will leave you now and wish you good luck in the future. Feel free to tell all your friends about what happened here today."

He pulled out his pistol again and held it up.

"Tell them about the day the Sendero came to town. Tell them about the man with the silver Beretta, and about how you hope he never has to come back again, eh?" He laughed as he walked back to his jeep.

24

Although they passed another wooden house before the sun disappeared behind the mountains, they saw no one, and Jack was as certain as he could be that nobody had seen them. With darkness approaching, he was now less concerned about being spotted than about their ability to continue paddling at all. They both seemed to be managing okay physically, but as they approached the narrower valley between the mountains, the river broadened and the flow of water slowed. Mudbanks regularly loomed out of the murk, and they found they often had to settle for drifting slowly, using their paddles just to guide them and keep them from running aground.

Despite their care, on one stretch they ran into no fewer than five banks in the space of half an hour, climbing out of the canoes on each occasion, and walking or wading with them until they found a deeper channel. The mud sucked at their feet, and the mosquitoes swarmed around Jack in a cloud, as if they had been following him all the way, just waiting for their opportunity. He occasionally felt things nipping or touching his legs, but was really too tired to care much about it.

Although their progress was slower than he had hoped, it was still better than tramping through the forest on foot. They managed to keep going until dawn, by which time his hands were raw from using the wooden paddle, and he felt his body bloated from thousands of swollen bites. Elena looked at him in the daylight with horror on her face.

"Are you okay?" she said. "You look terrible."

"Thanks," Jack mumbled. He was trying to think of a suitable reply when he spotted something downstream.

"Look – another river," he said, indicating with a nod. He frowned as they got closer. "Damn. It's flowing west. That's no good."

"It may bend round again," suggested Elena.

"Maybe. But I doubt it." He tried to recall the maps he had pored over a few months ago before leaving Cuzco.

He paddled into the left bank, levered himself out of the canoe, and staggered around trying to get some feeling back into his legs. Elena joined him, and they stood looking towards the course of the new river.

"No. It's definitely not right," Jack announced. "The one we're on now is already heading too far north. Look – the sunrise is way off to the right. This new river is bigger and faster, and I bet it'll keep heading northwest until it pours into the Huallaga.

"You are probably right," Elena reluctantly agreed. I have no clear picture in my head. I have to trust you."

"Well, I remember that the Huallaga and the Ucayali flow northeast roughly parallel to each other, separated by anywhere between thirty and eighty miles of primary forest."

"What's that in kilometres?" Elena asked.

"About fifty to a hundred and thirty kilometres."

"*Caramba,* there is a big difference between fifty kilometres and a hundred and thirty."

"True. But we can make an educated guess about where we are in relation to the two rivers. We've covered around forty or fifty miles in the last three days, during which we crossed the Huallaga. My guess is that we're probably no more than twenty miles to the east of it now, which is why I think these rivers flow into the Huallaga, not the Ucayali."

"*Cierto.* So what do we do? To paddle against the river will be hard work. Slow, also."

Jack nodded. "And apart from anything else, it looks like it would still be taking us in the wrong direction – back the way we came, more or less."

Elena looked at him for a few moments. "So you want to go through the forest again," she said matter-of-factly.

"'Want' is not the right word," Jack said, thinking about the daunting prospect of plunging back into the gloom for anything up to six or seven days. It was even worse now that they were descending to the floodplain, where the forest could be a vast, swampy nightmare, with densely-packed undergrowth and little food. But what was the choice? Following the river would mean an easier passage and a relative abundance of food and water... just until they ran into the Peruvian military, the Yanks, the Sendero, or angry locals looking for their canoes.

"There's no other option," he said finally.

Elena looked thoughtful for a second or two, and then shrugged. "We will need food and supplies," she said. "We'll have to take them from the nearest house. Then we go."

"That's a hell of a risk," said Jack.

Elena nodded. "*Si*. But as you say, there's no other option."

They stood in thought on the bank, with the early morning mist still rising from the river and evaporating from the trees.

Jack sighed his agreement. "Okay, sure. The journey will be hard enough with supplies, and probably impossible without them. We passed a house back there about ten minutes upstream. If we go back–"

She raised a hand. "Better if it's just me."

"What? Why?"

She smiled and shrugged. "Stealing is what I do. And if I cannot steal what we need without them seeing me, then I will call on them as a loyal member of the Sendero. They will provide me with what I want."

Jack started to protest, but Elena was already up and heading for her canoe. "Let me do this – believe me, I have lots of experience. Rest, and I will return in thirty minutes."

Elena's estimate proved wildly inaccurate. The morning wore on, and occasional sounds of civilisation floated across from various points of the compass. Jack hid his canoe by dragging it into a backwater a little further downstream, and spent some time scanning the far banks of the river they were about to join, deciding where would be the best place to start walking.

When she did reappear, there was no outward appearance of emotion, good or bad. She merely beckoned to him as she was approaching, indicating that Jack should join her mid-stream. When he paddled out to meet her, he saw two bulging flour sacks sitting behind her. He paddled quickly ahead as they emerged onto the new river, and turned upstream towards the spot he had picked to start the trek. The new river was flowing more quickly than he had hoped, and it was a struggle to make headway, but eventually they arrived at a tiny backwater there the current was negligible.

They pulled the heavy canoes up the bank and into the trees. Once they were satisfied that they were well hidden, they took a moment to recover. Elena produced two old but sharp machetes, and a couple of plastic two-litre bottles, each of them full of almost-clear water. After drinking from the bottles and with machetes in hand, they picked up a sack each, and headed straight into the jungle, as directly due east as Jack could figure.

The initial going was not as bad as he had feared, and they were still walking dry, but he knew this could change as they continued the gentle descent to the floodplain. He elected to take advantage of this progress as long as possible, but eventually they came to a halt, both of them exhausted.

They had arrived at a small clearing where a tree had fallen and partially taken down two others. It was good to see the sky, while they remained nicely shaded at the margins by some straggly palms that were fighting their way toward the light. They dropped the flour sacks thankfully, and sat down to drink some of the warm, sediment-laden water in their bottles, which now tasted like nectar to Jack.

After a few minutes, he upended his sack and urged the contents out onto the ground. He was amazed and delighted to find a lighter, a small cooking pot, half a pineapple, fishing line with hooks, a kilo of farine, a collection of threadbare t-shirts and shorts and a roll of thin plastic sheeting. Elena did the same with her own sack and out fell some bandage, a bottle of iodine, a newspaper, another kilo of farine, a hand of small bananas, a quarter-full bottle of cooking oil, and a full bottle of cashassa.

Jack pounced on the cashassa, picking it up with a smile.

"I haven't seen cheap alcohol on any survival lists before," he said.

"Medical uses," said Elena. "I prescribe it for the *cordura* - um, the health of the mind?"

"You're the doctor," said Jack, grinning in spite of everything.

They made a rough camp with some broad leaves to lie on. They ate the farine, the pineapple and the banana gratefully, and after agreeing it was unlikely anyone would be looking for them here, they rested, dozing in the shade for a couple of hours before deciding to push on again to cover as much ground as they could while the going was good and they still had daylight.

In the end, they walked only another two hours. When they came unexpectedly across a small, clear-water stream, they decided to stop and make camp. Elena got out the fishing line strung with hooks, and arranged it carefully along the water's edge, while Jack gathered the driest sticks he could find and started a fire with the aid of some newspaper soaked in oil. After making a rough framework of branches near the fire, he went down to the stream and stripped off. He bathed, washed out his overalls, pulled on a pair of the dry, clean shorts and a t-shirt, and returned to the fire, where he draped the overalls over the frame.

Elena came back with some more roots and leaves, having also washed and changed her clothing too.

"Dry clothes," said Jack simply.

Elena nodded. "*Estupendo.*"

They sat down together and passed the bottle of cheap drink back and forth, as they admired the fire.

"I still can't figure it out," Jack announced.

"Hmm?" said Elena absently, disturbed from her own reverie.

"Well, I know why everyone's after *you* – criminal, terrorist, traitor etc, right?" He paused, waiting for some sort of response. Getting none, he carried on. "But why me? What have I done? I mean, I understand that to you lot I was just a random gringo with a potential selling price on his head, but what about the army? They surely can't really believe I would be wandering around here helping the Sendero. And what about those Americans? What's their problem? And there clearly *is* a problem – I didn't just *imagine* the treatment I got, or the conversation I overheard. Unless I completely misread everything, they were happy enough to kill me. So what the hell is it all about?"

"I don't know," said Elena. "Maybe because they think that if you know me, you will know what I know?"

"That's crazy. I'm a victim, not some sort of co-conspirator."

"Co- what?

"Er, *cómplice?*"

Elena nodded. "Of course you're not. But they don't know that. They only have your word. They have a lot to hide, and they are *paranoico.*"

"No 'innocent until proved guilty', then?"

She laughed. "I know that expression. Do you know 'shoot first and ask questions later'?"

Jack nodded and smiled. "Sure I do." He thought for a few moments. "Okay, so tell me Elena, what exactly *do* you know that could get me dead?"

She sighed heavily. "*Bien,* where do I start?" She thought for a second. "What do you know about our government?"

"Not much, really. Right wing, of course, and friendly with the Americans..."

Elena laughed. "Friendly with the Americans? They're *working* for the Americans!"

"Bullshit. They just want U.S. trade barriers reduced, and some help with infrastructure investment and that sort of stuff. It's perfectly normal."

"*Está bromeando!* Did you know that our President's election campaign was paid for by the Americans? Did you know that as soon as he was elected, ten American companies established billion-dollar operations in Lima with businesses owned by the President or his family? Did you know that all *remesas* – all, um...?

"Consignments."

"*Si.* Di you know that all consignments of cocaine out of Peru were held up for months, and then a week after the elections the military contacted the producers and gave them a *cuota* for their exports? Said that if they agreed, no one would interfere with the consignments? In exchange for a big percentage of the product, of course."

"And how do you know all this?"

"Because, as I said before, we are a political party. We have representatives in the government, and we have other political sources. We are also a producer and exporter of cocaine."

"Naturally," Jack intoned, the disgust clear in his voice.

Elena's eyes flashed. "You are no-one to judge us, gringo. Drugs are a problem because your world makes them a problem. I do not like it, and if there was another way, I would take it. So..."

"Okay," said Jack holding up a hand. "But even if it's true–"

"*Es verdadero,* Jack; you can be sure it's true. And things are changing again now. Something new is happening."

"What do you mean?"

"I don't know exactly, but someone is setting up big production facilities in Peru. All our coca base used to go to Colombia or Brazil for processing, but now, someone is trying to do it here in Peru. All of it. And they cannot do that without the military being part of it. There is too much. It is too big an operation."

"So I'm a threat because...?"

"Because if you tell this to someone, they might believe you. Killing you is the obvious solution, and the only thing that surprises me is that they did not kill you immediately."

"They didn't kill *you* on the spot."

"No, but only because I would be good propaganda, to convince people the government is working hard to stop drugs and terror. And of course no one will believe anything I say."

Jack nodded. "Yeah, I wondered about that." He thought for another moment. "Well, maybe they wanted to find out how much I know; who my sources are, and so on."

"Perhaps, although the longer they keep a gringo, the more complicated things get. Better to just kill you straight away and burn the body." Elena spoke matter-of-factly, as if this were part of daily life.

Jack looked at her for a second. Her eyes were cold, distant, unemotional. It shocked him.

"It must be something to do with the Americans, then," he said. "That's who they took us to see, after all."

"Yes. Maybe they did not want to do it without the Americans' agreement. But I do not understand why."

"No. but it's obvious to me that there is some sort of official US involvement in whatever is going on. God knows what, but–"

"Shh!" Elena hissed.

Jack looked at her as she cocked her head to one side and listened intently.

"Fish!" she said, suddenly grinning. "Back in a minute." She promptly stood up and ran off towards the stream.

Jack found that he was salivating at the prospect of cooked fish, and his train of thought was derailed in a flash. For a few seconds there was just the heat, the crackling wood, and the black, white and red of the fire. A few mosquitoes whirred, and some howler monkeys called to each other in the distance. A bead of sweat broke, and rolled slowly down the side of his face. The pale branches and leaves of the nearby trees glowed in the light from the fire, while in the background, darkness enveloped everything. Although he was staring into the fire, Jack saw the blackness, heard the silence, and felt the vastness of the ancient forest.

Then suddenly there was Elena crouching before him with two glistening catfish in her hands and a huge smile on her face. The fire seemed to burn in her dark eyes, exaggerating her feline presence. Jack would hardly have been surprised if she had started to purr.

"How do you like it?" she asked, waving the fish at him and laughing.

25

After another three days of grindingly hard slog through increasingly boggy forest, the wonderful catfish Elena had prepared was a distant memory. Jack was becoming increasingly anxious about his decision to head for the Ucayali. What if they were at the point where the two rivers were farthest apart? It could take another week to get anywhere even close to their objective. What if they had been wrong when they identified the Huallaga? What if they were walking round in circles? He stared ahead, trying to gauge the position of the rising sun, and he noticed a broken, misty curtain of light in the distance, lying to the right of their path. As they moved closer, he became hopeful it might be a river. Maybe the Ucayali already? His heart leapt at the prospect, and in spite of trying to maintain his calm, his pace quickened.

Two hours later, they were standing by the banks of a small river. It was good to be in the open again, but this was clearly not the Ucayali. Jack estimated its width at around a hundred feet, compared to the thousand yards to be expected of the bigger river. Nonetheless, it was clearly navigable by small boat, and it looked like it was heading east. Two things crossed his mind – the first was that this was their highway to the Ucayali; the second was that if that were the case, its banks would be populated.

As he discussed their options with Elena, the sky began to darken, and a distant rumble of thunder reached their ears. Elena looked up briefly and shrugged in her usual unruffled way.

"I think we should float down the river," she said. "We will get wet in the rain anyway, and it will be a easier than cutting through more jungle."

The suggestion was perfectly reasonable – with tied-up bundles of branches as buoyancy aids, it would be an easy ride. But Jack's imagination was playing games with him. He stared at the muddy water. As best he could guess, it was flowing at about walking pace. Was that a good speed for caiman? What about piranha? Electric eels? When he reluctantly expressed his concerns, Elena laughed, as he knew she would. It was no decision at all, really. If they continued walking, they would have to wade across the river every time it twisted back on itself. It would be hard going, take as long or longer, and they would get just as wet.

He forced a smile. "You're right. It has to be done."

Aw, crap.

They ate some more food and spent time gathering their bundles of sticks and branches. Re-emerging by the riverbank, they heard the sound of the wind high in the canopy, and looked up to see the tree tops bending, and leaves and debris fluttering and spinning down to the river. A minute later, the first heavy drops of rain began falling, and by the time they had tied their bundles together, wrapped them in plastic sheeting, and arranged their sacks to keep the critical stuff as dry as possible, the storm was upon them. The dark clouds were back-lit with flashes of lightning, the thunder seemed to press down on them, and the water in the river boiled with the torrents of rain that fell. They were soaked to the skin in less than a minute, and visibility was reduced to a few yards. Heart firmly in his mouth, Jack followed Elena into the middle of the river, finding distraction in the fact that the water felt pleasantly warm in comparison with the rain.

He clung to his bundle and fell in line behind Elena as she alternated between swimming and floating. The current seemed a little stronger than his original estimate, but it could not be fast enough for Jack, who for the first thirty minutes was bracing himself for an attack by something unseen in the murky water. The storm passed, the sun re-emerged, and the minutes turned slowly into hours. Jack relaxed. He had more or less forgotten about the other animals he was sharing the river with and was thinking about how much ground they were really covering, when the sound of a motor pierced the blanket of relative silence. It sounded raucous and close, but as they swam quickly to the margins of the river, it became clear that it was still a long way off.

"*Peque-peque,*" Elena announced, and Jack recognised the reference to the ubiquitous river transport in Peru – a long wooden canoe with a noisy little motor balanced on the back, coupled directly to a long propeller shaft. He found himself holding his breath as he listened to the sound of its gradual approach from downstream. However anxious it made him, Jack realised that the noise marked the beginnings of civilisation: where there were motors, there were towns and villages, with the possibility of electricity, phones, internet, boats and all the rest of it. At best it could represent freedom; at worst, an opportunity to get food, clothing and equipment. The only minor problem was that all the inhabitants were, essentially, the enemy.

They heard the motor slow and stop, and after waiting for a few minutes, they made their way back to the middle of the river. Then, after less than an hour, they rounded a bend and had to make a dash for the banks again. Before them lay a long spread of cultivated plots, as far as the eye could see, on both sides of the river. A half-dozen or so houses were dotted about, on either side. It would take a long time to detour around them, with an ever-present risk of being spotted, and with no certainty of what they might find around the next bend.

Jack's eye was drawn to some canoes tied up along the banks, secured to rickety little wooden piers. There were a handful of peque-peques too, which he gazed at with some degree of longing. They crept out of the water and into the tree line, and after an urgent discussion, they decided the best plan would be to wait until dark, steal a peque-peque, and try to put in as many miles as possible during the night. Decision made, they ate some food and then made their way cautiously to a good position to await nightfall. As the light eventually began to fade, a few more canoes arrived in the settlement and tied up, and Elena nudged Jack.

"It has to be now," she said. "Everyone will be eating. Later, some of the men may decide to go fishing again."

Jack felt horribly exposed as they crept towards the nearest boats. The light was disappearing fast, but it was not dark enough for him. He agreed with Elena's reasoning, however, and he knew that looking out from a house in which there was any sort of light would make it virtually impossible to see anything moving against the background of trees.

Their chosen craft had four simple bench seats and was bigger and heavier than Jack had anticipated. Elena left him to check the little engine. He had seen the same engines used in Peru for everything from pumping water to generating electricity to powering boats. The couplings were different, but the engines were the same. Everything looked okay, and there was plenty of fuel in the separate fuel tank. He nodded to Elena, then they pushed the craft out into the water and hopped in. It was much more stable than the canoes they had used before, and the freeboard was a generous couple of inches, so they were not constantly shipping water as they paddled silently downstream past all the houses.

By the time they reached the far end of the settlement, the last vestiges of daylight had disappeared completely, and with significant cloud cover, they paddled cautiously onward, hoping that no-one was going to miss their peque-peque tonight.

If Jack had known they would spend more time getting out and pulling the boat than paddling, never mind using the motor, he might have opted to just continue floating down the river. Sandbanks and mudbanks proliferated, most of them hidden just below the surface. On bends, he found them easy to predict, but they appeared seemingly at random along the straight sections, too. At one point, maybe a couple of hours into their journey, as Jack levered himself out of the canoe again and stood rather heavily on the sand bank they had run aground on, there was a smacking, splashing sound and something large surged quickly past them. Jack froze in his tracks, hanging on to the canoe with his right hand. If he had any doubts about what it was that had startled him, they were quickly removed when a whole series of similar sounds repeated along the banks. They had reached caiman country.

"It's okay," Elena hissed from behind him. "They are only babies."

He heard her laughing intermittently over the next five minutes or so, especially whenever he flinched or jumped at any splashing sound. He consoled himself with the thought that in England she would probably be terrified of hedgehogs or Yorkshire Terriers.

Things got easier as they proceeded downstream. The moon, hidden until now behind clouds, made a sudden appearance directly overhead, helping them navigate as the river wound on. Hour after hour. They stopped briefly to eat and rest, and Jack found that without the noise they made paddling or wading, the forest seemed to close in on them. When they continued, they found it was still too dangerous to use the motor, both because of the noise and the prospect of hitting a bank at speed, so they just kept their steady paddling rhythm going.

When their moment of triumph came, after ten straight hours of paddling, they were too tired to exalt in it. It was still well before dawn when they came upon a row of houses on the left bank, with some sort of path running along the riverbank, and an occasional electric light strung under a tree branch. Keeping well to the right, they realised the river had widened slightly and that it appeared to be much deeper than before. Then, as they slunk silently past the community, they felt the current change and start to push them back upstream. It was an unnerving sensation and Jack could not initially understand what was happening. Instinctively they dug their paddles in and paddled to the point of near exhaustion, fearful of being pushed into the margins and overturned. Then without warning, the canoe spun round once, spun again, and they found themselves spat out onto a much larger, swifter-flowing river.

They glided quickly past the rest of the village, with Jack desperately trying to start the little motor. One – two – three pulls; an adjustment to the choke; a check of the fuel tap, another pull – another.

Elena was struggling to keep the canoe heading out into the middle of the river, and losing the fight. They were being rapidly pushed towards a stand of partially submerged trees.

"Come on, come on," Jack muttered to himself. Another pull. Another...and the motor burst into life. It coughed, nearly stopped, then picked up again and began to run smoothly.

He engaged the propeller, there was a loud clunk, and he rammed the throttle lever to the stop. Elena fell backwards off her seat, and Jack swung the canoe sharply away from the trees, missing them by inches.

Elena lay on her back for a few seconds looking up at the Milky Way, and then slowly raised herself on her elbows.

"Ucayali?" she asked

"Ucayali," said Jack, gazing at the far banks with a grin.

"*Gracias a Dios.*"

"Amen."

26

The noisy little Brazilian Army Embraer plane stopped with a lurch on the apron of the military airfield in the jungle city of Iquitos, Peru. It taxied slowly to the hangars, and stopped next to its little sister, a Phenom 100 private jet that Adam Torres had flown in on two hours earlier. Before the blades had stopped spinning, the door opened, the steps were deployed, and a woman in uniform descended to the tarmac. At the same time, three SUVs pulled up next to the plane. Torres jumped smartly from the passenger side of the lead vehicle and walked round to meet the woman.

More people descended from the plane and from the vehicles, but all eyes were on Torres and the woman who had just flown in to meet him. He was the taller of the two, but not by much. She was at least five foot nine, with an athletic build, and most people would have put her in her mid-thirties or early forties. She had short black hair, a well-lined face and a hard mouth. Her sharp brown eyes were made more striking by the heaviness of the black make-up she wore around them. Her posture was erect, alert, assertive – she looked like she was permanently ready to defend against attack, and like she would make a formidable opponent.

"*Buenos días,*" she said in Spanish with a thick Portuguese accent. "Señor Torres?" A confirming nod from Torres prompted her to continue. "*Eu sou Márcia Ferreira, responsavel pela Polícia Federal em Tabatinga.*" She held out her hand.

"*Muito prazer,*" Torres responded. He extended his hand and they shook. His Portuguese was not native like his Spanish, but it was perfectly fluent. He stood in relaxed pose, but his face was set in its customary unreadable expression.

The group standing around them could glean little from the exchange – the words, the postures, the looks – except perhaps the feeling that two predators were sizing each other up after meeting for the first time. When the business-like greetings were done, and various other introductions effected, the small group proceeded to one of the hangars, where food had been laid out on a long table in an office built along one side.

"Please excuse the squalor," said Torres, as they all sat down at the table. "But I thought we should keep this within the confines of the base."

"Exactly right," agreed Ferreira.

Ten people sat down to eat, and as the initial awkward moments passed, the conversation turned to neutral, non-sensitive topics. Ferreira and Torres sat opposite each other in the middle of the long table and spoke pleasantly about the state of Brazilian football and how the cost of living was getting so high across the South American continent. Once they had finished the simple meal, however, Torres got up and walked over to a large desk near the back of the office. A projector clicked on and Torres tapped for a few seconds on the keyboard of a small laptop until a slide with a list of numbers appeared on the screen beside him.

He picked up a few sheets of paper, glanced through them, nodding, and then spoke to his audience for several minutes, summarising, matter-of-factly, the joint plan for the drugs seizure to take place at the Santa Rosa/Tabatinga border. As he talked, he revealed further details on the slides. It would be on a scale so far unparalleled in the region, involving the boarding and searching of fifteen passenger and fishing boats, the arrest of twenty-eight traffickers, and the confiscation of nearly seventy thousand pounds of large-brick cocaine, as well as US$1.2m in cash, and the usual collection of arms and mobile phones. There were a few low whistles as the scale of the operation sank in.

He spoke briefly of the main responsibilities on the Peruvian/American side and confirmed the chain of command and the main communications protocols.

"The eyes of the world will be on us, and it will be another demonstration of the effectiveness – Peruvian and the Brazilian effectiveness mainly, with some help from us – of our joint operations along the borders."

When he had finished, Torres handed over to Ferreira, who

confirmed the responsibilities for her team and described the necessary details. Afterwards, Torres suggested that the military and police officers pair off and take some time to discuss minor details with their opposite numbers, and invited Ferreira to accompany him on a short tour of the base.

"It's been a long time Márcia," said Torres quietly, once they were outside.

"Eleven months, I think," Ferreira acknowledged.

"It seems like you have a good team."

"I do. I trust these people as much as I can trust anyone."

"That's good to know," said Torres. He paused for a second before continuing. "And me? Do you trust me as much? We're all part of the same team on this one."

Her expression barely changed as she thought for a few seconds. "Senhor Adam, I trust you every bit as much as you trust me," she finally said.

Torres' deadpan expression cracked momentarily into the semblance of a smile. "Well, in the two years of our partnership I've had no cause to doubt you at all."

"Precisely."

They walked towards the end of the apron where it joined the runway, and then stopped. Torres turned slightly, checking the surrounding area before he spoke again.

"I regret that this operation is necessary," Torres began. "But it's a sacrifice we must make to keep things on track."

"Yes of course. I understand that. But it's not going to go down easily in some places."

Torres nodded in agreement. "I know. The most important question is, can you keep the organisation in place on your side?"

"Yes, but I'll need a little extra time before our next operation. I'm going to lose some key players, after all."

"Yes. Me too." He paused. "But essentially, everything is green for this, right?"

"Affirmative," agreed Ferreira.

Torres nodded. "Excellent." He looked around again, inclined his head slightly towards the barracks and held out his arm as an invitation to Ferreira to continue their walk. "Perhaps you are going to the LATAM security conference next month?" he asked.

"It can certainly be arranged."

"Good. I was thinking that perhaps we could confirm details of future operations at that point? If it's enough time for you, we would only lose a few weeks before we are back on track."

"It's plenty of time, yes." Ferreira nodded.

"Agreed, then?"

"Agreed."

They shook hands.

"There is just one other thing," said Torres.

Ferreira's expression hardened slightly, although she remained silent.

"It's nothing. A gringo I'd like to find, that's all."

Ferreira raised an eyebrow.

"Really, it's just a minor inconvenience. It should be resolved within the next few days. However – just as a precaution – perhaps you could ask your people to watch out for any odd-looking gringos travelling alone through your area?"

"Can you give me more detail?" asked Ferreira suspiciously. "All gringos look odd to me."

Torres shook his head and shrugged. "No need to over-complicate things. But if some Brit on his own – or maybe with a female companion – appears out of nowhere, acting strangely, just let one of my people know and we'll deal with it directly."

"Senhor Torres–" began Ferreira.

Torres held up his hand. "Really – it's not a problem."

Ferreira looked at him closely for a few seconds. "Very well. We'll keep an eye out. But if this is something that could compromise our operation, you must let me know."

"*Sim Senhora*," said Torres, nodding. "*Pode deixar*." Trust me.

They made their way back to the hangar, where the officers seemed to be working enthusiastically with each other. There were questions from some people, a final offering of coffee and biscuits, and fifty minutes later they all re-emerged into the sunlight.

The military turboprop's engines were already warming up as they made their way across to it. After stopping for a final round of handshakes, the Brazilians walked to their aircraft and the Peruvians retired to the hangar to watch the plane taxi and take off.

Torres could not stop a rare smirk of satisfaction from creeping across his face. All was now in place for an operation that would be headline stuff – as the Peruvian Adviser had said, 'significant news' – around the world. With a potential street value in excess of US$10bn, the cocaine haul would be billed as the largest drugs bust the world had ever seen. A marvellous example of international cooperation: a huge amount of drugs and arms destroyed; lots of narcos taken off the streets; money repatriated. Of course, as everyone present at the meeting understood, only a small percentage of the drugs and arms confiscated would be destroyed. The rest would be apportioned between the various interested parties. A considerable amount of it would become Torres' private property, and once it was fed back into the system – a slightly modified system, albeit – it would make him exceedingly rich. The Americans did not really care what happened to it – they just wanted attention taken away from their own plots and schemes. As long as the good people of the US of A and their representatives kept on voting lots of money into ongoing initiatives to help their new Peruvian buddies, Torres would be left to his own devices.

Of course there was the loss of the cash that would be seized, and the men that would be sacrificed. It would be inconvenient, for sure, and normal operations would be disrupted. But the loss would be made good in a few short months, and everything would be fine. Then Torres would get himself decently wounded, reluctantly accept his Silver Retirement Medal and paltry pension, and disappear. The rest of them could go to hell, Brazilians included.

He watched the plane roar down the runway and lift off into the pure blue sky, wobbling slightly from the thermals generated by the city to the north. Just a little turbulence before a perfect flight, no doubt. A minor irritation.

A minor irritation.

His smile faded as he contemplated the damned gringo again – McCrae, they now believed was the name – and the girl. It was a concern, certainly – more so than he had let on to Ferreira, perhaps. But it could still be resolved – *would* be resolved. True, the forest was a big place in which to find someone, and the pair had been lucky so far. But all roads led eventually to an airport or a communications tower, and Torres would soon have every one of these within a five hundred mile radius covered.

As for McCrae's supposed friend wandering around somewhere in Cuzco, Torres already had someone on the guy's tail twenty-four seven, and his phone and email were being monitored. Although there was a possibility, however small, that the army would find McCrae first, Torres felt more relaxed now he had a backup plan. Any phone contact with McCrae, and they would know where the bastard was within minutes. Whatever the order of events, it was only a matter of time before both gringos and the damned Peruvian girl were nailed.

He suddenly realised he was still staring into the sky, with the Peruvians standing around awkwardly, waiting for him.

"*Vamos*," he said, turning and forcing a smile.

Everyone began to walk back to the hangar, Torres trailing the group. His eyes narrowed in concentration as he visualised how things would be done. To some degree, it was unimportant – as soon as McCrae's position was known, he just needed the three eliminated – but there was no way he could leave it up to the Peruvians.

God forbid.

No. Some finesse was required. There were people he could rely on to do the job cleanly when it came to it, and he called them to mind now. He nodded very slightly as he came to a decision. His next stop would have to be Cuzco.

27

With the motor running at a little less than full throttle, the canoe seemed to race at breakneck speed down the river. Having left the cloying darkness of the forest behind, the bright openness of the wide, brown river was invigorating. Unfortunately, with no shelter from the sun, Jack's skin was burning even through his shirt, so he was grateful when they were at last able to slip into a narrow floodplain channel half an hour past the last signs of life they had spotted. Hauling the canoe into the margins, they climbed the low bank into the shade of a stand of trees trailing tangled lianas into the water.

"Well, we can't do twelve hours a day of this, that's for sure," Jack gasped. He kicked the leaf litter around to make sure he could sit without being eaten alive by something, and let himself down gingerly onto the cool earth.

Elena was already kneeling, removing things from her bag and laying out her line of hooks on the ground.

"*Es mejor que morir*," she said flatly, and started testing the knots on the line one by one.

"Ha ha. Yes, it certainly beats dying," agreed Jack, "but if I sit in the canoe in the sun for much longer, I may die anyway." He carefully pulled his sweat-soaked shirt off to reveal a lobster-coloured, blistered neck and shoulders. His face was also burnt and the skin on his arms was raised in long strips from wrist to elbow.

When Elena glanced across, she did a double-take, and Jack saw the look of shock on her face.

"*Madre de Dios*," she whispered. "First the mosquitoes, now the sun. Your skin must be as thin as *papel fumar*. I don't know how you gringos have survived so long."

"We do just fine, thank-you," said Jack, but without much conviction.

Elena sighed. "Hmm. Well, you are right, anyway: either you need to be covered, or we will have to travel at night." She paused to redo one of the knots on her line. "But it is more dangerous in the dark. We would have to slow down."

Jack nodded. "I know. But I've been wondering about doing it in stages. We could set off at, say, four a.m., go until nine a.m., rest until three p.m. and do three until eight. That's still ten hours. Maybe a hundred miles a day?"

Elena screwed up her face in thought. "How far are we from Brazil? Do you know?"

Jack shook his head. "No idea. I've a few markers in my head, but we haven't passed any of them yet."

"Markers?"

"Yes. *Puntos estratégicos*." He closed his eyes and tried to visualise the last map of the area that he had studied. "We ought to be somewhere between the two major towns of Contamana and Requena. After Requena, we come to the mouth of the Ucayali, and from there to Iquitos, it's only about fifty miles. Eighty kilometres, in your currency."

"Eighty kilometres is a long way in a peque-peque. And how far from Requena to the river mouth?"

Jack screwed up his face as he marked off the distances in his head. "Another eighty kilometres?"

Elena looked at him and sighed. "Iquitos to Brazil?"

"Four hundred."

"*Pucha*. And we don't know how far we are from Requena."

Jack shook his head. "No. But it can't be more than about three hundred," he announced brightly.

"Uh-huh – and that's all kilometres – my currency – right?"

Jack nodded.

"So we can be eight hundred kilometres from Brazil?"

"Approximately," Jack agreed.

"Well, *puta mierda*," Elena announced, raising her eyes skyward. She gave him a sardonic smile. "That's 'sonofabitch', in *your* currency.

Jack ignored the jibe, frowning in concentration as he continued picturing the map in his head. He was already trying to remember his planned route onward from the Brazilian border, but he had not committed it to memory like the one for the Peruvian leg.

"Yes. That's about it. And those are straight-line distances, don't forget."

For a second, Elena looked like she would explode in anger, then she sat down and started laughing and shaking her head. "Eight hundred kilometres. You're a crazy gringo, you know?"

Jack managed a weak smile. "Yeah, so you told me. Anyway, like you said, it beats being dead, right?"

She smiled back at him, perfect white teeth shining from her smooth, mahogany face and dark eyes scrunched up with humour just above her high cheek bones. Even the recent scar that ran down her cheek could not mar an uncomplicated grace that made Jack sit and stare at her for a few moments.

But she was still a terrorist. Unpardonable; unforgivable.

"So what do you think?" he asked sharply, breaking the spell.

She shook her head. "I think it is too dangerous at night, and we would travel so slowly it would take months. I think we must travel during the day. Maybe we can find a faster boat, and make a cover for you. That way we can go faster, and rest at night."

"But if we steal a bigger boat, aren't we more likely to be chased? The locals would take a lot a more notice, and wouldn't they be more likely to get the police involved?"

"The Police? No – people here despise the police. They are no better than the narcos, and sometimes much worse. Here, people solve problems their own way." She thought for a moment before continuing. "But the communities do talk to each other, and you are right that people would notice a big boat more."

"You think people here could already know about us stealing this canoe? Or the other ones?"

"I don't think so. We have come very far, very fast." She smiled. "Even I am impressed."

"We were lucky, certainly."

Elena shook her head emphatically. "No. Luck is earned. You found the way. I know many people who could not do that. I could not do it." She laughed. "So no-one would think that we could come this far by now, and I am sure that nobody here will know about us."

"Good. And I hope the army and the Americans – and whoever else they're working with – are all still wasting their time looking for us on the Huallaga."

"I am sure of it. But I don't know for how long. The army is not completely *burro*."

"No. Nor are the Americans," said Jack thoughtfully. "They would be crazy not to watch for us further downstream." He thought for a moment. "Everything eventually feeds into the Marañon River, so unless they're idiots, they'll be watching the Marañon near Iquitos."

Elena considered for a few seconds.

"Probably further upstream of Iquitos, too – the river around the city must be very busy, so it would be easier for them to search where there is less traffic. They will hope that if we don't die in the jungle or get picked up on the Huallaga, they will find us before we get to Iquitos."

"And they'll have put the word about too, presumably?"

"Of course, although perhaps not near here. They will not think anyone would be mad enough – or maybe even able enough – to cross from the Huallaga to the Ucayali. Not as fast as we did, for sure."

"Okay. So for the moment we probably have a breathing space."

"We can breathe, yes – for now. If we are careful, and if we stay with our canoe, we will probably be safe. But word will spread. The longer we are here, the more dangerous it will be. Especially for a gringo. You need to keep out of sight."

"Not just me, Elena," said Jack somewhat defensively. "They'll know all about you, too."

"Ha ha. Yes, but at least I look like a Peruvian, not a... a beetroot with blond hair." She pointed at him and laughed, and Jack found it impossible not to join her. For a few moments they laughed together like kids in class, alternately shushing each other and then giggling and guffawing.

When they had recovered their composure, Jack accompanied her down to the river to watch her string the fishing line along the bank. There was a good twenty feet of it, with hooks at evenly spaced intervals of around two feet, each hook on a leader of about a foot. Elena baited the hooks with bits of leaf and insects she grubbed out from round about. When she was finished, she tied the end of the line to a sapling at the river's edge, then walked back, quickly laying the hooks in the river along the bank. She squatted down with the line wrapped around her left hand and running through her right.

"I like to use bigger hooks and leave them for an hour, but with these smaller ones, you must remove what you catch quickly, or the piranha will strip it off for you."

Jack watched the line quiver. Elena did nothing for a moment and then she quickly jerked the line up and onto the bank, dragging out two small fish, and a red piranha thrashing away on the hook furthest from them. She trapped the line under her foot and deftly removed the first two fish, but before she got to the piranha, it dropped onto the bank and flapped into the water, the line severed and the hook still in its mouth.

"Not bad," she said, and smiled. She pointed to the tail of one of the fish, and Jack saw that most of it was missing – chewed off. "That's why you have to be quick."

"So why didn't they attack us when we were floating down the river?"

"We're too big. Probably smell bad too."

"Speak for yourself," said Jack.

Elena thought for a second. "Ha ha. Very funny, Mister Jack. But all gringos smell bad. Here we wash twice or three times a day; gringos hardly wash at all." She pinched her nose and made a face.

They set off again a little after two o'clock. They were in good spirits – rested and fed with fresh fish and farine. Jack was covered with all the available cloth they could find. After three uneventful hours, they rounded a bend to find their first sizeable community. It was big enough to have a track running for half a mile or more along the riverside, with a row of wooden houses on stilts behind it and one or two brick buildings, including a church. They could see that it had been built on the south side of a smaller river flowing into the Ucayali from the east, and to Jack's delight he could see a series of telegraph poles with electric cables running between them, and a communications tower near the riverfront with mobile network dishes near the top.

They stopped to consider their options.

"They have phones. I can get in touch with my contact, Greg, in Cuzco" said Jack emphatically.

Elena nodded. "Hmm. Okay, but we also need food." She kicked the red plastic can of fuel at her feet. "And supplies."

"Can we bluff our way?"

"Bluff? What means 'bluff'?"

"Bullshit. Lie."

"Ah. You mean can *I* bluff our way, then." She thought for a few moments and then shook her head doubtfully. "I don't see how."

"You managed last time," Jack pointed out.

Elena snorted. "Scaring one poor woman on her own is easy. I can't do the same thing to a whole community. And I can't think of any bluff that would explain why I am travelling downstream in a wooden canoe with my clothes like this" — she pulled at her filthy, tattered shirt — "and with no supplies, no money, and no phone. I cannot buy anything, and they don't give things to people for nothing in these places."

Jack thought for a while. "Well, maybe you could pass as a tour guide," he said, eyeing her up and down. "You know – for gringos. You could say there was an accident and one of them is injured. You lost your pack with your GPS and phone and stuff. You just need to borrow a phone to contact your base."

Elena rolled her eyes. "But they would expect me to at least know where I *am*, wouldn't they?"

"You can bullshit that. Tell them you're coming from Contamana, exploring floodplain channels—"

"Flood-what?"

"Floodplain channels. Um, *canales de la planicie – llanura inundable*. Tell them it's for TV – Sky, National Geographic, or something."

"Hah hah – yes, even here they know National Geographic." She considered for a moment. "Okay. Well, maybe we will not get any supplies, but we might get a phone call. If you think that is the most important thing..."

"I'm sure of it, Elena. If we can get through to Greg, he can bring in the British embassy; the British press. They'll get us out."

"They'll get *you* out," said Elena, dryly.

"No. *Us*. I will tell them you are my rescuer or something. Really, Elena. I won't abandon you."

She looked at him for a few seconds, thinking.

"Okay, well I suppose we must try it. The only alternative is to steal everything at night. For some of the supplies, that may be possible, but not for a phone. There's probably only a few phones in the whole village."

They backtracked several hundred yards, paddling hard against the current, until they found a suitable spot to unload their meagre gear and where Jack could wait in reasonable comfort for several hours. Elena memorised the phone number and the English message Jack gave her, and prepared to leave.

"Good luck," Jack said, as she got into the canoe.

"Luck? We make our own luck, no?" She grinned, started the motor, and was off. A few minutes later, she was lost to view as she followed the river to the left. As she rounded the bend, the noise of the motor was instantly muffled, and quickly faded to a tenuous background hum. Fifteen minutes later, on the edge of Jack's consciousness, he was aware that the hum had stopped.

He busied himself organising the few bits and pieces of gear they had, and collecting dry wood for a fire, in case he should have to spend any time here. Afterwards, he ate a mouthful of farine and sat down to look again at the map he had taken from the cabin.

DUMAR T.AE, HEP 1-11, 15m.

The writing on the piece of paper. Holding the map up to the light, he could clearly see the pinholes in it. He thought back to how the pins had been joined together with the lengths of cotton, and found the single pin hole on the coast to which he remembered all the other pins had been linked back. Some sort of distribution reference? Telephone maybe, or data... or power links – yes, electricity to run the equipment being used at the sites, perhaps? But it seemed unlikely – the energy demand would have to be either phenomenally high or particularly critical to need that sort of planned supply laid on. Most of the construction stuff could easily be generator-powered, and if they could bring in earth-moving gear, they could bring in big generators. He could not really see how what he was looking at was much of a big deal at all – just a lot of big sites run from another one on the coast. So what?

As for the words and letters, they meant nothing. The name Alexander Dumas – famed among English-speaking schoolboys for all the wrong reasons – came to mind, but little else. He had reached no conclusion by the time the shadows lengthened and the sun set behind the distant mountains. The now familiar slapping, splashing sounds of the river could be heard from all around: it was the time when the rainforest was at its most active, including the bats, the fish, the caiman, and the mosquitoes. There was no moon visible tonight, and when the darkness crept in, it was very dark indeed, even on the open river.

He sat in the blackness, too tired and sore to be that bothered by the clouds of mosquitoes homing in on him. His body had become a little more used to them, so that no longer did the bites come up in lumps that left him feeling like he was on fire. Or maybe it was just the physical and mental stress that meant his much put-upon senses had re-prioritised things for him. And talking of priorities, he realised his whole being at the moment was tense – straining constantly to catch the distant sound that would tell him Elena was on her way back. He tried to relax, but it was impossible. What was taking so long? She must have had at least an hour now to talk to the locals. Surely she could have negotiated what they needed in that time.

He considered lighting the fire, and when the noise of the caiman came too close, he even got as far as igniting the lighter flame for a second or so. But he resisted the temptation, still hoping that Elena would turn up soon. He returned the lighter to his pocket. He thought about what Greg would do when he got the call – if he got the call. Would he take it seriously? He must do, surely: after two weeks with no contact at all, he should at least be *considering* the need to alert someone. He closed his eyes. It was pointless speculating, and he would know soon enough.

Come on Elena - where are you?

28

The cheap mobile phone vibrated and buzzed for the third time in a dank room on the first floor of the cheap hotel in Cuzco. The bed covers moved and were finally flung aside as a man sat up and grabbed the phone. He peered at the number as he pressed the 'answer' button.

"Hello? Um, *buenos noches*?" he said groggily. He listened for a second or two with a puzzled expression on his face.

"What? Who? What's that about Jack? Jesus, do you know what time it is?"

"Sorry señor, but Jack really needs help," came a woman's strained voice through the static.

The man started to get to his feet.

"Okay. Sure. But is he alright? I mean–"

"He is good. He says to tell you 'England will win'."

"Ha-ha – fat chance. If–"

"But please listen. He is in very bad trouble."

"Really? What sort of trouble?"

"There are people after him. After us. They try to kill us."

"What? But that's crazy. Who the hell–"

"There is not time. Please listen!"

"Okay, okay – go on."

"We cannot stay here. We are on the Ucayali, going to Iquitos – Tabatinga – to Brazil."

"Right..."

"Jack asks you to get to the British and tell them. He said to say 'something big is going down'. It is very big. The army, the narcos, even the Americans."

"Okay, um, what was your name?"

"Elena."

"Right Elena, I understand. But this is madness. Can I not talk to

Jack?"

"No. He is hiding. He is too obvious. Look, I have little time. We really *really* need your help. *Muy muy importante.*"

"Okay. Don't worry. I'll phone someone first thing in the morning."

"No, no! You must go to see them. Talk to them. Where are you now? Are you in Cuzco?"

"Yes."

"*Mierda.* I do not think there are embassies in Cuzco. Okay, phone first if necessary – but then you *must* go see someone in person. *Rápido.* Jack says if you have to travel, he will pay."

"Don't worry. Tell Jack he can rely on me."

"And remember – do not go to the Americans. They are involved."

"Okay, okay. But how will we find you?"

"We are between Contamana and Requena. A village called Tierra Nueva. We will look for something at the villages we pass. A flag or a sign. Jack said you would know."

"Okay. Hmm...," he paced across the room as he thought, before snapping his fingers. "A British flag, then, how about that?"

"*Eso.* Perfect."

There was a pause and some other voices could be heard in the background.

"I must go now," said Elena. "Thank you very much."

"Tell Jack I'll sort everything out. Don't worry. Take care, okay?"

There were more voices, some static, and then the line went dead.

The man paced up and down the little bedroom for a few minutes, and looked at his watch. Finally he went to the bathroom, took a shower and put his clothes on. He collected his gear, organised his rucksack and left the room.

In the now unattended lobby of the hotel, he reached behind the counter and picked up the phone directory, then he went and sat down. He frowned as he skimmed through the phone book with increasing urgency, until he finally found an entry for *Consulado Británico in* Cuzco. He smiled and breathed a long sigh.

He took out a pen and tore a strip off one of the blank pages of the phone book, writing down the address of the consulate. Then he replaced the book behind the counter and after a few minutes struggling with the heavy wooden front door, managed to open it. He walked out into the narrow cobbled street and turned right. The lighting was dim, but it was enough to see all the way down to the Plaza San Pedro, where there were some people and cars passing.

A few moments after setting off in the direction of the plaza, he heard a car approaching from behind, and he automatically stepped up onto the little pavement. The car rolled alongside, and through the open side window he heard the driver call out.

"Taxi, *señor*?"

As the car stopped, he bent down and peered in at the driver. Who said Peru was inefficient? He handed him the piece of paper with the address of the Consulate, and the driver smiled and gave him a thumbs-up.

"*Si señor. Vamo.*"

"*Cuanto?*"

The driver shrugged. "*Veinte.*"

"Okay." He returned the driver's thumbs up and got into the back of the car. He cursed as he squeezed his tall frame into the inadequate space, and sat with his head bowed slightly to stop it banging on the roof with every pothole.

Less than five minutes later, they drew up next to what looked like a building site.

"*Llegamos*," announced the driver.

"Where? *Adónde?*"

The driver pointed to an alleyway to the right. "*Doscientos metros, señor.*"

"Oh. Great." He paid the twenty Nuevo Soles and got out of the car. He was surprised to see the driver get out too. He nodded and smiled uncertainly at him, and the driver smiled back, producing a pack of cigarettes and putting a cigarette in his mouth. Another thumbs-up was exchanged as he started walking towards the alleyway.

The driver waited until the man had passed by, and then returned the cigarette pack to his pocket. He quickly reached inside his jacket with his other hand and produced a silenced pistol. A sharp spit from the gun, a spray of blood and tissue from the head, and the body of the tall foreigner collapsed in front of the car. It twitched once, twice, and was still.

Putting the gun away, the driver bent down and searched the corpse, removing the phone and money he found in the trouser pockets. He ripped the rucksack off and threw it to one side, then dragged the body to a gate in the wall at the passenger side of the car. He knocked, and the gate was immediately opened from the inside. Another man appeared, and between them they manhandled the body through the door. The driver went back and quickly rifled the rucksack, taking any documents he could find, and then he handed it to the other man, along with the gun he had used. The other man accepted these, looked round quickly, and went through the door himself and closed it behind him.

The driver got back into the car and drove unhurriedly away. As soon as he was on the main road again, he pulled over. He made a call on his phone, and stared at the passport in his hand as he waited for it to be answered.

"*Cumplido*," he said simply. Done.

29

There was a huge splash not two yards from where Jack sat, and his heart nearly leapt from his mouth. Bugger this – it was time to light the fire. He pulled the lighter out of his pocket, but before he could get it near the kindling, he heard the wonderful, distant background hum of a peque-peque. Elena!

The hum got steadily, oh-so-slowly louder, until finally the canoe rounded the bend and the noise level suddenly doubled, as if someone had just opened a door. There was the flash of a torch. On – off, on – off. It must be Elena – no-one else could know where Jack was. He flicked on the lighter to give the same signal, and in less than a minute, there was Elena jumping ashore. In the silence after she turned the engine off, her whispered words were quite clear.

"All okay. We have more fuel and more farine. Come on, let's go!"

She sounded agitated, her voice urgent.

"Problems?" he asked.

"No, I don't think so. I don't know. They were very kind, but there were some who were suspicious. I had to *inventar* many things about our story, and I don't know if they made sense." She smiled. "They gave me twenty litres of fuel to get me back to my injured clients, and four kilos of farine – and the torch. Generous, I think."

"Yes, certainly. Well done. And the phone call...?" He could hardly keep the impatience from his voice.

"It was a short call, but I'm sure your friend understood everything. He said he would phone somebody, but I told him he must talk face to face."

"Yes – good, good." Jack breathed a sigh of relief. "Thank God."

"But now we need to get past the village – get away. We cannot stay here."

"Yes, of course," said Jack, snapping out of his thoughts of imminent rescue.

"It should be easy," Elena continued. "The river is wide, and there are no houses on the other side. If we stay on that side, we can be past in thirty minutes – an hour at the maximum."

"Okay. Sounds sensible. Let's hit the road, then."

"Right. Oh – wait – there's something else they gave me." She turned and shone the torch briefly onto two plastic bags. Holding the torch in her mouth, she reached down, opened the first bag and pulled out from the middle of a bunch of loose leaves, two little wads of balled-up leaves, each a little smaller than a squash ball. She closed the bag again and handed a wad to Jack.

"Used it before?" she asked.

"What is it?" he asked, suspiciously. "Coca? No. Never have."

"Now's the time to start."

"Elena–"

"It's okay – it will not hurt you. Keep it in the side of your mouth until it is soft, then, um, *chupar e masticar*."

"Suck and chew. Okay..."

"Just a little. Occasionally."

Jack took it gingerly in his hand and looked at it until Elena snapped off the torch. He had heard about the use of the coca leaf for enhancing energy and suppressing appetite, but had not used it, even in Cuzco, where every man and his dog lived on the stuff. He smiled grimly. He *was* knackered after all, and pretty much permanently hungry. As Elena suggested, now was probably the time.

"Don't swallow it," said Elena, coming to his side and switching on the torch in search of their stuff. She held the beam steady to allow Jack to gather everything together, and they pushed the canoe out and hopped in. Jack sat at the back next to the engine, and Elena at the front. Once he had secured the propeller shaft so it was clear of the water, they paddled slowly round the bend, and Jack was surprised to the see the few lights of the village shine out clearly across the river in the distance.

"Bloody hell, it's like Blackpool illuminations," he groaned, although he knew that for anyone standing in the well-lit community, there was no way they could see across the half mile that separated the two banks. On the other hand, he and Elena would be able to see quite easily if anything was going on over there, as they slipped past in the dark.

Their paddling settled into a slow, steady, rhythm. Jack's cheek slowly became numb, and he began to feel more positive. His stomach stopped rumbling and he felt that he could paddle like this for hours – days, if necessary. For the first time in two weeks, and in spite of everything that had happened to him, he felt rested and calm. Paddling down the Ucayali in the dark in a stolen canoe suddenly seemed the most natural thing in the world.

The faint light from the distant community was just enough to allow Jack to see the red eyes of the caiman watching them as they paddled into the night.

Even with the village was far behind them, they continued their slow progress in the dark until, after running into a long series of mudbanks, they eventually found a place to ground the canoe and rest. The resident caiman dispersed noisily as the boat approached, which might have startled Jack except that he was just too tired to care anymore. The effects of the coca had kept him going for a while, but eventually he had spat out the wad, and now he was as weary as hell. If he was to be eaten by a croc, so be it: it was probably preferable to being shot, and he would not have to worry about the prospect of being burnt to a crisp again tomorrow.

They collapsed where they were, lying in whatever position afforded their limbs the greatest respite, and rested. Try as he might, Jack could not get to sleep, however. Instead he lay thinking, imagining what the British authorities might do when Greg contacted them, and trying to second-guess the events of the next couple of days.

Elena had told him that the agreed sign was a British flag, and he was happy about that. A union jack would be easy to spot around here: nearly every village had a church and a flagpole of some description, and as long as no-one objected to flying a foreign flag over their village for a while, all should be well. The only issue would surely be the logistics of the thing, and effort would surely be concentrated on the larger towns – Requena, for example, or maybe even Iquitos itself. He speculated idly about whether there would be enough British flags – did embassies keep a stockpile for emergencies? He smiled to himself as he lay looking up at the sky. The clouds parted for a few seconds, allowing the austere light of a gibbous moon to shine down and transform the scene into ghostly black and white. He pushed himself up on his elbows in time to see the whole width of the moon-kissed river, the towering trees edging the water, and ten or more caiman of various sizes, lying parallel to their canoe and looking for all the world like other beached craft. The absurdity of it amused him, and he watched until the clouds smothered the moon again and blackness returned.

He was still smiling vaguely as he pictured a map of the Ucayali between Contamana and Iquitos. They could not be more than two hundred miles from Requena now. Although progress at night would be pitifully slow while that beautiful moon remained hidden, by racing at full pelt during the day they should easily reach the town the day after tomorrow. The timing seemed perfect, and all they had to do was keep below the radar for another thirty-six hours or so.

He eventually slept, to be woken by Elena banging around in the canoe. He felt groggy and irritable, and his legs, which had been resting on top of the seat in front, were sore and stiff. It was still dark, although he could see the blackness slowly dissolving. They were on the water within ten minutes, and made good progress down the twisting river, slowly increasing their speed as the light spread. The noise of the motor drove huge flocks of egrets and heron up into the dawn sky every time they rounded a bend, and sent the caiman scurrying for cover.

When the sun finally appeared over the tops of the trees, Jack held up a makeshift cover to shield himself from the heat on the right side of his face and body, and cursed as the weight of the cover chafed at his sunburn.

"Here," shouted Elena.

She turned and stretched out her hand to him. In it lay another ball of coca leaves, and Jack could see that her right cheek already bulged. He hesitated only a moment before accepting, and promptly wedged the ball in between his lower teeth and the side of his mouth. After a few minutes the numbness slowly spread through his gums and a feeling of calm alertness overwhelmed his irritation.

Certainly he was uncomfortable. He was – or had been – desperately hungry. But things were working out now. Another day's cruise down the Ucayali – he smiled at the thought of them 'cruising' – and they would be within striking distance of Requena and the first real possibility of rescue. He turned and shared his smile with Elena, who held her thumb up in response.

Just a few more hours.

30

Torres' mind was filled for a moment with an image of the town the Major had described to him. Hot, humid, smelly, unsanitary. How people could live in those places was beyond him.

"This place, on the Ucayali River? How the hell did they get all the way over there?" He measured the distance from the site to Tierra Nueva with his thumb and little finger.

The Major shrugged.

"And how confident are you of this information?" Torres asked.

"A hundred percent. With the intercept already on the guy's phone in Cuzco, we were able to get all the call connection data quickly. We're just waiting to see if we have audio."

"But surely that's a given, isn't it?"

"Unfortunately not. Audio is a rarity here, because of the technical – and procedural – complications."

Torres raised his eyebrows and shook his head. "Bureaucracy." The word emerged reluctantly, through gritted teeth.

"Bureaucracy," the Major conceded.

"Major," said Torres, closing his eye and rubbing his temples, "I'm going to be *really* disappointed if there is no audio."

"Yes sir. Everything that can be done is being done."

Torres sighed. At least he had employed his own people in Cuzco, where things had gone perfectly: all traces removed, hotel room checked – even the guy's hotel bill paid. What a cheapskate, sneaking out without paying the bill. Damned gringos.

"Okay, so at least we know where our man is again. What's your plan, Major?"

"I've already ordered in two choppers and two patrol boats – one from upstream, one from downstream. They can't hide from us for long."

"Hmm. I need hardly remind you that he has already hidden from you for seven days," Torres said with barely contained sarcasm. "And managed to cross a hundred kilometres of barren floodplain. And has now turned up almost two hundred kilometres from where you were searching."

The Major's voice was strained. "Yes sir, but that's because there were too many variables. Now they have nowhere to go except downstream." He pointed to the map laid out in front of Torres. "To get anywhere else, it's over three hundred kilometres in any direction, through impenetrable jungle. If they decide to do anything other than follow the river, the jungle will take care of them for us."

Torres looked at the Major coldly. "Listen, whatever they might or might not decide to do, or wherever they go, I want a confirmed result. We will not leave this to chance. Understand?"

"Yes sir."

"Okay. So where's your other patrol boat coming up from?"

"Requena."

"Uh, let's see, that's here, right?" said Torres, tapping a small circle on the military map that had the symbol of a plane, a boat and a man next to it.

The Major nodded. "Around five hours away."

"Okay. Get on it then, Major."

"Yes sir."

"And Major..."

"Sir?"

"I want that audio."

"Yes sir."

31

J ack was surprised that during the first three hours of daylight they saw not a soul on the river, and were able to make good progress. The mudbanks, topped with scrubby, short-lived, dry-season vegetation, were clearly visible now and easy to avoid. It was getting hotter, but Jack's makeshift cover was proving its worth, and as long as they were moving, the breeze kept them reasonably cool. At one point, they passed a village of some size on the west bank. Although there was no sign to give it a name, Jack knew it could not be Requena, so they sped past, intent on covering as much distance as possible in the shortest space of time.

Eventually though, they felt the need to stop, stretch, eat and drink, so they picked a small channel on the northwest side of an island, and nosed into it. Running the boat up onto the mud, behind a stand of bushes and trees, they found they could just see the main river through the branches, but would be all but invisible to anyone on the main channel. They sat hunched on the canoe seats in the shade provided by the trees, and gulped down the rest of their farine with mouthfuls of Ucayali water. It was a welcome relief after the hours of unrelenting sunshine and the constant vibration of the engine.

Suddenly Elena held a finger up, tipping her head to one side at the same time. Jack listened, and soon heard the faint sound of an outboard motor in the distance. They hurriedly pulled their canoe further into the trees, and waited for the boat to appear, which it did less than a minute later.

Jack was shocked to see a camouflage-painted military patrol boat powering up the river, with an implausibly large canon mounted on the front and two small machine guns at the rear. The tiny wheelhouse was just big enough for one man, and there were three other soldiers at the back and one to man the cannon. At the stern were twin three hundred horsepower four-strokes, and the boat was planing as if the weight meant nothing. It shot past them and one of the men at the back raised his binoculars and appeared to be looking straight at Jack. The boat slowed. Another man turned and raised his binoculars. They were clearly interested in the little channel, and as the boat came off the plane and settled down onto the water, they talked among themselves, as first one then another raised his hand to point in Jack and Elena's direction.

Jack found himself holding his breath, as if the slightest movement would be enough to expose them. He felt the sweat form on his brow and trickle down into his eyes. He closed them and waited, releasing his breath as gently as he could. If they were spotted now, there would be no getting away. Not this time.

Finally, he heard the engines accelerate and he opened his eyes, half expecting the boat to swing round and head straight for them. Instead, he watched with relief as the engines continued to throttle up. The boat rose on the plane, and disappeared as quickly as it had arrived. He wiped the sweat from his brow and felt a sudden chill as he thought about what would have happened if they had still been on the river. With the noise from their own engine, they would never have heard the patrol boat's motor, and the first they would have known about it was when it came round a corner and it was too late to dodge or hide.

"Probably just a routine patrol," said Elena. She shrugged, but Jack could hear the tension in her voice.

It was Jack's turn to hold a finger up. "If it's just routine, what do you think *that* noise is, then?"

She stopped and they both listened to the unmistakable sound of a helicopter approaching.

Jack was less worried about being spotted by the chopper than by the patrol boat. They were well covered by the trees they had pulled under. But the hairs were up on the back of his neck. A patrol boat and a helicopter appearing a few hours after their stop was more than coincidence.

"Dammit," he said, as they sat waiting for the helicopter to pass. It seemed to take an age. It was clearly not flying point to point, but was executing some sort of search pattern, and appeared to be crossing and re-crossing the river. Glimpsing it once or twice through the branches, Jack was surprised to see how low it was flying. He held his breath as the sound came closer and closer...and then finally receded.

"Perhaps we should stay right here, during the daytime," said Elena. "I don't think that boat could get close to us without getting stuck, and the helicopter did not see us. This would be a good place to wait for dark."

"Okay," Jack agreed. "But tonight we have to make the best of it, whether we have bright moonlight or thick clouds. We can't be more than a hundred miles at the most from Requena. Even at walking pace, two long nights will get us there."

Elena regarded him for a moment.

"You are very confident about Requena," she said finally. "It might not solve our problem. Maybe Greg has not been able to contact anyone. Maybe no one will listen. Maybe–".

"I know all that, dammit," he snapped. "We'll worry about it when we get there."

He had not meant to be so short with her, but the truth was that he *was* setting a lot of store on things going their way at Requena. And there was no clear contingency plan – travelling all the way to Brazil by night seemed like a ridiculous proposition, but what else was there? He had to believe that the British authorities would do something. There might be delays – some difficulties with bureaucracy or logistics – but they would sort something out. All he and Elena had to do was avoid detection until they saw a British flag. That was as much planning as he could handle just at the moment.

32

"What have you got for me Major?" asked Torres, walking into the oppressively dark, dank operations room on the military compound.

The Major waited until Torres was standing next to the small computer and then he sat down and clicked the "play" icon on the screen. They listened in silence to the short conversation between Elena and Greg.

"Hmm. This changes things a little, Major," said Torres.

The Major looked at him blankly.

"I want British flags out in every decent-sized village along the Ucayali from Contamana to Iquitos, with a team of your people at each location. If anyone asks, it's a special military exercise, but I want everyone briefed on what to expect and what to do."

"Certainly sir."

"Which means," Torres said, emphasising his words, "That when we have them, I want the bastards held under lock and key until I get there – out of sight of everyone and without anyone having any conversation with them at all. Clear?"

The Major nodded. "Yes sir."

"Okay. Let's get those flags up, then."

KEIR FARRELL

33

The journey proved almost as slow and tortuous as they had feared, but at least they remained undetected. They were tired and hungry, even though Elena's fishing skills had enabled them to eat once – but their hunger would no doubt have been the greater had they not been sucking or chewing their small wads of coca leaves for almost two days solid.

They would have missed the town of Requena altogether had they arrived during the day: Jack had forgotten that it lay not on the Ucayali itself, but a mile or so up a small tributary. In fact, they arrived early on the third night after their encounter with the patrol boat, and they could not fail to see the orange glow in the sky from miles away, or notice the impressive levels of noise which floated down to them on the night air.

Holed up during the day, they had heard the big motors of a patrol boat burble past them a few times, and a helicopter scouring the area, but none of them came as close as on the first day.

They approached the mouth of the tributary cautiously along the west bank of the Ucayali, until they were within less than two miles of the twinkling string of streetlights marking the westernmost end of a waterfront that stretched into the distance towards the town.

"It looks pretty big," said Elena. "How many people? Do you know?"

Jack shrugged. "From what I remember, around twenty thousand or so."

Elena gave a low whistle, and Jack searched his memory for a second or two. "It has a large *Plaza del Armas*, a cathedral, several hotels, an airport, light, and phones," he recited.

They had already agreed that Elena would go in alone, Jack coming out of hiding only if a friendly reception was certain.

Jack nosed the boat into the banks and cut the engine. He got out and unloaded their stuff as Elena made her way back to sit by the motor. He started describing the flag to her again, but she held her hand up.

"Look, it is like nothing we have in Peru," she said with some exasperation in her voice. "Believe me – I will recognise it." She smiled. "And if there's no flag, I have our shopping list committed to memory."

Jack sighed. "Yes, yes – okay – I know. Go on then."

He was not looking forward to another hellish night on his own, padding about the tree line behind a mudbank, and he watched Elena go with a mixture of anticipation and anxiety.

She crossed the main river and made her way up the tributary to within sight of the town's port. Leaving the canoe and creeping in from the periphery, she excited no interest whatever in the locals. It was a Friday night, shops and stalls were still open, and a lot of people were drinking in the plethora of rickety little bars by the market. A normal night in a normal Peruvian Amazon town – or it would have been, without the presence of the disproportionately large number of soldiers patrolling the place. Walking to the large Plaza del Armas, the compulsory square around which every Peruvian town is built, and past the equally inevitable diminutive cathedral, Elena looked to her right at the communications tower. A huge British flag halfway up the structure could hardly be missed, even in the artificial light reflected from narrow, concrete-covered streets and tin roofs. Her face brightened when she first saw it, but the more she looked at the well-armed soldiers walking around and the heavy guard on the civilian communications tower, the more her expression clouded.

She found the market area, and wasted no time using the cover of the bustling, night-time activity to lift some money from a couple of bags, as well as some fruit, which she gorged on greedily as she did her rounds. She bought a litre bottle of water and polished it off in minutes. Next, she managed to acquire a modest nondescript skirt and a t-shirt, and paid a visit to a restaurant toilet where she washed her face and changed her clothes.

She spent time around the bars along the river, talking to people, listening to snatches of conversation and observing the subtly strained artificial levity at the bars where soldiers stood nearby. She appeared relaxed as she walked about or sat down for a few moments here and there. She walked slowly, with a very slightly stooped posture, and kept her face almost constantly in shadow. To the casual observer she appeared considerably older than her twenty-five years.

It was easy for her to pick up the information she wanted, and as she worked her way around it became increasingly obvious that the flag was a set-up. There was certainly no British presence here, and the gossip was that the military were using it as a ploy to trick some Sendero members. The irony of it was not lost on her.

By midnight she had stolen, bartered or bought everything on their list and more, and was walking briskly along the riverbank, approaching the spot where she had left the canoe. She heard a helicopter approaching from the direction of the town, and flinched as it flew overhead and switched on a searchlight. It lit up a huge swathe of the river, and as it arrived over the Ucayali, a patrol boat was caught momentarily in the light before the helicopter moved upstream. The boat trailed after it, remaining in shadow. She got into her canoe, placed the gear in the driest location, and stared thoughtfully back along the river to the town. Finally, she appeared to reach a decision.

She pushed off, started the motor, and headed upstream towards the port, keeping as close to the banks as she could, until she had passed a series of frail-looking wooden piers with canoes tied up to them. She cut the motor, moved up to the front of the canoe, and allowed the boat to drift back downstream, steering it when necessary with the wooden paddle.

She stopped alongside the first canoe she came to, and then worked her way carefully down a whole string of them, until she spotted a plastic fuel tank in one of them, which the owner had left connected to the motor. She reached in and lifted it up. It was nearly empty, but she repeated the exercise until she had found two full tanks, which she exchanged for their nearly exhausted ones. Finally, she pushed off and let the canoe drift silently downstream, keeping her eye all the time on the distant spotlight that intermittently bathed the patch of the Ucayali that lay between her and Jack.

No one saw the lone canoe drift slowly down to the Ucayali and continue downstream another two hundred yards. No one noticed as

Elena steered it into the margins and sat there peering out at the activity further upstream. She had picked a well-sheltered spot, but the canoe was still relatively exposed on this side of the river, where it was much more heavily populated, and the margins more cultivated. It was about half a mile to the other side of the river, and the search being undertaken by the military patrols was concentrated well over a mile to the west. She waited and watched for ten minutes and then she fired up the engine, and started across the river.

Jack had been listening to the noise of the patrol boats since they had arrived on the scene an hour or so after Elena had left. They were making a series of sweeps, switching on their searchlights every few minutes or so. Several times he saw small craft held in a beam of light while the patrol boats approached or even came alongside to investigate. There was a surprising amount of traffic around, and Jack knew that most of it would be people going fishing or bringing a catch back. The exercise went on for a long time, and eventually Jack grew bored with it, occasionally chewing on the remains of his wad of coca leaves until it became too bitter and he spat it out. When a helicopter joined in the search, Jack dug deeper into the undergrowth, making sure he could not be spotted under the protection of a low canopy of stunted, broad-leaved trees. His emotions rose and fell like a roller coaster as the chopper came closer, tracking its light up and down the margins, before moving slowly over to the other side and repeating the process along the west bank. The boats and the chopper were clearly in communication, as the searchlights regularly converged perfectly on hapless canoes in mid-stream. Jack realised it would take a miracle for Elena to get back to him across the river. It was obvious now that they should have stopped much further downstream, from where they would have been able to come and go as they pleased, unmolested.

He considered the possibility that maybe the search was being carried out by the good guys, or at least on the instructions of the good guys, but he did not really believe it. If there was a flag up and he was already being invited in, why not just wait until the flag did its job? Why buzz around wasting money trying to get to him a mile or so upstream? It made no sense. As the time dragged on, he became more certain that there was no flag in Requena, and no British presence. The wheels were working too slowly, and they were still being hunted by the enemy. Now they would probably have to make it all the way to Iquitos on their own.

Suddenly the helicopter swung round, its searchlight on, and headed downstream. A second later, the two patrol boats roared after it at speed. All the searchlights came on at once, sweeping along the line where the tributary and the Ucayali met. They had obviously been alerted to something. The helicopter started tracking to Jack's side of the river, and he tensed. He crept down to the shoreline, and strained to see what was happening, but all he could make out were the beam from the chopper's searchlight, the foaming white wake of the patrol boats, and a big pool of light up ahead of them.

He crouched there watching the commotion as all the lights converged on one particular spot. He could not make out what it was, although it must surely be a boat, and the patrol was on top of it within minutes. Then, as suddenly as the river had been brightly illuminated, it was plunged once more into darkness. This time, all the engines roared away at full throttle and the noise slowly diminished. The tiny navigation lights of all three craft could be seen heading off towards the town – the chopper gone within a few seconds, the noise of the boats fading more slowly. But what had happened to the boat they had stopped? Was it with them? Sunk? Carrying on unmolested? Surely they had either found what they were looking for or had just decided to call it a night. He fought against an awful chill in his gut as he peered downstream into the blackness. He strained to hear the sound of another engine; hoping to catch a glimpse of a canoe. Nothing. His mind was still in turmoil as he turned to make his way back to cover. He needed to think.

Torres was already deep in thought when he was interrupted by a young sergeant with a note for him. He read it and walked quickly to the comms room, where he almost snatched the microphone out of the duty officer's hands.

"Torres here. Go ahead Major. Over."

"The patrol at Requena just reported picking them up," the Major said, his slightly unsteady voice betraying his excitement. "They're bringing them in now. Over."

Torres' hard, unwavering voice responded. "Okay. Make sure they keep them away from everyone. There's a base outside of town, right? Over."

There was a pause. A long crackle of static.

"Affirmative. About ten miles southeast. Over."

"Transfer them straight to the base. I'll be there as soon as I can. Where are you – still at Contamana? Over."

"Yes sir. But I've already recalled the patrol here, and there's no more for me to do. I can be in Requena within two hours. Over."

"Copy that. Out." Torres gave the handset back. "Lieutenant, I need some transport. Now."

"Yes sir."

34

Minutes after the car had filtered onto the main road to Manaus, the traffic slowed to a crawl. Carla looked out absently at the mixture of shiny new buildings and tumbledown shacks with hand-written boards proclaiming their prowess in tyre repairs, if not in grammar. It had not rained in the city since she had left over a week ago, and the morning air was already hazy with heat, dust and fumes.

She reflected on her tour of the northern towns of Porto Velho, Rio Branco, Belem and Boa Vista. It had certainly netted her plenty of new recruits, but the problem would be keeping them all on board. The spontaneous reaction of a mistreated working class had breathed life into the Movement, but the poor soon drifted back towards the nearest politician waving a wad of banknotes.

She massaged her temples and sighed, catching a glimpse of the taxi driver looking at her in his rear-view mirror. She shuffled out of his line of sight. Just like her driver, the average Brazilian voter was generally swayed too easily by his baser instincts. It was understandable: for years Brazil was tyrannised as a colony, and more recently ruled by a military dictatorship. People were used to having little say in their daily lives except when it came to cheap alcohol, dancing and sex. The current crop of arrogant, ignorant, self-seeking politicians was just taking advantage of the complaisance of a people who had little understanding of, or interest in, the democracy in which they nominally participated – a people who had been trained to accept what they were fed without complaint.

The car inched forward, past the city's new football stadium, a stunning modern structure in the middle of an uninspired clutter of unplanned expansion. Probably half the money spent on the project had been stolen by successive tiers of politicians, and a good percentage of the rest passed to corrupt contractors.

"*Desviado*," she reminded herself, with a faint smile. Brazilians do not steal money, it is simply 'diverted'.

Her feelings of frustration and anger grew, as always, when she started to think about how dramatically unjust the country was, and how the members of a tiny elite were driving it straight into a brick wall while they spirited their stolen money out of the country and into Swiss bank accounts and American real estate. She made herself take a deep breath and let it go slowly, forcing herself to think more positively. The GCC had a real chance to change things. Her recruits were no longer confined to the poor and uneducated: now she had lawyers, doctors, university professors and civil servants. It was gaining recognition and credibility, and becoming a viable agent of change.

The car moved slowly through the traffic lights, past the bus terminal bizarrely built in the middle of the dual carriageway, and came to a halt again. She was now looking at a huge shop stuffed with Brazilian-made tat at elevated prices. Everything Brazil produced was tat, she reflected. No one outside Brazil would accept it, so it was foisted on an ignorant and desperate public while the Brazilian rich just illegally imported whatever they wanted. This would change too, she hoped. She dreamed of an open economy, with strong Brazilian businesses competing globally. With the corrupt and incompetent scum out of the way, they would rebuild Brazil and help the people realise their true potential.

She closed her eyes for a few seconds and concentrated on her breathing – now nice and steady. She felt herself relax.

Etapa por etapa. Step by step, she reminded herself. First, she had this mysterious secret meeting to go to. What would that bring? An alliance with a bunch of would-be military dictators might be expeditious, but she did not believe there was the stomach in the GCC for the ousting of one corrupt, elitist regime and the installation of another. Still, whether potential enemies or friends, she needed to see these people: talk to them; get a feel for them.

They had contacted her to confirm that someone would meet her at the Taj Mahal hotel, an obscure enough place, apart from having a revolving restaurant on the top floor. Unfortunately, it sat on the tree-lined, traffic-choked main road into the city centre, and her taxi was taking forever to reach it. The narrow, badly planned, poorly maintained roads were in contrast to those of her last stop, Boa Vista, where the main road all the way from the airport to the city centre was a vast, open, six-lane highway with few cars on it. It was still poorly maintained, but somehow when you had room to manoeuvre around the potholes, it seemed a great advance. The capital of the Brazilian state of Roraima, Boa Vista was largely forgotten or ignored by the hundred million or more people in the south. It might be on Brazil's international border with Venezuela and Guyana, but most Brazilians despised Venezuela and could not tell Guyana from a pumpkin. Nonetheless, Carla's stop there had been particularly rewarding – not only had she found lots of new members, she had also met an old friend and fellow member of the movement, who had been able to help her enormously on the last leg of the trip.

The taxi jerked to a stop and the driver wound his window down to shout abuse at a pedestrian he had nearly run over. Carla looked round to get her bearings again, and figured that if traffic permitted, she should be at the hotel in ten minutes. Her first priority would be to have a hot shower and some decent food.

In the end, the traffic did not permit, and she was twenty minutes late by the time she checked in. Hurrying to her room, she was barely in the door when she received the message she was expecting. She only had time for a quick shower before having to rush out and walk quickly round to the Rei dos Sucos juice bar to meet another contact. She was tired, hungry, and in spite of the hurried shower, hot and uncomfortable.

She sat down on one of the hard wooden stools bolted to the floor, and ordered a juice and some unhealthy but filling food. A few moments after it arrived, a young man sat next to her.

He picked up a menu and scanned it briefly, then placed it on the counter, sighed, and looked around nonchalantly.

Far too nonchalantly, Carla thought.

"*Boa tarde Senhorita. Gosta de goiaba?*"

She recognised the phrase with a mixture of excitement and irritation, feeling that they should have had something a bit more exciting than 'do you like guava'? She gave the required reply.

"*Sim. É bom pro estómago.*"

From a quick glance, she judged the man was in his early thirties, and she thought he looked – even smelled – military. His obviously well toned body, shiny black hair and bright brown eyes, made her think of an eager labrador.

The man looked away again after they had exchanged a brief nod and perfunctory smile, and devoted himself to catching the attention of the waiter and ordering a juice. Guava, Carla noted with amusement. She sat patiently, alternately reading and responding to imaginary texts on her phone, and eating her stodgy snack with very real appreciation.

"You are being followed," the man said, as he accepted his juice.

For a split second, Carla thought he was talking to the waiter.

"Hmm," she said, resisting the temptation to look around.

"Here," he said, tapping idly on a little sheet of paper he had contrived to place on the counter next to him. It was one of the shop's own order sheets, apparently identical to the one she had received just a few minutes ago, marked up with her order.

"Uh-huh. OK," she said, without moving her head.

She picked up her own order sheet and dropped it on top of the new one.

Apparently satisfied, the man drained his juice and got up. He picked his own order sheet up from the counter and went off to pay the bill.

Carla waited ten minutes. She finished her food unhurriedly, sliding the fake order from her right side to her left, picking up the real order and making a pretence of reading it, and ordering another juice. This was duly marked on the real sheet by the waiter, and no one noticed her fold the fake sheet a couple of times and palm it into her bag as she rummaged through it and pulled out the money to pay the bill.

She got up and walked to the little payment kiosk, looking as unconcerned as possible, but feeling tiny beads of sweat forming on her forehead and pricking her skin. Once she had paid, she made her way outside, and after a moment's hesitation, hailed a taxi. The hot afternoon sun, and her curiosity to see what was on the note, easily overcame her earlier resolve to walk back to the hotel. As soon as she was seated, she quickly withdrew the fake order to see what was printed on the back.

She read the bizarre series of instructions, and wondered for a moment whether she was being made fun of. She remembered the man's warning, and admitted to herself that the feeling of being watched had been strong throughout her tour of the north. She had to accept that the stakes were high and getting higher, for everyone involved in the current struggle for power in Brazil – and that included her. She blinked away the doubts and resolved to follow the instructions to the letter, starting with receiving a mobile phone from a tour guide at the Amazon Theatre the next morning at nine o'clock. Memorising the rest of the instructions, she balled the piece of paper, hesitated only for a second, turned her face away from the rear-view mirror and popped the ball into her mouth.

35

A rare column of sunlight chased the pigeons across London's Portman Square. From his third floor window, Simon Walker watched the leaden clouds roll quickly back in, and sighed. He sat down wearily at his workstation, dropping the papers in his left hand on top of a large untidy pile next to his computer. He laid the two sheets in his right hand directly in front of him and studied them for a few moments. Finally he shrugged, pushed one of the sheets to the side, and reached for his keyboard. Before he could start typing, he was interrupted.

"Hi Simon," said a cheery voice. "Got anything for me?"

It was the placement student who had been coming round dutifully every morning for the last two months looking for something interesting to do.

"Nope," said Simon, with an equally cheery dismissal.

It was a routine response to a routine question – except that today, for some reason, Simon happened to look up, after he had responded. He saw the girl looking wistfully at the discards next to the computer, and he felt guilty. Maybe it was the hangover he was nursing.

"Okay, wait a second," he said, lifting his chin off his hand. "Here – maybe you could take a look at this." He picked up the discarded sheet and handed it to her.

The girl was clearly taken aback.

"Oh," she said. "What is it?"

"It's a story." He hesitated. "It *might* be a story. Well, actually, it probably won't – ever – be a story. But it depends on a lot of things, including what *you* can make of it."

"Oh."

"Yes. Ever heard of Ed Stafford?"

"Yes. The guy who walked the Amazon, isn't he?"

Simon was impressed: few people remembered the names or exploits of any explorers beyond a few notables like Livingstone and Scott of the Antarctic. Fewer still knew much about contemporary ones like Stafford.

"Hmm. Well, now there's another guy – this guy." He pointed to the paper the student was clutching. "Who apparently has decided he's going to do the same thing, except quicker."

"Oh, wow," enthused the girl. "Sounds interesting."

Simon grunted. "Huh. Maybe."

He saw the questioning look and shook his head. "Look, there are lots of nutters out there who have these dumb ideas. Only one in a million of them can find their way to the GPS shop on a cloudy day, never mind achieving what they claim they will."

"I suppose so, yes."

"So there's not much point in writing about most of them, is there?"

"Right."

"Right. If I wrote about half the crap that comes across my desk, I'd be out of a job. You have to sort the wheat from the chaff – learn how to pick the winners."

"So you don't think this guy's a winner, then?"

"I don't know. Probably not, no."

"Why?"

Simon thought for a moment.

"No support."

"Sorry?"

"Expeditions cost a lot of money, and a lot of good projects and people fail because they can't raise the funds." He shrugged. "This guy is clearly doing his own PR." He pointed at the sheet. "So he probably has no organisation, no support, and no backers – he's a loner. Another heroic failure."

"A loser."

"No. Absolutely not. He's probably a great guy who just can't get support. Maybe he has no family, or he moves in the wrong circles, speaks with the wrong accent or has a glass eye or something." He paused to run a hand through his hair. "I admire him. It takes a lot of balls to do something when you've no back-up. But without it, your chances of success aren't much better than zero."

"So it's a waste of time, then, is what you're saying, right?" The girl looked uncertain.

"Probably, yes."

"Probably..."

"Well, it depends."

"On what?"

"On him, mostly."

"So..."

"So, it's probably a load of crap...but you never know your luck," Simon finished brightly.

The girl's shoulders sagged visibly as she contemplated the paper again.

"Listen," he said patiently, "there are a few things in his favour."

The student looked at him quizzically.

"Like what?"

"Well, like his military background, for example. Like the fact that he's already in Peru - he's actually on the move, and not sitting on his backside in a Borchester bedsit, amazing us with his dreams of future daring-do."

"Borchester...?"

"Alliteration; poetic licence. I'm a bleeding poet, okay?"

She hung her head a little, smiling. "Ah. Sorry. Well..."

"Hmm?"

"Well, now you're making it sound more promising. So why are giving it to me?"

"Ah. You mean why am I not writing it up and keeping all the glory for myself?" Simon laughed.

"Yes."

"Because I have another story here; another expedition, in fact." He tapped the piece of paper in front of his keyboard. "All the pieces are already there for me: they have sponsors, they have a PR team, they're half-way to the finish, they've supplied good attention-grabbing details, they're offering photos, nobody's run the story yet... Basically, it's a no-brainer."

The student nodded.

"Besides," Simon added. "I've another half dozen stories to wade through in the other pile over there." He indicated with a thumb.

The student was nodding thoughtfully as she re-read the press release on her own piece of paper. She turned the page over, turned it back again, and then gazed at it in quiet contemplation.

Simon waited patiently.

"So," he said at last.

The student looked up questioningly.

"So bugger off! Go do some digging on Mr Whatshisname–"

"McCrae."

"Whatever. See what you can come up with: family, friends, career, background – that type of stuff. See if he has some sort of website or blog; try to contact him. There's plenty of time – I doubt if anyone else will bother picking the story up at this stage – and let's face it, it took Stafford two years to cover the course when he did it."

Simon felt a rare flush of pleasure to see the girl's shoulders straighten and her face brighten as he talked. She was beginning to look quite enthusiastic about her day.

"Okay, I certainly will. Thanks, Simon," she said, almost springing to her feet.

You sentimental old fool, he admonished himself silently, and aloud "Well, don't get too excited about it – like I said, it may never be a story. But if you can come up with something vaguely interesting, we'll see what we can make of it."

She was already half way out of Simon's cubicle. "Yep. Don't worry – leave it to me!"

"Look for an angle," he called after her.

"No problem!"

He turned to his computer again and pushed his own story around on the desk. He could still hear the student's retreating footsteps pounding enthusiastically through the office.

"You're welcome," he growled quietly, and smiled.

36

T

orres' expression was as grim as the weather closing in around them. Because of violent thunderstorms heading in, all helicopters were grounded for the next few hours. His considerable clout apparently did not extend to risking Peruvian military aviation assets in bad weather. No matter. He was now on the fastest army boat they had out of Iquitos, currently covering ground at a rate of nearly seventy kilometres an hour according to the GPS reading Torres could see glowing in the darkness of the cockpit. Their bow wave was fearsome at this speed, and as they emerged from one of the pilot's shortcut channels, they nearly upset a boat caught unawares. Outside, the dawn light was just enough to navigate the broad river safely, and the pilot was holding nothing back.

The end of this ridiculous chase was almost at hand. With the gringo and the terrorist bitch out of the way, he would be able to breathe easily again. The Peruvian operation would snap back into its nice uneventful routine and allow him to get on with his own private business. He still had to finalise details of the upcoming drugs bust, an operation that would cost him his income on a couple of the month's trade, but which was nothing compared to what he would rake in once the dust had settled. And then he would be away. Someone else could do his day job, while he fulfilled his long-held dream. He closed his eyes and allowed himself to conjure up images of the new family home he would build in Nicaragua. It was the perfect revenge on the damned Americans. He even speculated idly on the chances of successfully blackmailing them later, with what he knew about their outrageous clandestine operations in South America, but he quickly dismissed the idea. They were not all fools, and if he showed up anywhere on the radar as a threat, he had no doubt at all about their ability to hunt him down. No. There would just be an early retirement and a nice, boring, ordered withdrawal from the Firm until he could disappear.

He leaned out of the cockpit, his face directly into the wind, bracing himself as they slid rapidly round the bends in the river. The early morning mist was ice-cold on his face, and made him feel alive and eager for the new day. Eager to be in at the kill. And that, he reflected, would be exactly what it was. There was too much at stake and there were too many complications for there to be any other outcome.

They had been on the river for almost three hours now, and he was anticipating the appearance of Requena around every bend. The early morning sunlight was throwing the towering thunderclouds in the west into sharp relief. They had so far escaped the tempest, and he had been assured that even if they were caught in the middle of it, they would not be slowed down for more than fifteen minutes or so.

He glanced at the GPS display again and watched the map spin around the pointer as they took the last big bend before the town. As they powered down the next long, straight section of river, signs of civilisation started appearing along the banks. The trees disappeared, cleared for pasture and planting, and ramshackle wooden houses on stilts stood well above the current level of the river. Emaciated cattle could be seen grazing in some of the fields. Small aluminium speedboats were shuttling back and forth up ahead, coming into and out of the tributary he knew must be the Rio Tapiche. Requena extended a couple of miles upstream from the mouth of this little river, and beyond it lay the airstrip where the prisoners were being held.

He stared at the simple wooden houses, trying to imagine what it would be like to live in one: a single room with a hammock or two. Electricity if you were lucky. Some of them might even have a toilet. He shook his head: most would not. How could people be content to live like animals? Surrounded by their own filth. Nothing to do except work, sleep and procreate until they died ignominiously, mourned only by their family and a few friends. It was barbaric. He watched as they passed a tiny canoe with three kids in it, not much older than six or seven. The little craft rode up and down on the huge wake from the army launch, and the kids looked neither interested nor afraid. Born to a life of drudgery, they were uneducated and ignorant – fit only for bearing more uneducated, ignorant children. He despised them all. Once he had his money, he hoped he would never see another god-forsaken hole like this again.

The launch decelerated and came down off the plane, burbling frustratingly slowly past the town, then picking up speed a little as they made their way to the army's own pontoon further upstream. They tied up alongside and Torres stepped out of the boat, striding up the long flight of wooden steps from the river to the small army base. A helicopter sat there, its blades firmly tied down and the aircraft itself anchored to the ground.

"Good morning sir," said a young Captain, saluting sharply and looking irritatingly radiant and healthy.

"Good morning," snapped Torres. "Where's the Major?"

"His chopper had to turn back to Contamana. Everything's grounded."

"Hmm. The launches?"

"Stood down – they're on their way back to Contamana too. We can't raise them or anyone else over there at the moment because of the weather."

"Damned country," muttered Torres.

"We've a truck waiting for you sir. Just over there," he pointed to a battered old dun-coloured Toyota pick-up, just the other side of the helicopter.

"Okay. Let's go, then. How long to get there?"

"Only thirty minutes, sir. It's not far at all really."

"Good. You can fill me in as we go. Have they said anything? Have they been told anything? Have they seen anyone?"

Torres opened the front passenger door to find a young grunt slouched in the seat. One look at Torres' face startled him into action, and he jumped out and ran round to the back to stand at attention. He saluted as Torres got in the front and the Captain in the back. Then he got in the other side and the driver roared off across the small field and onto a dirt track that seemed mercifully well repaired.

"So, Captain, what can you tell me?"

"No more than you already know, I believe. The three prisoners were brought in–"

"Sorry?" Torres broke in. "How many?"

"Three, sir."

"I'm looking for two."

"I'm sorry sir, I wasn't aware of that."

Torres' face set, but the muscles in his jaw twitched as he shifted slightly in his seat.

The Captain cleared his throat "Perhaps they picked up an accomplice, sir."

Torres straightened and stared out ahead. "Yes, Captain. Perhaps."

They continued in silence as the vehicle bounced uncomfortably along the dried-up track. Then the sky overhead suddenly darkened and within a few minutes a strong wind was bending the tops of the surrounding trees violently. There was a flash of lightning somewhere behind them and an almighty clap of thunder that vibrated through the truck. Heavy raindrops plopped lazily on the thin tin roof for a few seconds, and then the heavens opened. The driver slowed and stopped, unable to see anything in front. For a few moments it was as dark as night, and the rain came down like water from a gully. The wind rocked the vehicle from side to side, but passed in just a few seconds. Then a battleship grey sky engulfed them and the rain came on in impenetrable waves. The sound in the cabin was deafening, and water started to spit in from the air vents and the door seals.

It was twenty minutes before visibility improved, and then the windscreen wipers revealed a track littered with leaves and branches and running with water like a small stream. The driver urged the truck forward slowly, until they came to a fallen tree barring the way. Without a word, the three soldiers got out and started clearing the obstruction.

In the end, it was two hours hard work before the truck finally arrived at the airstrip. Torres' face was as emotionless as always, but he seemed to move like a prowling panther as he made his way from the truck to the Commandant's office. He was a well-built man, and the tension in his body made him appear even bigger. Few had ever mistaken the look in his eyes for anything more benign than pure malice.

As he approached the closed door, it suddenly sprang open, and another fresh-faced private saluted sharply as Torres entered. The Commandant rose to greet the new arrival, saluted him, opened his mouth to say something, and then hesitated. Instead, he manoeuvred his way past the CIA man, towards the door, and gestured somewhat awkwardly.

"Follow me, sir?" he finally managed.

Torres nodded.

The walk from the office to the brick-built barracks room left everyone with mud up to their knees. They finally stepped up onto the concrete veranda that surrounded the building, and approached the two guards outside the door, who stood to attention. The Commandant nodded slightly, and one of the guards rapped on the door.

After a short exchange of words, bolts were heard being pulled, and the door opened. A young soldier held the door for the Commandant and Torres. The other soldiers remained outside.

"Sergeant, our visitor needs to identify the prisoners," barked the Commandant.

The sergeant nodded and led the way to a wooden door with an iron grill in front of it. He opened a small hatch at chest level, and Torres bent to peer in. A second later, he stood up.

"Let them go, Commandant."

"*What?* I mean, er, I beg your pardon, sir?"

"Let them go. They're not the right people."

"Are you sure, sir–?"

Torres wanted so much to vent his anger and frustration on these deeply stupid people. They had been told to look for a Caucasian male and a female terrorist whose photo had been circulated. They had picked up an ugly-looking Peruvian male, a woman of maybe twenty – by the looks of her, pregnant – and a kid of around seventeen who looked scared enough to shit himself. How could they possibly be so completely, hopelessly incompetent? And how much time had this cost him in his search? It had at the very least given the chase about eight clear hours of freedom to continue their flight unmolested. He wanted to shout and scream and rage, but instead he simply shut the Commandant up by lifting his hand. "I'm quite sure, yes."

He turned and walked out of the room, scattering the soldiers as he opened the door.

"But sir," cried the Commandant, hurrying to catch up.

Torres only stopped when he reached the Commandant's office. He stood outside, waiting for the man to arrive.

"Commandant," he said, slowly and deliberately, "You have the wrong people. Let them go – just let them go, mind you – and get me a helicopter back to Iquitos."

"But everything's grounded–"

Torres held up his hand again, smiled thinly, and opened the door. "Shall we?" he asked quietly, ushering the man in.

When the two of them emerged a few minutes later, the Commandant's face was drained.

"Captain!" He shouted the short distance across to another wooden building, where an officer was already standing to attention. "Get on to HQ and get clearance for the chopper. I don't care how you do it, just do it. Put Pilot Officers Chavel and Geves on alert."

Torres strode off towards the truck, got in, and sat down heavily in the passenger seat. He locked the doors and stared unblinkingly through the windscreen, ignoring the sudden buzz of activity round the base.

Where were the bastards now, for Christ sake? If they got to Iquitos – if the merest hint of this got out – a lifetime of planning would be ruined, and his own life would not be worth crap. He frowned in concentration. First, he needed to arrange things so that wherever they were, there was absolutely no possibility of them communicating anything to anyone. Next, he had to make sure that the only way they could get to Iquitos was in one of those cardboard boxes that passed for coffins in this ridiculous country.

37

J ack shook his head, sat back and looked around. They were sitting on a fallen tree trunk by the side of a tiny stream five hours beyond Requena. After Elena had returned with a canoe full of provisions, tense and talking rapidly in Spanish, Jack had been infected by her fear and her urgency to get away. He had also been absurdly relieved to see her arrive back safely. Now, in the cold light of day, his thirst quenched and stomach full, he was coming down from a nervous high. Since they had started running full pelt at earliest light, the only moment of excitement had been when a huge army launch with a bow wave as big as a liner had shot out from the other side of an island and nearly run them over. It disappeared downstream as fast as anything Jack had ever seen on a river, and left the two of them catching their breath amongst the weeds. But that had been a few hours ago now, and his body and mind had been progressively standing down ever since.

"I agree it looks bad," he said, when Elena had told him everything she had seen in Requena. "But it should still be a priority to get a working phone so I can try to contact my guy in Cuzco again, or even get through to an English number—"

"You'll never get an overseas number," said Elena flatly, shaking her head.

"Okay, Cuzco then."

"*Correcto*," said Elena. "I agree." She thought for a moment. "But where are we now? I mean, how far is Iquitos?"

"We should be coming up on the Marañon River soon. Once we hit that, we can turn upstream a little way and stop at Nauta."

"I've heard of it."

"It's imprinted on my memory mostly because there's a road from there to Iquitos: sixty miles, almost direct." He smiled. "It was one of the first things I marked down to be a cinch, after all the crap I'd have to go through to get that far on foot."

"What is 'cinch'?" asked Elena.

"An easy option."

"Ah," she said. "I hope so." She smiled. "I think you were right about all the crap."

They both laughed, and sat in companionable silence for a few moments, peering out from the dappled shade of their hideaway.

"So why not go straight to Iquitos?" Elena asked. "You have obviously thought about it, no?"

Jack nodded. "The people who are after us obviously already know we're on the Ucayali, although they still don't know where. They're probably still betting on us not yet having reached Requena, which is to our advantage now." He paused, lost in thought for a moment.

"And?" prompted Elena.

"Well, I think they'll assume that even if we don't show up at Requena, we'll continue by boat all the way to Iquitos. I reckon the last thing they'll think is that we would double back, going upstream on the Marañon just to find the only highway in the whole of the Peruvian Amazon. If I'm right, and we can get to Nauta safely, I think we can probably enter Iquitos undetected by the back door, while all their attention is on the river."

Elena tilted her head slightly, and gave him an appraising look.

"That's good, you know. I like it."

"You sound surprised."

"Perhaps." She smiled. "No – just joking."

Jack smiled back at her for a second, and then got to his feet. "We should get going again. If I'm right, we're only a couple of hours from Nauta." He started packing up their meagre bits and pieces. "Of course, we still have another two hundred miles to cover, from Iquitos to the border."

"Perhaps I can help with that bit," said Elena.

"Oh yes?"

She nodded. "While you have been planning your things, I have been planning mine. You get us to Iquitos, and I will get us to Brazil. Okay?"

"And how are you going to do that, exactly?"

"I have friends."

"Dare I ask...?"

Elena shook her head. "You do not want to know."

Jack held up his hands. "Okay, it's a deal," he said.

"Good," said Elena, getting to her feet and offering Jack her hand. He took it. It was small and soft and feminine; not what he had expected at all, and he looked down at it questioningly. They moved a little closer to each other. He was so close now, he could feel the heat from her body. She looked up at him and he found himself lost in her brown eyes. He dropped her hand, moved his own to hold her round the waist. He drew her to him and she responded, arching her back slightly, putting her hands up to his face, stroking it, caressing it...

They both heard the sound at the same time, and froze for a moment in their embrace. An outboard, approaching quickly. They broke apart and rushed to pull the canoe as far as possible into the tree line, quickly throwing into it anything that had not yet been stowed. Then they moved cautiously down to the river, crouching and looking out in the direction of the noise.

As the seconds ticked by, it became clear that this was not a big motor at all, although it seemed to be approaching quickly enough. The reason became clear when the boat appeared around the corner. It was a small aluminium speedboat of maybe ten or twelve feet, with one man in it and a neat four-stroke outboard pushing it rapidly through the water. It was planing so high at the front Jack wondered it did not take off. It sped past, leaving a wake big enough to dislodge their own canoe.

"Wish we had one of those," said Elena.

"Yeah. And that's nothing to the speed of those army launches – never mind the damned helicopters. Time we weren't here."

Jack started manhandling the canoe back into the river, and Elena quickly joined him. As they pushed the boat out, their hands touched and they paused for a second. A momentary awkwardness mocked their renewed sense of urgency, and then passed. They leapt in to the canoe, Jack started up the motor, and they were underway again.

Jack automatically began to cover himself up to hide from the burning sun, until he realised there *was* no burning sun any more. He looked back and saw a spreading darkness. In the time they had spent resting and eating, what had been just a distant storm had finally rolled in. It spread across the rainforest, obscuring the distant hills, spilling rain as it approached. As he watched, forked lightning slashed across the sky and arced down to the forest. He heard the distant thunder, and felt it in his stomach.

They sped on in the unfamiliar coolness, stopping only once when they ran out of fuel and had to switch tanks. The new tank was not full, but Jack reckoned it was certainly enough to get them to Nauta.

A while later, he was just beginning to doubt his calculations when they suddenly emerged onto what had to be the Marañon. It was huge: a monster. Jack estimated it to be at least twice the width of the Ucayali, and right now, as sunlight burst through momentarily and lit up the forest beside them, he was stunned by the panoramic vista. The bright, sharp greens of the leaves and the bone white of the tree trunks and branches in the sunlight, stood out spectacularly against a backdrop of unbroken blue-black sky, with wisps and curls of mist and drifts of falling rain angling across it.

A cold blast of air hit them head-on, and Jack immediately turned the canoe and aimed for the closest trees. He watched as ripples blew across the surface of the smooth, brown river. The ripples turned to waves, and suddenly they were plunging through an angry, chopped-up surface. A few huge, heavy raindrops started to fall, the sunlight disappeared, and as they reached the margins Jack saw the trees bend towards them, shedding clouds of leaves and debris. Then they were well into the lee, running the canoe up the banks, looking out at a landscape changed dramatically. The rain came hissing through the forest and crashed onto the river. For a few seconds the mixture of cold wind, waves and rain reminded him of the Atlantic, and then things quietened down again. The wind dropped altogether, and there was just the darkness and the rain. It fell in unbroken sheets, cascading from the trees and filling their canoe.

They sheltered as much of their stuff as possible, but there was not a lot they could do in the face of this deluge. Jack initially tried sheltering under his cover, but the rain easily found its way through from above, below and from the sides, and after a minute or two he did what Elena was doing, and just stood looking out at it all.

The worst of the rain passed within ten minutes. They tipped and bailed the canoe, and got under way again, keeping the boat well in with the south bank, but maintaining a watchful eye on the north bank, where Jack expected Nauta to appear within a quarter of an hour or so.

Just from the quantity of river traffic, it was obvious they were approaching a large town. Two big barges were being pushed upstream, while aluminium speedboats and smaller canoes darted all over the place. Houses and farms appeared along the north bank, and soon the inevitable communications towers could be seen sticking up from the main town.

They stopped well downstream of the main port, picked a spot near a dirt road that obviously ran along the banks from the town, and pulled the canoe into the shore. They removed only what they needed from it, plus anything that might identify them, and left the rest in the canoe. Under Elena's amused gaze, Jack patted the prow of the canoe before climbing the banks to join her.

They stood just off the road, and Elena looked closely at Jack.

"You don't really look so much a gringo now, as long as your head is covered. I think that with me at the front, we should be okay."

"Really?" asked Jack doubtfully. "Even in the town centre?"

Elena shrugged. "I think so, yes, and if you're right about the road, perhaps we can avoid the centre altogether."

"The road's there for sure. It goes almost directly north out of Nauta. Sixty miles to Iquitos."

"*Excelente*. So we go straight for that. But we need supplies – we have money now, remember?" She patted her pocket. "And when we have a phone, I will call my contacts in Iquitos. People who know me. People who *owe* me, more importantly."

Jack nodded. "Sounds good. But what about the police? The army? Checkpoints and stuff? You are a wanted terrorist, you know." He smiled somewhat crookedly, and her expression changed from eager anticipation to mild irritation.

"We avoid them. We will enter the forest and walk right past them."

"Just like that."

"Certainly. If they are the regular units, they will be looking for trucks with big cargoes of drugs, not a few people walking in the forest.

He nodded. "Okay, well let's get on with it then."

"*Si si. Vamanos.*"

38

Their approach to the noisy town, still half drowned by the storm, went unremarked. As soon as they reached the market area, Elena bought a battered-looking mobile phone and a prepaid SIM. A few minutes' walk north of the market, they found a dark and obscure café where they could have something to eat and drink and Elena could use her charms to get information, and while she was talking to the café owner, Jack inserted the SIM and found a point to charge the phone.

They had agreed not to speak any English, and decided that Jack would keep his hat on all the time. He was seated now in the shade, with his back to the owner and the one other customer in the place. His understanding of Spanish was improving, but he could not catch all of what was being said, so when Elena came back and gave him a discrete thumbs-up, he was relieved. They waited five minutes or so before paying up and leaving.

Once they were walking and there was no-one within earshot, Elena gave him the news that the only functioning checkpoints on the road were the ones outside each town, that the road was in good condition, and that if they wanted to hitch a ride they should look for the side road called Ramal del Pedro.

"First, let me try to raise Cuzco," said Jack.

They stopped by the side of the road under the shade of a huge almond tree, and Jack dialled the Cuzco number. It rang a couple of times and was picked up. There was a pause, a slight buzz, and another pause, long enough to prompt Jack to say "Hello?"

"Hi there. Can I help you?" asked an overly-friendly, female American voice. Jack asked for his friend and the voice came quickly back at him.

"Oh, I'm afraid he's not available right now. Can I take a message?"

"Of course. Who am I speaking to?"

"This is, uh, Jill. I'm a friend."

"Okay Jill, well let me tell you..."

He trailed off, having already deliberately cut the connection while he was speaking. The hackles were up on the back of his neck. The words were too smooth, the delay was too long and the hesitation over her name was too unbelievable. A compromised plan and a missing plan organiser – no coincidence. He ripped the back off the phone and removed the chip.

"You know we don't have another one of those," said Elena, nodding at the chip.

"I know, but I think we're going to have to get one."

Elena looked at him.

"That was – supposedly – some friend called Jill," explained Jack.

"Ah. And your friend is somehow *indispuesto*?"

"Yes. Unavailable."

"Allow me," said Elena, holding out her hand. Jack gave her the chip and she doubled it over, flexed it a few times and tore it in half. Then she held out her hand again.

"The phone too?"

"I – we – have been working with these things for a long time. Here they have tracking by telephone – the actual *teléfono* – I mean, the actual *receptor* itself." She tapped the phone. "As well as through the card." She placed the phone on the ground and stomped on it several times, then picked up the bits of circuit board and threw them into the few feet of smelly water in a nearby gully.

Jack swore. "So if we assume this was set up – that they were waiting for me to call – they could already have a fix on our position?"

Elena nodded. "Perhaps. But you were quick to cut the line. It depends on the network and how many towers there are. And they need the details from the operator. It could still take some time, and it is not precise."

"But they'll identify Nauta."

"Maybe, maybe not."

Jack cursed again. "Sorry Elena. That was careless."

"Don't worry, Jack," said Elena, shrugging. "At least it explains what happened at Requena. They have your friend, and they know about the plan with the flags. Which means–"

"Which means the message hasn't got through. We're still on our own," Jack finished. He paused and looked down at the ground. A chill ran down his spine. "It also means Greg could well be dead."

Elena reached out and touched his shoulder, but Jack retreated slightly.

"I'm sorry, Jack," she said.

They stood in silence for a few moments, until Jack took a deep breath and exhaled loudly.

"Okay," he said finally. "*Vamos?*"

It took them another twenty minutes to get a second phone and card, and half an hour to work their way past the police checkpoint a mile or so from the port. Elena got through to her contact in Iquitos first time, and although the conversation was cryptic enough, she explained to Jack that help had been promised.

"We can trust them," she said. "From Iquitos, they will get us as close to the Brazilian border as they can." She paused. "But we have to get to Iquitos first."

The informal hitch-hiking-cum-bus-stop point was less than a mile past the checkpoint, and there was no apparent attempt to monitor it. They watched from a safe distance for some time, and saw a few people flag down pick-up trucks. Satisfied that there was no danger, they did the same themselves, and ended up squeezed into an old Chevrolet with a loosely sprung bench seat and little else. Elena explained to the driver that she was a guide and was taking Jack back to Iquitos. Assuming that Jack did not speak Spanish, the driver smiled at Elena.

"Yes. The buses and taxis are too expensive. No profit in it, right?"

Elena smiled conspiratorially. "*Exacto.*"

"You're lucky - I only charge a hundred. Some charge twice that."

"What?" Elena cried. "A hundred? My friend, we don't even want to go all the way to Iquitos."

The driver shrugged. "Sorry, but I have to charge the whole distance." He paused. "Where do you want dropped off, then?"

"Quistococha."

"Ah," said the driver, "Alright then."

"In case we fall asleep, can you wake us up ten minutes before we get there please?"

"Sure. It'll only take us an hour or so."

After a few comments to Elena, and five minutes trying his terrible English on Jack, the driver gave up and the three lapsed into a reasonably amicable silence for the rest of the journey. They left the truck at just after four thirty in the afternoon, and as they walked past a big blue sign announcing that they were entering the Quistococha Tourist Complex, Elena made another call on her phone.

"*Llegamos*," she said simply, when the call was answered. She listened for a few seconds. "*Convenido*." She rang off and then explained to Jack that they would be picked up here in ten minutes, and driven to a plane that would take them to a place called Caballococha, fifty miles from Santa Rosa and the tri-border with Brazil and Colombia.

"A plane? Just like that? Jesus, that's some contact, Elena."

Elena said nothing, but looked slightly uncomfortable, and Jack decided to let it drop.

"We'll get a local ferry to very near Santa Rosa, then we'll switch to a small boat again and if all goes well, we'll be in Brazil half an hour later."

"Brilliant," said Jack.

"You'll have to look after me, you know, when we get to Brazil – well, at least when we get to your people there."

"My people? Oh yes – you mean the embassy; the consulate, at least." He reached out, took her hand in his and squeezed it. "Yes Elena," he said, suddenly solemn. "I promise I'll look after you."

Elena squeezed his hand back and smiled.

He opened his mouth to say something else, but Elena's expression suddenly changed.

"That's our lift," she said, pointing across the road to a red VW pickup truck. "Come on."

It was dark when they boarded the tiny aircraft straight from a car that parked only a few yards away. Just like the car, there were only four seats. Unlike the car, there was absolutely no separation of the two seats at the back, where Jack and Elena sat in comfortable close proximity, with the pilot and co-pilot up front. After they had taxied out to the runway, the pilot turned to them and gave them some details of the flight, just like any good professional airline pilot.

"Good evening folks," he said in clearly enunciated Spanish. "While we're waiting for final clearance, I've just time to tell you that after take-off we will be climbing to our cruising altitude of three thousand feet. The weather is excellent, and our cruising speed will be just less than a hundred knots, so our ETA at Caballococha is one hour fifty-three minutes.

He looked more closely at Jack, did a quick double take, and then repeated everything in near-perfect English.

Jack wondered with some amusement whether he was a pilot with one of the Peruvian international airlines.

Moonlighting for the local contrabandistas, he thought. *Well, why not?*

"Seat belts fastened?" the pilot asked. "Prepare for take-off."

The aircraft thundered and bounced down the runway for what seemed to Jack forever, before finally juddering uncertainly into the air and climbing away at an uncomfortable angle. They banked to the left, straightened, and finally levelled out of their climb. The engine note decreased slightly and the little craft seemed to calm down from its original frenzy of rattles and vibration, making Jack aware of how tense he had become. He breathed slowly and forced himself to relax.

Since being picked up at Quistococha, no one had asked them who they were or what they were doing, and this studied lack of interest continued on the plane. No questions, no conversation, just the drone of the engine. They both dozed fitfully throughout the flight, and were wide awake again by the time the aircraft jolted to a halt at their destination.

A car was waiting for them, and they left the airfield just as they had entered the one in Iquitos – without seeing another soul.

The car bounced down a narrow dirt track leading from the airstrip, and emerged after a minute or two in what appeared to be a residential area. A few turns later, they arrived at a grubby pier. It was small, disorganised and poorly lit, and the most impressive part of it was the long wooden platform that served as the dockside. A large passenger ferry displaying the name Herreras IV along its white prow was tied up alongside. Their driver pushed a hammock each into their hands, wished them luck, and sped off, leaving them to walk up the narrow wooden gangplank to the passenger deck.

No one said anything to them, and they just slung their hammocks along the deck with the rest of the passengers. Jack was amazed that there had been no problems, no hitches, no delays. In a country not well known for its efficiency, it seemed that the drug smugglers, terrorists and general underworld were way ahead of the government in terms of organisation.

Elena went off to speak to a few of the other passengers while Jack leaned over the rails and watched the activity along the riverfront. Ten minutes later she came back with two cans of beer and a grin on her face.

"We arrive in Santa Rosa tomorrow at dawn," she said. "Then we just need to beg, borrow or steal another canoe to cross into Brazil – it's only half a mile."

Jack took the can and popped it open. He stood there for a moment, almost lost for words.

"Elena, I don't know what to say. I can't really believe we've made it. And the last four hours have got us further than the past five days. Amazing what a few contacts can do." He raised his can. "Here's to contacts."

"Here's to us," said Elena.

"Yes. That too."

The beer was ice cold and tasted wonderful. He drank half of it with his eyes quite closed, and when he opened them again and put the can down on the rail, Elena was smiling again.

"Ever made love in a hammock, gringo?" she asked him.

39

Torres had spent twenty years working for a country, a people and a government he loathed and despised, merely as an expedient to exacting his own calculated revenge. He had long since mastered the art of masking any emotion he might feel, and he performed his allotted duties diligently, almost robotically, without sweating the day-to-day stuff, because none of it really mattered to him. Who cared if a criminal was or was not caught? Who cared if a few Americans did or did not die? But now, just as all his careful planning was coming to fruition, and when he could almost taste approaching victory – now his anger and frustration were threatening to break out. As he listened to each reported failure on the part of his own organisation or the police or the military in Peru to catch these damned people, he grew steadily more agitated. He was bottling it all up, and the growing tension never left him, even in his bed as he tried to sleep.

He was still wide awake at 2:00 a.m. when his phone rang and a voice alerted him to new information being received. He levered himself out of bed and stretched for a few seconds to try to unknot his muscles, then he sprang for his shower. Afterwards he dressed rapidly, grabbed a piece of dry bread and a carton of juice, and was off to the comms room in the small army base in Iquitos that was hosting him at the moment. As he entered, a communications officer saluted, and the radio operator held out a headset. Torres took it and put it on, grateful that this must be a normal 'duplex' line for once – almost like a phone.

"Torres. Go ahead," he said, talking sharply into the microphone.

"We have information on the targets. A local agent loyal to the–"

"Oh just get on with it, for god's sake," snapped Torres.

There was a moment of confusion.

"Sir?" came the voice again.

"Yes, yes. Okay. Proceed," said Torres, more calmly.

"Sir. We have information that they have boarded a boat – MV Herreras IV – arriving in Santa Rosa tomorrow morning at 5:30 a.m."

"How reliable is this information?"

"Very. Positive ID from someone who has seen the woman's photograph. The report also says she is accompanied by a man confirmed to be a gringo. The informant is a local who knows the vessel and its captain and was able to confirm the destination and ETA."

"Okay," said Torres, handing the headset back to the operator. He turned and paced up and down the room for several minutes.

"Do we have secure facilities here for raising our colleagues on the Brazilian side?" he asked to the room in general.

"Yes sir," said one of the more alert sergeants in the room.

"Okay. Get me Lieutenant Colonel Ferreira."

He paced up and down while the connection was made.

The sergeant finally nodded. "Line 3 on the desk phone," he said.

Torres walked briskly to the metal desk, snatched up the receiver and punched the button for line 3.

"*Bom dia Senhora*," he said smoothly.

"*Bom dia* Mr Torres," came the slightly ruffled reply. "*Tá muito cedo.*"

"Yes, I apologise for the hour," continued Torres in Portuguese. "But I have information that I need to act on now."

"Go ahead."

"I have an extra two suspects to pick up on our drugs operation, but they are arriving at Santa Rosa tomorrow at 5:30 a.m."

"But the raid is scheduled for the day after tomorrow, as you know."

"Yes, but all the assets are in place and all the boats are nearly fully loaded."

"*Nearly* fully loaded is not *fully* loaded, Senhor Torres. Besides, some of the players will not arrive until tomorrow."

"A detail, I believe. We know where they are and we can link them. They can be picked up any time."

Ferreira sighed. "But this was not what was agreed. It will be difficult to arrange the pick-ups, and the whole thing will be messier." She paused. "In any case, Santa Rosa is in Peruvian territory – you don't need us. You can do it as a separate operation, can't you?"

"That's true, of course, but it would be much better for everyone if we were seen to be working together on everything."

"Yes, indeed," said Ferreira. "Much better if you need to cover your ass."

"I can assure you—"

"Oh skip it." There was slight pause and a small sigh. "*Meu Deus, amigo*, what you're asking is almost impossible." She paused and let out a sigh. "You know, if I can pull it off – and it's a big if – there will be significant additional costs involved." The emphasis she placed on the words 'additional costs' left no room for doubt in Torres mind: this was going to cost him some more of his precious cut. He hesitated only a second. *So be it.*

"I – we – will fund those extra costs with pleasure."

"Hmm." Another pause. "Okay. I make no promises, but I will see what I can do. I'll come back to you in an hour, okay?

"Excellent."

"Very well, then."

The line clicked off.

40

"It's so beautiful," Elena said quietly.

Jack nodded.

"It's strange," she continued, "but I've rarely seen the dawn breaking except through a tangle of trees."

They were looking out over the prow of the big wooden passenger boat as the earliest light began to spread gently across the sky. Directly above them, the dark, blue-black velvet sky was still sprinkled with stars that faded out as the darkness slid into progressively lighter shades ahead of the boat. When they looked back, they could see the sunlight already colouring the storm clouds red, pink and gold, while thinner white veils of mist approached in waves. The still waters provided a perfect mirror for the whole image, framed by a thin border of forest extending from either side and touching across the distant river ahead and behind.

"Yes." Jack spoke softly, to no-one in particular. "It's like the past is fading away and a new future's being painted over the top." When he caught Elena looking at him he turned. "What?" he said, self-consciously.

"I did not realise you were such a sentimental man, gringo." She smiled.

"Ha ha. Yeah, well, sometimes..." He put his arm round her and they watched as the slowly brightening sky began to reveal a huge expanse of civilisation gouged out of the forest along the north bank, while the south bank remained almost devoid of activity.

The boat plodded steadily on, and as the light of day intensified, the river showed its true muddy brown colour. Traffic started to appear, with little canoes and speedboats zipping across the channel between the Peruvian island in the middle of the river, and the Colombian banks to the north. Jack knew that just a little further ahead, those banks would become Brazilian, the border between the two countries running crazily through the middle of the sprawling urban mass.

He watched a couple of speedboats flying towards them from ahead and to the north – probably from Brazil. At those sorts of speeds, it would take them only five or ten minutes to cross between there and Peru.

That close to safety.

As he followed their path, he tried to recall from his detailed planning so long ago, exactly where Brazilian customs was located. He thought he remembered them being somewhere in the middle of town. It didn't matter, really – as long as they got a boat to land them on Brazilian territory, they should be safe enough until they could get to the authorities.

His eyes narrowed as he tried to calculate the line the speedboats were taking. It looked like they were coming from the central area of Tabatinga, which he could see still had some street lights on. They would be going across to the town of Santa Rosa, and he glanced across to the right towards the little Peruvian town. He looked back at the boats again, and then again at the town. Those boats were not heading to Santa Rosa at all.

Shit.

He nudged Elena and pointed.

She spent a second or two using her hands to try to block the glare of the rising sun, and then she swore. "Brazilian. Feds," she said. She turned and looked over to the south bank, then grabbed his sleeve.

"Look – army!" she said, fear rising in her voice now.

Another two boats were flying towards them from the Peruvian side, upstream of Islandia.

"Shit - they can't *all* be in this, can they?"

"All of them, Jack – the Brazilians, the Peruvians, the gringos. They will search the boat from top to bottom. We need to get away, *now*."

They turned together and walked urgently towards the back of the Herrera IV, trying not to run, looking for a possible escape route. Jack's heart was in his mouth.

"We'll have to jump," said Jack.

Elena nodded.

"Look," he continued, pointing to the north bank, "It's only a few hundred yards to that side – that's Colombia."

"As long as it's not Peru," said Elena, beginning to run. "*Vamanos!*"

They raced to the back of the boat, down the stairs to the lower deck, and then to the stern, where there was a small kitchen area with easy access to the river from a platform no more than a foot above the water.

Adrenaline coursed through Jack's body. Part of him wanted to stay on the boat; the other half knew that if they did, they would probably be dead in a few hours.

"Jump as far out as you can, Elena – away from the propeller."

She nodded.

Jack looked quickly along the banks.

"There's a floating petrol station there – see it?"

"Yes."

"We'll meet there, right?

A couple of crew had finally turned up to see what passengers were doing in their galley.

"*Oi?*" one of them said. "*Essa área tá proibido.*"

"Okay Jack. I'll see you there. Let's go!" Elena shouted, and immediately dived into the water.

Jack hesitated only a second before following her with a dive as far beyond the boat as possible.

Under the water, he could hear the heavy churning of the big propeller on their boat, fading now, and the higher-pitched buzzing of other smaller craft getting louder. He held his breath as long as he could before he broke the surface and looked round. He could see Elena about ten yards away, swimming strongly at an upstream angle to the floating petrol station. He cursed himself for not picking something further downstream, as the current was much faster than he had thought.

He dived again and swam under water until his lungs were almost bursting, before breaking the surface once more. As he looked back, he could see a group of speedboats now clustered around the Herrera, with a soldier or police officer standing prominently on the bigger launch and talking or arguing with the boat captain and crew.

"Oh God, stall them – stall them," Jack prayed, taking a lungful of air and submerging to swim in the same direction as Elena.

He surfaced thirty seconds later, hearing the whine of a motor closing in. He quickly gulped more air and dived, this time instinctively turning back across his track and upstream. He prayed that Elena would do the same thing.

He struck out, hearing a cacophony of buzzing, growling sounds closing in, then passing within what seemed like inches of his head. When he could last not a second longer, he came up, gasping for air. He had not travelled far at all, but the boats had continued on past him. And past Elena as well, he hoped. He peered across the water and saw immediately that Elena had not turned, and was now surrounded by the boats.

"No!" He called out. "Oh God, no!" His voice was drowned out by the noise of the outboards. He immediately started swimming towards her position. He had no idea what he was going to do, but he was not going to abandon her. The boats had closed in and were now between him and Elena. He could not see her. He stopped for a second to call to her, and saw two of the men on the lead boat stand over the prow and raise their rifles.

"No!" he screamed. "Nooo!"

Multiple shots rang out, and Jack started swimming again as fast as he could towards Elena. All his senses were strained to focus on Elena and what was happening ahead, and he was only vaguely aware of the zing of an approaching outboard motor. At the last moment he turned, trying to get away from the sound, but he turned the wrong way. The sound exploded in his ear and he felt a heavy crack to his head, then everything faded – everything except the image of Elena's face pleading for help, and a sickening knot in his stomach.

Elena...

41

"**S**hooting unarmed suspects in front of a boat-load of witnesses is either incompetence or desperation." Márcia Ferreira stood with her arms crossed, in a pose that was more schoolmistress than police chief.

Torres' cold, impassive face cracked slightly, but he said nothing.

"I don't believe you are incompetent Adam," Ferreira continued. "Which just leaves desperation." She sighed. "Look, I need to know what this is all about, and I need to know right now, or our partnership is over." She paused and looked pointedly at him. "So..."

They stared at each other for several seconds, and finally Torres nodded curtly. "I can tell you it involves my government and the Peruvian government." He paused, and his lips puckered slightly as if he were calculating something. "And I can tell you that the woman is – was – a wanted terrorist by the name of Maria Fernandez."

Ferreira nodded. "I know the name. Fine. No tears shed there, provided we get a body, a positive ID, and some favourable press coverage. But the report I received mentioned *two* people."

"Yes..." Torres' hesitation stretched into several seconds of silence.

"I must know what the implications are for me and my team," prompted Ferreira.

"Let's just say he's an enemy spy," Torres finally said.

"A spy? Spying on what, and on whose behalf?"

"Spying on some of our operations in Peru."

Ferreira's eyes narrowed slightly.

"For the Europeans," Torres added.

Her eyes closed briefly and she shook her head. When she looked at Torres again it was with a flush of pure anger. "So let me get this right. You sabotaged our joint operation–"

"I sabotaged nothing," snapped Torres. "We got all the targets in Tabatinga and Islandia, as well as the materials and money. It was a huge success by any standards. They'll probably elect you president on the strength of it."

Ferreira was not mollified. "You *risked* our joint operation, just to cover the termination of this spy."

Torres said nothing.

"An operation which – being such a huge success – will be the focus of just about every country between here and China that has an interest in drugs and terrorism."

"An operation which this man was threatening." Torres seemed oblivious to Ferreira's sarcasm.

"Really? Threatening how, exactly?"

Torres stood rigid, as if he were addressing one of his CIA superiors. "I can't tell you that, Márcia."

Ferreira sighed. "Right. Then we have nothing further to discuss, and you can consider our agreements cancelled. And that includes the funds from the last Caribbean operation and whatever you hoped to get from this one, since I must remind you that all the merchandise and money is locked up for the moment on sovereign Brazilian territory."

The muscles in Torres jaw twitched, and a momentary flash of anger showed in his eyes as he contemplated the potential loss. "Godammit, Márcia," he finally said through gritted teeth. "He's a Brit, okay? He was travelling in company with Martinez, and we have reason to believe he knows about our undercover ops in Peru."

"Including your own get-rich-quick schemes and our joint deals?"

"Possibly."

"Possibly?"

"Yes, *possibly*. I don't know that until I find him, for Christ's sake."

"But if he *does* know, then his organisation already knows."

"He has no organisation."

"What?"

Torres hesitated. "He's a tourist."

A cry of strangled outrage escaped Ferreira's lips. "*Puta merda*, is he a spy or a tourist, Adam?"

Torres eyes flashed. "Does it really fucking matter? The point is, while he's alive, he's a serious threat to us *all*."

Ferreira looked closely at Torres for a second, before she took a step back and snorted. "Jesús, you're taking out British tourists, and you've got *us* involved in it – *me* involved in it. Murdering tourists on Brazilian soil—"

"Peruvian soil."

"Peruvian – Brazilian – whatever. It doesn't matter, does it? It was a joint operation, with my assets in plain view. I don't fucking *believe* this." She turned and paced up and down, her hands clasped tightly behind her back. The sound of her boots on the concrete floor of the huge empty aircraft hangar echoed sharply.

"He has to go," said Torres flatly.

Ferreira stopped pacing, "You're assuming he didn't drown."

Torres shook his head. "Until I have a confirmed result, he's still a threat."

"You haven't had a confirmed result on the girl, either, have you?"

Torres waved his hand dismissively. "No. But I've seen the video. She went under in a pool of blood. If she survived the shooting, she'll have been eaten alive."

Ferreira looked at him.

He sighed. "Look, even if she did survive, she's *persona non grata* with just about everyone – the Sendero and Tupac are after her, as well as the police, the military and my people. She's untouchable, and no-one would believe a word she says. She's the least of my concerns."

Ferreira scowled. "We still need a corpse."

"It'll turn up."

"Hmm." Ferreira thought for a second. "And your tourist. Whatever happens to him, you're assuming he hasn't spoken to anyone else."

"He hasn't."

"How can you be so sure?"

"We've been tracking him for two weeks."

"Two weeks? You've been after him for two *weeks*?" Ferreira put her hand to her forehead, and massaged her temples. "So let's get this straight, Adam. You lied to me at our last meeting, you risked our joint operation and our personal deals, and now you're telling me you couldn't manage to pick him up in two fucking *weeks*? Who am I dealing with here? Sponge Bob fucking Square Pants?"

"The only assets I had were Peruvian army," Torres hissed, before taking a deep breath. "Look, all I need to do is nail this guy fast, and the problem disappears. Permanently."

"What do you mean all *you* need to do? The truth is *we* need to nail him, Adam." She regarded him coldly. "This is way out of line. You dropped me in the shit, and I don't know what I'm going to do about that." She turned and paced a few steps. "Okay. First things first," she finally said, returning to stand in front of him. "You need to get some friendly press on this right now, and I'll do the damage limitation on my side. Focus on the result of the busts and we'll bury the shooting."

"We're already on it."

"Right. I'll also authorise a small team of yours to enter Brazil. You can bring them in today. In the meantime, get me a description and any other details we need to know, and I'll supervise our own search operation."

"Thank you."

"Don't bother thanking me – I'm not doing it for you." She looked at him sharply. "This isn't over, you know. And you'd better make sure this guy turns up dead – in Peruvian territory – pretty damned quick."

42

Torres sat at the sparklingly clean, glass-topped desk in his office in the austere US Embassy building in Lima, and spoke in clipped tones over the secure line. It was late, and he had only just arrived from Tabatinga. He was tired, and the bright LED lighting was giving him a headache. As he listened to the speaker's reply, he held the mouthpiece away from his mouth and breathed deeply. He could not afford to sound uptight. He was used to these conversations lasting less than a couple of minutes, and being confined to simple statements of fact. In the last ten minutes, he had been grilled not only about the project deadlines and the in-country politics, but about the loss of several U.S. workers, the disappearance of an American in Cuzco, and about some hazy, unofficial reports of tourists being mixed up in their operations in Tabatinga. Less than four hours after receiving official congratulations on the success of the biggest joint drugs operation in history, he was suddenly being hounded by a bunch of nervous desk jockeys.

"Yes – I have heard the rumours, sir, but my assessment is that even if they are accurate, there is no connection to us or our operations." He tried to sound unconcerned.

"Hmm," the voice came back, sounding less than convinced. "So you would categorically say that these reports are pure fantasy. Is that right?"

"With all due respect, sir, that's not what I said. The situation here is relatively volatile. It was volatile at the beginning of the project, and it probably always will be volatile. The rumours should be checked out, of course, but even if there is some truth – however tenuous – in the stories, I believe my task is to manage our operations in such a way that both they and the Company remain secure. I don't believe–"

"Thank you," the voice interrupted. "I don't need a lecture on your responsibilities. What I need is for you to investigate, assess and resolve. I need you to keep a lid on anything – anything – that might adversely affect this project."

"Certainly, sir."

"And I need you to make sure that we don't end up reading this shit in the newspapers over breakfast with our colleagues."

"Yes sir," Torres managed, his eyes looking skyward in frustration.

There was a pause on the line.

"You've been doing a great job over there, you know."

"Thank you."

"But you know how critical things are now."

"Yes sir," Torres said, maintaining his calm. "And everything is going to plan, as I reported."

"Okay. But let's get this crap tidied up, right? We don't want to hear anymore about–"

"Of course not," Torres interrupted a little too quickly.

"We don't want to hear any more about it," the voice continued slowly, "or anything else that might draw unwanted attention."

Torres rolled his eyes and grimaced. First Ferreira, now Langley. *Assholes.*

"No indeed, sir. Don't worry – it's all under control."

"I sure hope so." A pause. "You know, there are a couple of people who think it might be time for you to come in."

There it is.

"With all due respect, I think that would be counterproductive at this stage." He could not afford to let this happen. Not now.

"That's for us to decide," the voice snapped at him.

Careful. He had to tread lightly.

"Yes, of course. If you think that's best, it's fine by me." He paused to leave a nice space for his next words. "But I'll need to effect some introductions first."

He did not elaborate. They all knew that the hardest links to manage in the whole chain were the Peruvian Presidential Adviser and the head of the tamed Sendero. Sure, when the time came, they could be removed – but for the moment they were irreplaceable, and the only person they would deal with was Torres. Torres had made sure of that. It was his ace-in-the-hole, and the fact that they had let him get away with it confirmed in Torres' mind that they were a useless bunch of fat slobs. He smiled in the awkward silence. The time it would take to get someone here, show them around, and get a working relationship going was simply too great at this point. With go-live just around the corner, no one would be insane enough to disturb the delicate network and put everything at risk.

"Well, we have a contingency for that," the voice continued, creditably smoothly. But the pause had been too long.

Bullshit.

"Of course." Torres hoped his amusement did not come through.

"But I'll talk to them. Convince them we should leave things as they are for the moment. I know you're the best option we have for getting through to completion."

"Yes sir." Torres kept the reply simple and unemotional.

The rest of the conversation comprised the usual platitudes and was over in a few seconds.

As he replaced the receiver, the ghost of a smile on his face faded, and the habitual cold, unemotional expression settled in again. He was not stupid. All he had really achieved was a stay of execution, and if he did not take advantage of it right now, the next contact would either be to order him in or add him to the 'missing Americans' statistics. He had three things to do now – produce a credible explanation for the missing American, find the girl's body, and wipe that damned Brit off the face of the earth. He had someone he could rely on for the first task, and he reckoned the Brazilians would pick up on the second, so that just left the Brit.

He pulled a thin file across the desk and opened it. It had come through one of his personal contacts, and had cost him a small fortune. It was not a patch on one of their own searches, but it was the best he was going to get.

He opened the file and started reading.

'McCrae, Jonathan Michael' it said at the top.

Thirty-one years old. Born in Donegal, Ireland, and orphaned. Raised in Bristol, England, the only child in the family.

Probably spoiled rotten.

Poor school grades; good at sport.

Yeah, it figures.

He scanned through to the next page, where Jack's military career was laid out. He was not surprised to learn he was chasing a war vet., but the fact that the guy was ex-special forces was a kick in the gut. Anyone who did four tours of that sort of shit in Afghanistan and Syria was not someone you wanted to underestimate. On the next page was another surprise. He was not just a war vet., but a *decorated* war vet. Huh - damned people - always poking their noses into things that were of no concern to them, and half of them mentally unstable. He read the citation: a Military Cross for 'conspicuous gallantry' saving a couple of his squad members after an ambush in Syria. Never got past Staff Sergeant, though, before he quit. Strange, that. Twelve years in the army and he just ups and leaves – he flicked to the next page – to become a fitness instructor in Scotland? Makes no sense. He went straight into the army aged seventeen. It must have been like family to him, after both adoptive parents died within six months of each other. So he devotes all that time to his new family, sees a lot of action – even gets himself a degree – and starts crawling up the ladder. And then suddenly, six months after being decorated, he bugs out to go and live up some mountain in Scotland. Weird. Unless he suffered some trauma... Yes, that was probably it - post-traumatic stress, perhaps. The guy had probably gone soft. Maybe things weren't so bad after all.

The last page was about his short and no doubt very boring time as a fitness instructor, and his activities before he left for Peru. There was a blog, and Torres turned to his laptop and called it up, together with a text file he had received of social media posts and emails. He spent half an hour going through it all, but it was mostly mind-numbingly dull, self-conscious stuff, although it all pointed to the happy fact that Jack McCrae was a loner. No family and no friends.

He closed the file, picked up one of his phones, and dialled.

"Sir," a voice answered his call.

"Any sign?" he asked.

"Negative."

"Okay. I'll be back in Tabatinga by tomorrow night."

He reopened the file to the most recent photograph of Jack, and flicked between it and the summary that concluded, in capitals 'NO KNOWN RELATIVES OR FRIENDS.' So, a stressed-out ex-grunt with no-one to care about him. Aw, what a shame.

His eyes narrowed.

Open season.

43

Jack's first conscious feeling was of acute grief, although he could not immediately understand why All he could think of, as awareness slowly returned, was that it was too bright, that his head was hot, and that his lower body was cold and wet. He tried to open his eyes but they refused to obey, so he just lay still. He concentrated instead on the awful feeling of sorrow that seemed to physically weigh on him, and then suddenly he remembered. Elena. She was gone. Murdered. The images of the shooting came to him, and his mind played them over and over again until he felt sick. He wanted to shout – to rampage and roar – about it, but he lacked the strength. He squeezed his eyes tight shut, and felt them burn behind his eyelids.

His mind began to clear. What had happened after Elena...after that? How had he escaped the same fate? He tried to raise his head, but all he succeeded in doing was to make it slide off whatever it was resting on. His face smacked into soft, yielding wetness. Water poured into his mouth and up his nose, and he instinctively rolled over and pushed himself up on his hands and knees, opening his eyes and coughing. He crawled out of the water, and turned himself to sit on the mud. The bright sunlight blinded him and his head throbbed even more.

He was sitting at the mouth of a stream that was dribbling a pathetically small amount of water into the main river in front of him. He had been deposited on a little bar that divided the two watercourses. There was no doubt in his mind that the wide, muddy river he was staring out at now was the same as the one he had jumped into from the passenger boat – the Marañon, as they called it in Peru, or the Solimões, in Brazil, or just the plain old Amazon.

He shuffled up a little, and moved and stretched the muscles in his neck and body, finding that they were stiff but otherwise okay. He thought strenuously about standing up, but his legs would not yet move properly. Worried about being caught in the open, he craned his neck to look behind him. There was no sign of any civilisation, so he contented himself with passing a hand across his face and then his head, where he discovered an impressive lump. He checked the rest of his body, and saw that everything was in one piece, including a large leech that had attached itself to his thigh. He reached down, slid the animal off, and threw it in the river. For a few seconds he stared unblinkingly at the blood trickling down from the wound, and then he took a deep breath. He had to try to focus and think clearly.

First of all, where was he? Which country was this? His hopes rose when he considered the possibility that he had actually made it to Brazil, but then as more of the details of the shooting came back to him, his frustration returned. The first thing Elena said when he had pointed out the boats to her, was 'Brazilian Feds'. He remembered seeing the incongruously bright, Brazilian flag patches on the uniforms of the soldiers in the boat. It had obviously been a joint operation: Peru and Brazil – maybe Colombia too – with some insidious American influence behind it all.

He lay back again, utterly despondent. Whatever country this piece of mud was in, he could not be any deeper in hostile territory. A thousand miles from just about anywhere – north, south, east or west. In a country – whichever it was – hell bent on killing him.

He spent the next few minutes talking himself round to a less negative point of view, but his heart was hardly in it when he finally dragged himself to his feet and walked unsteadily inland. What chance did he realistically stand? Neither by nature nor nurture was he any sort of criminal, thief or liar. The fact that he had come this far was due in no small part to Elena and her ability to procure food, clothing and supplies. He had been able to ignore the inconvenient fact that she had lied and stolen for them, from one end of Peru to the other, and he knew that if she were still alive, she would already be off getting what they needed in the nearby communities. If he were to survive, he would have to try to do the same, and then what? How could he risk another confrontation? He would just end up reacting like he always did – hesitating, or losing himself, or whatever it was that happened to him – and this time he'd wind up dead.

He reached a narrow dirt track that stretched away in both directions along the riverbank. Behind this, he found a clear area where a line of scrubby bushes and trees kept him hidden from view. He stripped off his clothes and hung them on a branch to dry, while he collected his thoughts. The warmth on his chapped white skin, punctured in a thousand places by insect bites, felt wonderful, and as he checked himself over carefully, he decided that feeling sorry for himself was not an option.

So what *were* his options? Lie down and die? Head for the nearest civilisation and try to organise a phone or some internet? Run for it? He dismissed the idea of looking for Tabatinga or Santa Rosa, or even Colombia's border town of Leticia. His chances of remaining undetected long enough to acquire a phone or a connection, make contact, and then wait to be rescued, were stupidly small. He would just be making it easy for his enemy. On the other hand, sitting around here was tantamount to doing the same thing: rolling over and letting them come find him.

'*Okay Jack. I'll see you there.*'

Elena's last words came to him, and suddenly there was a knot in his stomach. The rendezvous – the floating petrol station! What if she *was* alive? What if she had somehow escaped and was there at the station? He pictured her crouched in the shadows, watching and waiting. He had not actually seen her die, had he? *He* had survived – why not Elena? His heart beat faster, even as his mind's eye played the scene of the shooting over again. They *must* have hit her – two boats, a half-dozen rifles, an easy target. But they *could* have missed. It was a small chance, admittedly, but a chance nonetheless. Suddenly, the decision about what to do was easy after all.

He dressed and started walking along the track, upstream towards where he was sure Tabatinga lay. His best chance lay in acquiring a boat, waiting until dark, and making his way to the floating petrol station. If Elena was there, then they would be back on track with the original plan; if she really had gone, then he would turn back and head downstream again and get as far away as possible before planning the next move.

He had not been walking more than ten minutes when he rounded a bend and saw below him, along the river bank, a few floating houses. Next to these was a bigger tin-walled shed that sheltered a wooden boat, a smaller version of the one that had brought them to Tabatinga. Beyond this, there were several canoes and launches pulled up on the mud, and he stopped for a minute to see if there might be some way of getting to one of them.

The closest one was an aluminium speedboat with a small outboard and the inevitable red plastic fuel container sitting on the rear bench seat. If he could get to it – and if he could get it away – and if the engine started – and if there were any fuel – it would do the job. That was a lot of 'ifs'. The alternative was to carry on and hope a better opportunity presented itself, although he knew there would be more people and a greater chance of being discovered as he approached the town.

A bird in the hand...

He decided to wait until dark, and after making careful mental note of the position of everything at the riverside, he retreated across the track and dug himself in. It would not be long now – the sun was already on the other side of the river and going down.

He spent his time trying to remember the detail of his original route, and working out how long it would take to get to the Brazilian city of Manaus, the first major population centre on the Amazon, in an aluminium speedboat. He had reached no satisfactory conclusion by the time the light faded enough for him to creep across the track again.

He found it easy to get down to the boats undetected in the spreading gloom. The aluminium boat he had picked out was old and battered. It was about twelve feet long with a handy-looking 15hp two-stroke outboard. It was loosely secured to a simple wooden stake, and Jack had no problem releasing it. He took a paddle from another boat and placed it carefully in the aluminium one, and then bent to the task of pushing the boat out of the mud. He was concentrating so hard on dislodging it that he did not notice the two men creeping down to him, nor the heavy wooden paddle that nearly split his skull open and left him slumped over the prow of the boat he had been trying to steal.

44

Elena's Brazilian contact had a good vantage point from a safe house upstream of Tabatinga. In fact the house was more of a shack nailed to a floating wooden platform, tied up among other similar *flutuantes,* along the Colombian side of the tri-border. It was barely habitable, but anonymity was the order of the day, and this place oozed it.

He had brought provisions, and he re-stocked the ancient refrigerator that buzzed and gurgled in the corner of the one-roomed cabin while he kept half an eye on the Herrera IV's stately downstream progress. The battered binoculars he had been using sat on top of a small wooden table, next to a bottle of cheap rum and two shot glasses, a small grab-bag, a couple of mobile phones and a Smith and Wesson M&P.

The Herreras was almost drawing level with the flutuante now, and he glanced at the rum and then looked at his watch. He shook his head slightly before walking to the fridge, opening the door, and pulling out a small carton of juice. Just as he was shutting the fridge door, the sound of some sort of commotion carried across the river, and he opened the window shutters wider and looked out towards the noise.

He saw people lining the sides of the Herreras, pointing and shouting, and he watched as Police and Military speedboats came alongside, red lights flashing and sirens sounding intermittently. He stretched across and exchanged the carton of juice for the binoculars, as the speedboats suddenly backed off, turned, and raced upstream. He saw them converge on something in the river, and focused the binoculars in time to see that there was someone in the water. The magnification was too poor to be able to identify them, but he had little doubt it was Elena and her friend who were in trouble. Without taking his eyes off the scene, he pulled a stool across, sat down, and rested the glasses on the window sill to steady them. He gritted his teeth as he watched the soldiers raise their automatic rifles and fire at the defenceless form in the river. The head went under, and even from this distance, the stain of red that spread across the water was clearly visible. The boats slipped steadily eastward, their occupants scanning the river as they drifted, but the man in the flutuante focused his attention on an area further upstream and closer to the banks, following the line of swirling currents and eddies. He held his breath as he pivoted the binoculars a fraction of an inch at a time, and then he stopped, his eyes narrowing. A head broke the surface once, twice, three times – just long enough for someone to take a gasp of air each time. The man watched closely now, covering an area closer to the banks and a good hundred yards upstream of the retiring boats, and then he leapt up, grabbed his pistol, and ran from the flutuante. He thundered down the steps and jumped into his own little boat. He started the engine, cast off and sped downriver.

It was a close run thing, in the end. He caught the body twenty yards from the riverbank, at the edge of a whirlpool well known in the area for swallowing things a lot bigger than the average human being. The body was floating face down and quite limp now – a few minutes later and it would have disappeared altogether.

It took him a long time to drag the dead-weight into the boat, but he smiled with relief as the figure coughed and retched and struggled feebly to get up, before finally lying motionless in the bottom of the boat. As he restarted his engine and turned upstream, he realised he had been spotted by a few fishermen along the banks. He slowed, and turned in a wide circle to bring him within a few yards of them, then he ran slowly along the riverbank, looking at each of the men in turn, pulling out his gun and showing it clearly, and holding his finger to his lips. It was unlikely that anyone would want to help the Feds, but these people would certainly recognise him, and knowing that he had seen their faces would guarantee tighter lips.

At the flutuante, he shouldered the body and carried it up the steps and into the shack. He laid it on the only bed and quickly checked it over. It was a girl. She was older by a few years, and her face was deathly grey, but he recognised her as Elena Lopez. She was still breathing, and he saw little blood, but her top had a hole in it, to the side of her belly, and it was clear she had been shot. He felt her pulse, which was slow but steady, and shook her gently.

"Elena. Elena," he said.

There was no response.

He drew the stool up to the table, took the pistol from his pocket and placed it on the table, and sat down. He picked up a phone and dialled a number. The call was answered almost immediately.

"*Bom dia Doutor. Tenho um caso urgente,*" he began.

When he had finished the call, he got up, threw a thin sheet over Elena, and walked to the window again. He scanned the scene carefully with his binoculars, but appeared to see nothing of interest. The Feds and the Military had withdrawn downstream, the Herreras had arrived in Santa Rosa, and there was no longer any sign of the drama that had just taken place, nor of the person Elena had been travelling with.

He closed the window shutters, switched on the tiny incandescent light dangling from the ceiling, and sat down again at the table, facing the door, with the pistol within reach. He poured himself some rum, drank it back in one gulp, and settled into his chair.

45

Elena was vaguely aware of someone touching her, and moving and turning her where she lay. She felt little pain, but drifted in and out of consciousness in spite of her best efforts to clear her head. She had no idea where she was and was finding it difficult to remember what she had been doing.

There were two people speaking, and she heard most of the conversation, but as hard as she tried to speak, she got no further than *thinking* the words.

"That's it?!" She heard someone cry in amazement. "She's been shot, doc! Shouldn't you be operating, or something?"

She remembered now. The river – the police – the sound of gunfire, and the sudden pain in her back.

"She has, yes. And she's a lucky lady, whoever she is..." the one with the deep voice said. Obviously the doctor.

"You don't want to know," the other man said. The voice sounded vaguely familiar, but she could not quite place it.

"Er no, of course not," the doctor said quickly. "Anyway, the bullet entered through her back, a few centimetres from her spine, and exited on her right side, missing the intestine by about the same amount. She lost some blood, of course, but nothing too horrendous."

She did not feel lucky. Anything but. She had almost made it – they had almost made it.

They...

Her memory suddenly snapped back into place. Jack! What had happened to Jack? Had he got away? She wanted to get up, to talk. She needed questions answered. She fought uselessly against an overwhelming fatigue.

"Like I said – a lucky lady," the deep voice said. "The wounds should close nicely, but she'll be sore for a few days. She needs to take those antibiotics too. The only thing I can't do is check for any foreign matter left inside, but my instinct tells me it's clean.

"Can she be moved?"

Can I be moved? Can I even move myself, dammit?

"Up to her, really. I gave her a mild sedative, though...,"

Oh, you did, did you?

"...she needs that little rest. Once she's finished the drips and woken up, she'll probably be good to go."

"Amazing."

The bed bounced slightly – presumably the doctor getting up – and she heard him setting something down somewhere.

"There are some bandages and ointment there, and the antibiotics – make sure she takes those without fail, okay?"

"Sure."

There was a sigh. "Compared to what you usually bring me, this is a mere scratch."

"Okay doc. Thanks as always. Usual form of payment, okay?"

"No problem. Take it easy."

She heard the shuffle of feet, the door opening and closing, and the receding footsteps, as she lay paralysed, still fighting off a deep desire to sleep. She did not want to sleep. She had to get up and find out what was happening. To find Jack.

Jack...

Her hearing seemed suddenly to fill with sound of her own heartbeat, and a warm darkness tugged at her solicitously. Her facial muscles twitched in agitation for a few seconds before she finally succumbed to the midazolam and morphine.

46

Jack slowly came to, feeling cold and with the stink of stale urine in his nostrils. A tropical thunderstorm seemed to be raging inside his head, and he reached up to find that he had acquired another huge lump on his scalp. When he moved his head gingerly from side to side he could feel something cracking or flaking, and felt mud or dried blood or something stuck to his hair and on the skin of his neck.

He sat up and got a fresh noseful of the stink of piss and shit. He reached out and felt a smooth, curving coldness.

I'm in a fucking toilet, now. Jesus, what next?

He stood up gingerly, pressed himself against the wooden wall, and reached out with his foot. He found the other wall, as he expected, about three feet away. He felt to his right and found a door, and then a handle. He tried it but it was locked.

He stopped to run a hand over his face.

I've had enough of this, he thought wearily.

The events of the last few weeks flashed through his mind and stopped at Elena. He thought further back – a lot further back. Back to his career in the army, and to his childhood. Is this how it was to end? Waiting for death in a shit-house in the middle of the Amazon?

Who the hell put him in here, anyway? It seemed unlikely to be the army, the Brazilian Feds or the Americans. Perhaps it was just the locals who had caught him stealing their boat. Maybe he could explain his way out of it. Or maybe not – his Portuguese was negligible. Of course, they might call the police, and that really would be the end of him.

He pressed himself against the door and felt it give. A good push and either it or the lock would give. He decided to give it a try, but just as he was bracing himself, he heard footsteps outside, and a light came on.

"Mr Ma-cry," came a voice. "Mr Ma-cry. We know who you are. Do not try to be the smartass. We shoot you if you will try to be the smartass. You understand?"

Jack stood back as the door was unbolted and opened. He blinked in the light, and walked out with his hands up.

Two men were pointing automatic rifles at him, and a third stood in front of him, a pistol in his hand.

"Who are you?" Jack asked, his voice coming out as a croak. "And who is Macry? I don't know any Macry."

"It does not matter who we are, Mr Ma-cry. And we are not fools. We know who *you* are and we have friends who will be very pleased to see you. Come," the man said, waving his pistol at Jack and beckoning him forward.

They walked past a small wooden house, onto a track. In the moonlight, Jack could see they were very close to the shore where he had spotted the boats. An SUV was parked on the narrow track, and Jack was prodded towards it. As he looked at it, his brain went into overdrive. They were close to Tabatinga, he was sure – perhaps only a few minutes away by car. Once they had him in the vehicle, it would be all over in ten or twenty minutes. It would be hard to escape from the car, and at some point they would surely either knock him over the head or tie his hands, or both. Anger suddenly boiled in him, and the mist descended. Sounds seemed to fade, although he could still hear his heart pounding in his ears, and the only thing he could see was the back of the man with the pistol, up in front. His throat went dry and he felt cold. He blinked. They were within a few feet of the car. Now was time. He stopped walking, and the men shouted at him, and prodded him in the back. As he started forward again, he glanced behind to see the men. As he had hoped, they were now far to close behind him – a mistake Jack was about to make them regret.

"Wait!" he suddenly shouted, spinning round and putting his hands up. The two men behind had to jerk their weapons up to avoid colliding with him. He grabbed one of the weapons, and used his weight to swing the man at the end of it into his partner. As he fell, the man released the gun to Jack, and Jack jumped behind the SUV as the man with the pistol fired at him. The shots went wide, and as soon as there was a pause, Jack fired a short burst towards the group, immediately rolling out to the tree line. One of the men cried out, and when Jack looked from behind a tree, he saw two men running for the cover of the SUV, and one lying quite still on the ground. Looking more closely, he could see that the man on the ground was the one with the other rifle. That just left one man with a pistol. Jack crouched and moved as quickly and quietly as possible along the tree line to put himself closer to the downed man. As he did so, one of the other men tried to retrieve the rifle on the ground.

Don't do that, you idiot, thought Jack, even as he aimed and fired. The man crashed heavily to the ground, immobile, and Jack was already moving further up the tree line. He fired three short bursts at the car, shattering the windows and blowing out the front tyre. He saw his opponent dive for the other side of the car, and Jack used the advantage to run and pick up the second rifle. He grabbed it and continued running forward on a diagonal to the right, so that he finished up on the other side of the track. His opponent was now in clear view, and apparently had not even seen Jack's move. Jack withdrew the magazine from the first gun, and dropped the gun. Then he quickly brought the second one to bear.

"Drop it!" Jack shouted.

"Fuck you, gringo!" the man responded, as he crouched and began firing wildly with his pistol. Jack fired a burst, more to encourage the guy to keep firing, than with any hope of hitting him, and after a few seconds he clearly heard the click of an empty chamber. He immediately broke cover and charged the man, wailing like a banshee.

The man was on his knees fumbling for something in his pockets – another magazine, Jack reasoned – and was not prepared to defend himself when Jack delivered a solid blow to the side of his head with the butt of his rifle. The man collapsed.

"Damn," Jack grunted. He wanted information from the guy, and now it would be impossible. He picked up the pistol and a new magazine which lay on the ground, then he walked around to where the other men lay. One was clearly dead, the side of his face having collected a bullet. The other one was moaning softly, holding his stomach. A pool of blood was spreading underneath him.

Jack bent down to him. "Who are you?" he asked.

Nothing.

"*Quien son ustedes?*" he tried.

"*Ayuda, ayuda,*" the man moaned feebly.

"*Habla, o yo le mato,*" Jack hissed. Talk, or I kill you. He pressed the rifle to the man's head.

"*Traficantes,*" the man breathed. "*Traficantes. Juro!*"

"Why do traffickers want me?" Jack continued in his pidgin Spanish.

"Everybody wants you."

"Everybody?"

"Yes. Sendero, police, army, everybody."

"In Peru," Jack said.

"And Brazil."

"But why?"

"I don't know. I swear, I do not know."

"Fuck."

"Help me," the man moaned.

"Someone will come," Jack said dismissively. He was sure their gunfight would attract a lot of attention in due course. Time he was somewhere else.

He ran down to the boats, picked the one with the best looking engine, and pushed it out. He jumped in and climbed to the back. The current took the boat and turned the stern downstream. Jack primed the engine, made sure everything was connected, checked the choke and the throttle, and as he turned to get in a good position to pull the starting cord, he saw one of the men running down to the water's edge. It had to be the guy with the pistol – Jack obviously had not hit him as hard as he thought. He gauged he was too far away to shoot at him with either a pistol or an AK, so he concentrated on getting the engine started. He heard the motor of the other boat splutter into life, just before his own engine caught.

Damn. If he turned upstream, the man would be on him easily, so he had to either use the distance advantage he had now and continue downstream, or turn and go back to disable the guy. As he paused for a second to think it through, a single shot rang out. It sounded like a rifle. Where had the gun come from? The vehicle, of course! Jack cursed his own incompetence, and suddenly heard the voice of his old army instructor.

"*What do you need – a fucking nursemaid, McCrae?*"

If he had known that Jack had also forgotten to remove the petrol cans from the other boats, he would have been on him like a ton of bricks.

He smiled grimly at the thought, and turned the throttle to maximum, racing away downstream and hoping he had the speed and fuel to out-distance his pursuer.

47

Elena awoke to the gentle creaking of the floating house, moving gently up and down in time to the wake from a passing boat. Remembering the previous night, she was immediately scared she would be unable to speak or open her eyes, and she sat bolt upright, cursing the sudden pain in her side.

"Ah. Awake at last," a voice said from somewhere outside. She looked round as the door opened and the contact she had spoken to on the phone stepped inside. Five years since she had last seen him, and he had not changed a bit.

She smiled. More wince than smile. "Yes. And no doubt it's thanks to you that I woke up at all."

The man gave a slight shrug. "What are friends for?"

Elena shuffled gingerly to the side of the bed and put her feet on the floor. The man tutted at her, took a cup of water and a tablet from the table, and walked over to stand next to her.

"Take it easy, will you? You were shot, and—"

"I know," she interrupted. "I'm a lucky lady – a bit of rest, drips, antibiotics, and I'm good to go, right?"

"You heard us talking last night?"

"Yeah. Seriously weird. I could hear everything, but I couldn't respond."

"Certainly not your usual form." The man laughed, then his face grew more serious. "Listen Elena, I don't know why everyone suddenly wants you so badly, but your life isn't worth shit here at the moment. It's not just the Peruvian military after you any more – the Movement wants you, the Brazilians want you... There's even a rumour the Americans want you."

Elena sighed. "Not just a rumour."

"Jesus. Well, I don't know what it's about and I don't want to know. The point is, you're an untouchable at the moment. There are very few people who are going to risk having anything to do with you."

"I know. I really appreciate it, you know–"

The man held up his hand. "Don't, Elena, please. I did what I had to, and I'm pleased to have been able to do it. We're quits now, you and me, but I'm out of it."

"Sure. I understand – don't worry."

The man looked down, and then turned and walked over to the window. "It's not just me anymore. I have a wife and kids now. I want something better for them than all this... this crap, right?" He opened the shutters as he spoke, and a blade of bright daylight cut into the room. He remained with his back to Elena, looking out on the river.

Elena nodded. "I understand. Really. It's okay."

"Hmm," he muttered. "Right." His tone became more positive. "Well, I've left some things there for you on the table – clothes and stuff like that." He pointed at the table. "I got you a couple of clean phones and a half-dozen new chips. And since the only way you're going to get out of here now is by boat, there's a half-decent one tied up alongside. It looks like a piece of crap, but actually the motor's brand new. I'm also leaving you my favourite Smith and Wesson, a box of ammo, and a five thousand Brazilian." He paused, still with his back to her. "Listen, you know how to find me, Elena. If you're really in trouble – I mean really, *really* in trouble–"

Elena held up her hand to interrupt him. "Yeah I know – call someone else, right?" She smiled.

The man turned, grinning, obviously relieved at her response. "You got it."

She stood up and walked over to stand in front of him. They embraced, and kissed on both cheeks.

"Good luck, my friend," the man said gently.

"Sure. You too."

He turned and walked towards the door.

"Look after those kids, right?" Elena called after him.

As soon as the man left, Elena busied herself getting cleaned up, redressing her wounds, and changing her clothes. She grabbed some cold food out of the fridge and then sat at the table, setting up her phones with the special sims and initialising them. She felt good – far better than she had a right to feel after being shot and half-drowned less than twenty-four hours earlier. She looked down at her poor, mistreated body, full of scars and bruises, and raw red in places, and the words of a song her father used to play, floated through her head.

A quien dios ama, le llama. Only the good die young.

She hung her head, lost in bitter-sweet memories for a moment. Maybe it was true. Suddenly her head snapped up again.

What about Jack?

It was time to get busy. She took a scrap of wrapping paper from the table and made some notes. She had contacts, and contacts were the only way she was going to track Jack down or get out of here.

She sat for almost fifteen minutes writing down names of people who might help her here, and further downstream in Brazil. Everyone she could think of – the good, the bad and the ugly – from the last eight years in her underworld universe, went on the list. Next, she went through the list and refined it. When she had it down to four people – two here, one in Peru and one in Brazil – she wrote down exactly what she wanted to ask, and then picked up one of the phones.

There were only two failsafe phone numbers she had memorised – people whose help she knew she could count on in her Peruvian network. The first number didn't pick up, the second was a coded message which gave her another number. This additional number was an extra step in the same sim-based, VoIP system they had used for the last two years, and Elena had a high degree of trust in it. She used a second phone with a different SIM to dial the number. There was a perfunctory and well-rehearsed greeting. Apart from a slight lag, the connection was good.

The two parties on the line identified themselves, then Elena read from her notes to briefly explain her problem and what she needed. The other party confirmed, and finished with another coded message. Elena also provided her own coded message, and the conversation was over in less than thirty seconds. She immediately switched off the phones.

"Triangulate *that*, assholes."

All she could do now was wait as the word went out to her contacts.

After six hours, she had received just two calls. The first one was an offer of help in Brazil if she could get herself to a town called São Paulo de Olivença. The caller gave her a time, a place and a name, and she had been half-heartedly preparing for the trip until she received the second call.

It came from a very reliable Colombian source, and when she heard the news, Elena could not keep the emotion out of her voice. Some traffickers had reported to their dealers that they had captured 'El Gringo'. Fortunately, by the time anyone got there, one of the traffickers was dead, one of them wounded, and the gringo had got clean away downstream.

Jack.

She asked for details and was given a location and a contact on the river. Risking everything, she left her sanctuary at dusk, zig-zagged painfully slowly down the river, avoiding the police and the military, and picked up her contact at the southernmost tip of Islandia, before crossing into Brazil and being led to the exact spot.

She was not able to speak to any of the surviving traffickers, and there was nothing at the site to confirm it was Jack, but she felt it in her gut. And she instinctively knew Jack was capable of what these people were talking about. She had seen it in him right from the start. He knew his way around weapons, and although he had gone out of his way to play everything quietly, she had seen that look. It was a look that haunted people who had dealt with conflict – with violence and death. Something in the eyes, the set of the face, the way they held themselves. She felt her spine tingle. It was Jack.

Now she had to make a decision. She had been told that Jack had been chased downstream for 'about an hour', and that the trafficker pursuing him had broken off because he was nearly out of fuel. She had to decide whether to go after him or... or what? She had used up her favours here already, and someone would feed her to the lions soon enough. Few people knew about the firefight at this point, but she knew someone would start blabbing about it very soon. Everyone and everything was a commodity to be traded here, and information about herself and Jack would be no different.

Her guide was anxious to be gone, and she finally nodded to him. She offered him some money, but it was declined, as she knew it would be. There were still a few – a very few – who could not be bought. They shook hands, and he turned and vanished into the night.

She quickly walked back to her boat, and pushed off. If she was to catch Jack, she would have to move by night. If the information she had been given was accurate, he had a minimum of forty kilometres head start. She would make slow progress, and she would have to try to guess when he would move and where he would stop. Her eyes bored into the night, as if by concentrating hard enough she would be able to see him. He was out there, somewhere.

I will find you, Jack.

48

Simon scrolled impatiently down the news results for Peru. The little article the placement student had prepared lay beside the computer on the desk. It was pretty good – much better than he had hoped – and her research had dug up a few interesting background details, but in spite of her not unimpressive abilities, she had ultimately come up against a brick wall. Jack McCrae, fitness instructor, decorated ex-soldier of no fixed abode and with no known living relatives, had gone seriously missing.

From what they could glean, he had met someone else in Peru who had accompanied him on one leg of his expedition. The two of them had blogged regularly, but had then gone off the air. McCrae had blogged almost daily for the initial six weeks of his travels and then stopped abruptly; the other guy had continued for another couple of weeks before he too had stopped. There had now been no news of them for three weeks – no word about McCrae in well over a month. All they knew was that he had set out from the city of Cuzco to descend the drugs-and-terrorist-infested valleys of Peru, hoping to emerge at the other end on his way into Brazil.

Simon's news searches and his contacts elsewhere had returned only one oblique reference to foreigners in Peru. It did not appear to lead very far, but it did set Simon's news hound senses tingling. The original short Spanish text was hot from a Peruvian blog that rambled on about the massive drugs bust in Tabatinga – already splashed across every self-respecting rag in the world, and wholly uninteresting to Simon – but also talked about some gringos jumping out of a passenger boat near Peru's border town of Santa Rosa. The author was clearly connecting the two events, although he was dancing carefully around the connection, and his final general observations on the rights and wrongs of unlawful killing were just uncritical waffle. There were a few pictures as well: one of the boat in question, full of people and lined with hammocks; one with army and police launches zipping across the water; and another showing two dots in a brown river, with the caption '*Os gringos huyen de lo ejército*'. 'Gringos flee from the army'. A final fuzzy photograph showed military boats in the distance, soldiers standing on the prow with their weapons raised, although it was difficult to make out much detail.

Simon's intuition had rarely let him down in the course of his 15 years as a journalist. It was nagging at him now, making his head hurt as usual. No amount of digging – no contacts made, no official enquiries, no internet searches, phone calls, emails or anything else – had provided any more information on what had happened to the potentially uninteresting and clearly insane expedition to the Amazon. Now, suddenly, two gringos had popped up in the middle of the biggest drugs bust in history, in a poxy frontier town on McCrae's planned route. Simon had never been a big believer in coincidence.

On impulse, he collected up his papers and walked round to the Managing Editor's office. He was prepared for a fight. It was not his job any more to go haring off after stories, but the fact was that he could not send the student, and he had no one else available right now. It would be down to him, and he could feel in his bones that the story was a good one.

The Managing Editor looked through the papers as he listened. He nodded a couple of times and waited until Simon had finished his pitch.

"It could be absolutely nothing, Simon."

Simon nodded. "Yep, it could. But I doubt it. If I'm right, there's human interest, local interest, crime, drugs, guns, blood and guts – you name it, it's all there."

"Hmm. Maybe."

Simon sighed. "Look, even if I'm wrong about these guys, there are still at least a dozen possible emerging stories out of Brazil, Peru and Colombia: the drugs bust itself–"

The editor dismissed this with a wave of his hand.

"Narco-terrorism then. Organised crime, corruption, political meltdown in Brazil, the environment. These are just a few to whet the appetite, right?"

"Hmm, and none of which you are qualified to report on."

"Why not? I've been to Peru before. I spent nearly two years in South America. Have you forgotten I speak Spanish and French, too? And I've worked business and politics. Whatever happens, I won't come back without a story."

The Managing Editor thought for a second, and then nodded. "Okay. If you can find someone to cover you – deal with your reporters – you've got a week. I can't give you any more."

"Perfect," said Simon, almost jumping out of his chair. "You won't regret it."

"Humph," was all Simon heard as he turned and walked briskly through the ever-open door of the big man's office.

49

Carla was already impatient to leave. She had been sneaked into the tiny town of São Paulo de Olivença two days ago, on one of the army's jet boats from Manaus. The 700-mile non-stop trip up the Amazon had taken an extremely boring and uncomfortable day and night, with the unrelenting noise and vibration of the big diesel motor making rest itself a tiring exercise.

The meeting that had taken place on the day of her arrival had been overflowing with high-ranking military officers in civilian clothes. She recognised at least six of them – some retired, some still serving. What they talked about during the discussions was for the most part sensible enough, and Carla certainly understood their frustration with the government. They invited her comments with respect to the possibility of the current regime reforming itself and leading the country out of disaster, and she was happy to state that the majority of the anti-corruption movement felt that there was little hope indeed.

How did she feel about the more militant side of the Movement? About what had happened in Brasilia when this element had got out of control? Did she not feel that the ongoing frustration might lead even more of the Movement to become radical and militant?

She understood their frustration, clearly. She also despaired of the current regime; of the majority of the current crop of politicians. But she certainly did not feel that militancy was likely to be productive. She felt that democratic pressure and eventual legal and political changes brought about through the anger and actions of the electorate were the best way forward.

Yes, she agreed that with things the way they were, there was absolutely no prospect of any economic recovery in sight. She acknowledged that there was a serious risk of the return of hyper-inflation and of vast swathes of the middle and lower middle classes being reduced once more to poverty, their meagre gains over the past years reduced to nothing, and their educational progress stymied.

But did she feel that the Movement would be kindly disposed to an abrupt change in power if this were brought about through a democratic impeachment process?

Well, she felt that there was a considerable groundswell of opinion that this was a viable way forward, yes. She offered no opinion on whether she felt it was appropriate or not.

"I am here simply to represent the Movement," she said to one particularly impertinent enquiry. "My own views are neither here nor there."

The majority around the table clearly felt that her statement was tantamount to support for impeachment of the current President – a man who himself had taken the reigns following the impeachment of his predecessor – and the discussion moved on. Now, as things progressed, the statements seemed to become more guarded, and she noticed a few anxious looks passing when someone began talking about how the change might be effected. It was generally acknowledged by all, however, that the solution – one which they all quite clearly seemed to believe stopped short of dictatorship – was to 'help' the political opposition impeach the current president and then lend all their military weight to a specific candidate in exchange for his or her later "cooperation". By implication, this weight would include the Movement. No one mentioned who the specific candidate might be, and gentle probing failed to evince it, although Carla thought she already knew. In any case, she was more concerned to try to gauge whether they might perhaps be prepared to go further if impeachment proved unsuccessful, and the lack of answers to some of her carefully phrased questions left her with very little doubt about it.

She was, in the end, not sure whether to be more alarmed at the solution being proposed or at the thinking behind it, but she did realise the enormous power these people represented, and was loathe to dismiss it in another fit of the righteous indignation she was wont to indulge in. Instead, she made all the right noises and agreed to carry the message back to her people, which for their part the military clearly also saw as being a key to their potential success. So in the end, everyone danced happily around, and made vaguely positive murmurings until Carla was – very graciously – invited to leave the meeting at a certain point while discussions turned to "other matters".

After a good night's sleep in a private room at the barracks, the next day she had again been politely received by the senior military commander. He told her they felt it was safe enough now to move her to Manaus in a C-105 transport plane returning from Tabatinga on a routine re-supply mission within the next twenty-four hours.

"A little more comfortable than the jet boat," the Commander joked. "Or at least, a lot quicker."

He also explained the decision not to fly her back directly to Brasilia, since they felt her sudden disappearance in Manaus and equally sudden reappearance in Brasilia after so many days would prompt too many questions.

"Instead, we've arranged to leak some information that suggests you had a liaison with a "good friend" who spirited you off for some, er, 'fun', at a jungle lodge near Manaus."

Carla nodded. It was a sensible precaution, although she was keen to get back to Brasilia now, and was disappointed that the promised help to get her there had evaporated. She was also annoyed to be told that the telephone contact with Brasilia that she had been guaranteed was not possible, because of 'technical difficulties' To cap it all, she noticed the predatory gleam in the Commander's eye when he mentioned the word 'fun', and wondered whether he could contain himself long enough for her to get safely out of his office door.

He plied her with a PR pack of all sorts of nonsense, gave her a model of the C-105 transport she was to be smuggled back to Manaus in, and put his hand on her back as he ushered her smoothly towards the door. Prepared for the kiss on the cheeks that might be a prelude to something more, she pulled open the door so that the farewell was in full view of the guards outside, and the Commander finally just held out his hand for a handshake.

That had been yesterday, and although this morning she was up early, showered, dressed, fed and ready to depart by eight o'clock, she was then informed that there had been some complications, and that a local anti-drugs operation had meant the C-105 was currently sitting on the tarmac at Tabatinga with its cargo bay being 're-purposed', whatever that meant.

So she mooched about her room, until she could stand it no longer. Then she went and asked for access to a computer, but was told it would be impossible 'for security reasons'. Finally, in a pique of boredom and frustration, she went for a long walk around the barracks. It was on her walkabout that she learned from several indiscreet comments that the anti-drugs operation had somehow unearthed a gringo spy, and that half the armed forces in Tabatinga had been tasked with finding the suspect. What or who exactly was being spied on, and for whom, no one seemed to know, but she was told in no uncertain terms that the guy was a dangerous, desperate criminal who would stop at nothing to destroy the country.

She dismissed it as part of the Military's inherent paranoia, a legacy from the days of the military dictatorship, when all sorts of appalling schemes were launched to settle and level the whole of the Amazon rainforest. Vast tracts of land had been given to the rich and powerful or their friends – all of them either in the military or with strong military connections – in exchange for vague promises that they would clear the forest thereon. The justification for this had been a concern that the bordering countries of Bolivia, Peru, Venezuela, Colombia and even British and French Guyana could be secretly invading under the very noses of the Brazilians. Encouraged both covertly and openly by the USA, the dictatorship had been quick to seize on communism as a threat against which to unite the people, although the reality was that the ruling elite hated the Americans and despised their own people just as much as they did any potential communists.

In the meantime, military bases were set up throughout the Amazon, in what were considered the most strategic locations, and between the threat from the phantom invading forces directed by the Russians on the one hand and the threat from the phantom invading forces funded by the Americans on the other, the military's tentacles spread quickly throughout the Amazon Basin. Thirty years later, the whole of the north of Brazil was still subject to the vagaries of rich and corrupt civilians, and a macho military with pretensions.

She kicked her heels until lunchtime, her sanity finally saved by finding something to read in the ten-book-and-a-pile-of-porn base library. She was still reading it at three o'clock, when she was told that there was still no confirmation of the time – or day, for that matter – of arrival of the transport plane. She was both anxious and annoyed, since the other military bigwigs that had been there seemed to have been somehow spirited away. She gave up on the book and went to talk the Commander again.

"I really need to be away from here," she explained earnestly. "Is there any other way I can get transport?"

The Commander sighed, and looked put-upon. "I don't know. I suppose if you're desperate–"

"I am."

"Okay, well I guess I could get you quietly onto the regular commercial boat, if you like."

"What about security? Does the boat get stopped often?"

"By the Police, you mean? Not from here, usually, no. You normally only get stop-and-search near Tabatinga and close to Manaus. If you got off somewhere before Manacapuru, you'd be fine. Anyway, I take it you have your own, um – you know, that your papers are...?"

His voiced trailed into nothing, and Carla found it amazing that after hosting a potentially treasonous meeting, the man was pussyfooting around the question of fake IDs. "Of course," she said rather testily.

"Good. Well, give me the name and ID number and I can get you on board, no questions asked. Just turn up tonight and sling your hammock. Okay?"

Carla was not 'okay' with it at all, but it was the best that could be done, and having accepted it, she was more inclined than ever to get off the base and go for a walk. Such was her moral advantage at this point that she easily overcame the Commander's groundless objections, and he gave the relevant authorisation. She was restricted to going down to the river, just over a mile away, and told to avoid the road to the right, which would take her into the town. After being kept waiting another half an hour, she was finally handed a non-descript old mobile phone and told how to contact the base, and was turned loose with strict instructions as to her route and the time to be back.

As she walked around two sides of the base perimeter, she saw all the cameras on which she was no doubt being watched, and the guards in the little towers who would no doubt be following her every step. Try as she might, she could not love her country's military. The meeting had certainly gone well, and there were obvious positives to be taken from it, but as she walked away from the camp, out of its rigorously controlled environment and finally out of view of the cameras and sentries, she felt a huge sense of relief. Of just being free. That was until she turned a corner and found her way barred by one of the officers from yesterday's meeting.

Holy shit, she thought.

He did not waste words, which came a blessed moment before Carla started freaking out.

"I have a message for you from Marcos," he said simply.

"From *who*?" Carla managed, recovering her poise.

"He said to say '*menina certinha*'." Goody two-shoes – the affectionate name Marcos used to give Carla, and which only the two of them would know.

"O-kay..." she said. "So why didn't he contact me himself?"

"Too risky. Phoning through to the base is difficult and their mobile connections hardly work at all."

Carla pulled out the phone she had been handed.

"Ha. You'll not get far with that thing. Have you used it?"

She nodded. She had already tried it twice on the way down from the base before giving it up as a bad job. It was annoying, but no major issue – she did not feel under any real threat here.

"It's also not secure."

"Not secure?"

"Not from the people who gave it to you," he explained.

"Ah." Carla nodded.

"I have my own system." He pulled a phone out of his pocket and waggled it. "Take a walk with me?" He asked, standing to the side and gesturing with his hand.

She shrugged. "Sure. I was going that way anyway."

By the time they reached the riverside, and the officer had said goodbye, she was not sure whether to laugh or cry. The idea of Marcos having an insider at the military's meeting, and not telling her, was annoying enough. The fact that she had suddenly been given a time, a date, a rather bizarre place, and a mission to aid and abet terrorists in the middle of the jungle, almost beggared belief.

Carla was the one person in the Movement who consistently

rejected militancy in all its nefarious forms. It was she who had kept the group from being overrun with radicals with only their own interests at heart. It was, in fact, the one thing that stood between Marcos and herself as co-founders of their organisation: Marcos' belief that the ends justify the means, versus Carla's guiding principle of never doing evil that good might come of it.

She found a place to sit by the riverbank and contemplate the swirling Amazon. She could always decline, of course. On the other hand, she was sure Marcos would not ask something like this of her if it was not important. Huh – important, certainly, but morally acceptable? Ends justifying means?

"What are you doing to me, Marcos?" she said aloud.

The big question was, how much did she trust Marcos not to ask her to compromise her own ideals? She went back over the years they had known each other and the decisions they had made together. They had, on occasion, fought each other to a standstill on some points, but they somehow had managed to fit all the pieces together in the end. To her knowledge, never once had he lied to her.

She sighed and nodded slowly. He was, when all was said and done, an honourable man. Besides, she knew he thought her attitude was sometimes too unbending, and her need for order too overwhelming. Perhaps on this one occasion, she would play the hand and see what happened.

Okay Marcos, I'll buy it. You got me.

She got to her feet and started on the long walk back to the army base. She had no doubts about being able to bluff the Commandant. She would just go back and say she had thought it over and would wait for an available plane – and hope the damned plane did not turn up until after she had made contact with this Lopez woman.

50

It was a long night. Hyped though Elena was, the blood she had lost from her wound made her feel weak, tired and nauseous. For food, she had to be content with mouthfuls of farine and some goats' cheese, washed down with warm juice and water. She had difficulty concentrating in the dark, and more than once she ran the boat aground because she was sticking too close to the riverbank. She also had to make several long detours across the river to avoid lights that looked like they might be patrols.

By the time dawn came, she was exhausted. She did not have Jack's navigation skills on the river, and had never seen a map of the area. She had been told São Paulo de Olivença was two hundred kilometres downstream of Tabatinga, and, unless she could find Jack, that was where she was headed. She was not sure how far she had come, and had no idea what lay ahead. She passed a few small communities on the south bank, but was sure Jack would want to put as much distance as possible between himself and Tabatinga, so she carried on.

There were huge islands in the middle of the river, and she was sure she had gone the long way round them a few times. She would have to stop somewhere, if not to rest, then at least to avoid any patrols. In the end, her rest stop chose her, rather than vice versa.

She was approaching what looked like another island, with the main channel to the left and a much narrower one to the right, when she saw across the river, swarming upstream at a great rate, a group of three military craft. She did the only thing she could and dived for the small channel immediately, hoping they had not spotted her. She opened the throttle and sped as fast as possible down the winding channel, tensing against the sound of big motors or helicopters chasing her down. The channel seemed to go on forever, but eventually, as she rounded a bend, she saw a string of wooden houses perched precariously along the banks. Beside one of them was a tiny stream, and without thinking too much about it, she aimed the boat straight at it. She stopped the engine as soon as she entered it, and raised the propeller clear of the water, allowing the boat to grind into the mud. She leapt out, ran up the little bank, and found herself in the yard of a small house surrounded by grubby children playing among the chickens. Several dogs came bounding over to her, one of them clearly prepared to defend the house. At the same time, a tall, thin man emerged from the house with a shotgun. In spite of the danger, Elena was more concerned about the military, and could not resist looking back up the river. When she turned round again, she saw the man looking the same way. He looked back at her, then lowered his gun and beckoned her forward.

"*Passa, Oscar!*" he called, and the menacing-looking dog sat down, allowing her to edge past.

"Who are you running from?" the man asked, once they were inside, with the door closed. He was an old man, and his skin was lined so much it looked like crinkled, brown wrapping paper. He still had a full head of grey hair, cut short. He was dressed only in a pair of threadbare shorts.

Although her Portuguese was perfectly serviceable, Elena said nothing.

The man shrugged. "It doesn't matter. You can shelter here for a few hours."

"Thanks," Elena said.

"I'm afraid I have nothing to offer except some fish and *farinha,* but I'm going across to Belém do Solimões later for some provisions."

"Oh, there's a town?" Elena asked. "How far is it? What size is it? Are there any, er..." her voiced trailed off.

"Police?" the man prompted.

Elena flashed an angry look at him. "I was going to say 'facilities'."

"*Desculpe, querida.*" He said. Sorry dear.

"It's okay," Elena said quietly. "No problem." She was too tired to do her strong-and-ruthless-terrorist act, and she had a good idea this man would take no notice anyway.

"You can see the river for quite a long way from the window," the man said. "Sit here, and I'll make coffee."

She sat on a rickety stool and gazed back upriver. So far, nothing had come after her. The old man put a pan on a rusty gas cooker and added some water, coffee powder and a lot of sugar.

"You can rest in here," he said, pointing to a fairly dust-free corner of the room. I'm going fishing now, but I'll be back before–"

He was interrupted by the playful screams and whoops of the children outside.

"Before nightfall," he continued. "I'll tell the children to go play somewhere else – they're not mine, you know." He seemed to find the idea amusing, and his face creased into a broad grin. "I can take you across to the town when I come back."

Elena's concern showed through.

"You can trust me, dear. Your life is your own. I've no interest in selling anyone out. If you don't want to stay, that's okay too."

He smiled again. "But at least have a coffee."

By the time he had finished making the coffee, Elena was almost asleep. Her head rested on her arms, which were folded on top of the little window sill.

"Here you are," the man said, handing her a coffee.

"Thanks," she said. "I'll stay, if that's okay. I don't think I'll be moving out until dark."

"Fine. We can go across to the town together. It's only twenty minutes upstream. I'll be staying there the night. I'll tell them you're my niece or something. They'll believe whatever I tell them. Then you can do whatever it is you need to do and disappear, okay?"

Elena nodded and drank her coffee. It had so much sugar in it you could stand a spoon in it, but it tasted good. She smiled wanly at the man, and looked round.

"If you want to sleep now, go ahead," the man said. "I'll wake you when I return." He stood up, reached up to a shelf, and pulled down a roll of cloth. "Pillow," he said, handing it to her.

Five minutes later, she had abandoned her usual caution and mistrust, and was fast asleep on the floor.

51

It was just before dusk when Elena and her host left the rickety wooden house. The old man carried a white rice sack down to the boats and placed it carefully in his little canoe.

"Fish," he said.

There was no motor on the canoe, so he simply clamped his hand onto the side of Elena's aluminium boat as she followed the meandering channel.

"How do you manage without a motor?" Elena asked him, seeing that the current here was quite fast.

He smiled. "I get a lift there. It's easier coming back."

Stupid question.

Within ten minutes they were on the main river, and the old man pointed downstream.

"The navy and the Feds will be at the other end of the island," he said, matter-of-factly.

Once they cleared the island, she could see the lights of the town on the other side of the river, maybe a mile away. The last vestiges of daylight showed that there were no patrols on the river at this point.

They made their way across sedately, and by the time they had tied up to one of the tall poles sticking up out of the muddy banks, the only light came from the bare incandescent bulbs strung along a small platform that clearly acted as the community's port.

"Wait here for a couple of minutes," the old man said, "then bring up that sack and walk up the path to the first building you come to."

Elena looked amused. "Beast of burden, huh?"

The man nodded. "You are my niece. I am an old man."

She duly waited, and when she thought enough time had passed, she hefted the rice sack full of fish onto her shoulder and struggled up the slippery path.

When she emerged at the top of the bank, she stepped onto a

crudely built road that stretched into the distance, and along the north border of which were the grubby façades of a straggly row of wooden houses.

The village was larger and busier than she had imagined, with lots of people walking about, and dozens of children laughing and screaming. She saw the old man talking to someone at a large wooden building that looked like some sort of store, and he beckoned her over.

"Francisca," he said. "This is my great friend Paulo."

She walked over and bobbed her head, unsmilingly. It was the same demonstration of deference she was used to in indigenous villages throughout Peru, and she figured it would serve just as well in Brazil. The man Paulo looked her up and down as if inspecting a horse.

"Welcome to the town, dear," he said. "Put the fish over there by the door."

As she obliged, she listened to the rest of the conversation.

"My friend," the old man said, "I'd like to stay the night, if you don't mind. Do you have a room?"

"For you both?"

The old man nodded.

"Sure. You can use the cabin behind the usual place. There are two beds there," said Paulo.

"A big thank you, my friend," said the old man. He beckoned to Elena to follow, as he turned and began walking along the road.

"Coming for dominoes later?" Paulo called after them.

"Sure, if you don't mind losing all your money again."

Both men laughed, and Elena walked behind the old man as he led the way through the village.

The cabin door was closed but not locked, and inside they found a neatly swept earthen floor, a small sink with some shelves next to it, and two beds. The toilet would be outside, of course. There was a candle on one of the shelves and the man lit it with some matches before he closed the door.

He smiled at her. "What time do you want to leave? Do you need any provisions?"

Elena shrugged. "As soon as possible, I think. And I don't need anything really, apart from some water and farinha. Unless anyone has any coca, of course."

The man gave her a sharp look, but then he seemed to think of something, and his expression softened. "You mean leaf, of course."

Elena nodded.

"Don't even mention it around here. This is an Indian community. It's already been ravaged by alcohol and drugs, and the police and the *Cacique* are trying to stamp it out completely."

She recognised the Indian word for the leader of the community. "Oh sorry – I didn't know."

"There is also a type of monastery here – monks from some church or other, trying to convert the Indians and make them good, god-fearing members of society."

The sarcasm in his voice was obvious.

"You don't approve," Elena said, matter-of-factly.

"My dear, I've lived around here for nearly seventy years. I've never seen much good come out of a Christian yet. It's even worse when they get together in groups." He suddenly laughed. "You know, the Indians believe the monks have some great magic that stops them being attacked by jaguars and caiman. I think they probably just smell bad and taste worse."

Elena laughed too. She thought of her own experiences with indigenous communities in Peru. Maybe some things were the same all over the world.

"Anyway, I suggest you come down to the bar with me–"

"Bar?" Elena interrupted. "I thought, um, you know..."

"Oh sure. Alcohol's prohibited, but only when the Police or the monks are around. The monks are away on some religious crusade somewhere, and the Police have gone to Tabatinga for some reason."

Elena was pretty sure she knew the reason, but looked blankly at the old man.

"And the Cacique?"

"Hmm. Well, let's just say that he's a 'practical' man."

"Ah."

An hour later, they were back at the store. A large shutter had been opened at the front, and a few tables had been set out. Paulo and a group of other men were already playing dominoes very noisily, while some of the women-folk stood around looking on. There was a bottle of cachaça on each table, and lots of small shot glasses. The air was thick with cigarette smoke.

Elena huddled together with the other girls and women, listening to their gossip and nodding and being as pleasant as she could. She was careful not to say too much, hoping to reduce the number of questions about where she was from. The old man asked for water and farinha, and ordered Elena to take it back to the cabin, and she took a long detour to go down to store it in the boat. She took care to place money for it in the cabin, leaving enough to thank the guy for his help.

She was tempted to leave right then, but she felt she owed the old man a final thank-you, so she returned to the store, where she was surprised to find that nearly everyone had left. The old man was concentrating on his tiles, and Paulo, seeing the enquiring look on her face, explained that everyone had gone to play – or watch – football. He suggested she might like to go too, but she simply smiled, shook her head, and went and sat in an empty hammock that was slung near the door. She just wanted to catch the old man's eye for a second, and then she would slip away to the boat. Unfortunately, he was still concentrating on his dominoes, his cachaça, and on exchanging some banter about local events, and she was unable to attract his attention.

Ten minutes later, she was ready to give up and sneak away, when something in the conversation caught her attention.

"...forbidden to talk about the new stranger," Paulo was saying.

"Oh? But why?"

"No idea. He just walked out of the jungle, apparently. Looked in pretty bad shape. There were only a few women around, and when they couldn't understand a word he was saying, they figured he was a new monk. They led him to the monastery, and he's not emerged since.

"So he's a gringo, then," the old man said, finally glancing across at Elena.

"Yes. Anyway, the Cacique went to see him, and he has official approval. But we're to leave him alone and not talk about him at all."

"Strange."

"Yes. I reckon old Manoel has taken leave of his senses. He always did drink too much *yagé*."

Both men laughed, although the old man gave Elena an odd look, and then winked at her.

"Can we go see him? Try to talk to him at least? You said he's up in the monastery building? I've never even been there. You wouldn't catch me anywhere near those buffoons."

"I know what you mean, but they're not so bad, some of them."

"Hmm. I don't know, Paulo, I really don't." He banged a domino down on the table.

There was silence for a few seconds while both men studied their tiles.

"It's up there, isn't it?" The old man asked, with apparent disinterest.

"Huh? Yes," said Paulo distractedly. "A ten-minute walk, straight up the road from your cabin. But we might as well wait for Father Jonathan and the rest of them to return. They'll be back on the boat from Tabatinga tomorrow lunchtime."

The old man looked over towards Elena, just in time to see her slip into the shadows behind the store.

52

"**N**o Ma'am," the lieutenant responded to Ferreira's question. "Nothing. He's fish food by now, Ma'am."

"Hmm. Show me again on the map all the areas you checked."

The man loaded a detailed satellite map on the screen.

"This is from yesterday. You can see where the levels are already changing quite quickly." He pointed with his pen. "The areas marked in red are where we concentrated our search for the body. These are the areas where sediment – and anything else – is normally deposited. We went all the way up to here." He pointed again, this time to a tight bend in the river. "That's over eighty kilometres, and it's the first horseshoe bend. Our people say it's almost impossible for anything that heavy to get any further – or even that far, Ma'am."

"No clothes? No belongings? No sightings? No gossip? After three full days?"

"No Ma'am."

Ferreira shook her head. "We cannot assume he's dead. Extend the alerts down to Tefé. Tell them the guy is alive, armed and dangerous. A matter of national security." She waited for the lieutenant to finish noting down her request. "And get me the military base on the secure line, will you?"

"Yes Ma'am."

She walked in to her office, sat down, and waited for the secure phone to ring. She looked out at the Police barracks and the town beyond. Here she was again, devoting all the division's resources to making sure the well-oiled wheels of underworld trade carried on rolling. Last month it was riding shotgun on a huge drugs consignment; last week it was faking a drugs bust; this week she was supposed to eliminate some poor innocent who knew a bit too much about something or other. What would it be next week? The truth was that most of the criminals and police in the border countries were part of the same team, and fuck everyone else. She was one of them, and she was not proud of it. It was just a question of survival. She was starkly conscious of the fact that her drive and determination – and her skill and ruthlessness – had got her and her whole family out of the mud and put them in good houses in decent places. Her husband had left her eight years ago, but she had not given up nor given in. Their daughter was studying law in São Paulo, and their son was travelling around Europe, all through her efforts. Her parents and her sister lived very comfortably together in the most expensive condominium in Manaus, and various other family members were doing very well thank you. Márcia herself had two apartments fully paid for in the States, and the money left over was squirreled away in bank accounts abroad. Not exactly a fortune, but a very tidy sum indeed. And the bottom line was that no damned gringo was going to spoil it now. The phone rang and she snatched it up.

"Good morning, sir," she said straight away. "I'm calling about operation Jacaré."

She listened for a few seconds. "I know sir, but this is considered a real threat, and we need assistance from all parties."

She nodded vaguely a few times.

"Yes. Our American friends are still in the country. Our authorisation gives them a week – renewable – and a lot of leeway to act as they see fit to protect our joint interests. We also have a search under way, and I must advise that so far nothing has turned up."

She listened for another few moments.

"That's very much appreciated Sir. We've been concentrating our resources in a one hundred kilometre radius of Tabatinga, but joint ops could help by casting a net further downstream."

She paused again, listening.

"No sir. No dirty work necessary – just let us know, and we'll clean everything up."

She fiddled with the papers on her desk.

"Yes sir. As you say: between the hammer and the anvil. No doubt between us we will have everything resolved within the next day or two."

She stood up as if she were about to salute.

"Yes. Thank you sir. Goodbye."

She hung up and turned to look outside again. She could just see her own modest house perched on the hill behind the barracks, and she thought about her beautiful Atlanta apartment – her favourite, and the place she hoped to retire to one day.

No one was going to spoil all that she had worked so hard for. But she had to admit she was weary of the whole thing. Maybe when this operation was all over it would be time to slip away and start enjoying herself. Life was too short for much more of this crap.

She got up and walked out to the main office.

"I'm going out for a while. I'll be back by ten thirty," she announced.

"Yes Ma'am," said the duty officer.

Outside, she got into her inconspicuous grey car and drove off the base, bumping along the potholed roads until she found a little stall along the side of the road. She stopped, wound down the window and called out *"Tem celular, amigo?"*

The man rummaged around in his little stall and held up two mobile phones.

"Dá quanto?" asked Ferreira.

"Cem a cada." A hundred each.

"Ha! Nem sonhando, cara. Cem pros dois." She could get them for half that in the town centre.

The guy shook his head unconvincingly, and she knew she had a deal.

"E me dá cinco chips de vinte," said Ferreira, with an air that assumed everything was agreed.

The man pulled out the chips and plodded across to the car.

Ferreira handed over the cash, took the phones, and drove quickly away without saying any more. She drove round the block, stopped to put everything in a briefcase, and made her way to her house.

Inside, she hunted out the right charger for one of the phones and called the operator to register her chip with a false ID. With this done, she left the phone to charge and blended herself a juice with fresh pineapple and banana. She stood drinking it by the kitchen window, which looked over her barbed-wire topped wall down to the river to the south. From afar, it looked idyllic, with the sunlight bouncing off the little tin roofs and the river sparkling as it sped east towards the Atlantic. But Ferreira saw only squalor, graft, disease and death.

After fifteen minutes of charge, she checked the phone's battery level, disconnected it, and returned to her car. She drove to the north of the town, crossed the border into Colombia, and stopped, checking to see which service the phone was connected to. Then she sent her text message. She hung up and waited, and five minutes later her phone rang.

"Hi," came the voice of Adam Torres.

"*Buenos dias,*" Ferreira responded.

"*Notícias?*" Torres asked, switching smoothly to Portuguese.

"Nothing. You?"

"Nothing. I have to assume he is still alive."

"I have my people checking up and down from Tabatinga to Tefé. I'm told your people have arrived in Manaus."

"Yes. They can coordinate better from there."

"Good. The army have promised help, and I will be going to Manaus tomorrow. I've also asked for help from friends in Brazilian Intelligence. They will contact your people soon."

"Thanks, although I'm sure–"

"Just do me a favour and take the offer, Adam," Ferreira interrupted, raising her eyes to the ceiling.

There was a pause and then "Okay, Márcia. Just as long as they don't get in my way."

"They won't. Anyway, we'll need all the help we can get if the guy manages to get as far as Manaus."

"Fine. As you wish."

There was petulant quality creeping into Torres' voice that Ferreira found worrying.

"You know," she began slowly, "that if he's not picked up by the time he gets to Manaus, our problem gets bigger by a factor of about a million, don't you?"

"Márcia, whatever happens, I'll get him."

"Well someone will have to get him, certainly, Adam. For your sake, I really hope it's you."

53

Jack had been poring over a small-scale map of the state of Amazonas which he had found pinned to the wall of the incongruously large, well-equipped house. Now he sat back on his stool, resting his head on the wall behind, and looked up at the high ceiling and the single bulb that cast a feeble yellow light around the room. He had discovered that the building was laid out with eight bedrooms, all clearly in use, although the place was deserted at the moment. There were two larger rooms with tables and plastic chairs, and a huge kitchen/dining area with three gas cookers and two gas fridges. It had running water and a feeble twelve-volt electricity supply that fed the bulb he was staring at now. Leather-bound bibles with the title 'New American' were piled in various places. He also found a storage area housing tools, supplies and equipment, but which was lacking the one thing he needed most: petrol. He searched everywhere, but apart from a chainsaw with a thimble-full of the stuff in the bottom of the tank, there was not a drop to be found.

Appealing though the relative comfort of the house was, Jack could not afford to be stuck here for several days. When he had first spotted the village, his only thought was of fuel. He left the boat upstream and approached on foot through the forest, but his attempt at stealth had been made a nonsense of by a group of women and children bathing at a stream that bordered the settlement. Fortunately, they did not seem put out by his appearance. He had left behind the rifles he had collected, and his pistol was concealed in his waistband. Besides, the women were a lot more interested in his hair and eye colour than in where he had come from or what he was doing.

He could hardly understand a word any of them said, and was puzzled to be led to the house, shown where he could have a shower, and then left quite alone. Puzzled he may have been, but he was not going to look the gift horse in the mouth. The first thing he did was open a fridge and get stuck into as much cold food and drink as he could manage. Then he took a shower and attended to the most battered bits of his body. He even found a pair of scissors and a razor and got rid of his beard. He worked rapidly at everything, pistol close to hand, his mind working overtime on some sort of plan. He was so lost in thought that he was caught completely unawares when he emerged from the shower to find an old man standing in the door of the bathroom. They looked at each other, and both of them glanced down at the chair that stood between them, where a dirty black Beretta lay on top of Jack's meagre pile of clothes.

The man ignored it, and launched into a language Jack did not recognise, as Jack hurriedly towelled himself and put his clothes back on. He decided to leave the pistol on the chair for the moment. Suddenly the old man switched to Spanish, and, like changing the language on a TV channel, Jack found he could suddenly understand a good part of what was being said. He smiled and nodded, to indicate that he was following what he was being told, and the old man seemed satisfied. He continued to stand in the doorway, however, clutching an ornate sort of thin club, and finished his piece in slow, formal Spanish. When he had done, he looked at Jack and said *entiendes?*

Jack nodded. Yes, he understood. He was welcome in the community provided he respected their customs, and there would be a meeting tomorrow that he was expected to attend. There had not been the slightest hint of emotion in the words or in the man's face, and no mention of the house Jack was staying in, nor of the pistol.

The man bowed slightly, and turned to leave.

"Er, excuse me, but can I buy some gasoline?" Jack blurted out to the man's retreating back.

"No. No gasoline until next week."

"Sorry?" Jack thought maybe he had misheard.

"Until the boat comes next week, we have no gasoline."

Jack watched the old man walk stiffly away. Perfect. A whole community without a drop of gasoline. Maybe that was why the bible owners had run off.

That was three hours ago. Now he turned his attention back to the map. He could see that the next town of any size downstream from here was 30 miles away, which he calculated he could cover with eight hours paddling through the night. He had already packed a bag, taking food and drink from the fridges. He had also found some cheap-looking but serviceable clothes, a pair of training shoes, and a large straw hat that with the slightest tilt of his head hid most of face. He sighed, folded up the map, and placed it in his bag. Then he put down some of the Peruvian money he and Elena had split. He lifted the bag to his shoulder, took a quick look around, and left the house by the kitchen door. As he descended the steps to the ground, and reached the relative darkness of the moonlit night, he thought he heard a noise back at the house. A creak – maybe a step – on the wooden veranda? No matter – in a couple of seconds he would be engulfed by the trees and lost to anyone behind him. He strode on, quickly but quietly.

"*Alto!*" A woman's voice.

Too late now. I'm out of here, thought Jack as he made a dash for the tree line.

"*Pare!*" The voice repeated.

Something clutched at Jack's stomach. The voice. He knew that voice. *Her* voice. *Elena? Here?* Impossible.

"Stop!"

His heart was suddenly in his mouth and he turned and started running back. His eyes were stinging, his throat was dry, and his head pounded.

"Jack?"

"Elena!" The word escaped his lips in a breathless cry as he exploded through the forest margin and saw her standing at the foot of the steps.

She stood rooted to the spot for a second, and then rushed towards him. He scooped her into his arms and held her as if the sun and the moon would surely fall from the skies if he let go. They kissed, and he picked her up and carried her to the house and up the steps.

"How did you...?" she began.

He just nodded. "And you...?" He could not trust his cracking voice to say any more.

Tears streamed from Elena's eyes, and suddenly all Jack wanted to do was smother her in kisses.

Explanations would have to wait.

54

After hurrying to organise their boat and equipment, Jack and Elena had been on the river all night. Not only did they have the spectre of the army on their tail, but Elena's first rendezvous was scheduled for eight o'clock that morning in São Paulo de Olivença, just over a hundred kilometres downstream. The instructions had been clear and simple: the contact would be at the appointed place at eight o'clock in the morning for two days in succession. If Elena could not make it by the second day, she would be on her own.

"So tell me more about who we're meeting," Jack said, as they groped their way carefully along in the dark. They had slipped easily past the patrol boats to the east of the village, and made good time until they came to a stretch of river that was so thick with floating weed and grass they had switched off the boat's engine. The only sound now was the slurp of their paddles and a few distant splashes along the river bank.

"The contact? I don't know her," said Elena.

"Her?" said Jack, somehow surprised.

"Yes. She's an associate of someone – of a Brazilian friend – I used to know. They're part of a Brazilian protest movement.

"What, another terror– er, *underground* organisation?"

"No," Elena said, with some exasperation in her voice. "It is not the same at all. This is the famous Brazilian anti-corruption movement, the GCC.

"Ah yes," Jack said, "the famous GCC..."

Elena tutted. "Well, I didn't expect an ignorant gringo to know about it, but it's famous in South America."

Jack smiled. "Okay, I believe you."

"*Bueno.* He and some others created the movement a few years ago, and now it's very big. When I knew him, he was involved with

Sendero and some other organisations in Peru and Colombia. At the time, many of us were thinking that maybe we could join forces. Become an international organisation."

Jack thought for a few moments. "I can see the appeal of that. What happened?"

"Oh, a lot of arguing and fighting. No-one could agree on how to organise things. My friend lost interest and went off to concentrate on Brazil. I haven't seen him for five years or more."

"And you trust him."

"Implicitly."

"And this woman – the contact?"

Jack could just about see Elena nodding, up in front. "If he sent her, I trust her," she said in a tone that invited no further comment.

Jack sensed there was more to this story than Elena was telling him, but he decided not to pursue it. They were going to need all the help they could get if they were to carry out his nascent plan.

He had studied the map and decided that if they could make it to the major city of Manaus, with access to phone and internet, it would be all he would need to start unravelling what was going on and get the word out. Manaus was also a physical gateway out of the nightmare, since the city had a road link to Venezuela and Guyana to the north, as well as international river and air services. But it was a hell of a long way, and they would need somewhere to hide, as well as transport and supplies. Hopefully the person they were going to meet would provide some or all of this.

The sky was lightening in the east now, and a sizeable community was just coming into view, spread along the south banks – their destination, Jack felt sure. Unfortunately, there was also a small flotilla of vessels heading towards them, and even from this distance, it was clear they were military. Jack scrambled to start the engine and turn their boat around, and they ran back upstream, dodging the weed, until Elena spotted a narrow entrance on the other side of the river. They raced across and pushed into the stream as far as they could, hopping out and pulling the craft up the banks, then covering it with anything that came to hand.

It took another five minutes for the ships to pass. The largest one of the three had a helicopter perched on the back of it, like some giant insect, while the other two were more like over-grown patrol boats.

Between them, they could easily cover the whole river from one side to the other, and if the chopper had been in the air as well, he and Elena would have stood little chance of evading detection. As it was, they simply waited another fifteen minutes and then nosed carefully back onto the river to continue their journey. There was little traffic now, except for a handful of fishing boats.

Elena was to look for a blue floating house along the waterfront, and stop two hundred metres upstream of the house, by a large fallen tree. As the early dawn colours fused to a more homogeneous yellow daylight, the predominant reds and whites of the ramshackle waterfront housing came into focus, but one place in particular stood out.

"It has to be that one, right?" said Jack, pointing to a large, ramshackle, floating house painted a garish light blue. It was the last house upstream of the town, and they could clearly see a huge fallen tree between them and the house.

He opened the throttle and they headed directly towards the tree, searching the banks for some sort of reception. Jack was disappointed when they found there was no-one to meet them, but he knew it was an irrational response – they were at least an hour early, after all.

The river bank was a sheer drop of more than twelve feet, and after securing the boat to the bleached-white branches of the fallen tree, they climbed out onto the enormous trunk and made their way carefully up onto dry land. They brought their pistols and their food and water out of the boat. After scouting the area and finding a track that must surely lead to the town, they positioned themselves further downstream and well out of sight, and settled down to wait.

55

Jack yawned. "I don't know about you, but I could use some coca leaves about now." They had been waiting for the best part of an hour, and the warm sun and the sound of the river pushing past was having a soporific effect.

Elena smiled. "I don't think it is common in Brazil," she said. "In fact it's not even that common in Iquitos. It only grows high up."

Jack nodded. "Yes. More's the pity."

"*O que?*"

"I said 'more's the pity'."

"What does it mean?"

"It means–" The faint sounds of footsteps in the distance interrupted him, and they both turned their heads towards the source, while Jack reached back and snatched his pistol from its hiding place.

A woman came into view on the narrow path. Jack and Elena had positioned themselves so they could see well down the track, and it soon became clear that the woman was alone. She walked slowly, passing Jack and Elena in their hiding place, and finally stopped by the fallen tree, peering down towards the boat. Then she looked around carefully, and called out in Portuguese.

"*Elena? Marcos mandou uma mensagem,*" The Portuguese pronunciation was strange to Jack's ears, although he thought he knew what she was saying.

Elena looked at him and held her finger to her lips.

"*Todos nascem iguais,*" the woman called. She waited a few seconds and repeated her message in Spanish. "*Todos nacem iguales.*" All are born equal.

A slight smile had formed on Elena's lips, but she waited until the woman had repeated the expression once more before she levered herself up and stepped onto the path. Jack followed her, concealing his pistol in the waistband at the small of his back.

"*Mas algunos son mas iguales que outros*," Elena said, and the woman spun round, the expression on her face flitting first from anxiety to relief, and finally to suspicion, as she considered Jack.

"Elena? Marcos said it would be just one person," the woman said.

Jack raised his hands palms out, to try to show he was no threat.

"Carla?" said Elena.

The woman nodded.

"This is Jack McCrae," Elena said in Portuguese. Then she asked if they could speak in Spanish, so Jack could understand.

"Sure, why not," said Carla, "but someone had better tell me what the hell is going on."

Carla led them along the path and down to the blue floating house. When they got inside, they found it equipped with nothing more than a couple of stools.

"It's not pretty, but it is safe," Carla explained. "It belongs to another contact here."

"*Another* contact? Just how many people know about us?" asked Jack, with a look of concern.

"Well at the moment I'm the only one who knows about *you*. As far as I was concerned I was asked to help one person – a terrorist-turned-political refugee – named Elena Lopez."

Elena raised her eyes at the word terrorist, but remained silent.

"I see," said Jack. "Well, if you don't feel you can help–"

"I didn't say that," Carla snapped. She paused, a look of anger flaring briefly before she checked it and sighed. "Okay, so who *are* you, then...?" She folded her arms and stared at him. "Where are you from, and what are you doing here, mixed up with a terrorist–"

"*Jesús*," Elena interrupted. "Look, Carla – or whatever your real name is – I'm not a damned terrorist, okay?"

The two women regarded each other with narrowing eyes, until Jack broke the spell by clearing his throat loudly. "Right, er, Carla, if you really want to know..."

Carla nodded.

"It's a long story."

"Take your time," said Carla. "We're quite safe here for the moment."

Over the next half hour, Jack went through the whole story in his halting Spanish, until in the end they were left with the same questions he and Elena had been puzzling over since escaping from the site.

"So it's drugs, isn't it? It has to be, right?" said Carla.

"It seems that way," agreed Jack, "although it must be on a massive scale – I mean, with the Sendero, the Peruvian Army, the Brazilians and the Americans all working together. State-sponsored drugs running?"

"It doesn't surprise me at all," said Carla. "And it doesn't surprise me that Brascons is in it up to its neck, too," she added, referring to the company logo that Jack told her he had seen at the site.

"Oh? You know it?" asked Jack.

"Certainly. It's a huge Brazilian construction group," Carla explained. "It's all over South America and beyond. It was implicated in the corruption scandal that brought down the Brazilian president, and it's one of the companies we've been going after for the last two years.

Elena blinked. "Really? I'd never even heard of it."

"Probably because they use a lot of different names in different countries. But it's all the same business – the holding company for all their high-value contracts is registered in Panama. It could be behind the whole thing."

Jack shook his head. "I don't believe it," he said. "This is on a scale bigger than any single company. Think of the organisation and planning required, not to mention the complexity of the logistics. Then you have the problem of keeping it all quiet – paying off terrorists, the military, entire governments. No company's *that* big."

"Microsoft? Google?" Elena challenged.

Jack nodded thoughtfully. "Okay, so maybe it's possible in theory. But think about it – if the company were behind it all, and trying to keep it secret, it wouldn't have its employees running around with company logos, would it?"

"I suppose not," said Carla.

"So it's probably just a contractor, innocent or not."

"Not," said Carla.

Elena nodded. "Yes. They're probably just making so much money out of it all that they don't care what it's all about."

"But I bet they know," said Carla.

"For sure."

Jack groaned. "Which brings us back to the fact that we *don't* know." He massaged his temples. "All we have is a notion that three or more countries are working together to manufacture and distribute drugs. But why this enormous construction site? And the other sites marked on the map? Construction on a massive scale, but for what, exactly?"

"Drugs factories," Carla suggested.

"No. The works are far too big," said Jack. "Besides, what are all the connecting lines for?"

"Bringing electricity in," Elena said.

"I thought about that, but why go to all that trouble, when you can build generators – or even whole power plants – on site?" said Jack.

Elena thought for a few seconds. "Power plants are noisy, and pollute the environment."

Carla sniggered. "You think these people care about that?"

"Possibly," said Elena. "They would if they were trying to keep things quiet. If you start building power plants everywhere, the noise and smoke will soon have people talking."

"Yes," mused Jack, "But laying hundreds or thousands of kilometres of power lines everywhere is hardly low profile, is it? Not only that, but surely these sites are big enough to be seen from space. I mean, satellite imagery can soon spot a large construction site. So much for keeping a low profile."

"Well, when you think about it, who needs to keep things quiet anyway?" said Elena. "Peru has been planning to build dams all along the Huallaga and the Ucayali." She shrugged. "Maybe that's all they are – dams being built by Brascons or a sister company. All quite legal, and no-one would be concerned except for the environmentalists – and no-one takes them seriously in Peru."

Jack shook his head. "No. I thought of that, but all the sites are high up in the mountains – well above the level of any of the main rivers."

The three of them sat in silence for a few moments, before Carla spoke.

"So, from what you say, the only way to find out more is to get to Manaus and civilisation, right?" she said.

Jack and Elena nodded.

"Right. I'd better go and organise that. I'm afraid you'll need to be patient for a few more hours, and wait until dark. Will you be okay? Do you have anything to eat?"

"We have some supplies," said Elena. "We'll get by."

"Good. I'm going to see what sort of transport I can arrange. I probably won't be back until it's time to go – maybe late tonight. I can't come any earlier without arousing suspicion."

"That's fine Carla. We'll eat and rest," said Jack.

Carla nodded. She turned and walked to the door, cracking it open and taking time to look carefully outside before slipping out and leaving Jack and Elena alone.

It was almost midnight when Jack followed the two women up the alarmingly springy passenger boarding ramp of the Coração Sagrado VII. No-one challenged them, or even paid them much attention in the clothes Carla had brought for them. Jack wore a pair of cheap long trousers to cover his still-white legs, and a black T-shirt. He also had on his large straw hat. He had removed his blond stubble, and the skin on his face, arms and hands had long been burnt and darkened by the tropical elements. Both women believed he could pass as Brazilian on a brief glance at night. Carla and Elena were dressed in poorly fitting jeans and unflatteringly baggy t-shirts, although they still could not avoid receiving a few lecherous looks on the way down the street.

"We've got a *camarote*," Carla announced, as she stopped by a cabin and unlocked the door. "It's in someone else's name, paid for by my colleagues. The captain and crew don't really care who's in it, as long as it's paid for." She reached in and switched on the light, which flickered to the rhythm of the boat's diesel engine, throbbing away far below them.

"Wow. A real bed," said Jack, seeing two double bunks inside, with thin, evil-looking mattresses lurking on them. In between the two sets, was a space just large enough for an adult to squeeze into, and there was a dirty-looking air-conditioner jammed into one wall, with the front of the casing missing. "Air-con, too," Jack exclaimed. "Bloody hell."

"Hmm. Sort of," agreed Carla. She threw her bag onto one of the bunks. "There should also be a bathroom a couple of doors up. I'll fetch the food, so that we can eat in here, and we won't have to leave the cabin much until we get to Anamã – two days downstream. I've been guaranteed there'll be no police or military interest in the boat up to that point."

"Guaranteed?" said Elena, with a note of suspicion.

Carla nodded. "Guaranteed," she confirmed, and then saw the look of scepticism on their faces. "Look, you'll just have to trust me, okay?"

Jack had a dirty, unimpressive hold-all that Carla had provided, into which he and Elena had bundled some clothes and toiletries. They had also quietly added their weapons, deciding against mentioning these to Carla, and this had fleetingly raised the question of whether or not they should just ditch the things altogether. Jack thought about it for all of three seconds and announced that actually there was no fucking way he was going anywhere without his pistol, to which Elena responded that in this case there was no fucking way she was going anywhere without hers.

As he placed the bag on one of the bunks, a sudden increase in noise and vibration from the engines announced that the next leg of their journey had begun.

56

Torres' jaw muscles tightened visibly, as he snatched up the phone to answer the call.

"Yes," he said simply, and listened, nodding occasionally. His cultivated poker face twitched like it was having trouble containing its owner's frustrations, and his eyes narrowed in concentration.

"Okay. I'm on my way now," he said finally, and disconnected. His eyes closed for a couple of seconds and then he turned to gaze out of the window of the unmarked military SUV at the streets of Manaus. He found them, as he found those of any other South American city, dirty, crumbling, badly built, smelly, and peopled mostly with uneducated, petty criminals. The girls looked nice though...

The vehicle bounced through a security gate and jolted his wandering mind back to the problem in hand. It had been easy resolving the Cuzco missing man mystery, especially when they discovered the guy had been heavily into 'medicinal' plants. A sad case of a misfit pot-head presumed dead after disappearing into the jungle in his relentless pursuit of the next hallucinogenic plant. So for now, in both his diplomatic and Agency roles, Torres was off the hook. On the other hand, he knew that just one word out of the Brit would kick the whole thing off big-style – and the odds of containing it were lengthening with each passing hour.

In spite of having flags up along half the length of the Amazon, and teams of divers hunting for bodies along a stretch of river extending fifty miles downstream of Tabatinga, nothing had been found except for a couple of corpses of Tabatinga low-lifes.

They rattled down a metal slipway and came to a halt on a wide pier. The two men in the front seats jumped smartly out, one of them opening Torres' door for him. He stepped out and followed the men across the pier and up some steps to a small building fronting the river. The door opened and a member of his own team stepped out to greet him.

"Good location," Torres acknowledged with a slight nod before entering the building. He greeted the other people there and looked round at the facilities. There were several computers set up along two rows of desks, and a rack of networking components was alive with flickering red, amber and green LEDs, while four large-screen monitors occupied most of one wall. From the windows he could see the sprawling, chaotic port of Manaus, with brightly-painted passenger boats moored along the various piers or driven onto the mud along the riverside beyond.

"Forty-eight hours, you said...?" Torres looked at the senior member of his team.

"Yes sir. Total comms blackout. It was Flávio who arranged things," the man said, nodding towards one of the Brazilians who was tapping away on a computer.

"Thanks. We owe you one," said Torres in Portuguese.

The man stopped typing and turned to face Torres. "A pleasure," he said, smiling.

"And in the meantime?" Torres asked no-one in particular.

"There are men spread across the port area," one of the other Americans said. "All in radio contact with us here. We also have a list of registered passenger vessels coming from upstream, and we're tracking every one of them." He paused to point at one of screens on the wall, then moved his finger to the next monitor along. "We're tied in to the port's security cameras, and we have three drones up between here and the meeting of the waters. We also have an alert out with the local police and we can get patched in to most of their camera network if needed. We have satellite as well, obviously."

Torres nodded. "Is everyone aware what to do when we have a positive ID?"

"Yes sir. Immediate take-down and removal."

Torres nodded again. "Okay then. Let's find the bastard."

57

Once the boat was under way, Elena decided it was a good time to visit the bathroom. With the increased noise from the engines and the rattling of their air conditioner covering the sound of any conversation, Jack felt at liberty to talk openly to Carla.

"So, Carla," he said, in his faltering Spanish. "What's your story?"

"We can speak in English, if you like," she said.

"My god," cried Jack. "Does everyone in South America speak three languages?"

Carla laughed. "No. Most people have trouble with just one."

"But you...?"

"I did a lot of travelling between Brazil and Argentina when I was younger. Spanish came easy. Then I decided to learn English...you know, when I got into politics."

"I don't see the connection."

"I figured that fighting corruption would be better done from an international platform. That means English. Simple, really."

"And...?" said Jack.

"And what?"

"And is it?"

"It will be, for sure. We're still just at the first stages."

"Ah yes, your movement. The GCC, isn't it?"

"Yes. Have you heard of it?" Carla said with genuine surprise.

Jack decided not to lie. "No. Actually, Elena told me."

Carla laughed again. "Ah well, we'll get there – just give us a little more time."

"I don't doubt it," said Jack. He thought for a few seconds. "So I suppose you and Elena are kind of in the same business, in a way?"

"What?" Carla snapped.

"I mean, you're both fighting against corrupt governments, for example." Jack suggested.

"But our movement is not a terrorist organisation, and I am not a terrorist like she is."

"Elena is not a terrorist," Jack responded, a little more vehemently than he intended. He tried to dial the emotion down a bit before continuing. "Elena has never been convicted of anything, Carla. And she's a freedom fighter, not a terrorist."

"Oh. Sorry. I didn't realise." The note of sarcasm was unmistakable.

"That's because you don't know the history," Jack said, as neutrally as possible.

"No, I mean, I didn't realise you two were…"

"What are you talking about?" cried Jack. He felt the colour rise in his face, and was thankful for the dim lighting. "And what's that got to do with anything, anyway?"

"Nothing. Nothing," said Carla. She sighed. "Look, sorry, but I don't hold with violence or extremism of any sort. It's not my game and I don't believe it's ever necessary. We have some people in our movement who disagree with me, and it's a constant battle trying to stop things getting out of control."

They lapsed into silence for a few moments.

"So where is your movement based?" Jack asked.

"Huh? Oh, well, in Brasilia, of course. The political capital, you know?"

"Yes. Of course." He thought for a few more seconds. "So how come you're out here in the middle of nowhere, helping someone you believe to be a terrorist?"

Before she could respond, the door opened and Elena came in.

"The bar's open upstairs," she said in Spanish, and threw her towel on the bunk above Jack. "Anyone want to risk a drink? Carla? You think it would be a problem?"

"It should be okay, as long as we don't get into any conversations," said Carla. Yes, sure. Jack?"

"Don't need to ask twice," he said, sitting up.

They made their way outside and climbed the steel ladders to the very top deck, where there was a tiny bar offering water, beer, cachaça, and not much more. Behind the bar was a long, wide space with a few plastic tables and chairs, all open to the skies. The fibre-glassed floor curved awkwardly down to the sides, around which ran a thin metal railing, and as Jack and Elena walked towards the stern, they had to step over several discarded tarpaulins and flotation devices.

Carla called out to them from near the bar, in Portuguese simple enough that it was quite understandable to any Spanish speaker.

"*Duas cervejas?*"

Elena nodded, and Jack turned and stuck up a thumb. Then, conscious that he was exposed to full view where he was, he led Elena quickly to the nearest table, where they pulled out some chairs and sat down.

"*Beba com moderação,*" said Carla as she walked across and placed the beers on the table.

"Do what?" said Jack.

"Drink in moderation," said Carla and Elena together.

Elena looked at Carla with some surprise. "You speak English?"

"She does, yes," said Jack. "And since both you guys seem to be regular polyglots, do you mind if I stick to English when possible? You can speak to me in Spanish or English, but Portuguese is confusing me – a lot – and my spoken Spanish isn't exactly fluent."

"*Realmente? Nunca me habia notado,*" said Elena and laughed mischievously.

"Very funny," said Jack.

Elena smiled. "Sorry Jack. Sure – it's no problem for me."

"It's okay with me, too," said Carla. "Spanish and English it is."

They touched cans and took long draughts of the ice-cold liquid.

"God, that's good," said Jack.

Carla and Elena nodded.

They sat for a few minutes, just enjoying their beer, and then Jack looked around carefully, and leaned forward.

"So, Carla, you were going to tell me about why you're here? I'd be very interested."

Elena put her can on the table.

"Yes. Me too," she said.

Carla took a long breath and started into the history of the GCC and her part in it, together with the other founder. She told them she was 'up north' as part of her drive to get new members, and told them about how she had been invited to attend a meeting in São Paulo de Olivença.

"It's a long way to come for a meeting," observed Jack.

"Hmm. Well, not for the military," said Carla guardedly.

"What?" cried Jack. "You were here meeting with the *military*? The same military that nearly killed Elena and is presumably still hunting us down?"

Carla stared at him. "I didn't know that at the time. And anyway, they're hardly the exact same, are they? A lot of the people at the meeting were risking their careers – possibly their liberty – to get together to discuss what might be done about the intolerable levels of corruption in Brazil."

In his sudden anger, Jack ignored her comments. "So you're considering dealing with a group that's probably helping to run an international drugs ring, and that's apparently happy to kill innocent people to protect their interests, right? If that doesn't make them terrorists, what does?"

Carla put her drink on the table and sat back. "Listen, I have never, nor will I ever, ally with extremists or radicals who condone violence. I was simply here to see what these people had to say for themselves, so that we could decide how to deal with them."

"So why are you helping me?" asked Elena. "Or didn't you know–" she looked around quickly before lowering her voice and continuing, "that I'm a wanted member of the Nuevo Sendero Luminoso?"

Jack smiled at Elena's sarcasm, and Carla threw her head back and took a deep breath before looking at Elena again.

"I know who you are, Elena, and I did ask myself that question before agreeing to meet you. The truth is, I probably wouldn't have helped you if the request had come from anyone other than the leader of the GCC."

"Marcos," Elena stated flatly.

"Yes. Marcos." Carla said with some surprise. "You know him personally? He didn't say."

Elena nodded. "Yes. From the days when he rubbed shoulders with the Sendero – and Tupac Amaru and the FARC, for that matter."

"Oh. Well, a lot of that was before my time, although when we were setting up the GCC he would occasionally disappear for a few weeks to 'visit friends' in Peru."

"Yes. He got frustrated with the in-fighting between all the various groups, and eventually cut the ties."

Carla nodded. "He told me."

"Mind you, it's odd you never saw him as a terrorist, because I can assure you he was in the thick of it at one time."

Carla sat forward again. "Yes. I know. But he's never once given any indication that he'd go down that path in Brazil, and he knows I wouldn't stand for it if he did."

Elena looked at Carla carefully. "You two are, um...?"

"What? God no," Carla stammered, staring at her beer. "No, no."

She suddenly looked up at Elena with a worried expression. "Why? Did you   I mean, were you...?"

Elena shook her head. "Oh no. Not me and Marcos." She laughed. "It would never work – we're too much alike."

"Then why...?"

"Why was he prepared to come to my aid? Well, let's just say he owes me one."

"Must be a big one," Jack chipped in.

Elena would not be drawn. "If we get out of this, the debt will be paid."

At this, Carla abruptly rose from the table and walked off to the bar without saying a word. Jack looked at Elena and she gave him a 'no idea' shrug. They sat in silence for the couple of minutes it took Carla to return with more beer. She banged the cans on the table, then picked up her own can, opened it, and took a long swig. She sat down and placed the can on the table.

"Elena," she said, quietly. "Let's get one thing straight here. If you get out of this, Marcos will still owe you one, right? The only thing that will change is that *you* will owe *me* one."

"O-kay...," said Elena, fingering the pull top on her beer can.

Carla sighed. "Do you see Marcos here?" she asked.

Elena hesitated, then smiled. "Fair enough," she agreed. She opened her own can and raised it.

"Carla," she said, "thank you."

Jack raised his own can. "Yes. Thanks. I owe you too, right?"

Now Carla looked embarrassed.

"Oh, forget it. *A próxima rodada é sua, tá?*"

Jack looked puzzled.

" 'The next round is yours'," Carla translated, tipping her can to Jack.

"Ah," said Jack.

"Or yours," Carla added, looking at Elena. She shrugged. "Well, one of you, anyway." She laughed.

"Okay, Carla – you got it," said Jack. "A próxima rodada."

They banged their cans together and drank the toast.

Nearly two hours later, there was no sign of the bar closing, although by now the three of them were the only customers left. Carla got unsteadily to her feet and staggered off to the bar again. This time she returned with a plastic rubbish bag as well as three more beers. As she swept all the empties into the bag, Jack and Elena pushed their chairs back a little, to give her access, until finally Carla dropped the bag by the side of the table and sat back down.

"I think this will have to be my last," she said a little groggily. "Not used to it."

"Yes, me too, said Elena. I need a decent sleep."

Jack just nodded.

"You know," said Carla, "the more I think about this, the better it gets. I mean, I wasn't going to say anything, but when I left you to rest earlier, and went back to the base, I decided to check something I'd noticed in passing, but hadn't paid much attention to."

"At this military barracks, you mean?" asked Jack.

"Yes. The thing is, I don't think it's an ordinary *quartel* – barracks."

"Go on." said Jack.

"Well, I know I've had a bit to drink now, but the thing is, it has this sort of, uh, port thing, as well."

"Port thing?" Jack asked with amusement. "Well why not? Armies do often have patrol boats, you know."

"Yes, but this port – hidden away in a black-water lagoon off the main river – is constantly busy. It's not just the odd patrol boat. There are plenty of civilian boats coming and going, and a lot of boxes and crates coming off – and being loaded. There's an office, a warehouse – there's even a little crane by the side of the docks.

"Okay..."

"So, I'm thinking it could be a drugs distribution centre. Or at least illegal goods or something."

"Hmm," said Jack. "But it could also just be food and the usual supplies."

Carla shook her head firmly. "No. These are big quantities. Besides, why would they be loading stuff onto civilian boats?" She paused. "Anyway, the whole place is odd."

"Odd how?" Elena asked.

"Well, to begin with, this is not a frontier, which would be where any genuine Amazon military base would be, wouldn't it?"

Jack nodded. "That would be the logical place, yes."

"Yep." Elena agreed. "If you look at maps of Peru's border regions, you can find bases in the most obscure places – obscure until you see that they're right on an international border line."

"Right. So, this place is not exactly on a border, is it?" She leaned forward and tapped the table with her finger. "But it *is* conveniently close to the borders of two of the most famous drug-producing countries in the whole continent, right?"

Jack and Elena nodded.

"Right. It's also near a town, so its traffic is hardly noticed, mixed up with the town's traffic. It has a large port facility for no apparent reason, as well as access to a big airstrip – big enough for military transports. It has power, communications...it has everything you could want if you were a major drugs distribution centre."

Jack grunted. "Jesus, everyone in South America is running drugs."

Carla shrugged, but did not smile.

Elena nodded. "Certainly. If they're not running or dealing, they're benefiting from the supply – directly or indirectly."

"It's obscene," said Jack.

"Well don't be too hard on us," said Elena. "We're only supplying what the western markets demand, after all."

Jack rubbed his face. "Yes, yes, I know. Go on, then, Carla."

"Well that's it," she said, and took a slug from her can. "The more I think about it, the more I think we've just sailed out of the biggest – at least, one of the biggest – drugs distribution centres in the whole country. In the continent, perhaps."

"So how do the other people all fit into your new plan?"

"Who - you mean the other countries? Well, the Peruvians, that's obvious: they have as much to gain as anyone else. You said yourself, Elena, that the drugs and smuggling operations are controlled by the Peruvian military, right?"

"Right."

"So, they also have an agreement with the Brazilian military. Probably with the Colombian and the Bolivian and the Venezuelan military, too."

"It's incredible."

"Why is it incredible, Jack? It's all about money. Everyone in Brazil is corrupt. Probably in the other countries, too. Why is it incredible?"

"I don't know. I – um – I had higher expectations, maybe?" said Jack, as he felt the vertiginous effects of looking down from the moral high ground on which his family and army life had placed him – a hitherto comfortable spot where he could be sure that everyone was basically decent and honest at heart. His foster parents had hammered an exaggerated sense of fair play into him and burdened him with the notion that 'what goes around, comes around'. Anything that bucked that trend was an abomination and could not last long in a fair and honest world. He had spent his whole life believing it all, but suddenly felt betrayed; bereaved. He shook his head. Maybe it was just the beer.

Carla snorted. "You had high expectations? Oh dear – Brazil will soon cure you of that."

"I think perhaps Peru got there first," said Elena.

Jack groaned, but managed a smile.

There was an amiable silence for a few moments, during which they drank some more beer, and then Jack put his can down.

"Right," he said. "That's it for me. I'm feeling maudlin."

"What?" Elena and Carla chorused

"Maudlin. Sad. Sorry for myself."

"Ah. Well don't worry Jack – you'll get through it. We'll all get through it," said Carla.

"Yes," said Elena, nodding.

With a glint in her eye that was more than just the alcohol, Carla held up her can of beer. "Yes. *You're* going to get through it, Jack, so that you can expose all this to the outside world and bring down the stupid Americans. Elena, *you're* going to get through it to bring down the crappy Peruvian government, and *I'm* going to get through it to bring down this piece of shit Brazilian government."

A final toast, and they threw their cans in the plastic bag and wobbled off to the cabin.

Jack held back a little, and when Carla was descending the steps and almost out of sight, he reached out and pulled Elena towards him to kiss her. Locked in their passionate embrace, they did not see Carla's amused expression when she popped her head up to see where they had got to.

"I can see you, you know," she called in Portuguese, before turning to descend again.

58

They had left the shelter of their cabin and were lining the rails of the top deck to get some fresh air. The Sagrado Coração VII had been pounding down the middle of the Amazon River to take full advantage of the downstream current, when it suddenly slowed and turned towards the riverbank. There seemed no reason for it, and Jack and Elena exchanged anxious looks.

Carla's questions to the crew elicited only "Anamã", although no amount of squinting into the distance could distinguish anything resembling a town. Just a tiny channel, half hidden behind a stand of towering, lifeless trees whose half-submerged trunks and branches quivered in the swirling current.

"That doesn't look very wide," said Jack doubtfully.

The captain slowed the boat to a crawl in order to guide it through the narrow access, and ten minutes later, they had moved from the muddy brown channel into the mouth of a small blackwater river along whose east banks a town finally appeared.

"We'll get some food here and hire a fast boat to take us to Manacapuru," said Carla enthusiastically. "Once we get to Manacapuru, I'm on home ground."

In the end it took them just under four hours to get to Manacapuru by fast boat, racing north to Caapiranga, changing to another river taxi, then heading east through tiny, breathtakingly beautiful, flooded-forest passages navigated at breakneck speed.

"Oh to be a tourist," Jack said at one point

Elena laughed. "We can always come back again, later," she said.

"Ni verga!" Jack cried, raising his eyes heavenward. "No way!"

They emerged onto the broad expanse of Manacapuru Lake, and an hour later they finally stepped up from the boat onto the creaking wooden planks that served as a stairway to the town's main road. Carla was anxious to get into the town and find a taxi, but they ducked into a little roadside cafe to grab a hot, sweet coffee and some toasted cheese curd sandwiches while she made some phone calls.

As they waited, Jack and Elena watched storm clouds roll in from the east, until the sky was almost black. The cold, pre-rain wind blew their plastic cups off the table and the first spots of rain banged loudly on the corrugated tin roof. Carla put the phone down and stood up.

"We'd better go," she said, and they gathered their things together. As they walked increasingly quickly towards a group of VW vans caked in red mud, she talked to Jack and Elena. "I can't get hold of the people I need locally, but I've put the word around to a few colleagues I can trust. Let's see if anyone knows anything about what's happening in Peru. If there's information out there for us, we'll have it soon."

"Can we dial out on that phone?" asked Jack, raising his voice against the increasing background hiss of the approaching rain.

"Outside Brazil? On this service, no. But we can organise that when we get to Manaus."

They had almost reached the first van when Jack pulled them up. "There aren't any checkpoints or anything on this road, are there?" he asked.

"Not usually, no," said Carla. She pointed at the sky. "Besides, this is Brazil – the police don't do anything in the rain." She smiled.

They threw themselves into the van just as the rain arrived, and were on their way with ten other wet and steaming people, by four thirty. They did not speak to each other at all during the journey, and no one tried to speak to Jack, for which he was thankful. Someone grumpily suggested that Elena put her hold-all in the back of the van, but after looking at the savage grasp she had on it, and the equally savage look on her face, they backed off. Finally, at seven thirty that evening, everyone squeezed themselves out of the van into the suffused orange glow of the sodium lighting around the coach station in Manaus.

While Carla paid the driver, Jack and Elena stood by the side of the busy one-way road, watching an incredible volume of traffic roaring down its three lanes. It had rained here, too, and the noise of the traffic seemed to be doubled by the constant hiss and squelch of tyres on wet tarmac. Before they could fully adjust to it, Carla was urging them down the road towards the seedy-looking Hotel Arara. There was only one six-bed room available, and they took it, paying extra so they could have the place to themselves.

While Elena placed her bag carefully on her bed and started rummaging around in it, Carla threw hers on the floor and flopped down on one of the beds. Jack took a piece of scrap paper he found in the bin and looked around for something to write with.

"Carla?"

There was no response.

He went closer, heard her rhythmic breathing and realised she was out for the count.

"Do you have a pen, Elena?" he asked.

Elena was already on her way to the bathroom with a toothbrush and soap in her hands. "No, sorry."

He did not want to disturb Carla, so he decided to open her bag. He saw what he was looking for, and as he went to pick it up he could not but help notice a large roll of one-hundred-Real banknotes and a whole collection of identity documents. He stared at them for a few seconds before closing the bag.

While Elena went off to the bathroom, he sat down on the cheap plastic chair beside the wobbly chest of drawers, placed his paper on top, and started to write. He noted some names and phone numbers first, then drew a line down the centre of the page and began to write notes on everything he could remember seeing or hearing over the last month that he thought might be important. Finally, he turned the page over and wrote a summary of what he was going to say to the people he would phone.

"It's an elevator pitch," he mumbled to himself as he finished.

"What's that?" Elena said, coming up behind him.

"Oh sorry – just talking to myself. I'm trying to get my story straight so I can convince someone to help me. It just struck me that it's like preparing a sales pitch."

"*Tono de venta?*" Elena nodded. "Yes. It is not an easy story to believe."

Jack shrugged. "*She* believed it," he said, nodding towards Carla, who was now lying on her back snoring.

"Yes. But circumstances – and Marcos – helped. The people you will be phoning will be sitting at home in comfort and safety, a million kilometres away. Who *are* you phoning, anyway?"

The cash and the ID cards in Carla's bag flashed through his head, and he looked across at her briefly, before turning back to Elena and putting his finger to his lips.

"Just a few people I know."

Elena looked a little puzzled, but spoke quite normally. "Oh. Okay. Should we try to get the number of the British Embassy or something?"

"Consul. The British Consul, it would be. There's no embassy in Manaus. I would remember if there was."

"Okay – consul, then."

"Sure, if possible. Although if we had a computer, it would be a lot simpler."

"Huh? What's that about a computer?" Carla's sleepy voice interrupted.

"Ah, good evening Carla," said Jack brightly. "I was just saying that if we had access to a computer, things would be a lot easier."

"Oh. I see. Well, I'll have to go out to get you a different phone and make my contacts," she called out. "I'll see what I can arrange. Will you two be okay stuck here for a couple of hours?"

"Yeah sure. Don't worry about us."

"If you give me five minutes to get ready, we could all go to that place next door and get a pizza before I go."

"Good plan."

After eating something that tasted of dough and had a texture like cardboard, they finished their meal with a beer. They talked through what they might need, and Elena insisted on giving Carla some of the money she had received in Tabatinga. After making them promise they would head straight back to the room when they finished their beer, Carla left. Jack pulled out his piece of paper and pen, and set it on the table. Elena ordered more beer, and they decided to remain at the table keeping an eye on the comings and goings at the hotel.

"Are you suspicious of Carla?" Elena suddenly asked.

Jack shook his head. "I'm suspicious of everyone," he said.

"Me too?"

"You especially."

She threw him a hurt look, and he leaned over and kissed her. She pulled him closer, and the entanglement might have lasted a deal longer had they not been interrupted by the arrival of the beers.

"You should see the quantity of money and fake documents she has in her bag – it's like a spy kit or something."

"Yes, but she explained that. She's under threat from all sorts of people."

"Hmm. Well, I think it was a useful reminder that the fewer people who know about what's happening, the better."

"Shoot first..."

"Ask questions later. Yes."

Elena nodded her approval. "You're becoming a Peruvian after all."

Jack scowled, and pulled his paper and pen nearer.

He read his notes to Elena, making a few additions and corrections, then concentrated on remembering the points on the wall map he had seen. He recalled now that the single coastal point had been marked ENAPU. A line led from there to the midpoint of another line that ran roughly southwest/northeast along the mountains, and then four shorter lines sprouted at right angles from this. At one end of each of these short lines were pins, labelled AO, BO, CO and DO respectively. Each of these was joined to a paired pin marked AE, BE, CE and DE, and there were more pins joined to each of these, with a whole collection of them strung out somewhere – he could not remember any more detail. He also vaguely remembered a few other points, but could not remember their precise location in relation to the others.

As he went over it once again, with Elena, it seemed to him that maybe he had been looking at the thing the wrong way round. They had talked about it being some sort of route to distribute something from a single point – electricity, as they had speculated – when it could just as easily be to collect something for delivery *to* a single point. Not electricity, obviously – why deliver bucket loads of energy to a remote point hundreds of miles from anywhere – but something else. So – minerals? Oil? Gas? Surely not. Anything like that, and it would have been splashed across the papers everywhere, instead of apparently being covered up. You certainly would not kill innocent tourists over it, would you? So, could it really be drugs? What was Peru internationally famous for, but coca? He decided to test the theory on Elena.

"It's the only thing that makes any sense," she agreed. "Organised drug production and distribution. It would explain a lot about what's happening in the Sendero and politically in Peru. But I don't see how they would use these lines, whatever they are."

Having decided what the product was, they then wrote down the players as he saw them – the narcos, the Peruvian military and, for some reason, the Americans – probably the CIA, if you believed their bad press. So far, so good. But then there were the Brazilians, who, if Carla's theory about Brascons was correct, were happily beavering away doing themselves out of their cut – unless they were getting something else out of it, or just did not have the full picture.

Finally, Jack wrote down the words from the piece of paper he had found at the site – *DUMAR T.AE, HEP 1-11, 15m* – and the name of the site manager, Charles Johnson. Unless they were using false names, surely someone would be able to pin down a guy working for the American government in Peru called Charles Johnson.

They looked through it all again and then Jack dropped the pen on the table in frustration. It made no sense. No-one would believe him. Drugs? Really? Transported how, exactly? He shook his head.

"It's no good, Elena, we need to know *exactly* what those lines and points are. We need to know what the Brazilians are up to, and we need a plausible link to the USA."

They ordered another beer and brooded. Jack thought about everything that had happened to them. About his friend in Cuzco, and how close they had come to taking Elena away from him. It made him angry again. Maybe everyone on this bloody continent would kill their grandmothers for a few dollars. Maybe that was just the way it was here – life was hard, nasty, unfair and cheap, and no one knew a better way. But the Americans – what was their excuse? He remembered that cold, cynical voice talking to the site manager. What were the words? *They will just disappear, that's all. My problem; my responsibility.* It was not a voice he would forget.

He looked over the two telephone numbers he had written down. One was an old mate from Dublin – *had* been a mate, until they had lost touch a few years ago. The other was the number for the place where he had worked after he left the army, although again it was over four years ago. He stared at them and was appalled that these were the only contacts he could muster. No other friends, no family, nothing. He sighed and took another pull of his beer.

"Are you okay?" said Elena, putting her arm around him.

It snapped him back to reality. The lack of names was the result of actions and attitudes taken in the past. The result of past experiences he could do nothing about. In the here and now, against some pretty ridiculous odds, he had someone that rang all the bells and pushed all sorts of buzzers in his jaded head, and made him feel that life was worth the living. He turned to her and allowed her eyes to take him in and caress him. He suddenly felt overpowered by conflicting emotions, and he reached out to her, embracing her before she could see his discomfort.

"Jack, I can't breathe," she gasped, after a few seconds.

"What?" he cried, shocked. He drew back.

"Sorry. Sorry. I..."

She reached up and touched his face. "I know, Jack. It's okay."

They were interrupted by the blaring of car horns announcing that a taxi had had the audacity to stop on the main road near the hotel. They looked over and saw Carla emerge from the rear door. She looked around, pulled some bags off the back seat and closed the door, then put her head down slightly and walked quickly to the hotel. They continued watching the road for several minutes and then they saw her come flying back out of the hotel entrance, looking around wildly, a worried expression on her face, before she saw them and walked calmly but quickly over to them.

"I was worried. I thought you would be in the room."

"Sorry. Just sitting here thinking. You want a beer?"

"You want a phone, a computer and some internet access?"

Jack sat bolt upright.

"Really? Already?"

"Yes. It's all there."

He almost knocked the chair over as he jumped up. "Let's go!"

He had to maintain his calm while they paid the bill, but his heart was bursting as they ran up the stairs to the room.

59

The Sagrado Coração VII limped into the port of Manaus at ten o'clock at night, late because of an engine failure midstream on the Amazon. It had taken two hours to fix, and the boat drifted way past the Paracuuba shortcut the Captain usually took. After fixing the engine, they had to come the long way round. Then, just as they were crossing the famous 'Meeting of the Waters', with the city in sight, they were held up again when the Federal Police and the Navy boarded the boat to check everyone's ID and the boat documents. In the end, the delay was of more concern to the passengers than to the captain, whose official cargo was largely ignored and whose ten kilos of cocaine and eighty thousand cigarettes still lay undisturbed below.

He had chosen not to mention to the Feds or the Navy the three people who had disembarked in Anamã, since he did not much care who they were or what they were doing. However, he knew the information could be valuable, and once the boat was secured and the passengers had left, he pulled out his phone and dialled a São Paulo de Olivença number.

"*Fala*," came the curt answer.

"Sagrado Coração. *O Comandante se encontra?*"

"*Espere*," the voice said, and hung up.

The captain looked at the phone and shrugged. He placed it in its holder by the wheel and went to organise the unloading of the legitimate cargo. He forgot all about it, until one of the crew tapped him on the shoulder and handed him the ringing phone. He took it and pressed the button.

"Sim, senhor Comandante," he said after a couple of seconds. He moved away to a quieter part of the boat where no one could hear him, to continue the call. Yes, the girl the Comandante had paid for had joined the boat. But did the Comandante know that she had brought two other people with her? No? A guy – a gringo? And another woman? He described them as best he could and then told the Comandante that they had left the boat at Anamã, before the boat was boarded. Yes, boarded by the Federal Police and the Navy. They had some other gringos with them, too, the Police. No, he did not know who they were. No, he had not told them anything – he thought the Comandante might want to know first.

He listened for a few seconds then smiled a little.

"Sim Senhor. Obrigado Senhor. *Prazer*."

It was another hour before the message got to the military commander in Tabatinga, and a further twenty minutes before it got to Colonel Ferreira. It took Ferreira thirty minutes to contact Adam Torres, who at that moment was standing in his operations room in Manaus, less than four hundred yards from where the Sagrado Coração VII was berthed.

"Godammit. I knew it," Torres snarled, when he heard the news.

"And they could be in Manaus already," Ferreira observed.

"That fast?"

"Yes. They would have needed a little luck, but I've already checked it out. If they were quick picking up a boat, it wouldn't take them that long."

"Okay. We need to find the bastard right now."

"Bastards. Plural. Don't forget there are now three of them."

"I don't know how that damned woman survived — you're sure it's her?"

"The description fits."

"What about the second woman?"

"A political activist. If she disappears, no-one on the establishment side is going to kick up a fuss. But she knows the territory – she's a Brazilian – and they say she's smart."

"And you're sure they're acting together?"

"I think we have to assume so, yes."

"Right," said Torres, and then paused for a moment. "First thing – can your people put up road blocks? I mean, without it becoming a national scandal?"

"Certainly," said Ferreira. "We can block all the roads in and out, and control access to the ports and the airports. We'll tell people at the ports it's a military exercise, and we'll have our army friends helping. The airports are easy, of course. We'll also set up random roadblocks throughout the city and tell everyone it's a 'blitz' on drink driving or something. It's not uncommon."

"Okay. The internet and the phones will all go down in a few hours."

There was a short, strangled, coughing noise from Ferreira before she spoke. "I see. Can I ask how you–"

"It doesn't matter," Torres cut her off. "It's all taken care of." A hint of pride crept into his voice as he continued. "I'm not playing games here, Márcia.

"Clearly not."

"And the intelligence guys you lent me have been very helpful," Torres added. "They tell me we can bill a temporary blackout as a military exercise, if it comes to it."

"Yes, that's probably true," said Ferreira, the tension in her voice easing off slightly. "Although communications in Manaus are so crap that everyone's used to regular outages anyway." She paused. "Apart from the ones who use satellite."

"Yes, that's an issue, but I'll see what I can do to scramble satellite links too. You just close down the transport."

"I'm already putting it in hand, and I'll be on my way to Manaus in an hour or two, to manage our side."

"Good. We'll be able to coordinate better if we're both here in the city."

"Yes. It's also an easier place to run from, if it all goes to shit."

"It won't," Torres cut in. "It ends here, Márcia."

He hung up and spun round to where the Brazilians were working around one of the computers.

"Change of plans. The bastards could already be arriving in Manaus. I want more people at the port right now, and at any other place where it's possible to disembark.

"But sir, that could be anywhere between CEASA and the Ponta Negra - that's forty kilometres of riverside!" said one of them.

"Get more people then," snapped Torres.

The Brazilians looked at each other, and the senior one finally nodded. The other one picked up a phone and started to dial.

"I also need that blackout in force right now," Torres continued.

The senior Brazilian shook his head. "Sorry sir, that just can't be rushed. It has to be coordinated by colleagues in Brasilia."

Torres glared at the man, who held his hands up in mock surrender. "Okay, I'll see what I can do, sir."

Torres forced a smile. "Great job."

"No promises, though."

Torres nodded and turned to look out the window at the brightly-lit docks and the hundreds and hundreds of people milling about. He turned back abruptly.

"And for god's sake let's get more people down there right now, okay?" he said, using his thumb to point back over his shoulder.

60

After fifteen frustrating minutes trying to get through to his UK numbers, Jack gave up trying. The number Elena had found for the British Consul in Manaus did not work either. He put the phone down and shook his head.

Elena looked across. "No luck?"

"Not a thing."

"The Consul?"

Jack laughed bitterly. "No. No Consul."

"But that number's definitely correct."

"I'm sure it is. Don't worry about it. In my experience, few consuls like being contacted by their fellow countrymen."

Carla had already set up the computer.

"I bought the display model, so it already has all the apps on it. Pirated, of course." She smiled. "It's all working fine – I've already looked through my emails."

"Oh. Anything?" Jack asked.

She shook her head as she passed the computer to him. "Nothing that stands out, but I've downloaded a couple of responses to look at when you've done what you need to do. To be honest, I'm more likely to get something by phone."

Jack nodded and took the laptop, while Carla picked up the phone and sat on her bed. She had offered it to Elena, but as Elena pointed out, she had already used up all her favours. Unless they were heading back to Peru, it was down to Jack and Carla now.

Jack drafted a paragraph relating key events and facts from his written notes, and then searched the internet – a painfully slow process over the mobile network – for the addresses he wanted. They included the British Embassy in Brasilia and any British newspapers for which he could find something better than a 'general enquiries' email address.

He heard Carla talking quietly to one or two people, then he saw her stand up, pacing backwards and forwards as she listened to someone. He focused on his own priorities – if she found something, she'd share it soon enough.

She had already warned him how poor the internet connection would be, and that he might lose it any time. She emphasised this by reminding him that the electricity supply could cut out as well, and he had every reason to believe her, especially after seeing how slow the connection was. He decided to limit himself to the six addresses he had already found. He still had to take the time to set up a new email account, his assumption being that someone would be monitoring his old ones, and then finally he copied and pasted his text into an email and pressed the 'send' button.

At the same moment, Carla uttered a mouthful of expletives, looked at the phone with disgust, and started dialling again. Jack watched her with some amusement as she listened with obvious impatience, dialled again, then again, and finally threw the phone on the bed.

Jack looked back to his screen. He had been trying to navigate to his blog page, to copy his email to it, but the page would not load. He tried another page, with no luck.

"It's down," he said, finally. "The bloody internet's down."

"Did you get your messages sent?" asked Elena.

"I don't know. I pressed 'send' and then loaded another page straight away. I didn't see any confirmation of the send, and the new page froze."

"*Não acredito*," Carla cried. "*Meu Deus*, my friends, they really want you badly, don't they?"

"What do you mean?" asked Elena.

"It's not just the internet," she said. "The phone's not working either, and one of my contacts told me they've started putting roadblocks up around the city and at the main roads in and out."

"Shit. We've got to get out of here," Jack said. "Sorry Carla – you shouldn't have helped us. You should just disappear. You can probably still get away. We can take it from here. You should go – really."

"Are you kidding?" said Carla. "If they've tracked us to Manaus already, they've connected us. The Feds have been looking for an excuse to pull me in for the past three years, and I've just given it to them. So what am I going to do? Where am I going to go?"

"What about the people you know here?"

Carla shook her head. "I can't get them involved. There's only one guy from our movement here that I can really trust to help, and I've arranged for us to see him at nine o'clock tomorrow. I've also got a contact operating out of Boa Vista, north of here, and he's on standby in case we need him."

Jack sighed. "Chances of getting to Boa Vista if we leave now?"

"If they've just put up roadblocks, they'll be searching everything on the interstate roads – besides, a two hundred kilometre stretch of the road to Boa Vista is closed at night, where it goes through an indigenous Indian reserve. The airport is out, and there are no boats to Boa Vista at this time of year."

Jack thought for a moment. "Elena, no physical address for the Consul, I take it?"

"None."

"What about the local media – any help?"

"You've got to be joking. They're all in the government's pockets – at least in this part of Brazil. I wouldn't trust them to cover yesterday's weather."

Jack shrugged. "So all we can do is wait to see your contact. How can he help, do you know?"

"He'll think of something. His business is all about staying one step ahead of the law."

"He's a crook?" said Elena, with some amusement.

Carla scrunched up her face. "On the contrary. He just spends a lot of time making sure no-one in the GCC is *labelled* a crook. He knows his way around, that's all."

They talked for another half an hour, and decided there was little they could do until the next day. After checking the phone and the internet again, they lay on their respective beds and tried to get some sleep.

Jack woke up sweating, even with the air-conditioning on. It was just turning daylight, and he had the image in his head of the half-completed email 'send' screen on the computer. He got up quietly, checked the phone and switched on the computer.

The phone was dead, and while he was waiting without much hope for the computer, he began going over their options again. If he could not get a message out from Manaus, would Boa Vista – a smaller, even more remote town – be any better? They would have to get there without their move being anticipated, or the same thing would probably just happen again. Maybe it would be better to try for Brasilia or São Paulo? Or perhaps they should miss out Boa Vista altogether and head straight for Venezuela.

He sat up in the chair, shaking his head. "Out of one tin-pot kleptocracy, into another," he mumbled.

"Hmm? What?" came a disembodied voice from one of the other beds.

Jack looked over and Carla threw back her sheets and sat up, tousling her hair.

"What's the matter?" she asked sleepily. "Still no internet?"

Jack looked at the message on his browser, and shook his head. "No. No phone; no internet."

"Well, they can't keep the whole city cut off forever, can they?"

"To be honest, I'm beginning to think these bastards can do just whatever they want," said Jack.

Carla got up and went to the bathroom, switching on the TV as she went. Jack heard her brushing her teeth and then heard the shower going, before the presenter on the news channel started speaking. He leaned across, picked up the remote, and turned the volume up.

Elena slept on, tossing and turning a few times as the volume increased, and finally pulled the pillow over her head.

"We still have our rendezvous at nine o'clock," Carla called from the bathroom. "All we have to do is get a taxi to the city centre – it's only fifteen minutes away."

Jack nodded distractedly, his attention on a news item that seemed to be talking about problems with the telephone network.

"Carla!" he suddenly called. "Come and have a look at this, will you?"

Carla shot out of the bathroom in an instant, a towel more or less covering her, and Jack turned up the volume further. Elena threw her pillow to one side and sat up to look.

They watched the news story for a minute or two until the subject changed.

"So," he asked. "What's going on?"

"They're saying that a freak electrical spike at the main – what, exchange? hub? – in Manaus, has temporarily knocked out communications. They're working on it and hope to restore service as soon as possible, blah, blah. Complete nonsense."

"It might be nonsense, but they'll use it as justification for spinning it out as long as they need to," said Jack.

"Yes. At least until they end up with a riot on their hands," Elena added.

Carla laughed. "A riot? What, here in Manaus? You're joking. Nobody ever complains about anything here. No one ever does anything. How else do you think the useless pack of lying, stealing, morons gets to stay in power for so long? Look at–"

She stopped when she saw Jack smiling at her. "Sorry," she said. "Sore point."

"I know."

"Anyway, at least we know that sitting around waiting isn't going to do us any good," she added brightly.

"Damned right," said Jack.

"So let's eat and get going then," said Elena, throwing back her bedsheets.

They quickly got themselves organised, and were about to leave the room, when Jack remembered his conversation with Carla from the night before.

"You said you'd downloaded some responses?"

"What? Oh – yes. I forgot," said Carla.

"Let's bring the computer then," said Jack, grabbing the laptop and following Carla and Elena out of the room.

They sat on stools in the damp, dingy breakfast room where some French bread drooped in a bowl next to a grubby thermos of coffee and a pile of plastic cups and plates. While Jack and Elena tore into the bread, Carla ignored it in favour of booting up the laptop and scrolling half-heartedly through the emails she had downloaded. Suddenly she stopped, peering intently at the screen for a few seconds. She turned the laptop round and pushed it across the table towards Jack.

"Is that your map, by any chance?" she asked.

Jack recognised it straight away: a series of paired points along the

Andes, a larger number of apparently random points to the east, and a single point on the coast.

He nodded. "Where did this come from?"

"Contact of a contact. The email's behind it."

Jack brought up the email and read it. It was in Spanish, but he could understand most of it. He read that the map had been appended to a confidential project report emanating from a government office in Lima. The details were unavailable for some reason he could not make out, but the author of the email gave a name – DUMAR – a timescale of five years, and a staggering estimated value that he or she had written in uppercase.

"DUMAR TAE," said Jack, tapping the screen and looking at Elena.

Elena leaned towards him. "Yes. The words on the piece of paper at the site. Same as the project name."

"So that confirms it," said Carla.

"Seems to," said Jack, "But it still doesn't tell us what it *is*. No other information?"

Carla shook her head. "Not yet. They only passed *that* on because of the amount of money involved."

"Elena, does any of this stuff mean anything?" Jack asked, indicating some technical language that he found impossible to translate."

"Let's see," she said, pointing at the screen. "Well this bit says that full details are only available on a 'need to know' basis."

"Hah. I'll bet," said Jack.

"Other than that, there's not much, no. But..." she scrolled to the map. "I can tell you that the point there, marked ENAPU, is a port facility. ENAPU is the government's port authority."

Jack nodded. "Oh. Well that confirms that it's more likely we're looking at something being collected there, not distributed from there."

"Yes. Drugs," said Elena, matter-of-factly.

"Hmm. But from all those different points? Why? And what are these paired points here?"

Elena stared at the map for a while. "I don't know. The letters don't mean anything to me. Could be anything. Roads? Railways?"

"Too straight. It would be impossible to build anything that straight, from the mountains to the coast."

"Nothing's impossible, Jack," said Elena.

"Very improbable, then."

"An oil pipeline, then?" suggested Carla.

"Or gas. Yes – could be. But then why all the secrecy and why are all these bastards trying to kill me?" Jack shook his head. "No, I still don't get it."

"Sorry, Jack." Carla shrugged. "That's about all we've got at the moment.

Jack looked thoughtful. "It's okay, Carla. I just need to think harder, that's all."

"I looked at the other emails. Someone clipped and analysed all the top stories coming out of Peru in the last year, which is potentially impressive, but I don't see anything remarkable in them. Do you want to see the list? It's in Portuguese, of course."

"Yes please."

Carla took back the laptop, brought the email to the screen, and scrolled down until she came to the list of the top twenty news stories, with the number of occurrences next to each item. She skimmed through it and then pushed the laptop across to Jack again. He could understand most of the headlines. None of the stories jumped out at him as particularly relevant, and the themes were unremarkable for South America – drugs, corruption, inequality, border disputes, displaced peoples, oil spills, the environment, US trade, Chinese investment, Brazilian investment, and so on.

"Well there's the oil, anyway – so it's hardly a secret is it? US trade, of course...the Chinese...what about this Brazilian investment?"

Elena read through it quickly and then shrugged. "Couple of big businesses like our friends Brascon setting up subsidiaries or something. Nothing out of the ordinary."

"Nothing about the dams you said they're supposed to be building all over the place?" asked Jack.

"No. Nothing."

"Well that's odd in itself, isn't it, if it's such a big infrastructure project?"

Elena nodded. "It is, yes. There was a lot of interest in it last year – for the last five years, really."

"Hmm. Anything else?"Jack asked Carla.

"Not really, I had one other email about some internal government bickering over inward investment from the USA. It's about fifth on the list there."

Jack scrolled down and read through it with Elena's help.

"Arguing over who gets to steal what, no doubt," said Jack.

"Exactly. But it's a bit odd that we don't actually know where the money is being applied – at least officially. It's all just tagged as being for 'infrastructure'."

Jack sighed. "Okay. So, nothing to really get our teeth into, but all worth thinking about. Back to the map."

He brought the map back up and studied it for a few minutes. The scale was very poor for detail, and he wished he could zoom in just a little, or overlay the points on a decent satellite image. He looked at all the points again, and at the larger dots and the nonsensical abbreviations. He felt he was missing something obvious.

"We really need to get going," Carla said, standing up.

Reluctantly Jack switched off the laptop and they made their way back to the room.

Jack and Elena had only one small shoulder bag, and it only took a moment to pack, but when Carla spotted their guns, she insisted they be disposed of.

"The place we're going to has metal detectors," she told them. "And any sight of those will get you noticed very quickly. They're a liability."

Reluctantly, they stripped the guns down and wrapped them in a sheet. Elena volunteered to go out and dump them, and was back within ten minutes. A few minutes later, they were all outside in the heat of the day. Jack was amazed at how hot the city was, and before they had even found a taxi, he could feel the sweat beading on his forehead.

"We're meeting my contact at the theatre – the opera house," said Carla. "There, we'll be surrounded by foreign tourists, so no one will even notice you, Jack." She waved down a white taxi. "And if anyone can get us out of here, this guy will. Trust me."

Jack watched the taxi pull up. He was not quite sure who he could trust at the moment, and he could feel the enemy closing in on him.

"We should be there in fifteen or twenty minutes," Carla said, opening the back door and climbing in.

Jack took a deep breath, got in, and closed the door.

"Teatro Amazonas," Carla said to the driver.

Carla's estimate of how long the journey would be did not take account of the almost stationary traffic.

"*Não sei como eles podem fazer isso na hora do rush,*" the taxi driver complained.

"*O que?*" Carla asked.

She talked for a few moments to the driver, and then sat back, looking worried. She turned round in her seat briefly to exchange looks with Elena, and then started talking to the driver again. Meanwhile, Elena pointed casually out of the window on Jack's side, talking away in Portuguese. She only interrupted her flow for a second to say to him very quietly "Roadblocks in the city centre," then she returned to her pointing and her Portuguese.

Jack played along, looking out of the window and nodding and making enthusiastic noises, then he turned his attention back to the windscreen and the view up ahead. If there were the slightest hint of any roadblock, they would have to make a run for it.

By the time they had crawled up Rua Dez de Julho and were finally approaching the rear of the theatre, it was after nine o'clock and Carla was looking at her watch impatiently every few seconds.

Jack could just make out what he assumed was the theatre in the distance. He was craning to get a better look at the striking pink building and the brightly coloured dome that topped it, when Elena nudged him. He looked back towards the road and saw the now familiar uniforms of the Federal Police further up the street. Elena gently touched Carla on the shoulder, and once she had seen the danger, Carla spoke to the driver and paid their fare. It was a commendable impression of unhurried nonchalance, but Jack could hear the tension in her voice. As soon as she had paid, Elena and Carla opened their doors and they all got out and started making their way through the traffic, to the side of the road.

"*Senhora! Senhora!*" Jack suddenly heard from behind them. "*Senhora! Seu computador!*" the voice was now a shout. "*Seu computador!*"

"*Porra!*" cried Carla. "I forgot the laptop, and it looks like we got the only honest taxi driver in the whole of Manaus."

The shouting attracted the attention of a couple of Police, who were now looking in the direction of the taxi. The three of them had reached the broad, tree-lined Avenida Eduardo Ribeiro, and they ducked down this and tried to blend in with the few pedestrians on the street in front of the Palace of Justice. Jack saw one of the Police walking to the taxi, but they did not seem to have noticed Carla, Elena and himself.

Carla pulled at his arm, and they quickly crossed the busy road. The lights had just changed, and they got in the way of a few cars as they crossed. Horns blared. They walked as calmly as they could up the steps at the back of the theatre, and as soon as they were out of sight, they sprinted along the side of the building and walked through the main tourist entrance.

"Right," said Carla, as they walked into the lobby. "We're going to buy some tickets, meet our contact near the lobby steps, and then we'll all go on the guided tour. If anything happens, we split up. I'll cover for you as best I can, but we mustn't give my contact away, okay?"

Jack and Elena nodded.

"Here we go, then."

61

Simon Walker had already spent three days in Tabatinga and Santa Rosa, chasing up potential leads. Many years earlier in his career he had spent time in Peru, and he found that nothing much had changed there. No real surprise. He had, however, expected more of Brazil. As the supposed powerhouse of Latin America, he thought it would somehow be better than its poorer neighbour. Instead, all he saw was the same mindless bureaucracy, inefficiency, lack of planning, lack of thought, corruption and downright laziness for which the whole continent was famous. Struggling with a communications system so pathetic it defied any explanation or logic, it had taken him two days just to track down the blogger he had come to speak to – his main lead. But on the third day, he struck gold.

In a very smelly riverside bar, he met Fábio and his friends, nearly all of whom had apparently been on a ferry when the military had come charging towards them early on the last morning of their journey from Iquitos to Santa Rosa. They had all been wide awake and getting ready for their breakfast, so they had all seen the people jump from the boat and swim for it.

"*Dos extranjeros?*" Simon asked in his best South American Spanish, holding up two fingers. The lads were Brazilian, but fortunately, they all spoke fluent Spanish, and understanding was not an issue.

"No. One was a gringo; one was Peruvian."

"Or maybe Brazilian," one of the guys said. "She was the one they were shooting at."

"Who was shooting?"

"Who wasn't? There were Brazilian and Peruvian military there. They opened up like it was a turkey shoot or something."

"Without any provocation?"

"She was just swimming, man."

"And no-one knows anything more about her?"

"Someone said she was Sendero. Elena Lopez. Dangerous and all that. But she didn't look that dangerous. She was just swimming, for fuck sake."

"And the gringo. A guy, right?"

They all nodded.

"What happened to him?

"No idea. Everyone was watching the military shooting at the girl. When we looked around again, he was gone."

"Drowned?"

"Probably. There were some speedboats – you know, *lanchas* – zipping around there. They didn't see anything, and he was heading straight for them."

"But no body?"

"Not that we heard about. The police, the army, the navy were all over the place for a few days afterwards. But if they found anything, they didn't tell anyone."

"And that's all you know, then."

"Pretty much, yes. Although João here has a friend in the PF–"

"Sorry – the what?"

"The Polícia Federal. The Feds. The guys that look after the illegal drugs and weapons and stuff coming across the border," Fábio explained.

"Yeah. 'Look after' is right," João added, laughing.

"Okay..."

"Well, apparently it scared the crap out of the local commander, and she's been running around with a face like death for the last few days."

"She? What's her name?"

"Ferreira. Colonel. She's the boss around here."

"Ah yes. I already tried to interview her. No luck."

João shook his head. "You'd not get anything out of her anyway. Best to stay away."

"Why? She's the police, right?"

"Yeah, man, but...say, where are you from?"

"England."

"Right, well, I don't know how it works in England, but here, the PF organises everything – the drugs, the arms, the vehicles – you know, they kind of control it."

"Control as in stopping it...?"

João looked at him as if he were a small child who had just asked if it was true that the sun went round the earth. "Man, everyone knows you can't stop all this shit coming across the border, right?"

"Right."

"So it's better to organise it so that some comes through, but only a limited amount. For a fee, naturally. No-one gets hurt and everyone's happy, right?"

"Sure. So how does that work, exactly?"

João was not too clear on the details, but he knew there was a quota system and that all the illegal stuff in the quota came through to a processing plant and was distributed from there.

"Everyone gets a cut, I suppose – the Peruvians, the Brazilians–"

"The Colombians?"

João shook his head. "I don't know. They're a bit different, you know?"

"And your friend doesn't know anything more about the gringo, or why the commander is so scared?"

"No. He's only a grunt. People say the two in the ferry were trying to get stuff through without paying their dues – you know, get around the quota system." João made a face.

"But you don't think so?"

"It doesn't make much sense, does it? I mean who gives a shit? You just pick them up, take their goods and knock them on the head somewhere quiet. Job done. No need for shooting on sight or sending in half the army to look for dead bodies."

"So what do you think?"

"I don't know, really."

"Information," said one of the other guys, and Fábio nodded.

"Yeah, they must have had something on the PF – and the military, for that matter. They just wanted them dead so they couldn't talk to anyone," said Fábio, matter-of-factly. "Stands to reason."

The rest of the evening was spent buying lots of drinks for the lads, and the only other thing that came up was when João, recovering admirably from a deep state of drunkenness, suddenly remembered that his friend said there were other gringos 'in on it' – that some special force or other had come in from Peru. His friend had helped with the paperwork – special joint operations or something.

"Not Peruvians?" Simon asked.

"Oh sure, Peruvians. But there were definitely gringos, too – Americans. Definitely. My friend told me. 'Place is crawling with *Americanos*, he told me'."

Eventually, when he had squeezed everything he thought he could out of them, Simon left. He paid the huge bar bill, gave something to Fábio, and walked back to his hotel.

He woke with a mild hangover at four o'clock in the morning, and decided to write up his notes and try to figure out the implications of the Americans being involved in this...whatever-it-was.

He had a shower and sat on his bed thinking it through. Everyone knew the Americans were all over the continent, and had been since forever, and of course if the guy who had died was a Yank, and had been involved in the drug trade, that could easily explain their presence. In this case, no story. But if he was *not* a Yank - if he was one of those two Brits - then *that* was a story. Peruvians, Brazilians, Brits, Yanks and narcos. Death in the Amazon. All good stuff, as it were.

Unfortunately, it seemed he was not going to get much more information here. His next stop would have to be Cuzco, the last place the guys were known to have been. Decision made, he was putting his stuff together ready for an early exit in the morning, when he heard footsteps on the wooden floor outside and a soft knock on his door.

"*Si. Quien és?*"

"Fábio."

He opened the door and saw an obviously hung-over Fábio, wavering slightly and smelling of stale nicotine and alcohol.

"Come in."

Fábio propped himself up on the door frame. "João's brother came in when he got off duty."

"Oh yes?"

"Yes."

"And?"

"My friend, I have hot news. Very hot. But I need some money, you understand?"

"Shhhh, Fábio," said Simon, putting his finger to his lips. "Come in, for god's sake." He encouraged Fábio by pulling at his arm, until Fábio finally lurched in and stood rocking gently to and fro.

"Money?" asked Simon, after he had closed the door. "Er, sure, Fábio. But the most I can let you have is maybe a hundred Reais. I don't have a big budget, or anything."

"Oh. Okay," said Fábio, deflated. Then he suddenly brightened. "Look, *Señor* Walker. I like writing. You know my blog? Everyone reads it. It's pretty good, don't you think?"

Simon nodded. It *was* pretty good, but he put the readership in the hundreds, rather than the millions.

"Okay. Then how about you give me two hundred for the lead and if it comes to anything you get me in as Latin America correspondent?"

"But you'll need to speak English, Fábio."

"I do," said Fábio in English.

"So why are we speaking in Spanish?"

Fábio shrugged. "It's not good to lay all your cards on the table, is it? I speak Portuguese, Spanish and English." He smiled broadly. "And a bit of Japanese." He spoilt the effect of his revelation a little by coughing noisome fumes all over Simon, who backed away and turned his face from the blast.

"Okay," he replied. "I'll see what I can do. But you realise it's not my newspaper."

"You promise?" said Fábio, apparently not caring whose paper it was.

"I promise."

"And the two hundred?"

Simon went to his suitcase and came back with the money in his hand. He held it out.

"Okay, so what's the news?"

"The gringo's alive and in Manaus."

"What!?"

Fábio snatched the two hundred Reais from Simon's hand.

"Yes! João's friend was there when the news came in. The Colonel is so spooked she called up the military. She and some army guy have commandeered a transport plane to get them to Manaus!"

"Are you sure about this?"

"A hundred percent. I swear on the grave of my grandmother. It was confirmed by another friend who saw them leave."

"Right. I've got to get to Manaus."

Fábio shrugged. "But there's no plane today."

"What? Nothing?"

Fábio smiled. "Nothing," he said confidently, and then looked thoughtful. "Although there are usually some private planes coming and going."

Simon looked at his watch. It was barely five o'clock in the morning. Surely there must be something available today. "So how do I find one of these private planes?"

"Ah! Leave it to me," Fábio cried. He suddenly looked almost sober, and a predatory gleam twinkled in his eye. "If you cover my expenses, I'll get you one."

"Fábio..." said Simon. He shook his head despairingly. "Look, I can give you a hundred Reais max."

"Two hundred."

"A hundred and fifty, and that's as much as I can afford. Honestly." He held up his hands. "Speaking of which, whoever's flying will have to take a credit card."

"*Vichi Maria*," Fábio muttered, raising his own arms, and shaking his head. "You don't make it easy." He looked serious for a moment and then a broad grin broke across his face again. "But I'll get you a plane!"

62

They followed Carla into a small room off the main entrance hall of the theatre, where she bought tickets for a tour, and then they walked back and went further into the hall. A guide was speaking in Spanish to a group of a dozen or so tourists, and they hung around at the periphery of the group, apparently following the guide's comments and nodding as he pointed out various aspects of the austere marble and granite interior. An unremarkable middle-aged man materialised next to Carla, and as the guide started ushering the group through to the main auditorium, the four of them held back slightly and walked up the steps together.

Carla spoke quietly to her contact while the tour made its stately progress. She briefly introduced him to Jack and Elena as 'João', but after that, Jack and Elena were left to stand around trying to look interested in the guide's observations. In spite of everything, Jack found himself following the gaze of the tourists taking in the intricate panels and the ornate, four-tiered balconies. He looked up with them at the huge chandelier suspended from a ceiling painted to look like the Eiffel tower seen from directly below. They were moved gently on up the stairs to the ballroom, and eventually arrived at the level of the upper tier of boxes. People wandered in and out of them freely, and Jack, Elena, Carla and João occupied one on their own.

Jack could understand the gist of the conversation.

"It's not going to be easy, Carla, even like that," João was saying.

"I know," said Carla, "But this is a challenge – and an opportunity – we have to accept."

João nodded, and looked at Jack.

"Jack," he began. *"Meu amigo, a cidade inteira tá confinada pela polícia."*

Elena stepped in to translate. "He says the whole city is secured by the police."

João waited for Elena, nodded, and continued. "*A única opção–*"

He was interrupted by the sound of loud voices reaching them from downstairs.

"*Merda. A polícia,*" he said.

"Sorry João," Jack heard Carla say. "Go. You must get away."

João looked from Carla to Jack and back. "*De um a dez, Carla, a importância?*" Importance on a scale of one to ten?

"*Onze,*" said Carla, unhesitatingly.

João nodded, then grabbed her arm "Follow me, then. Quickly."

He led the way out of the box, turned right and walked briskly down to the next levels. The voices were louder now, and footsteps could be heard on the stairs as they entered the last box on the first tier.

"*Desce, desce!*" said João, pointing to the stage.

They looked anxiously down at the platform, but João promptly climbed over the small balcony, hung there for a second, and then made his way down the remaining ten feet, using the beautiful stucco decorations as handholds.

Carla was next, but she hesitated, looking at Jack and Elena. The sound of heavy footsteps came from the corridor outside. She seemed frozen in place, and Jack shouted urgently at her.

"Go on!" he cried. "Go!"

As she swung herself over the rail, a police officer entered the box. He saw Carla disappearing over the balcony edge, and stepped forward. He was so focused on Carla, he was taken completely by surprise when Jack grabbed him bodily, and used his own forward momentum to push him over the balcony and onto the platform 12 feet below. He landed heavily, rolled off the stage and lay still.

Jack and Elena immediately swung over the balcony together and followed Carla down, running across to the back of the stage to join her.

Suddenly the hollow, muffled silence of the auditorium was rent by a sound like a crack of thunder, and bits of plaster clattered down from the ornate ceiling far above. The four on stage instinctively ducked.

"*Pare!*" came a shout from above, and Jack saw several Police up in the boxes, one of them with a raised gun. He also caught a glimpse of another figure rushing into the auditorium at ground level, and heard a cry of '*Fora! Fora!*' – outside! – before he followed the other three off the stage and down into the bowels of the theatre. Down and down they went – much deeper than Jack had imagined. There were shouts and the noise of people running around behind them, and then they emerged in a large, dimly-lit basement area. João ran straight to the far end, while Jack pushed the heavy fire door to, and wedged bits of scenery in the mechanism. João darted behind a crumbling old pier, and started stamping on the ground. A slab of stone shook very slightly and there was an echoing sound from beneath it. João nodded, bending down to it, and they all rushed to help him scrape out the loose cement and sand that held the stone in place. It seemed to take an age, and they could hear shouting and banging behind them, at the door to the basement. Finally, they were able to lever up enough of the stone to get a purchase on it. They had just manhandled it to the side when they heard a harsh female voice from the steps behind them.

"*Pare! Pare agora, ou eu atiro.*"

They looked up to see Colonel Márcia Ferreira stepping carefully down the last of the dusty steps to the basement, holding a pistol trained on Jack.

KEIR FARRELL

63

"The gringo at last," said Ferreira in heavily accented English. "Apparently you are a very hard man to kill."

She stood braced, holding the pistol with both hands.

Jack put his hands up.

"Look," said Jack, "All I want to do is get home. I don't even know why you want me. I just want to go home!" The last words came out as a strangled shout of anger and frustration.

Ferreira sneered. "*Tá brincando, meu amigo.* Just tell me, who are you working for, huh?"

"I'm not working for anyone."

"*Pelo amor de Deus,*" cried Carla, "He's just a fucking tourist!"

"Bullshit. What sort of tourist goes walking through the VRAE – the home of the biggest cocaine growers and producers in the world? Why would a tourist do that, huh?"

"I'm just on an expedition – *was* on an expedition. Walking the Amazon – source to sea?"

Ferreira blinked, and Jack saw something he hoped might be doubt cross her face for a brief moment. Then she laughed. Her radio was squawking, and she took one hand off her gun. Watching the group the whole time, she fiddled with a knob on the radio, until it clicked off.

"Walking the river? What is the point of that?" she finally said. "It's so stupid. It's like walking the Atlantic. We have such things as boats."

Jack shrugged. "It's already been done once. I just wanted to do it faster."

"It's true!" said Carla. "It was just another crazy gringo idea. He didn't do anything. He was just in the wrong place at the wrong time."

"Oh Yeah?" Ferreira suddenly looked tired. "And you – what about you?" She pointed at Carla.

Carla started to say something, but Ferreira held up her free hand.

"Don't bother, *querida*. I know all about you, Carla da Silva. A right pain in the ass to the government – you and your lot."

"Damn right we are. The government's no better than a gang of crooks. And you know it."

Ferreira held up her hand again. "Spare me the lecture. I've been living with the scumbags for a lot longer than you."

Carla opened her mouth again, but Ferreira had already moved her attention on to Elena.

"As for you, Miss Fernandez – I know all abut you, too. You're a fucking terrorist, for the love of god."

Elena put her chin out defiantly. "The name is Lopez. Elena Lopez. And *anyone* who disagrees with the bandidos that run our governments is labelled a terrorist. All we want is justice for our people and an end to the corrupt, fascist pigs that steal our lives and think of nothing but their pockets – the end of them, and the people who help them and protect them." He eyes blazed and she even moved forward a pace.

Ferreira swung the gun towards her. "Don't even think about it, dear." Holding the gun trained on Elena, she looked at Jack.

"Right, gringo – you've got ten seconds to convince me why I shouldn't just blow your heads off right now."

Jack took a breath. "Look, er, *Colonel*," he said, squinting to see Ferreira's name badge, "I was just on an expedition. I was kidnapped, for Christ's sake – I got away – the Police found me – thought I was a terrorist or something – gave me to the Americans – they made the same mistake. I've been running ever since. I haven't done anything, and I don't know anything. That's it. All of it!"

Ferreira's pistol dropped very slightly. Jack saw the look of doubt return, and she shook her head. "Jesus you gringos piss me off, you know that? The world is struggling to get by, and you think it's fun to go off on pointless journeys, walking through our back yards. You have too much money and too much time on your hands."

She lowered her gun another few millimetres. "You and your damned governments are always telling us what to do, when you've made such a mess of your own countries. And look at you all – hundreds of years killing and stealing, and now you've all gone soft and useless. It's pathetic."

Now that she had spoken her piece, the fire in her eyes seemed to die.

"Anyway," she said more quietly, "it doesn't matter if you *were* innocent. You know far too much about our operations now." She paused. "And for that matter, Miss Lopez and Miss da Silva, so do you. And you there at the back, too," she said, calling over to João, who had managed to more or less hide himself behind Jack and Elena. "So come on, make your move, so I can kill you all with a clear conscience."

Carla stepped forward, and Ferreira raised her gun again.

"And you?" Carla asked defiantly. "Whatever your name is." She leaned in to read the name on the badge. Colonel Ferreira, right?" Hearing her name seemed to unsettle Ferreira, and Carla pressed the advantage. "What are you doing while you're supposed to be protecting the poor working people of this god-forsaken country – people like me, right? Stealing our money and making yourself rich off other people's misery. On what planet is that acceptable, do you think?"

"I do what I have to do," Ferreira growled angrily. "Don't you judge me. I'm not one of your political elite, stealing billions and living a life of luxury."

Jack lowered his hands slightly, walked a small step closer, and moved a fraction to the right, out of the firing line.

"For God's sake, woman," cried Carla. If you kill us, you'll be murdering innocent people. Does that really not mean anything to you anymore? Nothing at all?"

The gun came up again. Jack found himself watching it closely. He felt a cold sweat forming. He could no longer hear what anyone was saying or see what was happening around him. There was just the gun and the woman pointing it. He saw how she was holding it, and saw the hesitation in her eyes.

"You are full of shit," the woman finally said. "All of you." She looked up at the ceiling and breathed out heavily, puffing out her cheeks. The gun came down again.

Jack found himself drawn forward, his eyes riveted on the gun…

And then the woman suddenly just dropped it to her side. "Go on," she said simply. "Get lost."

For a second they all stood there in silence, no one moving a muscle. Then João backed slowly towards the hole. Jack remained, staring at the woman. The sweat was pouring off him, and he had to blink it away as it ran into his eyes. Carla and Elena stood next to him.

"Go on! Get the fuck out of here!" Ferreira shouted at them.

The spell was broken, and they turned back to the hole. João had already descended, and as he stood over the opening, an up-draft of stinking air made Jack's soaking shirt feel like ice against his skin.

Carla dropped in next, and scrambled down. Elena went after Carla, and Jack followed her, almost slipping on the rungs of the rusty iron ladder. When he reached the bottom, he found himself in water up to his knees. All they could see was the glow of João's torch in the distance and the dim light from the basement overhead. Jack watched as the stone was pushed slowly back over the hole, and suddenly a voice called down to them.

"*Têm dez minutos.*" Ten minutes to get the hell out of it.

The stone fell back into place with a dull thud, and they were off and wading after João as fast as they could.

64

Adam Torres sat in the back of the car like a statue, staring out of the side window. The vehicle was unmarked, but they had at least stuck a light on the roof and switched on the siren. It did not matter – the other drivers could not get out of the way even if they wanted to. So they sat there, the car virtually stationary now, with the aircon doing a poor job of keeping five big suited and armed men cool.

They had been on their way to the private airport near the coach station. Torres had been sceptical of the sighting that had been reported, but a single gringo chartering a plane out of Tabatinga was at the very least unusual, and he decided to follow it up personally. Apart from the military driver of the dull green SUV, he had taken just three other people - two CIA agents, and a Brazilian ABIN intelligence officer.

They made reasonable progress coming out of the city, and were within a few minutes of the airport when news of the second sighting came through. It was painfully obvious to Torres that this was the genuine article, and he immediately ordered the car turned round, but the moment they reached the main road back into the city, they found themselves in something that resembled a supermarket car park on Saturday morning more than a three-lane carriageway.

The cars shuffled forward another few feet before coming to a halt again. Torres wound down the window and looked out.

"There!" he said. "That guy on the bike!" He pointed out the side window. "Get me a bike!"

The Brazilian agent immediately realised what Torres was pointing at and where his thoughts were going. He opened his door and leapt out, at the same time keying his radio.

"Unit 358. We need some bikes at our location," he called into the radio. He strode between the cars towards the traffic cop seated on a

Police trail bike on the forecourt of a petrol station. He pulled his badge out, holding it in front of him as he approached. Torres was already out of the car and following him.

He quickly explained the situation, and the officer on the bike keyed his own radio. He spoke to his control, eyes widening when he heard the response. He slowly slid off the bike and started removing his helmet, and by the time Torres arrived, the bike was his. Torres ignored the proffered helmet and hopped straight on the bike. He pushed the starter button, crashed the foot pedal into first, and sped off.

The traffic cop and the intelligence officer watched open-mouthed as Torres threaded his way through the long lines of cars and buses, and by the time another group of Police arrived on motorcycles, Torres was out of sight.

He raced between the stationary lines of vehicles, straight down the main road to Manaus, ignoring the lights and the other traffic police. The outermost lane of three was supposed to be a bus lane, but even this was completely blocked. Negotiating three lanes of traffic creeping forward in vague Latin American-style lines was hot, hard work. He knocked all the newspapers out of the hands of a newsboy standing in the middle of Avenida Constantino Nery, and clipped dozens of wing mirrors on his way through. When he got lost, he took off across the grassy square of the Praça da Saude, drove the wrong way up a one-way street, crossed another square to arrive almost within sight of the theatre, twelve minutes after taking the bike. At the Praça do Congresso his luck ran out when he burst out from the square straight into the path of a yellow postal van. It was only a glancing blow, but it was enough to put the bike on its side and Torres on the floor. The van driver opened the door and began to get out, but Torres was already up and running down Avenida Eduardo Ribeira. Two minutes later, he was approaching the front of the theatre, which was already surrounded by Police with sub-machine guns and automatic rifles. A police captain watched Torres approach, and held his hand up to stop him.

Torres brought out his ID and thrust it at the officer, who looked at the sweaty and dishevelled Torres sceptically, and took the card.

"I am here on behalf of the U.S. government, on license by the

Brazilian Federal Police—"

"I know who you are, sir," the man said calmly, handing back the ID. He launched into a matter-of-fact account of what was happening, and confirmed to Torres that there were three suspects inside with Colonel Ferreira. "The Colonel ordered us all outside, to create a cordon around the building," he concluded. "No-one is allowed in or out, sir."

Torres listened impatiently. "Get her on the radio, then," he said, snappishly.

"Can't sir – no signal inside."

"What? Well then how do you know she's okay?"

"No shots have been fired, Sir. And anyway, I have my orders direct from the Colonel."

Torres shook his head. "Jesus Christ," he mumbled, pulling out his Sig P226 and setting off towards the theatre.

"Sir!" the officer shouted, raising his own gun. "Sir! I am ordered to stop anyone entering or leaving the building, by force if necessary."

Torres was oblivious to the verbal protestations, but the sound as the man slapped the cocking lever on his MP5, had an instant effect. He stopped, looking back to see the captain's gun levelled at him. Two other police officers had raised their semi-automatics. He put his hands in the air and walked slowly back towards the captain, until he was standing with his chest tight up against the muzzle of the gun.

"Listen," he said quietly, staring unblinkingly into the man's eyes. "This whole operation is vital to the interests of my government, your government, the Peruvian government, the Federal Police and the military. I am here at the request of Colonel Ferreira to assist in bringing down these terrorists. It is vital that I get into the theatre right now, and you cannot imagine the shit you will be in if anyone so much as harms a hair on my head."

He turned and started walking back towards the entrance of the building. Behind him, the Policeman lowered his gun for a second, and then raised it again, aiming it carefully.

At that moment, Colonel Ferreira emerged from the entrance. "Captain!" she called. "Get your people in to search the whole building."

As the Captain spoke into his radio, she walked briskly towards him and Torres.

"They disappeared," she said, shaking her head. "But they must be hiding in there somewhere. I followed them on to the stage and lost them behind the set."

"Yes Ma'am," the Captain responded. "We've had the building surrounded and all exits are covered."

Torres listened to the exchange, flashed the Colonel an angry look, and began striding towards the entrance.

The Captain started to raise his gun again, but Ferreira held out a hand to stop him. She saw the emotion on the man's face. "Everything okay, Captain?"

He nodded slowly. "Yes Ma'am, but it wouldn't take much to persuade me to drop that arrogant fucker where he stands."

Ferreira stood for a moment looking him in the eyes, and then she shook her head. "No, Captain. Brazil needs another dead body like it needs another bent president." She smiled faintly and walked away from the building, leaving the man with a slightly puzzled expression.

"Yes Ma'am," he said quietly, and then more loudly. "Orders, Ma'am?"

Ferreira waved her arms vaguely at him as she walked away.

"Ma'am...?"

65

The only light now was João's torch, as the fugitives splashed quickly along the stinking underground passage.

"Are these the sewers?" asked Jack. "They're pretty impressive."

Up front, Carla spoke to João, relaying some of what he said to Jack.

"They call it the 'galeria dos ingleses'," she said. "The English Gallery. It was built as a sewage system by the English, back at the beginning of the twentieth century, but it's not really used."

They stopped at a junction, where smaller tunnels branched off. Drips, ticks and scratching sounds echoed from every direction.

"Ratos e jacaré," said João, as he shone his torch around the walls.

"Rats and caiman," said Elena. "Great."

João studied some paint marks high up in the tunnel walls, spoke rapidly to Carla, and led off again. A minute later they turned into a huge chamber.

"I didn't know anything about them," said Carla. "Most people don't. João says there's a whole network of chambers and tunnels they use at low water. He says that although it's not quite lowest water now, we can get all the way to the riverside by following the signs on the walls and the downward slope of the chambers." She spoke briefly to João again.

"This is the main chamber now," she said. "It runs all the way down the main street in Manaus, Avenida Eduardo Ribeiro. I can hardly believe it."

They were clearly descending now, although the water level was getting slightly lower. Up ahead, there were some big splashing, thrashing sounds which sounded just like caiman moving around along the river banks at night. Jack hoped they were moving away from them and not towards them.

They were walking at quite a fast pace now in the shallower water, and João spoke breathlessly to Carla.

"We're going to branch off in a moment, so we don't emerge right by the main port," she translated. "The next bits will be a bit more cramped, okay?"

They were not only more cramped, they were falling to pieces. The water was deeper, and bricks and debris were strewn across their path. In the end, it took them fifteen minutes to make their way down the foul-smelling passages until they fell out of the exit and dropped into the dark waters of the Rio Negro.

They swam until they reached some mud flats, covered in debris and filth. João led them to a dilapidated, boarded-up floating house, and then left them for a few minutes while he went in search of a boat, returning in a dirty white jet-boat powered by a noisy diesel. He ushered them aboard, and sent them down to the back near the motor, where they could not be easily seen.

Carla translated as he crouched down and explained what was happening.

"We're being taken to Lago do Aleixo. It's about twenty minutes away," she said, glancing at her watch. "From there we go on without João, in transport that will get us around the police barriers to the north of the city, and he's going to arrange a truck to take us as far as the Federal checkpoint at the other side of the indigenous reserve on the way to Boa Vista."

She thanked João, and he turned and walked back to join the boat's pilot. "That will be João's part played," she explained, "but I'm confident my Boa Vista contact will pick us up from there, okay?"

"Okay. That's great, Carla. Thanks," said Elena.

"Yes. Brilliant job," said Jack, nodding.

The pilot reversed the boat out into the mainstream of the river, where they turned and accelerated through the maze of floating petrol stations and boats of all sizes flitting around the port. Once past the busy local commercial and passenger area, the pilot throttled up to full speed and they were soon powering down the river towards the Chibatão container port and beyond. The boat had the noisiest diesel engine Jack had ever heard, and they were pressed right up against it, making conversation impossible.

It was a long twenty minutes before they were deposited on a broken concrete ramp, at the top of which a battered old jeep awaited them.

They shook hands with João, and Carla gave him a brief hug.

"Thanks," said Jack, grasping the man by the arm. "I owe you."

Carla translated and João spoke briefly again, breaking out in a smile.

"Yes. You do," said Carla. "Maybe when he comes to England..."

They left after another firm handshake and smiles all round.

The journey in the Jeep took them more than an hour and a half over some good roads and some very rough trails. Eventually they emerged onto a long straight road, which Carla told them was Interstate highway BR174 to Boa Vista.

Their driver made a few phone calls on the way, and when he eventually pulled in to a small driveway, Jack was not surprised to see another truck waiting for them.

They thanked the driver of the Jeep and got into the cab of the truck. After speaking to their new driver for a few minutes, Carla explained that they would be dropped just this side of the next police checkpoint. It was about two hundred miles up the road, on the other side of the Waimiri-Atroari indigenous reserve.

"Then we'll have to walk, to by-pass the barrier and reach the village of Jundiá," Carla explained. "I'm arranging for someone to pick us up from there and take us the rest of the way to Boa Vista."

"That's brilliant, Carla. But what are our options from there?"

"Ah, well then I have a real card up my sleeve."

"You seem to have quite a few."

"Maybe, but I hope this is the last one we'll need. My Boa Vista contact does flights into Guyana. With luck, we'll be out of Brazil before midnight.

"Where have we heard that before?" said Jack.

66

It took two CIA operatives, a Brazilian intelligence agent and a dozen other Federal police officers nearly two hours to find the tunnel, and only after high-powered lights, sniffer dogs, crowbars and two theatre staff were brought in to help.

Torres peered down into the darkness, shook his head, and left the theatre. Outside, he sat in a car with his team, who had arrived at the theatre twenty minutes after Torres. They had already asked for plans of the sewers and been told there were none, but that the network was "extensive".

"Jesus, what is it that makes these people so incompetent?" cried Torres. "Is it the heat? The air? Something in the fucking water?"

He ran his fingers through his thinning black hair.

"So what you're telling me is that they could be anywhere in this goddamned city, correct?"

"I'm afraid so, sir."

"And what about communications? Could they have got anything out yet?"

"Unlikely. Everything's still down, although there's a lot of pressure to bring it back up. Roads too – all the routes out are blocked, but the barriers in the city are causing a big stink."

"Compared to the stink those terrorists will make if they get away, it's nothing."

"Yes sir, I agree. But the public are getting pretty ticked off, and the Brazilian authorities are wavering."

"Jesus, the Brazilians are always wavering. There's no coordination – no organisation. They've all got their hands in one cookie jar or another, and they couldn't give a shit about anything but that. Fuck the people; fuck the country. They're worse than the fucking Peruvians."

"Yes sir."

"Yes. Well I'm going to get these bastards with or without anyone's help. You just work on keeping communications down and transport tied up for another night at least. I'm going to make sure our net is spread wide enough to pick these assholes up if they manage to get out of here."

"Yes sir."

"Okay. Let's go, then."

67

S imon seriously doubted he had ever had a less comfortable flight in his life, even as a young reporter shuttling back and forth between São Paulo and Rio de Janeiro, or bumping around the British Isles. Four hours squashed up against the cold, hard plastic that barely covered the plane's ice-cold fuselage, had cut off circulation to parts of the body about which he was usually quite unaware. When the door of the aircraft had finally been opened, he could hardly move to get himself out.

They flew in from the southwest of the sprawling city, and descended rapidly over the new sports stadium built for the World Cup. The pilot just had time to point out Manaus' decrepit coach station, which as far as Simon could see they had avoided hitting by mere inches, before they skimmed over a white wall and bounced unexpectedly onto a scruffy little runway. The plane slowed to a walking pace before turning and coming to rest beside a hangar.

He was amazed to find the Federal Police at the postage stamp-sized airfield. Federal Police with body armour and submachine guns. They stopped him, searched his meagre baggage, and asked him what he was doing in Brazil. In Tabatinga. In Manaus."

"Just researching a story," Simon said in Spanish.

"What sort of story?" one of them asked.

Simon smiled. "*A cobra grande*," he said. The giant snake. He held out his arms to indicate something big.

The officer shook his head and looked exasperated, but said nothing. He was asked to take a seat and wait. He watched as one of the officers talked to someone over the radio.

Eventually he was released, without so much as a please or thank you, and someone from the private airline he had flown with called him a taxi. He asked for the nearest hotel and a gruff taxi driver dumped him at a ghastly place by the side of the coach station.

Twenty minutes later, he was sitting in his room with a cup of coffee, his laptop open and his satellite terminal balanced precariously on the window ledge to point to the Inmarsat 3 satellite.

He waited for his emails to download and wondered how on earth he was going to find the Brit. All he had was a report that he had been spotted somewhere in Manaus. He was itching to get on the internet and scour all the sources he could think of for information, but the connection was inexplicably slow and he wanted to see if any of his contacts had come up with anything for him. He finished his coffee and saw that his emails had finally all downloaded.

Most of it was useless, distracting, annoying, social media crap, but in the middle of it all was an email from a colleague at work with the cryptic title 'Saw this and thought of you :)' At this point it merely piqued Simon's curiosity, but as he scrolled down to the forwarded message, his throat went dry. He skimmed over it and then narrowed his eyes and concentrated on the detail.

It was an email that had come in less than twenty-four hours ago, and it was from Jack McCrae himself, without a doubt, although the name was not mentioned in the email. At a paragraph long, it was hardly comprehensive, but it did spell out fairly clearly that the guy believed he was in grave danger, and also identified the nature of that danger. The gist of it was pretty crazy – potentially the stuff of fantasy or paranoia – and if he had not just come from Tabatinga with his head stuffed with unfulfilled story potential, he would undoubtedly have consigned it to the bin. As it was, he would do what he could to verify the substance of it, while trying to track down his gringo in the flesh.

All he had to go on was that McCrae had made it to Manaus. He had – very sensibly, perhaps – not mentioned in his email exactly where he was, or where he was going. Simon looked at the email again, scanning the list of recipients. There were four other newspapers on the list, none of whom would have anyone in place here. In fact, the likelihood was that none of them would be remotely interested in the somewhat bizarre story. Even if they were, it would take them time, which meant that for the moment Simon was ahead of the game. He intended to keep it that way. He also saw the address of the British embassy in Brazil, and shook his head: the chances of an official running with the story were on a par with the chances of discovering the secret of the universe in a dog biscuit.

He replied briefly to Jack, simply telling him that there was someone in Brazil ready to assist, and providing the name of a free email encryption service. Then he got down to the serious business of tracking down likely sources of information from Peru, Brazil, Colombia and the USA. He still had contacts from the time he had worked in South America, and he sent out feelers to São Paulo and Lima. He also had his own networks in Washington and New York, and he was confident that if there were the merest sniff of something strange going on, one of the guys would dig it up.

As he went methodically through his list of potential sources, an obscure Associated Press news story caught his attention. Apparently there was some sort of joint security operation by the UK, France, Canada, the Guyanas and Trinidad being carried out, based out of Georgetown, Guyana. It was slightly odd that no details had been given, but other than that, it was only relevant because in the grand scheme of things Georgetown was not that far away. He filed it away for future reference.

As usual, he sat glued to the computer screen for far too long, and by the time he had finished following mostly useless leads across the internet, he was hot, sweaty, tired and sore. He knew that the rest of the day would be spent running up his newspaper's satellite phone bill and monitoring his email for anything that would give him his next lead. Time to take a break, have a shower, and get something to eat.

68

J ensen was furious. "But who authorised this? It's *my* operation. No-one—"

"Calm yourself down, Robert. It's not *your* operation – it's *our* operation."

"It was the General, wasn't it?" Jensen fumed. "He's paranoid, dammit—"

"That's enough, Robert," the man said, raising his voice. "It doesn't matter who did it, the fact is that the check has made it crystal clear PERGEN is not playing this game straight."

"But we've no real evidence of that, sir." Jensen had handled Torres for five years, and was reluctant to accept that he was anything but on the level.

"Oh come on, man. The missing Americans? The money from the drugs bust?"

Jensen stared across the desk, challenging him.

He breathed deeply, passed a hand over his bald head, and finally reached down and withdrew a thin folder from one of his desk drawers. He removed a single piece of A4 from the folder, placed it on the desktop and turned it towards Jensen. He continued holding it between forefinger and thumb.

Jensen sat forward to read it, and the blood drained from his face as he reviewed the information contained in the ten lines of typed text. He grimaced and shook his head, but said nothing.

The bald man sighed, withdrawing the paper and placing it carefully back in the folder. "Right now, he's in Brazil, working with a handful of people chasing someone down.

"Who?" asked Jensen.

"We've no information on that yet. But it's nothing the hell to do with the project."

"I don't know what to say—"

"Save it, Robert. Fact is, the project's compromised, and we're pulling out."

"But we can resolve this," Jensen insisted. "Sure, we may have to..." he trailed off as the bald man shook his head firmly.

"Robert, this is a POTUS-sponsored project. If we don't kill this off now, the fucking President of the United States is at risk. It's over."

"Jesus," was all Jensen could manage.

"I've already authorised all the measures we planned for this eventuality, and nothing can stop it now. Within 48 hours everything will be squeaky clean."

Jensen's eyes glazed over as he thought about all the planning, the thousands of hours, the billions of dollars, the lives, the past – and his future.

The man stood up and waited as Jensen got slowly to his feet. He held out his hand and they shook.

"See you in Committee as usual. Other than that, I won't be speaking to you again."

Jensen nodded dumbly.

"Good luck Robert," the man concluded, sitting down again and turning to his computer. "See your own way out, will you?"

There was nothing left to say. Jensen turned and walked towards the door.

69

Jack awoke from a troubled sleep, his unconscious mind disturbed by a sudden change in the monotonous tone of the truck's engine.

"We were just about to wake you," said Elena, seeing him open his eyes. "We're almost there. Are you ready to go?"

He nodded, yawning, and then shook his head to clear the grogginess. "Yep. Ready when you are."

Elena, sitting in between Jack and Carla, had her bag on her lap, and she placed it now so that the opening was towards Jack. When Carla turned her head to speak to the driver, Elena slipped something across to Jack. It was wrapped in a rag, and as he accepted it he realised it was his pistol, all put back together again. He glanced at her questioningly and she turned to him.

"Didn't think the metal detector would be working," she whispered, and grinned.

His eyes twinkled with a mixture of humour and exasperation, and he blew her a kiss. Without looking down, he checked the safety and then shifted his weight a little so he could quietly stuff the gun into his waistband.

The truck slowed even more, pulled in towards the side of the road, and finally squealed to a stop with two wheels on the verge.

Carla continued speaking to the driver, and Jack was able to understand most of what was said.

"Just head straight into the trees. Keep going and you'll pick up the trail, then turn right." He gave them the thumbs up, and Jack leaned over and shook his hand.

"*Gracias,*" he said. "*Obrigado.*"

"*De nada. Boa sorte,*" the driver said, smiling at Jack's Portuguese.

"Right – come on!" said Carla, and flung open the passenger door, dropping to the ground and then holding the door for Jack and

Elena. The driver got out the other side and started checking his tyres as if he was worried about something.

"Let's go?" urged Carla as soon as they were all on the ground. Jack swung the door shut and they followed her straight off the road and into the forest.

Once they were a good distance from the road, Carla stopped. She turned to them. "It's supposed to be around two kilometres to the checkpoint from where we stopped. All we have to do is walk ten minutes into the forest, then turn to the right and keep going – we'll be parallel to the main road – until we get to cleared land. The other side of that is the village of Jundiá – we should see the houses. We just walk to the left of the houses and onto the road. I spoke to my contact in Boa Vista, and he'll be waiting for us there in a black pick-up. It's probably around five kilometres in total, okay?"

"Sounds fine," said Jack.

"Easy," said Elena.

"Glad you think so," grumbled Carla, moving off again. "I was brought up to sit behind a desk, not to walk through the jungle."

"I thought you said you grew up here," said Jack, with some amusement.

"I did, yes," said Carla. "And like most of the other locals, I spent my time *avoiding* the jungle, not looking for it."

They walked on in silence, through what appeared to be primary forest, although once they turned north, a few discarded plastic water bottles and an old flip-flop suggested that other people before them had had reason to avoid the checkpoint.

They made good progress, since it was terra firma and there were no major obstacles, and they emerged from the tree line in a little over thirty minutes. The sun was getting low now, but here in the open they could see well, and another forty minutes brought them to a dusty road. The promised black pick-up truck was waiting for them less than a hundred yards away.

A big, balding man squeezed himself out from behind the wheel and came striding across to Carla, embracing her and kissing her on both cheeks. He stood beaming down on her, a great smile on his round face.

"*Puxa, Carla, que bom te rever!*" he cried, hugging her again. He finally turned from her and held out his hand to Jack. His grasp was solid, but sensitive, and Jack looked into a broad, open face.

"This is Roberto," said Carla.

"*Muito prazer*," said Roberto, shaking hands with Jack and Elena.

"*Igualmente*," Jack replied, tagging his name on at the end.

Elena nodded non-committally.

"You're American, right?" Roberto asked Jack, in perfect English.

"No. British."

"Oh dear – sorry." Roberto smiled.

"No problem," said Jack. "You're forgiven."

They got quickly into the car and bumped along the road to the junction with the main BR174 Manaus - Boa Vista highway. Roberto pointed to the right.

"Police," he said.

In the gloom, Jack could just make out a cluster of huge sheds and a few articulated trucks parked up a long way down the road. He listened as Carla explained very briefly to Roberto what was happening, Roberto making intelligent comments and questions as she went along.

"None of this surprises me," Roberto finally announced. "In Brazil, everyone is corrupt. You must know this, Jack, no?"

"Maybe, Roberto, but what about in Peru – and the U.S.?"

"Hmm. Well, Brazil does not have a monopoly on corruption, you know. Still, it is strange, I agree."

Jack shrugged. "Very. But in any case the Brazilians are in it up to their necks – at least it seems that way."

"So Carla tells me. And of course if it is true, it could be the tipping point our own organisation is looking for."

"I understand that. I just need to get the hell away from here and get the story out."

"Jack, I have to say that we would appreciate some political links – you know, evidence of the involvement of our politicians in this. Perhaps you could..."

"Roberto, you're talking as if I'm some sort of spy," Jack cried. "I'm not. Really, I'm not."

Carla touched Roberto's shoulder. "He's not, Roberto."

"No, no, of course not. Sorry Jack. We will get you out, of course. Don't worry." He smiled. "Still...," he muttered, as he got back to concentrating on the drive.

"So what is the plan, Roberto?" asked Carla.

He smiled. "Ah, well, it is too late for today, of course – it will be ten o'clock or later when we get to Boa Vista. But you will stay in my sister's house tonight – she is not here – and tomorrow we will go to the airstrip at midnight."

"Are they not monitoring all the airstrips?" asked Jack.

"Not this one, Jack. This week, it is at the farm of my friend, near the Rio Cachorro, fifty miles from Boa Vista. Next week, it will be somewhere else."

"Roberto is in the business of 'unofficial imports'," Carla explained.

"Yes," said Roberto. He glanced at Carla. "But not drugs," he added. "I don't do drugs. Well, maybe cigarettes, sometimes. But I am not like the people who are trying to kill you. And I am not stealing money from my people, like the *bandidos* in Brasilia."

"I understand, Roberto," said Jack.

"We are just trying to make a living. Did you know it is impossible to run an honest business in Brazil, they tax you so much? It's ridiculous – the tax rates are so high people cannot pay them. So what does the government do? It raises the tax rates even more, to make up for the taxes the people do not pay because the tax rates are too high. Stupid people."

Jack nodded sympathetically, and Roberto opened his mouth to continue.

"Roberto..." said Carla in an admonishing tone.

"What? Oh, sorry, Carla. But it makes me very angry. These people are idiots. And you know what they do with the taxes they get? Instead of spending the money on education and health and housing? They steal it! The bastards steal it and send it to Switzerland! They are *escória*, my friend. They are scum!"

Carla nodded. "Yes, and now we find that while the politicians are stealing our money, the Police and the Army are dealing in drugs." She laughed bitterly. "What a country."

What a country indeed, thought Jack.

"But what about our friend Colonel Ferreira?" said Elena.

"Who?" asked Roberto.

Elena gave Roberto the detail of what had happened in the basement of the theatre, and Roberto shook his head. "Hah, there must be something in it for her," he said. "She wouldn't do that for nothing."

Carla nodded. "Yes. I don't know what, but there's something behind her action. I wouldn't trust her at all. She's just like all the rest of them. Don't you think so, Jack?"

"Probably," Jack agreed, although he was surprised at the fact that they dismissed the act so easily.

Carla and Roberto talked on and off throughout the journey north, while Jack and Elena sat quietly in the back. Elena was not given to wasting words, and Jack was happy to get some more thinking done. They stopped at one point to eat and freshen up a little, but it was another long and tedious ride in the dark. Jack's thoughts drifted over the thousands of miles he had now covered on this seemingly never-ending flight from persecution. As usual, the more he thought about it, the more frustrated and agitated he became.

Almost as soon as they arrived at the modest little house just off the BR401, Jack was onto the internet. Mercifully, it was still functioning. Roberto apologised for the speed, but Jack knew it was probably no slower than any other internet connection in Brazil. At least he could check his emails and track down some more addresses he had thought about.

The email page was desperately slow to load, so he started writing down a few search phrase ideas. Finally, a ping told him that the email page had loaded. He looked at the list of emails, and his heart leapt when he saw one from a reporter who said he was interested in the story and was already in Brazil. The message was simple to the point of being abrupt. It gave the name of the newspaper, and then said 'In Brazil now. Interested in your story. Can help, but need exclusive.' Its style was oddly like a telegram, but to Jack, it was poetry. At the bottom of the email was a link that said it offered free encryption.

He was tempted to rush out a reply, but before writing anything, he sat and thought about it. What were the chances that this was from an enemy – that it was some sort of trap? No – Jack was using a new email address with a non-identifying name; the sender's IP address was in Europe and the receiver's was listed as being located in Rio de Janeiro. There was nothing to connect sender and receiver before the email. Jack had even avoided using his own name in the email he had sent out, instead pointing the recipients to his blog page.

After Jack had dragged some more details of the planned clandestine operation out of a somewhat reluctant Roberto, he wrote out the minimum information he thought was required, beginning with 'Offer of help accepted. Exclusive guaranteed.' He stated that there would be three people flying out of Boa Vista, destination Lethem airport Guyana, ETA 01:00 the day after tomorrow. He also added 'Now have some details of Peru operation. Can also provide details of Brazil side, but need more on U.S. connection.' This time, he signed the email off using his real name.

Carla left him to it, but Roberto hovered in the background looking anxious. At one point, he went outside for a few minutes and came back saying the weather looked like it was closing in, and that he was worried they would lose the internet connection at any moment.

"How long do you still need?" Roberto asked.

"I don't know, Roberto. I still have to encrypt the email and send it. Maybe fifteen minutes at most?"

"Okay. Well, I would be as quick as you can, if I were you. The clouds are getting pretty thick out there."

Jack nodded absently, concentrating on his task. He signed up for the sender's suggested online encrypted email service, and was amazed to see how simple it was. In the end he managed to send the encrypted mail in less than five minutes. He sat for a second without doing anything, waiting for confirmation, and when it came through he felt a wave of relief flood over him. He went back to the search engine page and started looking at the results from his last query.

Roberto, who had gone outside again, suddenly burst in. "It's going to rain. If the signal hasn't gone yet, it'll be gone any minute now."

Jack looked at the screen. He typed in "test" and pressed the search button. Nothing. Damn. He shook his head.

"Sorry, my friend," said Roberto, seeing Jack's despair. It'll be back later, for sure."

70

With nothing else to do in Manaus except write and research, Simon had gone to bed early, and he woke early too. By four thirty he was showered, dressed, and sitting in front of his laptop reviewing emails. He had that strange feeling of anticipation and excitement in the pit of stomach that he had felt years before whenever he found himself on the trail of a good story. For the sake of his poor guts, he had forced himself to sit quietly and relax until he had munched through the meagre offerings in the room's tiny fridge and drunk two bottles of mineral water. Now he hunched forward and watched impatiently as his satellite hub connected to the Inmarsat service and slowly dropped his new emails into his in-box.

A good haul: eight responses from the USA, three from São Paulo, one from Lima and even one from an old colleague in Bogota. But what really caught his attention was the last item on the list – a link to an encrypted email server.

Simon quickly logged in to get the email, and devoured the brief contents. His man was in Boa Vista, heading for Lethem. And he had passed on a time and a location. First things first, then: what where the options for getting to Lethem? He did some quick research on Lethem, which seemed to be a typical frontier town, on the border with Brazil – probably full of barely legal people doing barely legal things and drinking a lot of their barely legal income away. It was, however, just seventy miles northwest of Boa Vista, and was therefore an obvious choice for getting out of Brazil in a hurry. He loaded up a satellite image of the roads from Manaus. Six hundred miles to the border with Guyana – out of the question. He looked briefly at the flight options to Guyana from Manaus, but gave up when he saw how complicated it was. Instead, he sent an email back to the office asking someone to figure out what could get him to

Lethem by midday or maybe two o'clock at the latest, then he turned his thoughts to the other information in McCrae's email.

Apparently, McCrae was happy with the idea of the exclusive. That was nice to know, although Simon felt a twinge of guilt about demanding it. Still, if he returned from all this without an exclusive, he would find himself – rightfully, in his opinion – hung out to dry. So, that was one thing less to worry about.

Next, the guy was offering some sort of corroborative evidence of Peru and Brazil being in on the deal, whatever that meant exactly. It was shaping up nicely as a good story, but they still needed more details of exactly what was going on – and as McCrae said in his email, they needed something that would tie the U.S. in. Everyone knew that Peru was corrupt, and Brazil had already been exposed as the all-time-number-one country of sleaze. They could end up simply uncovering a bit more of the iceberg: vaguely interesting, but not particularly newsworthy.

He allowed himself to dream for a few seconds. A provable case of U.S. government-sanctioned international drugs trafficking was definitely the Holy Grail here. It would be the biggest scandal of the decade – maybe of the century.

While he waited for a response from the office on his flight options, he started looking through his other emails, hoping that maybe something else had come in that would help. His Lima contact had sent him a link to an article in the Lima Times about an American who had apparently disappeared from the face of the earth after heading down the Inca Trail from Cuzco in search of some hallucinogenic plant or other. The name seemed familiar somehow, but he searched for it and found nothing. He tried to look up Jack McCrae's blog, too, but that was reported as being down.

None of his other contacts had come up with much regarding Peru. Yes, there were all sorts of rumours about the drugs trade, but they were the same rumours as always – nothing new. There was also the usual gossip about just how much the Peruvian President was in the White House's pockets, and rumours about the exact amount of inward investment the country had succeeded in attracting on the back of the good relationship the two presidents enjoyed.

Peru was clearly doing very well for itself at the moment. While Japan and the East were throwing money into the pot to build port facilities, railways and the much-vaunted Trans-Amazonica Inter-Oceanic Highway, all concentrated in the industrial south, it seemed the Yanks were investing in port facilities, roads and other infrastructure in the north. There was some speculation that a new pipeline to one of the northern ports was for oil, but no evidence had been forthcoming of any significant new oil or gas reserves having been discovered. A well-kept secret, perhaps? Simon smiled. No such thing.

Meanwhile, everyone – the Chinese, Americans, Brazilians, and Germans among them – was in on the dam-building program approved by the Peruvian government. The number of dams was huge, and scanning one of the maps, Simon could hardly believe that any country – never mind Peru – could require so much electricity.

There were the usual political scandals, the usual minor reports on drugs and the police and so on – including the story he had originally picked up on – but nothing that triggered Simon's storyline senses.

He turned to the USA. Here, there was certainly more information; and there were more potential stories, including a couple that Simon filed away to follow up later - but nothing that helped at the moment. His eyes did narrow slightly at the fact that two of his contacts had identified a story about investments in port infrastructure near the Californian city of Salinas. He speculated on Salinas as a potential entry port for drugs. Certainly California had its drugs culture: it was a big market for Peruvian and Colombian cocaine. But he wasn't entirely convinced. As he read on, and followed through the links he had been supplied with, it looked more like the port project was something tacked on to a range of infrastructure projects throughout the region, which included a much-needed desalination plant. The state was suffering in the wake of climate change, and the government, still largely in denial over its own impact on climate, was under pressure to invest in the hardest-hit regions where unemployment in the agriculture industry was rising.

His eyes skimmed the list – leisure projects, business parks, reservoirs, a hi-tech research centre, and this deep-water port. So if it was bringing in a bit more cheap oil or gas, so what? Maybe they really had discovered more oil or gas in Peru, and had somehow kept it secret and were bringing it in via Salinas' new port. Great – but why would they want it hushed up? Commercial advantage, perhaps?

He spent some time researching the new port facility and trying to tease out any significant details. The best he could do was find some crazy estimates for the amount of money invested in the port, and a few conspiracy theorists' blog entries involving the presence of unlikely numbers of military personnel and a not-so-unlikely news blackout.

As he considered the possibilities, his senses started their faint tingling again. He could imagine drugs being smuggled in on oil tankers coming in from Peru. He could even imagine large quantities getting direct to the market. A great coup for whoever smuggled it. A good story, and certainly worth investigating, but it was a far cry from a government-sponsored drug supply line, built at staggering cost, kept entirely secret, and all done in the bright glare of the beautiful Californian daylight, with Peru and Brazil as supposed partners.

Anyway, where was the supply line on the Peruvian side? Sure, there were new roads. There was the new Trans-Amazonica, of course, but that was too far south, and heading to the wrong port. The big terminal port built by the Americans was in the north, at a place called Chimbote, and the only thing there was the reported pipeline – now looking increasingly like an oil or gas pipeline. Oil, gas, beer, whatever – all no doubt technically feasible, and all more or less desirable depending on your tastes – but a pipeline for drugs? It was bizarre – too bizarre. Impossible, surely. Nonetheless, his senses were still tingling – there was something here and he could feel it. There was a piece of the jigsaw missing - his view was obscured; the perspective was wrong. But it would come to him.

He flicked through the rest of the e-mails, but the only other personal email was a sarcastic piece from an old acquaintance in São Paulo, asking how he had ever survived in the business. Did he seriously believe that the governments, police and military of any South American country were anything but as bent as a 'nota de nove bobs'? Simon smiled at the reference to nine-bob notes, and of course his friend had a valid point. Anyone who had spent any time in South America knew it was entirely run by big-family mafia whose tentacles were all-pervasive. The rich and powerful conspired to keep the poor and uneducated in the slime while milking the country dry. Sad it might be, but it certainly was not bloody newsworthy.

He sat back, thought about it all for a few moments, and then sent a message to acknowledge Jack's email. He confirmed that he would be at Lethem when Jack arrived, and that he would dig around for information on the USA connection. More as a show of good faith than anything else, he passed on the information about the US investment in the port of Chimbote and the new or expanded deep-water port in Salinas, saying it was part of a complex that included a container facility, warehousing, and the desalination plant, as well as a lot of other infrastructure. 'Drugs? Oil? Nothing?' he added to the details, probably unnecessarily. He had also discovered that while the DUMAR on Jack's piece of paper did not seem to mean anything, and TAE could mean anything from 'Trial and Error' to 'Taegu, Republic of Korea', the most likely meanings of 'HEP' were either 'High Energy Physics' or 'Hydro Electric Plant', so he noted this down too.

As he was musing over how to sign off on his email – 'good luck' seemed way too trite – he received a mail from his office telling him that Manaus – Georgetown – Lethem was the only viable air route, and that internal flights in Guyana could only be reliably booked in-country. He sighed, pulled the satellite map up on the screen again, and looked carefully. The road from Boa Vista to Lethem looked reasonably okay. It was only seventy miles. How long could it take – two hours? Three at most? He dug around for scheduled flights to Boa Vista and found one that left in two hours from Manaus airport. Just under an hour's flying time to Boa Vista.

That would do nicely.

71

In spite of Roberto's confidence to the contrary, the internet did not come back on later, and Jack assumed someone was locking down communications here too. They might not know where he was, but they must be looking at Boa Vista as a strong possibility. He slept fitfully, and everyone was awake early.

Carla had been the first up, and had apparently gone to the shops to get some food – Jack saw her note on the otherwise bare breakfast bar, and read it without picking it up. Still groggy with sleep, he wandered into the living room and found Roberto hunched over a computer.

"Hi Roberto," he said, stifling a yawn.

Roberto jerked round in his seat. "*Putz*, you scared me, man," he said, looking genuinely shocked.

"Sorry," said Jack. He saw the Google search page on the screen and walked closer. "We have internet?"

"Yes. I was just coming to tell you. You want to use it now?"

"You bet."

"Here you go then. Help yourself. I'll make some coffee for us." He got up and walked towards the door.

"Thanks," said Jack, sitting down.

"Be quick though – we could lose it any time."

"Yeah, okay. Thanks Roberto."

In the event, all he had time to do was check his email and open the only message of any interest – an acknowledgement from the reporter. He read it through quickly. The rendezvous was agreed, at least. That was a relief – they were a step closer. He also read the information about the Chimbote and Salinas port developments. It all seemed to fit with the drugs scenario, although the fact that the Salinas port was supposedly just part of a bigger development was a bit off-putting. But then maybe it was supposed to be.

Clear as mud.

He started to type a reply, wrote two sentences and thought he would save it, and then found out the connection had gone down. He tried again, but it was quite dead.

"I got lost and it took me half an hour to find my way back," he heard Carla grumbling as she came through the door.

He cursed mildly, got up and walked out to the kitchen.

"Hi Carla," he said.

"Hi Jack. Sleep okay? There's nothing much around here in the way of shops, but I found some rolls and things."

"Yes. Sorry," Roberto said. "You could have taken the car..."

Jack stopped listening. He was puzzling over the site, trying to figure out if there was anything in a Chimbote-Salinas connection that made sense at all. He was trying to think clearly, and found the buzz of conversation in the background distracting, even downright irritating. Really, he just wanted to get going – or at least get a decent internet connection. Maybe there was something in town...?

"Is there an internet café somewhere around here?" he said suddenly.

Carla looked at him. "But surely they'll all be down, Jack, just like in Manaus," she reasoned, clearly thinking the same way Jack had been thinking earlier.

"Not necessarily," Jack said. "We had a connection there for a few minutes, didn't we Roberto?"

Roberto nodded. "But it obviously didn't last long. Did you manage to get anything done, Jack?"

Jack shook his head dismissively. "No. But surely there must be some places that use satellite. I would think satellite services would be more reliable and more difficult to interrupt, wouldn't they?"

Roberto shook his head. "Satellite? Here in Boa Vista? I doubt if there's anything like that. Even if there is, how would we know which ones they are?"

"Which ones what?" said Elena, blowing in through the door and heading straight for the coffee and rolls.

"Oh, it doesn't matter," Jack growled, frustrated by the negativity. "I'll tell you later."

No-one said much more. The plan for their flight to Guyana was already settled, and the conversation between Carla and Roberto turned to developments of the GCC in Brasilia and across the country. Jack and Elena sat down together by the large patio doors that led to the back garden. There was a coffee table there with bits of paper, magazines and a few pens stacked at one end, and Jack found a blank sheet of paper and pulled it across, while Elena ate.

He sketched the points from the map again, and the two of them stared at the paper together. Jack joined the clusters up to form lines. He wrote 'TAE' first, then scribbled it out. Now he wrote 'T.', and next to this 'AE-AO'. This was mroe precisely the form he had seen on the paper. Given that the letter 'A' was kind of a constant, he stared again at the 'E' and 'O'. They had been in his head so long now that he hardly thought of them except as abstract letters, but it struck him that they could be nothing more sinister than Spanish compass points – E for Este, or east, and O for Oeste, or west. He turned the paper to give it a better north-south aspect. The western end of something and the eastern end of something. A supply line, of course. So what?

"Useless bloody government," he heard Roberto complain in the background. "And of course now that it's the dry season, the river's almost disappeared..."

The reference to the Rio Branco suddenly gave Jack the idea that the strings of lines might fit the line of the Marañon River valley. He remembered there was another string further east on the map. The Huallaga? They could be looking at the lines of two of the main rivers in Peru, both flowing northwest, in parallel, for hundreds of miles, before descending east to join with the Ucayali in the Amazon Basin. He tested his theory on Elena.

"My geography is not good, but you could be right," she said, with little enthusiasm in her voice. "But so what? We already decided the sites were too high up to be hydroelectric dams."

Jack nodded absently, his finger tapping on the coffee table. "I know. But follow my logic, will you? First of all, let's agree that the lines really are some sort of pipeline."

Elena shrugged. "Okay."

"Well, it's not oil or gas – I mean, oil rigs halfway up a mountain?"

"*Cierto...*"

"So, there doesn't seem to be any reason for pipelines to be following river valleys, unless..."

"Unless they contain water?" Elena finished.

"Exactly." Jack nodded, pleased to have some support for his fledgling theory.

"But how? Why? I mean..."

Jack smiled. He remembered what he had seen and heard back at the site. The cave, the strange vibrations. It was fantastical, but the more he thought about it, the more convinced he was about what it represented.

"What if they were tunnelling through the mountains at that site, Elena?" He pointed at the scrappy map again. "If I'm right, these points could mark the ends of the tunnels, and we would have been at the eastern end of tunnel A"

Elena looked at him as if he were slightly mad.

"AE," Jack said, simply.

"But that's *loco*! Tunnelling all the way through the Andes? I think you have had too much sun, *mi amor*. Also, think of all the energy you would need, to pump the water up to the tunnels."

Jack nodded. "I *have* thought about it." He leaned forward, the tension in his voice increasing as he went on. "Look, Peru has been building dams all along these valleys, hasn't it?"

"Correct."

"How many dams, Elena? Any idea?"

She shook her head. "I don't know – maybe fifty or sixty, if they all get built? Remember they are already building along the Ucayali, too."

"Fifty dams! Hah! Think of all the energy that would generate. Peru only needs a fraction of that."

"True," Elena agreed. "They said they're planning to sell the rest to Brazil and Ecuador."

"Sure, but they could also use some of it to pump water up to the tunnels, couldn't they?"

"Perhaps."

"Yes. And you know the email I got from the reporter? He reckons HEP could mean Hydro Electric Plant. Remember the piece of paper said HEP 1-11?

Elena nodded.

"So, HEP 1-11 equals 'Hydro Electric Plants' numbers one to eleven."

"I suppose so, yes."

"They take energy from each plant and pump water uphill to a reservoir. It goes through the tunnel – 'T' for tunnel, right? – and away. If they can build a railway tunnel under the sea between France and England, they can bore a few wee holes through the Andes. From there, they could easily pipe it all the way to the coast. *And*, if I'm right about that, then how about the figure of 15m being a measure of capacity — as in 15 million cubic metres or litres or something?"

She stared at him, her expression changing slowly from one of bemusement, to one of wide-eyed, hit-with-a-brick surprise. Her mouth moved but no sound came out at first. She coughed and managed a croak. "The Americans are stealing our *water*?"

"Hardly stealing it. They're just doing a deal with the Peruvian government, who probably don't care or don't think it will make much difference – after all, most of the water flows through Brazil."

"But how do they get it to America? And why does America want it?"

"Ah," said Jack, smugly, and tapped his nose with his finger.

Elena growled.

"Salinas, California," Jack said.

"*Chistoso.* What do you mean 'Salinas California'? Salinas California *what*?"

"Something else I got from the reporter. It's a new port. Listen, the State of California is the so-called 'breadbasket' of the USA."

"*Lo granero.* Yes, I know."

"It's well-known for being in a constant state of crisis over its water, and it's also probably the closest part of the USA to Peru. So you just ship the water across, and carry on watering your tomatoes, or grapes..." He trailed off, a look of doubt crossing his face.

So why would they have a desalination plant at Salinas?

Elena looked at him. "What is it?"

He stared unseeingly for a few seconds and then the cloud passed. His heart leapt again. It was the perfect cover! A fake desalination plant – a plant with all that water passing through it, except it would be coming in on ships, not out of the sea.

He beamed at Elena. "Sorry – just thinking something through. That's it – it has to be!"

"Es *incrible*," Elena breathed. Her tone took on something of Jack's excitement as she continued. "And the drugs!" she hissed. "All the drugs go across with the water!"

Jack nodded. "The perfect plan. Money to pay for everything. Everyone a winner."

"The bastards will destroy the Amazon," Elena said flatly.

"Do you think these people care? Not only do they get their water, and money to pay for it, but they also suddenly control half of South America. With dams along all three sources of the Amazon, they can turn it on and off whenever they like. Who cares about the environment when you're making America – and a few Peruvian politicians and drug lords – great again?"

Anger flared in Elena's eyes. "Bastards. Finally, my government has sold our country to the gringos. They are a disgrace. I hate them." She paused, and glanced across towards Carla and Roberto. "And the Brazilians are as bad – either they don't know what is going on, which means they are stupid, or they are looking the other way in exchange for a share of the drugs business, which means they are twice as stupid."

"Yes – I'm still a bit puzzled by the Brazilians, but it all fits together too neatly for it to be anything else. In any case, they're clearly in it up to their necks."

"Yes. And *you* have seen the site and the maps, and the people. You've seen the Americans, Peruvians and Brazilians all working together. You've seen the whole thing. No wonder they all want you dead."

"*Us,*" Jack said. "They want *all* of us dead, remember?" His eyes narrowed and a grin spread across his face. "Well we're not fucking dead yet," he said, and banged his hand on the coffee table.

Behind him, Carla started. "What's the matter, Jack?"

He looked at Elena and quickly put his finger to his lips. "Sorry. It's nothing," he managed. "Really. I'm fine."

Roberto shook his head slightly and got up from the table.

"Take it easy Jack. I know it's frustrating, but you're nearly there. Just relax and you'll soon be home."

Soon be home. Soon be home. He was suddenly not quite sure how he felt about that. He was elated at solving the puzzle, and at having survived the pursuit across South America. He was also pleased at being so close to getting home. On the other hand, he was now awed by what they had uncovered, and weighed down by the responsibility of getting the news out safely.

He turned to Roberto. "Look, we really need to find an internet café, in spite of how difficult that may be. I need to get some internet access."

"Yes," Elena added. "Just drop us off at the main ones and we'll go in and ask. It's a small risk."

Carla looked at Jack and Elena for a second, and then at Roberto. "Yes, I agree. Roberto?"

"I, uh, well, I guess..."

"If it's too risky for you, Roberto, I'll take them."

He thought for a moment and then shook his head. "No. You're right, of course. Sorry – I should have thought... Right, I just need to go out for something first. I'll only be a few minutes, and as soon as I get back we can get moving. We'll find one somewhere, I'm sure."

In the end, Roberto only kept them ten minutes, which was long enough for them to agree on what Elena would be searching for online while Jack got an update out to his newspaper contact. By the time Roberto reappeared, they had some money, their notes, and their weapons, and were ready to go.

It took a fair bit of driving around until they finally found a "Lan House" which proudly announced that it had a satellite connection. Roberto went in alone, and when he came back he was able to confirm that their system was up and running.

It was all Jack needed. He and Elena got out of the car first, and as they were walking away, they heard Carla's voice and looked round to see her running towards them.

"Don't forget me," she said, a little breathlessly.

Jack looked at her for a moment. "Carla, you don't need–"

"Oh yes I do. I said I would help you, and that's what I'll do – every step of the way until you're safe. Three people doing internet research is a lot faster than one. Now let's go."

Jack shrugged his acceptance and the three of them walked up the external steps to a fourth-floor balcony from which double doors opened on to a dark room. It was full of dusty, screened-off desks with grubby black monitors on them. They paid for an hour each, and walked to adjoining desks.

Jack could feel the sweat beading on his forehead again, partly from the heat in the badly ventilated room, and partly from the prospect of unburdening himself and getting his message out to the wider world. The monitor displayed a login screen, and he entered the details from the torn piece of paper the attendant had given him. Nothing. He tried again. Nothing. He peered round the partition at Elena, who gave him the thumbs up. He sighed and got to his feet. As he approached the desk where the bored attendant sat, he heard a screech of tyres outside and car doors being slammed. Through the opaque windows he glimpsed several Federal Police officers advancing towards the building.

"Feds!" he shouted, and turned to Elena.

Carla was out of her chair in an instant. She strode over to the attendant. "*Tem outra saída?*" she shouted at him. He nodded dumbly and pointed over to the other side of the room at an inconspicuous door.

"Let's go."

Jack quickly turned and pulled the double doors shut, and then toppled the desks nearest the door onto their sides, partially blocking the way. Then he followed the girls out of the other door.

They were through the door before they heard the crashing behind them. They started down a flight of stairs and almost passed a large window looking out over a neighbouring building. Jack stopped to see if it opened. When it did, he urged Carla out first. She jumped down onto a flat roof, and waited for the next person. Jack helped Elena out and then squeezed through himself. Once out, he pushed the window closed again and dropped down. Together, they sprinted across the flat roof and jumped across to the next building, only a few feet away. There was a noise behind them. A shot. Jack felt something hit him hard on his left arm, and he stumbled and fell forward.

He tried to rise, momentarily puzzled when he found it hard to raise his left hand. Then he saw the blood, and a wave of pain radiated through his neck and torso. His experience told him it was only a flesh wound – painful, but not fatal. He reached round with his right hand and pulled his pistol out, then got to his knees. He saw Elena and Carla still running. They were already on the next roof, with two agents chasing them. The men were in crouched positions, zig-zagging towards the girls, and shouting something. He saw Elena turn and cast her eyes back and forth, clearly wondering what had happened to him. Carla had just disappeared from view, jumping down from the roof further ahead of Elena.

Don't stop, Elena!

She hesitated, and he saw her hand reach behind her back. He knew she was going for her gun, but his eyes also took in the agents levelling their weapons.

She would be dead before she could even take aim.

KEIR FARRELL

72

For a split second Jack was right back in Dublin – disorientated, looking on, but unable to move... and then suddenly everything snapped into focus. He was moving and thinking normally, but everything else seemed just slightly out of synch – slow, deliberate, and predictable. He saw everything so clearly – saw his targets perfectly in the dry, bright sunshine. Less than thirty feet away. He smelled a whiff of cordite lingering in the air from the earlier shot and it registered that there was little or no wind. He calmly evaluated the agents' attitudes and moves. They obviously thought him dead or incapacitated, and were concentrating entirely on Elena. Their backs were to Jack. The man closest to him was already braced in a firing position a couple of yards behind the other guy, who was still bringing his gun up. Jack raised his pistol. He could not use his left arm to support it, but he drew a careful bead, and fired twice. The first agent crumpled, and Jack swung the pistol smoothly across to aim at the second man. He fired three times, but a fraction too early, and the man threw himself to the ground and took cover.

Damn.

"Go, Elena!" he shouted, before several shots cracked and Jack heard the impact of the rounds on the small brick pier he was sheltering behind.

"Jack!" cried Elena.

"Just go! Get out of here, for fuck sake!" Jack cried out. "Get Carla away, and I'll see you back at the house!" Another volley of shots thudded on the brickwork. "Go!" he called again, willing Elena to see that the best course was for her and Carla to get the hell away while he was keeping this guy occupied. He picked up a small piece of reinforced steel bar that was lying nearby and tossed it out to his left, while he dived to the right, towards another brick pier. He tensed with the sound of another volley of shots, and was gratified to hear them impact well behind him. When he swung round the pier, he found his man exposed. This time he got the aim and timing right, and with two shots the man collapsed.

Jack quickly worked himself back into position to check on the first man, and found him lying unconscious in a lot of blood. He collected the man's gun and went back to the second man, who was quite dead. His bulky .44 revolver lay beside him, and Jack picked it up and threw it a good distance across the roof. He shoved the other gun in his waistband and ran towards where he had last seen Elena. He jumped down onto the next roof, and ran across that, but as he approached the other side of it he heard shots from ground level. He instinctively dropped to a crouch and dived behind the small parapet which bordered the roof. Crawling to where there was a gaping crack in the brickwork, he was able to see down to where a group of agents surrounded a body that was lying face down in the grass. Three things he took in straight away: the first was that the body was Elena; the second was that she was not dead, because she had her hands on the back of her head; and the third was that he could not get to her, since there were four men with her and at least another two at one end of the alley providing cover.

Shit.

He crawled to a corner of the building where he could see what was happening, and watched as Elena was handcuffed, picked up by the arms, and run towards the end of the alley, where several vehicles now converged and screeched to a halt. Another small team of people leapt out and split up, some of them heading in his direction. He cursed again, crawled quickly to the corner of the building, and jumped to the next roof. He ran across the tops of several more buildings and finally slid down into a deserted street. When he got to the end of the street, he dusted himself down, and walked as calmly as possible across the road. There, he looked around carefully before climbing awkwardly over a garden wall, and then raced along several gardens, keeping an eye on the buildings across the way, until he reached the spot he wanted, when he climbed up and looked carefully over the wall.

He had only miscalculated by thirty or forty yards. To his left he could see the internet building. Outside, were four police vehicles, and Roberto's SUV. They must have got him too, and there was little doubt that he and Elena would be in one of the police vehicles. A few armed men were posted around, and as he watched, an ambulance came flying down the road and skidded to a halt. The men pointed up at the Lan House, and the medics rushed up the steps.

He ducked down behind the wall again, and thought about his options. How was he going to keep track of the vehicles? He had no way of knowing where they would go, and he feared the captives would be subjected to some pretty brutal torture and a painful death if he could not get to them. He looked over the wall again, and saw the medics emerging from the building with a body on a stretcher. There was a drip attached, so it was clearly the surviving man. As he watched, a movement to the right caught his eye. His heart skipped a beat as he turned to look, but whatever it was had gone. He stared after it for a second before he realised what it was that had drawn his attention. It was a flash of yellow – the yellow of Carla's blouse? He dropped down from the wall and made his way back across the gardens before climbing up again, roundly cursing his injured arm.

He could still see the police vehicles, and he watched as one of them reversed a short way, turned, and sped off. The ambulance went next, and then Roberto's SUV. This left three cars, the occupants of which must be swarming across the roof tops by now, because there appeared to be no activity at ground level. He scanned the street carefully, and suddenly caught a glimpse of yellow again, at the downstairs window of one of the buildings. He shaded his eyes, moved further down the road, and eventually made out Carla's face. After waiting for a few moments, to be sure she was not being held by someone, he picked out some small stones and threw them across at the window. The first one that hit made Carla dive for cover, but she came back a few seconds later and looked out anxiously. Jack waved at her and she saw him. He looked up and down the road, and then signalled to her that it was okay for her to go to her left. She nodded, and Jack dipped behind the wall again and went in the same direction.

He met her at the point at which he ran out of gardens, and they found themselves together in a narrow lane.

"Elena?" Carla asked.

Jack shook his head. "They have her." Without waiting for any more questions, he beckoned her to follow him as he crossed the road and climbed a wall into another block of gardens. His injured arm was making the going hard, and Carla noticed.

"You're hurt Jack. Are you sure you're okay?"

Jack nodded. "Just a flesh wound. I can bind it later. Where is the house, from here? Do you know?" he asked.

"I should do – I walked all round here this morning." She took a moment to get her bearings. "Yes. It's two blocks that way," she said. "But where's Elena now? Where's Roberto?"

"I think they have both of them," Jack said. "Listen, somehow or other I need to follow those vehicles. Can you get back to the house on your own?"

"What? No. I want to go with you."

Jack shook his head. "No, Carla - it's impossible."

She was silent for a moment. "Okay, I tell you what, it'll only take us a few minutes to get to Roberto's place, and there's another car in the garage there."

Jack looked at her. "Is there?"

"Yes. He offered me the keys to it this morning."

It was the solution to Jack's immediate problem. "Alright, let's go then," he said. "But I'll be going after them on my own, Carla, okay?"

"We can argue about that when we get back."

They ran across more gardens, emerging on another road. When they crossed and tried to repeat the exercise, they found the next garden full of large, unfriendly and very noisy dogs.

"It's just there, four houses down," said Carla. "That's the back of the house, I'm sure of it," she said, pointing.

Jack looked around. "Okay. I think we can use the road. Just walk normally," he said. There were few people around the area, but anyone running would be sure to draw attention. They walked as far as a large, sliding metal gate.

"This the one?" said Jack.

Carla nodded. "Must be."

He tried to open it, and saw that it was locked, with a padlock on the other side. He did not want to risk walking any further on the road, so he motioned with his head to Carla. Grabbing a plastic bin, Jack pulled it over to the wall, stepping up on it and scrambling over the wall. They dropped down on the other side behind a huge jack-fruit tree.

They paused only for a second – just enough time for them to spot a figure through the patio doors at the rear of the house.

"*Porra* - it's Roberto!" Carla said, with a strangled cry. "How...?"

They both watched Roberto standing by the breakfast table. He had a couple of bags laid on top of the table, and there were some more bags on the floor. Next to these, the big floor rug had been pulled back, and as they watched, Roberto bent down and pulled something out of a hole. Banknotes. Wads of bank notes. The look on Carla's face changed from puzzlement to anger.

"*Filho da puta*," she spat. "*Pelo amor de deus.* I would never have believed it. Never."

"Sorry," said Jack.

"No. *I'm* sorry, Jack. This is *my* fault."

Before Jack could stop her, she was up and running towards the patio doors. She paused only to grab a rusting machete lying by a small storeroom, and then she was inside the house.

Jack swore, and pushed himself to his feet. Roberto was more valuable to them alive than dead, and he had little doubt that Carla could kill him with that machete.

As she ran full tilt towards the open doors, Roberto finally caught sight of her approaching. He froze, a look of horror on his face. He looked at the bags; at the floor; at Carla. He looked like he was trying to come to some sort of decision, and then she was there in front of him.

"You bastard, Roberto!" she shouted at him, raising the machete. Roberto held up his arms and backed away. He looked behind him, and appeared to stumble over something. Too late, Carla realised he was going for a revolver that lay on the arm of a sofa. He grabbed it and rolled across the floor, raising the gun before he came to rest, firing wildly. Jack was already running towards the door, pistol in his hand. He had no clear shot at Roberto, and his heart leapt into his mouth as he watched Carla scream and throw herself at Roberto. The heavy machete came down on his arm and Roberto howled, dropping the gun and bringing his other hand round to clutch the wound. The machete stuck in the wound for a second and then clattered to the floor, but Carla was already scrabbling for the revolver. Jack burst through the doors, and the two of them stood side by side, guns trained on the bleeding, whimpering Roberto.

"Help me. Help me, Carla," Roberto whined, as blood spread thickly from his arm.

Carla shook her head. "I can't believe you betrayed me, you asshole. Why did you do it? *Why?*"

"I had no choice. They told me they have my sister. They offered me money. They said they wouldn't hurt you – they only wanted..."

"Jack? They only wanted Jack? You idiot. They'll kill us all once they have Jack. Don't you get it?"

"No! They said they only wanted *him*. The American said so. He promised."

"American? What American?" Jack asked.

"I don't know! Torres, I think someone called him." Roberto grimaced. "Help me, help me," he cried. "Look!" He nodded at his limp and bloodied arm. The blood was still flowing, but Jack could see there was no major loss – it looked worse than it was.

Jack walked across the room, picked up the discarded machete, and came back to stand over Roberto.

"Roberto, I swear I'll hack your other arm off if you don't tell me everything."

The wide-eyed look of terror was enough for Jack. "Tell me about the American."

Carla remained quite still, her gun aimed at his head, while Roberto gave them a detailed description of the American. Jack's instinct told him it was the same man he had overheard in Peru. Apparently there was a team with him – some Americans and some Brazilians. They had no uniforms, but were all dressed in black. Some of them had their faces covered. They had picked him up while he was driving to an airfield. They had blindfolded him and taken him somewhere, putting a gun to his head and pulling the trigger, telling him it was a Russian Roulette game. It seemed clear Roberto had caved in straight away, and agreed to sell the three of them out in exchange for enough money to be able to disappear. He knew nothing much else of any use.

"And the plane we were supposed to get away in? Was that a lie, too?"

"No, no! Everything was arranged. It is still arranged! It wasn't supposed to happen like this. They were going to go to the airfield to pick you up, but when you started using the internet, I wasn't sure..."

"So you went off to tell them, you bastard," Carla cried. "That was your 'little errand', wasn't it?"

Roberto nodded.

"*Jesús,*" she said.

"So there's still a plane?" Jack persisted.

"Yes!"

"How do I know you're telling the truth?"

"Ask the pilot! His name is Soares, Fábio Soares He'll be there at midnight tonight. He'll wait for exactly an hour – if no-one turns up, he'll leave for Guyana. He has business there anyway."

"You realise that if you're *not* telling me the truth, Roberto, I swear I will find you and kill you. Do you understand?" said Carla.

"Yes, yes! I understand. But it's all true! You can contact him yourself. He has a legitimate business here – BV Importações. It's in the city centre."

Jack thought as quickly as he could. This wasn't getting him any closer to Elena, and the longer they stayed here, the greater their own danger. He hurried out to the kitchen and found some tea towels, which he tore into strips. Back in the living room, he pushed Roberto onto his front and tied his hands behind his back, ignoring Roberto's screaming.

"My arm! My arm!"

"Shut the fuck up, or it'll be your head next," said Jack. He rolled him onto his side, stuffed some more cloth into his mouth, and secured it with more strips. It would have to do.

With Roberto tied up, Carla finally lowered her gun, and they both backed away, walking over to the patio door.

Jack pushed his gun into his waistband and reached up to rub his face. He sighed heavily, and looked unseeingly for a moment at all the money on the table and on the floor. Without turning to look at her, he spoke quietly to Carla. "Everyone's corrupt, right, Carla?"

She saw what he was looking at, and nodded. "In Brasil? Pretty much everyone, yes."

"Right. You remember the woman at the theatre?" he asked. "Ferreira, I think?"

Carla nodded. "Colonel."

"What are the chances of contacting her?"

Carla looked puzzled for a moment, then nodded again. "Should be easy enough to track her down."

"Good, because I'm thinking that she just might want to help us – and if she doesn't, we have all this lovely money available to persuade her."

"Sure. If we had phone or internet access."

"Yeah. I've been thinking about that, too." He walked across to the fixed-line phone he had seen sitting on a small table by one of the windows. He followed the line to the point where it was fed through the external wall.

"Back in a second," he said, and left the room, reappearing a few minutes later. He picked up the phone, listening for a dialling tone. It was good. Of course it was good.

"It's fine," Jack said. "It was just disconnected."

Carla swung round and stared at Roberto.

"Help me, Carla," he moaned. "I'm dying."

"I doubt it," said Carla. "Not with all that fat on you, you lying bastard."

"Call an ambulance. Get me a doctor. For God's sake, Carla."

"Lie there and shut up. When and if we figure a way out of this, I might help you – but if you say another word without being asked, I will kill you myself. Do you understand me? I will kill you." She moved closer to him, aiming her gun at his head.

He grimaced and nodded.

With Roberto silent again, Jack held out the phone. "It's all yours, Carla," he said.

She lowered her gun, then turned and walked over to Jack. She put the revolver down on the table and took the handset from him. She closed her eyes briefly and took a deep breath. When she opened her eyes again, she looked quite composed. She sat down on the seat next to the table, took another long breath, and dialled.

73

Elna came round in total darkness. There was a strong smell of damp, overlaid with a faint scent of petrol. She was seated on a hard chair, and her chin rested on her chest. Her hands and feet were bound, and something restrained her chest. There was no noise other than her own ragged breathing. The room felt big – really big. Slowly, little sounds came to her: an irregular drip of water somewhere; an occasional creak of something overhead; and a hollow echo that accompanied each sound. She raised her head, the pain in her face, neck and left side ripping through her like a knife. She remembered that one of the bad guys had appeared out of nowhere and slammed the butt of his rifle into her. She had started to turn to meet the threat, and taken the full force of the blow on her left shoulder. She went down heavily on her right side, and the man had laid into her exposed side with a vengeance. The pain had been excruciating and she had blacked out for some time. When she regained consciousness, she was lying on the ground with lots of people shouting at her. Compliance under the circumstances had been a simple act of self-preservation.

She felt nauseous. As she looked around, she saw a few pinpricks of light above and to the sides. Her eyes fixed on them with relief, and as she stared, she tried to gauge the distance to the walls; the high roof. It was some sort of barn or warehouse.

She tested her restraints. They were secure, and as she moved, she realised that her shoulder muscles lacked a lot of power. Her left side throbbed with pain when she tried to move, and she started sweating in the still, humid air. An image of Jack came to her and she remembered his shocked and angry face shouting at her to get away.

Sorry, Jack.

She heard shuffling feet, then a key in a lock and the creak of a door opening somewhere behind her. A sliver of light to her right fanned briefly across the room and then snapped out. A dim light clicked on overhead, and she heard footsteps approaching. Her throat was dry and her heart began to beat faster.

"Ah, we finally get to meet," said an icy voice behind her with a smooth American accent.

The footsteps continued, and a second later the man stood in front of Elena. It was difficult to see in the poor light, but he was tall, with an angular face set in a sort of grimace that could be a scowl or a smile. His black hair was receding, leaving him a pronounced widow's peak that pointed down to a long, roman nose. He wore a dark jacket and trousers, and a dull-coloured shirt was open at the neck. Elena would have put him at around 40 years old, but he looked athletic. He stood with his arms folded, peering down at her.

Elena said nothing.

"You and your gringo friend have caused me a lot of trouble, you know." He had switched to flawless South American Spanish now. "You know, it's hard enough to bear this hellish continent from a decent apartment, but running around these barbaric countries after assholes like you is pure torture."

The ache in Elena's shoulder and neck was becoming more intense, and she flinched at the spasms when she moved her head.

"You don't need to worry about that little wound, Elena," the man said, reaching out and patting her arm heavily.

She gasped with the pain.

"*¡Jódete!*" was all she could manage to say.

"Oh dear. That's not very nice, is it? Well, I tell you what it is, Elena. All I want to know is where Mr McCrae is, and then you can go. Right?"

Elena was sucking in air through clenched teeth in an effort to control the pain.

"So, just tell me, okay?"

"What, so you can kill me? Sure."

He smiled. "Well, perhaps, perhaps." He looked over Elena's shoulder and nodded to someone.

Elena could hear more footsteps, and two other men appeared on either side of him.

"But there's a big difference – I mean a really *huge* difference – between a quick and easy bullet in the head, and having your teeth fed to you one by one, before your skull's squeezed until it pops like a zit. Don't you think, Elena?"

Elena struggled to keep the pain and her fear at bay. "Look, I don't know what the fuss is all about. The guy's just a tourist, for fuck sake. He doesn't know anything and neither do I."

"Oh I know he's only a tourist Elena. But he is a very annoying tourist.

Elena opened her mouth to reply, but the man wagged a finger at her. "And as for not knowing anything, well, I'm quite sure neither of you knew anything at all, to *begin* with."

"So?" said Elena in exasperation.

"Yes. It is all most regrettable really. It was those Peruvian idiots that dragged you into it. And I'm really so sorry, but you see it's certainly not true that you don't know anything *now*, is it?"

"Crap," Elena insisted. "We really don't know what's going on, dammit. And we don't want to know anything. We don't give a damn about you and your secrets."

"I really don't have time for this, Elena. You know *something* – however much or little it is – and you have no doubt told other people about what you know–"

Elena started to protest, but he held up a hand.

"Elena, I'm not stupid, you know. I heard what you said to Mr McCrae's little friend in Cuzco, for a start..."

"I contacted him to come and rescue us, that's all, you asshole. And what's happened to him? What have you done to him?"

He waved a hand nonchalantly. "I'm afraid he's gone, Elena."

Elena struggled with her bonds, feeling a fresh wave of pain and nausea wash over her. The bile rose in her throat, and she swallowed hard to stop herself vomiting.

The man watched in silence.

As the nausea passed, she found her voice again. "Scum," she managed, before vomiting the little food she had in her stomach. She continued to retch as the sweat poured off her forehead and stung her eyes.

"Hah," the man scoffed. "As a terrorist, *you* are hardly in a position to criticise *me*, are you?" He sighed heavily. "And I'm sure you realise that I simply can't have people getting in my way – in our way. Including you, and Mr McCrae – and any of your friends and family, of course."

Elena hung her head and closed her eyes tightly, looking within herself for some way to deal with it all. Someone grabbed her hair and pulled her face up, and Elena could see the other man approaching with something in his hand.

"Tell me, did they ever show that old movie in Peru, Elena? What's it called? Ah yes – 'Marathon Man'; *El Maratón de la Muerte,* I think – that's it," he said. "One of our great American films, of course."

Pliers. That's what the man had in his hand. A pair of pliers.

"Ah. I can see that they did." He smiled again. "Of course, we don't have all that sophisticated dental equipment here, so we'll just have to get along with what we've got." He folded his arms and stood back with exaggerated nonchalance. "Do you know how hard it is to get a perfectly good tooth out of a jawbone, Elena? With a pair of pliers?"

Elena instinctively closed her jaw tightly.

She suddenly felt a massive blow to the side of her head. It provoked a flash of white light and she felt herself going under, until she was jerked back to consciousness with the pain of pressure on her shoulder. She felt something hard forced into one side of her mouth, and when she tried to clench her teeth, she bit into something like wood. An arm was holding her head now. When she opened her eyes, her vision was blurred with sweat and tears, and all she could see was the outline of a face.

"You can change your mind any time you like, Elena. Save yourself a lot of pain."

Even if she had wanted to – and she felt that maybe she did – she could not speak.

She felt something clamp onto her teeth. There was a crunching and grinding. She felt bits of tooth enamel in her mouth. The clamping became a tugging; a pulling and pushing. It moved down to her gums. Bits of blood and skin and tooth and bone slid down her throat, making her gag, but the arm around her head held her firmly. She felt pressure on the tooth and on the gum. Metal on bone now, too. It went on and on. The pain increased, faded, intensified again, faded. Suddenly there was a peak of agony – like an electric shock. Another, and another. She squirmed and tried to scream, but she was choking on her own blood. Finally, she felt something give. Something was yanked from her mouth, and the arm that was holding her head suddenly let go. Her head fell forward as she coughed what she could onto her lap.

"So, Elena, what do you think?"

Nausea made her retch again.

"Tell you what," the man continued, "why don't we take a break for a few minutes so that you can think it over. My friends and I will go and have a nice cup of coffee, and you can reflect."

Elena heard something being moved round in front of her.

"And this, by the way Elena, is a hand-held hydraulic crusher. Latest technology, with a crushing force of three hundred tonnes. I'll leave it here on this little table so you can have a look at it while you think. You'll see that the jaws open quite wide enough for the average-sized head. Do *you* have an average-sized head, do you think, Elena?"

She heard him walk past her and then the footsteps faded. The light was switched off, and the door closed.

74

The two battered white Mercedes vans crunched slowly over the dry dirt-and-cinder surface. Their headlights had been switched off when they turned into the narrow side road, and they slowed to a stop a quarter of a mile from the gate that could just be seen up ahead, bathed in the grey moonlight.

"This is it?" asked Jack. He was sitting up front in the passenger seat of the second van, his arm bandaged and his stomach full of painkillers. The driver nodded. Jack looked at his new watch and switched on his portable radio. Someone had scrounged five of these, connected to NMFI wireless headsets under their black balaclavas. He and the Colonel each had one, together with the two drivers, one of which was Carla, in spite of Jack's protestations. He clicked his palm pressel and spoke softly.

"Alpha One. Comms check," he said. "Alpha Two?"

"*Copio*," came the reply from Colonel Ferreira in the first van.

"Bravo One, Bravo Two, Bravo Three?"

"*Recebendo*," came the responses – one from the extremely young guy that Carla's SOS had brought to their aid, with his own little private army and the nickname 'Vin'.

"Charlie One, Charlie Two"?

"Recebendo," from Charlie One, his own driver.

"*OK Jack*," came Carla's nervous whisper from the other van. Her anger over Roberto had played itself out and she had become more subdued in the few hours since they had left him tied to a chair. 'Will he be alright?' she kept asking. No-one noticed Jack's fleeting look of exasperation each time.

"*Copio e desligo*," Jack said, trying to adjust to using the Portuguese Ferreira had taught him.

Up ahead, in the back of Carla's van, the Colonel pulled her pistol out and checked her ammunition. She turned to the ten men and growled at them. "I'm not used to working with amateurs, and the people we're going up against are all pros – even the Feds. Like Jack said, all we've got on our side is surprise, and numbers. We lose either of those, and we'll be in trouble very quickly."

"Don't worry about my men, Colonel. They've been training for this for years," came Vin's indignant voice.

Ferreira shook her head. "It's unbelievable. I still can't get over it. Training for what – for attacking the police?"

"Not attacking – *defending*. Against anyone we have to. And although some people," he said, looking over at Carla, "don't like to know about us, we're the people who'll do the dirty work when the time comes, you can be sure of that." There was a wild gleam in his eyes.

Ferreira looked at him and nodded. "Okay, sure. Well, we've been over it all before, anyway." She turned slightly in her seat. "Carla, you have Jack's instructions. If there is no contact from us by 20:15, or if you are under threat, you get out of here and drive to Lethem."

Carla nodded. "Okay." She stared at the Colonel for a moment.

"What is it?" Ferreira asked.

"Nothing. I just still don't get why you let us go at the theatre; why you came here to help–"

"I'm doing it for the money," Ferreira snapped. "Okay?"

"At the theatre...?"

"Look, it's none of your damned business, right?"

"Okay – sorry. Thanks, that's all."

"Forget it, and forget me. I'll be out of Brazil myself in a few hours, and you'll never see me again." She paused. "It feels good to be doing something right for once, that's all."

She opened the rear doors and climbed down to the road, the men descending after her, all dressed in black, and all armed with brand new Brazilian IMBEL A2 assault rifles.

Jack looked back at his own small team of three in the back of the second van, and exchanged a thumbs-up with them. They had been over the plan again and again in the last five hours, using the maps the Colonel had acquired, and Jack had left her to communicate efficiently with the men, most of whom spoke only Portuguese. They all had their instructions: Bravo Two and Bravo Three teams, each of five men, had – Jack checked his watch automatically – eight minutes to get into position. Flashbangs to the north and south of the complex were scheduled for 20:00 precisely. Jack and the Colonel were betting they would find Elena in the main building – a disused concrete-and-steel grain store. If they were lucky, the diversions would draw off the opposition and give the Colonel and himself, with the three Bravo 1 men, a clear run to the centre of the compound. If not, they were counting on numbers and firepower to get them all in and out safely.

After a few seconds, he saw the men up front split into their teams and melt into the night. Carla started up her van and turned it around, nodding to him as she drove by, making her way back down the lane towards the main road.

"Okay. Let's go," Jack said quietly, and his own driver moved forward slowly, stopping briefly for Ferreira to jump in. As soon as she was on board, the van edged forward again, waiting for the moment. Suddenly, there were a series of loud explosions to either side of the building complex ahead, which was now outlined clearly. They driver floored the throttle, and the van surged forward, covering the quarter of a mile in a little under thirty four seconds. It crashed through the flimsy gates of the complex, slewed to the left and came to a halt inches from a Federal Police SUV that was blocking the doors of the target building.

"Shit," cried Jack. The idea had been to drive the van straight into the grain store. "Get them to move that fucking thing!" he shouted to Ferreira, as they all jumped out of the van.

"Va, va, va!" the Colonel shouted, barking orders as they ran towards the SUV.

White flashes and deafening explosions enveloped the buildings. These were punctuated by gunfire, firstly by single shots and then by longer bursts. A fire had started in one of the accommodation buildings, and thick black smoke was already drifting across the site.

The Bravo Two team appeared through the smoke to the north, while more gunfire erupted to the south. As soon as the team leader appeared, Ferreira pointed south. "Go help them!" As they started past her, she grabbed the lead man's arm and shouted at him "And don't just run up to them, or you'll get yourselves shot to bits, okay?"

The man nodded quickly and ran on.

The men in their own small team had now moved the SUV and abandoned it to roll downhill to the south of the site. One of the men was working on the large rolling doors and to Jack's surprise and relief he saw the doors begin to rise. They immediately rushed forwards and dived underneath, and less than two minutes after driving through the gates, they were inside. It took only another few seconds to locate Elena. She was seated at the far end, pale, covered in blood and sweat, but already grinning like a madwoman.

"Can't leave you alone for a moment, can I?," said Jack, as he cut through the ropes securing Elena.

"*O que...?*" she mumbled.

His head was next to hers as he cut the last of the ropes. "I said I'm never going to leave you again!" he almost shouted.

The ropes gave and she fell forwards into his arms, crying out in pain. He had to hold her up, and support her as he turned back towards the door.

"OK!" He called to the others. "*Cumprido, cumprido!*" He pressed the palm pressel and confirmed on the radio that the mission had been accomplished. He was about to add their codeword for immediate evacuation, when shots rang out. Fire was returned, and suddenly the building was filled with automatic gunfire, the noise and echoes deafening and confusing everyone.

Jack dropped to a crouch, covering Elena with his own body, and pulled out his pistol before searching to see if he could identify the enemy's location.

Someone grunted, fell to the floor. Several rounds kicked chunks out of the concrete near them, and he saw Ferreira bring her weapon up and fire several shots.

There were bits of machinery lined up along the right side of the building, and Jack grabbed hold of Elena by the shoulders and dragged her to cover. More shots, one clanging loudly off a nearby piece of machinery.

Suddenly he heard Ferreira cry out and hit the ground some distance away. He also heard at least one of their own men running back to the main door.

He spoke urgently into his microphone. "Alpha Two?"

He heard ragged breathing over the radio. "I'm okay," came

Ferreira's voice. "Go. Go..."

Jack scanned the building for her as they made their way towards the doorway. He thought he could see something, but as he moved to get a clearer view, a hail of bullets struck the equipment, floor and the walls. He dived back behind cover.

Gunshots now from the main door, and another answering fusillade of bullets from the enemy. Shouts from the same place.

"You won't get out, McCrae."

Jack knew the voice.

"You're dead meat. You and your drug-running bitch."

The same voice he had heard at the site. Cold and arrogant. Torres. It angered him, but not enough for him to lose his wits and respond. Announcing your location was dumber than dumb. He waited.

"Hey, McCrae! You—"

Jack added his own shots to the automatic fire that poured towards the man's location, and he could see from the sources that Ferreira and one other team mate were alive and still kicking. He hoped they would be firing and moving, to keep the bad guys guessing, but he knew there was no way he could move at the moment without abandoning Elena or exposing them to a wall of fire.

"Alpha One," he heard Ferreira whispering. "Jack. *Em cinco* – in five. Protect your eyes, then go."

"*Copio*," Jack said, starting his countdown.

In the deafening silence of a lull in firing, he thought he could hear her moving, wrestling with something. He turned towards the door, closed his eyes and tried to protect his ears.

The interior of the building erupted in blinding white light and a series of deafening explosions. He stood up, then crouched and snatched Elena up and over his shoulder, sprinting towards the door as a barrage of gunshots opened up from both ends of the building.

He slid to the ground and man-handled Elena under the door, emerging into a confusion of gunshots and smoke and small explosions. He picked Elena up and ran to the van, opening the door and laying her on the front seats. He gave a thumbs up to the driver.

"Okay! Go!" he shouted, then he turned and slammed the door.

"*Alpha One. Cumprido. Sai, sai, sai.* I repeat, *sai, sai, sai.*" He said into his microphone, ordering everyone out.

He heard the gears of the van grind as he turned and saw one of their own team returning fire from the cover of a door pillar. He ran towards them, but as he got to within a few yards, a massive explosion ripped through the building. A maelstrom of hot air and debris knocked him to the ground, and dull thuds churned his stomach and rattled his head. When he could focus again, he saw that most of the top half of the building had gone. The twisted and bent roll-up doors pointed crazily to the sky, and bits of masonry had been flung from what was left of the walls. A huge fire was burning now, and engulfed the remains of the interior. He could see all this, but all he could hear was a piercing, whining sound. The man he had been rushing to help lay crushed and mangled under bits of twisted steel, and half his head had been cleaved away.

Jack stared into the building, where the flames still burned fiercely. Nothing could have lived through it. What the hell had caused it? Ferreira had nothing with her that could have caused that sort of blast, so it must have been something that was sparked off by the flashbang she threw.

The whining in his ears slowly resolved into a voice. "Alpha One?" It was Carla.

"Alpha One," he acknowledged.

"What was *that*? Are you okay?"

"Yes. Okay. On my way out now," he said, already on his feet. As he turned to see where the van had got to, he stared in horror. It had moved only a few yards and was at rest now, pockmarked with dents and holes. A huge piece of steel girder had been speared through the windscreen, the tyres were blown, and the engine cover was missing.

He rushed to the van and yanked open the door. Elena was lying where he had left her, unconscious, with the girder only a few inches from her head. The mangled corpse of the driver was unrecognisable. He quickly dragged Elena out and got her over his shoulders again, then looked around wildly. Fire and smoke still obscured things, and explosions were still rippling around the site. He could also hear gunfire off to his right, although he knew the teams would have withdrawn. He looked at the gates – uphill, maybe a third of a mile. Hard going, and risking discovery. Then he saw the Feds' SUV further down the hill. It had come to rest against a fence, and looked to be in reasonable condition. He could probably force the lock or hotwire it – another skill the army had taught him in Afghanistan.

He made his decision and bolted for the SUV. As soon as he opened the door, he knew they were in luck. Someone had forced the steering lock when they were getting it away from the doors, but everything else was fine. He placed Elena in the passenger seat and got to work. Less than a minute later, the vehicle fired up. He threw it into reverse, turned the vehicle round, and sped towards the gates. As he approached, he could see figures milling about, but no-one fired at him. Perhaps they thought he was one of theirs. He was beginning to think they would make it through easily, when he glimpsed someone emerging from the smoke, just off to his side. It was a tall figure, and his eyes were drawn to it as he saw it calmly raise a pistol. Jack instinctively ducked, and a moment later bullets shattered the side window and the windscreen. Jack veered across the path and almost lost control before sitting up again and hitting the windscreen hard enough to dislodge some of the glass.

He could hear more shots being fired, but he was already through the gate and flooring the accelerator.

"Christ, that was bad," he swore. He clicked his comms on.

"Alpha One?"

Silence.

"Bravo Two, Bravo Three?," he tried.

"I've six people here," came Carla's voice.

Jesus, only six?

Before Jack could respond, Carla spoke again. "Should I wait, Jack?"

"No! They could be all over us in minutes. Go, go go!"

"Okay Jack. "On my way to the rendezvous, then."

"Good. See you there."

75

The old Toyota Bandeirante pick-up truck sped through the Boa Vista suburbs, with Jack in the back seat, trying to protect Elena from the worst of the vicious bumping and staggering as the suspension failed to offer much protection from the potholed and rutted roads. They had switched vehicles at the agreed meeting point a few miles from the scene of the rescue, and it was now just the three of them again, with Carla at the wheel.

Elena was battered and bruised, but otherwise unharmed, although she had been given a hefty injection of morphine to help with the pain in her face and her left side where she had fallen. It had clearly left her swimming in and out of consciousness, and occasionally she cried out or moaned when they hit the worst of the holes.

"Where are we?" she gasped, after the truck slewed to a crawl and crashed heavily into an enormous pothole.

"It's okay, Elena," Jack reassured her. "Just relax. We'll be there soon, okay?"

She shook her head feebly and winced. "*Aqua,*" she croaked.

Jack held her head up so she could drink from a plastic bottle.

"Be *where* soon?" she said, with a stronger voice.

"The airfield, Elena. We're flying out."

She pushed herself up in her seat and Jack could see her fighting the pain and the meds.

"How?" she finally managed. "No..." she began, but her voice failed her. She licked her lips and tried again. "I mean, who...?"

"Roberto," said Jack, anticipating the rest of her question.

Her eyes opened wider. "What? I thought they must have got him, too – you know, along with us. How–"

"Long story. Don't worry about it,"

"But I want to know. Tell me," she insisted. She pushed herself up more, so that she was almost shoulder to shoulder with Jack.

"He told the Feds everything, by the looks of it. In exchange for an awful lot of money."

"Not Feds," said Elena. "Americans."

"Okay, both then. Anyway, the original escape plan was genuine. The Feds – Americans – whatever – planned to ambush us at the airfield. Roberto apparently just panicked when he thought we were going to use the internet, and he contacted them."

"*Mierda*," Elena said. "His 'errand'."

"Yeah. Well, that's how they found us so quickly at the Lan House."

"Bastard," said Elena. "So how did you figure it out? How did you find me?"

"Elena, stop worrying about it. Save your energy. The important thing is that Roberto set up the flight, and never cancelled it."

"Okay, okay. But how do you know?"

"We had words with him. He told us, and he agreed not to cancel it."

"He agreed..."

"Carla persuaded him. She can be very persuasive, you know."

Elena laughed, but the pain from the movement showed on her face. "Yes, I'm sure she can. Where is she? What happened to her?"

"Still here," Carla called back from the driver's seat.

"Ah. *Que bom*," Elena croaked. "I thought maybe..."

"Oh no – you can't get rid of me that easily," said Carla.

Elena smiled. "Okay, but how did you know where I was? How did you get in? How–"

"Ferreira," Jack interrupted her.

"Who?"

"The police colonel. From the theatre? Carla tracked her down and got her on the phone. Told her everything. Ferreira was the one who found out where you were, flew up here, helped us organise everything. Without her, we'd never have got to you."

"Amazing. I owe her an apology. I thought... Where is she now?"

Jack hesitated, and she looked at him questioningly.

"What?"

"She was there. She went in with us to get you. There was a big explosion after we got you out of the building..." he said.

"Wow. *Loco*..." She was silent for a few moments, her head slowly drooping down to her chest, and then she suddenly snapped back upright. "So who else was involved? Just you guys?"

"No. There were a few others."

"Who?" Her head slumped again, and she muttered something incomprehensible.

"Leave it, Elena," Jack said. "Just rest."

"Huh?" She sat up again. "No! I want to know!" She shook her head slightly and looked at him determinedly. "Besides, we have nothing else to do, do we? Or do you have a travel game we can play?"

There was a laugh from Carla, and Jack sighed.

"Okay, okay," he said. "We had Carla's troops on our side. Her, um, private army."

"Her *what*?"

"It's *not* a private army," Carla retorted. "We just have some members of the movement who are enthusiastic enough to train for, well, any eventualities..."

"Hah! It *is* a private army, then," said Elena, suddenly wide awake. "Like the Nuevo Sendero."

"It is not like the Sendero at all," cried Carla.

"For fuck sake, let's not start an argument right now, please?" said Jack, cutting across a sharp intake of breath from Elena. "The important thing is that we are all okay." He turned to Elena. "Well, apart from you. I'm afraid you seem to have a fractured arm–"

"Oh - *that's* what it is," said Elena.

"Yes. And your mouth's a bit of a mess."

She nodded, and Jack could see her cheek bulge as she explored her wounds with her tongue. "Yes. Sore as hell," Elena agreed. "But it doesn't explain why I can't feel my lips."

"That's probably the morphine."

"Ah."

"It'll wear off soon. Maybe by the time we reach the airstrip."

"We're nearly at the turn-off now," said Carla.

"How long from here?" asked Jack.

"Another thirty kilometres after the junction – but in the dark, on these roads? It could take us an hour."

"Do we *have* another hour?" Elena asked. "Aren't they after us?"

"I don't know. Maybe not. We made a hell of a mess of the place where they were holding you, and there are bound to be a lot of people down..." His voice trailed off.

"Yes. But...? I can feel a 'but' coming." prompted Elena.

"There's something bothering me."

"Hmm?"

"The explosion. It seemed to be something Ferreira set off or that she caused with her flashbangs. Blew the whole of the main building to pieces, and everyone with it."

"Lit up the sky for miles around," said Carla.

"Yes. But when I was leaving, there was this guy that appeared from out of the smoke, calmly levelling a pistol and firing at us."

"Torres?"

"I don't know. I've never seen him before."

"I have, though," said Elena. "Tall, black hair combed back, thinning at the sides – arrogant-looking," she said.

Jack nodded. "Yeah. Seems to fit, but I couldn't swear to it. It was too dark and I was concentrating on getting through the gates. It was just that there was something about him..."

"Like some sort of predator," Elena suggested.

"Yeah, maybe. Something like that. I don't know."

"So?"

"So, I figured he was inside the building when it blew."

"With Ferreira."

"Yeah."

"Both dead, then."

"Yeah. Or both alive, maybe...?"

"A planned explosion?"

"Yeah. But it's a stretch. It would mean he was just waiting for us to turn up. Get us all in one go, right?"

"That's difficult to imagine, Jack," said Carla. "After all, the site was supposed to be secure or secret or something, wasn't it? They couldn't be sure we would find it. Unless..."

"Ferreira," Jack finished the thought for her.

"No. I don't believe it," said Carla. "It doesn't make sense. Besides, she's dead. You said it yourself."

"I *thought* she was dead," said Jack. "But we didn't see a body, did we?"

"And if it *was* a set up, what then?" said Carla.

"Then obviously we could be set up at the airstrip, too, couldn't we?"

"What choice does that leave us with?" said Elena.

"None at all," Carla said. "We've nowhere else to go."

Jack thought for a while.

"We should stop a quarter of a mile before the airstrip and hide the truck. We can walk the rest of the way. At the first sign of anything wrong, we'll take off across country. How far are we from the border, anyway?"

"I was studying the map earlier on," said Carla. "The flight to Lethem is around a hundred and fifty kilometres, but at its nearest point, the border can't be more than fifty kilometres in a straight line east."

"Good. So it should be doable. Elena – do you think you could make it on foot?"

"Are you kidding? To get away from these bastards? No problem!"

The truck lunged to the right as they hit another huge hole in the road, and Elena cried out in pain. Jack held her to him.

"We'll be fine," he announced confidently. "We'll be fine."

76

"**C**ommander," Torres growled. "You have five men dead or injured at the farm facility. The people – the terrorists – who did it, will soon be across the border in Guyana. I know where they're flying from, and where they're flying to. Give me a helicopter and I will stop them."

Lately, Torres was having difficulty controlling his anger and frustration. His poker-faced hardness had been replaced by a dangerously wild look, and he knew that if he did not master his feelings right now, his authority over these stupid people would be lost. The operation at 'the farm', as they called it, had been a disaster. He had no idea where McCrae had rustled up such a large team. It must have been the Carla woman Ferreira had warned him about. Now two of his three CIA operatives, plus a Brazilian intelligence officer and five Federal Police agents were dead or dying. It had almost been a total wipe-out. The attackers had jammed the radio somehow, and all their vehicles had been burnt out at the scene. They'd had to phone through to the barracks for support and a vehicle, and the idiots had kept them waiting for over an hour before a small team turned up. They had stood around, surveying the damage with their mouths open before Torres had managed to get them to take him back to their HQ in Boa Vista. Now he was confronting once again the dogged arrogance and ignorance beloved of those in power in Brazil. He decided to change tack.

"Please Commander. We all have good reason to want these people stopped. This is an international operation and *you* are the only person that can make the call. You are the man." He had to stop himself from raising his eyebrows at his own slime.

The man stood up and ponced around his office for a few seconds, basking in self-importance.

"Very well, sir," he finally announced. "In the interests of international security, I will authorise the use of our helicopter. My men are already assisting with roadblocks on the BR401 and at the borders."

And a fat lot of good may it do you, you prick, thought Torres.

"Thank you Commander. Your cooperation will not be forgotten."

After the Commander had made a call and briefed his second-in-command, Torres and his remaining agent were escorted to a waiting car, and driven the three miles to the small airfield which hosted a helipad and a couple of helicopters. In spite of the advance warning, no one was prepared when they arrived, and there followed delay after delay as paperwork was completed and the helicopter rolled out of its hanger. The pilot arrived looking bleary-eyed and irritated. He made them wait for his own inspection, and then finally they were on board and going through pre-flight checks as the rotors spun up.

When they had their headsets on and adjusted, the pilot talked to his control and they lifted unhurriedly off the concrete runway.

77

Carla brought the truck to a gradual halt, and switched off the lights.

"I think this is as close as we can get without being seen or heard," she said. "According to my map, the airstrip is on the other side of the next road we come to. To reach the gate, we take a left at the next junction, and then it should be around three hundred metres down, on the right hand side."

They descended in darkness relieved only by a pale moon that shone down occasionally when there was a break in the thick cloud cover. Elena rested against the side of the vehicle, breathing deeply and closing her eyes. Carla beckoned to Jack, and opened the passenger door to show him two semi-automatic rifles.

"They're for you. I don't like guns. Sorry," she said.

Jack's hand automatically went to his waistband to check for his pistol, then he collected the rifles and slung them over his shoulder.

"Thanks, Carla. I appreciate it."

"And don't forget that stuff, either," Carla said, waving towards the battered shoulder bag with Roberto's cash in it. "Ferreira's gone, I don't want any of it, and I sure as hell am *not* about to give it back to Roberto."

"Carla, it's a lot of money."

"Take it Jack. Do something good with it."

He still hesitated.

"If you don't, I'll burn it right now," she said warningly.

"Bloody hell. Okay – I'll take it, then. Happy?"

"Happy."

They moved off with Jack in the lead, and Elena close by him.

"Give me a gun, will you? said Elena.

"You're too weak."

"*Que tonteria!* I'm fine now, Jack."

Jack could tell by the sound of her voice she was determined, so he unslung a rifle and passed it to her.

"Too weak. *Huevada*," she guffawed.

Jack laughed. "Yeah – you're definitely feeling better, aren't you," he said.

When they reached the next road, the airstrip was laid out beautifully, dead in front of them. There was a low hedge, and then a long straight run of cut grass extending into the distance to their left. There was a large barn half way down, which Jack imagined acted as a hangar for the aircraft. After struggling through the hedge and onto the grass strip, he headed right, quickly covering the distance to the end of the runway, then they crossed the strip and they made their way slowly towards the barn along the opposite side. There was neither sight nor sound of any activity as they made their way down, until eventually they were right opposite the barn and could clearly see an aircraft sitting in the doorway. After waiting and watching carefully for five minutes, Jack was convinced there was no trap awaiting them.

"Okay. Let's go," he said, and they emerged from hiding to walk across the field.

"*Quem é?*" came a worried-sounding voice from the shadows, as they approached the barn.

"Fábio?" Carla called out, as they came to a stop.

"*Sim sim. Quem é?*"

"*Os amigos do Roberto.*"

"*Ah. Finalmente. Vamos, vamos!*" The man emerged from the shadows of the barn, and without paying them any more attention, started removing chocks from the aircraft wheels, and opening the tiny aircraft doors.

They walked to the doors, but the pilot suddenly stopped them, waving his hands. "*Armas, não!*" he said. No weapons!

He spoke hurriedly in Portuguese, and Jack could not follow what he said.

"He says the guns are too heavy and there is no room for them," Carla translated. "And he is too scared to risk being caught with guns."

"Okay, well, we're almost there, I suppose..." said Jack uncertainly, collecting the rifle from Elena and walking over to hedge by the barn.

He hid them in the undergrowth and returned.

"All done," he said.

"OK. *Vamos*," the pilot said, and beckoned them forward towards the door.

Jack felt Carla hanging back, and turned to her.

"I've done everything I can," said Carla. "It's up to you two, now."

"What?" Elena cried, as she realised what was happening. She turned to Carla. "No! You can't stay here. These bastards will come after you. You must come with us."

Carla shook her head. "No, Elena. It's you two they want. Once you've gone, I'll be fine."

Elena stepped closer. "Carla, I..." Her voiced trailed off, and she simply extended her good arm.

"I know, Elena. Me too." She smiled, and they carefully embraced. "Me too."

Jack gave them an exasperated look. "What the hell does that even *mean*?"

The pilot hovered at their side. "*Vamos, gente. Precisamos ir.*"

Carla laughed. "Never mind, Jack. It doesn't matter."

"*Agora!*" the pilot whined.

"Carla, thanks," Jack said. "For everything." He extended his hand, and Carla dodged it, giving him a hug and kissing him on both cheeks.

"No problem, Jack. I'll be watching the news. Nail the bastards."

The pilot raised his arms in the air. "*Pelo amor de Deus, vamanos!*"

"Okay. *Vá!*" Carla cried in irritation, and stepped away from the plane.

Two minutes later Jack and Elena were wedged into the rear seats and the engine whined, coughed, caught, and roared.

Carla was quickly lost to view as the plane bounced along the grass field, turned, and came to rest. The pilot quickly made some checks, the engine roared again, and then suddenly the brakes were released and they surged quickly forward. A few seconds later, they bounced into the air, the engine straining and everything rattling and vibrating like the whole aircraft was coming apart. Jack felt himself being alternately pressed down into his seat and then left with his stomach in the air as the plane bucked and skidded up through the clouds. They started to bank, and at the same time they broke through the clouds and Jack found himself staring out of the side window at a fairy-tale scene of fluffy cloud-tops suffused with diaphanous moonlight.

He turned to Elena, who was staring down through her own window. She noticed his movement and turned towards him.

"How are you feeling?" he had to raise his voice to compete with the engine noise.

"Not too bad. Still a little, you know, *tonto*."

"A little what?" he almost shouted.

"*Tonto*," she shouted back, making circular movements near her head with her finger.

The pilot turned to them and lifted a pair of headphones up, waggling them in his hand.

Jack found the passenger headsets and they both put them on. After a few clicks and false starts, everyone was connected. The pilot started talking in Portuguese and Elena translated for Jack.

"He says it's just under 160 kilometres, and we should be there in forty-five minutes," she said.

After turning, the plane levelled out and the noise and vibration eased as they reached their cruising altitude and speed. The worst of the cloud beneath them gradually cleared, and they sat in companionable silence, watching what they could see of the ghostly landscape pass below them.

Jack was not sure how he felt. They were still in Brazil, perhaps, but they would soon cross the border, and he would be a whole lot happier then.

78

As the pilot pushed the cyclic forward and the helicopter began to pick up speed, he spoke to Torres over the intercom. "Spotting a light aircraft in the moonlight is not going to be easy," he complained.

"You have radar," Torres grunted, matter-of-factly.

There was a patronising sigh from the pilot. "Not on the helicopter, we don't." A pause. "Sir," he added flatly. "All we have is basic air surveillance radar at our base. If they're flying high enough and fast enough, the radar might just pick them up, and our controller can then try to vector us in."

Torres muttered something under his breath.

"Do you know what type of aircraft it is, sir?" the pilot asked.

"No. No idea. But it's used for border hopping, so it's going to be small and slow."

"Hmm. Probably. But you'd be surprised, sir, at how sophisticated these people can be."

"My friend, I've been in this business a long time. It takes a lot to surprise me." Torres' harsh voice stopped any further chit-chat, and the pilot contented himself with reading back in clipped tones the probable departure point of the target aircraft, its estimated time of departure and its destination, all of which Torres had given him before they got airborne.

They crossed the Rio Branco heading northwest, and flew for another ten minutes, with the pilot occasionally talking to his controller, before his voice became slightly louder and more excited.

"We have a likely contact, sir," he confirmed to Torres. The tension and excitement in his voice came through clearly. "And I have a course to intercept." The helicopter banked very slightly and nosed down to put on more speed.

Torres nodded. "Time to intercept?"

"Approximately seven minutes, based on current airspeeds and courses. But he could slow down, or change direction, or even–"

"Good." Torres cut him off firmly, taking out his pistol. After his subordinate followed suit, Torres pulled the lever to release his sliding door.

The sudden wind noise and turbulent air inside the aircraft startled the pilot, and a split second of nervous input on the stick caused the helicopter to rock slightly. He looked over his shoulder, and stared in horror as Torres slid off his seat and sat on the floor, facing out, with his feet dangling outside. He saw the other agent doing the same. "Sir…," he began, the alarm in his voice clear.

"What is it?" snapped Torres. "If you have a problem with any of this, check with your commander, but for fuck sake don't bother me with it now. Just get us close enough to nail the bastards."

"Sir," came the brisk response. When the channel abruptly clicked off, Torres guessed the man was radioing his base. Trust them to give him a pilot with no balls. He contented himself with working out a way to secure himself with the seatbelt straps, and concentrated on the happy fact that they were still heading in the same direction and at the same speed. Maybe the guy had some balls after all.

The channel clicked on again. "It's authorised, sir," came the pilot's tense voice, "but I have to make clear that in the event–"

"Sure. Yes. Whatever." Torres cut in. "You're the boss. Now can we please go get the fuckers?"

79

"*Estamos em Brasil ainda?*" Jack asked, in his best Portuguese. He leaned towards the pilot from the cramped rear space.

"Yes, we are still in Brazil," said the pilot.

"What?" cried Jack. "I thought you didn't speak English."

"With my job, it would be strange if I did not."

Jack smiled and shook his head, and as he did so, he thought he saw a light or some sort of reflection off to their left. "What's that over there?" he asked abruptly. "A green light – there, to the left."

The pilot looked over his shoulder several times before answering. "Another aircraft. Converging with us or on the same course as us. No – converging." He suddenly leaned over and flicked a switch. "Better without lights."

"And how often do you meet other planes around here?" Jack asked.

"At this height, at this time, near Boa Vista? You make a joke, right?"

"Shit."

"That light's definitely getting closer," said Elena, with an edge to her voice.

"Right," the pilot said with an exaggerated calmness. "I'm going to do a slow three-sixty degree turn. We see what they do, okay?"

Jack felt it in his stomach as they started banking to the right.

"I've lost it behind us. Can anyone see it?" the pilot asked. No-one replied, and after a few seconds he continued. "Okay, we're coming round through one-eighty degrees now. If the other aircraft didn't alter course we should see him somewhere on our ri–"

"I see it!" Jack said. "To our right; slightly behind us. Green light and red light."

"Are you sure?" the pilot cried. "Green *and* red? No white?"

"Certain."

"Then he's heading straight at us. Hold on!"

The engine roared. The aircraft pulled up and started banking sharply left.

Jack tried to keep track of the other aircraft's lights, but they quickly disappeared below them. Then Elena called out. "Here! It's on this side now. I can see the lights. Now I can see the aircraft! It's a helicopter! It's really close now.

There was a soft thud on the fuselage. Another. A hole appeared in the ceiling and one of the small panes of plexiglass behind Elena's head cracked.

"He's firing at us!" cried the pilot, immediately starting to throw the aircraft about. He was banking alternately right and left, allowing the craft to descend and then applying power and bringing her up again. All the time his eyes were glued to the instruments.

"Can you see anything?" he said, breathing heavily.

"Nothing," said Elena.

"Nothing."

"We may have lost him. I'm going to descend further, but I'll be twisting about a bit. Sorry."

"Twist as much as you like," said Elena.

Suddenly a blinding light played across the cockpit window and they heard more thuds and dull pings. A bullet cracked the pilot's side window and buried itself in the control panel. Circuits could be heard shorting, and the tiny cabin was filled with the smell of burning plastic. Some of the instruments went completely dead. The pilot banked the plane away again and they heard more thuds, a little more remote – along the wing, perhaps.

"How far to the airfield?" asked Jack.

"I don't know now. Difficult to say precisely where we are after those manoeuvres. I need reference points or some stability. I think we're still approximately on course; certainly heading towards Guyana. That's all I can tell you."

He jinked the plane round again, and then his voice could be heard trying to contact their destination.

"Mayday, mayday, mayday. Lethem, this is Golf Mike November Sierra Romeo, a Cessna Skyhawk. We are being fired on by a helicopter. Repeat – we are under attack by a helicopter. We have lost some instruments. I intend to bring the aircraft in to Lethem if possible. We are at—"

A whole series of thuds ripped across the top of the aircraft. There was a strange explosive cracking noise from the engine, the engine note went up, and the whole aircraft started vibrating violently.

"Holy shit," the pilot cursed as he reached over and abruptly cut the engine.

"What are you doing?" cried Jack.

"Propeller strike. If I don't cut the engine, it will shake us to pieces in seconds."

The noise of the engine was replaced with a thousand rattles and whistles, and the noise of the wind squealing through the broken windshield. The pilot grappled with the controls and continued his mayday calls, and then they heard the helicopter approaching again. The searchlight appeared, and this time they could actually hear the sound of the gunshots being fired before the thuds hit them.

The pilot suddenly ripped off his headset and shouted to them. "Comms are out. I'm going to try to get us down, okay?"

Jack nodded.

"Make sure your belts are tight. I'll try to find somewhere safe to land."

Jack stared out at the moonlit landscape below. Where the hell were they, anyway? He heard another volley of shots; another series of thuds. The pilot groaned, and Jack looked over.

"It's okay," the pilot said, with an awkward smile on his face. "I'm okay. We'll get down – don't worry."

The plane's glide was reasonably shallow, but within less than a minute Jack could clearly see the trees they were descending towards.

"Come on," he heard the pilot say. "Fly, *meu amor* – fly."

Elena touched Jack on his shoulder. He looked round and saw that she was giving him the thumbs up. He nodded and smiled, and as he turned back, he saw the trees passing. There was a sound of something connecting with the underneath of the plane, then more shots; more thuds, and the plane bounced heavily onto the ground. It leapt into the air again, and Jack saw the pilot fighting with the controls. It descended, bounced once, bounced twice, slewed to the right, and then collapsed into the ground. It pitched forward, all the weight on the nose and left wing. Finally, the wing broke and the plane settled, coming to rest half on its side.

Flames started emerging from somewhere up front, and Jack fumbled with his harness, finally releasing it. He fell sideways onto Elena, and when she did not move or say anything, he realised she was unconscious. The pilot had already released his belt, but could not open his door, which was digging into the ground. He seemed unable to reach up to the other side door. Jack stood up carefully and by reaching over, he was able to release the mechanism that allowed the front passenger seat to slide forward. Standing on the inside edge of the pilot's seat, he finally managed to climb out. He then reached down through the door frame and helped the pilot up and out. Motioning the pilot to stay where he was, he then dropped back into the aircraft to get Elena.

With a sudden flare, the fire from the engine compartment started coming through from under the instrument panel, and the cabin started to fill with acrid smoke full of hot black plastic debris. Every breath suddenly prompted a fit of coughing, and he struggled to release Elena's belt and get her up to the door. She started to come round, and as Jack struggled, the pilot came back to help them. Between the two of them, they got her up and out, but they had to stop to cough and retch beside the aircraft. The pilot clutched at his side. Jack thought he could see blood spreading across his torso. Elena was on her knees coughing. A bright light passed over the top of them and Jack vaguely registered the sound of the helicopter landing close by. He looked around wildly for some sort of cover away from the burning plane, and then he lent his hand to Elena and helped her get to her feet.

"Go on!" he cried. "Get away from here!" He pointed to a small copse of trees twenty yards away.

As they moved off, Jack held his breath and leaned back into the plane again, emerging a few seconds later with the shoulder bag and his pistol. He ran after Elena and the pilot, catching them up easily, and they all dived to the ground behind a fallen tree. The pilot let out a strangled cry and sat clutching his side, while Elena lay on her back with her eyes closed, breathing shallowly.

Jack knelt down, and took a deep breath. He dropped the bag next to Elena, and checked his gun. As he slid the safety off, he saw the pilot looking at him with a strange expression.

"Sorry mate," he said, and shrugged. The pilot nodded and smiled at him, before groaning and closing his eyes in pain.

"I'll be back in a minute," said Jack with a lightness he did not feel. He turned back to the burning plane and the helicopter beyond. He could see the silhouettes of two men, one of whom he recognised as the tall man from the farm in Boa Vista. A cold fury gripped him, and he began skirting round the plane towards them. He watched the two men approach the wreck, exposing themselves to sight, and blinded by the light from the flames. They were either supremely confident or plain stupid. One of them raised his gun and fired several shots into the cockpit, which was now completely engulfed in smoke.

Stupid, Jack decided, calmly raising his pistol and aiming. Just as he pulled the trigger, one of the men spun round as if he had seen Jack, and dropped to the ground. Jack fired, and the second man staggered and collapsed to the ground. Without waiting, Jack moved swiftly onward, along an arc he had calculated would eventually take him to the helicopter. The other man could not be seen now. That was bad.

In less than a minute, Jack was within ten yards of the helicopter. The blades were still spinning and the pilot was peering anxiously out at the burning plane. There was still no sign of the tall man – the man that must surely be Torres. Jack was formulating a plan to flush the guy out when he heard a slight click off to his right. He spun round just in time to see a gun flash and feel a mule-kick to his right shoulder. The impact made him stagger, and he fell heavily to one knee. The gun had fallen from his hand and he knew he had only a second to locate it. He turned to search for it and felt something cold against the side of his head.

"Mr McCrae," Torres voice was almost dripping with venom. "Jack, isn't it? So nice to meet you, Jack. Your death is long overdue, you know. Long over–"

He broke off as the whole area was suddenly flooded with light. The headlights of several vehicles appeared and raced towards them. Jack pivoted on his knee and chopped Torres' legs from under him. Then he rolled away, ending up on his back. He tried to rise, but his right arm failed him and he fell back again awkwardly. By the time he had pushed himself up with his good arm and struggled to his feet, Torres had vanished. He looked back towards Elena and the pilot and saw someone moving in their direction. It must be Torres. He must have somehow seen where Jack had come from.

No!

Jack looked around for his gun, but it remained stubbornly hidden somewhere in the grass. There was no time. He had to move. He tried to run, but felt his legs heavy. He forced himself on, feeling his heart pounding as he staggered towards Elena's position. He was vaguely aware of powerful lights playing across the field and the noise of people shouting. His face burned with the heat from the fire as he passed dangerously close to it. Someone behind him was yelling something, but he ignored it. He could not allow Torres to get near Elena.

Not this time, you scum.

Then he saw him. Torres. Standing over the two figures lying defenceless on the grass. He was raising his gun. Jack gritted his teeth; felt his whole body tense and pulsing with anger. With a guttural howl he threw himself at Torres and brought him down. Torres fired so close to Jack's face that the sound deafened him and he caught the sharp smell of the bullet's propellant. Jack levered himself up. Torres lay still on the ground, and Jack looked at Elena and the pilot. The pilot had come round with the sound of the shot, and was getting slowly to his knees. Elena was still lying on her back, just as he had left her. As Jack bent down to look at her, the world seemed to grow darker around him. His head was swimming and he felt cold. He tried to fight it. He saw movement to one side – the pilot, staring at something behind Jack, a look of horror on his face. Torres! Jack tried to turn, heard someone shouting; challenging. He dropped to his knees close to Elena as a shot sang out from somewhere, and then he fell forward, his face buried in the grass a few inches from Elena's head.

He lay still for a moment, trying to decide whether he was dead or alive. In the background he heard the helicopter start to spin up again, then falter.

Still alive. Got to get up.

With a supreme effort, he stood up, swaying on his feet but otherwise quite unable to move. Someone behind him shouted a challenge.

"Stop or I'll shoot!"

Jack was so taken aback by the incongruously broad Scottish accent, that he froze more out of curiosity than fear.

"Show me your hands," the man continued.

Jack raised his left arm away from his body, but the right arm refused to do anything, and hung uselessly at his side. The pain was intense, but he could feel the blood drying on his skin. He would survive.

"You're kidding, right?" he whispered hoarsely, as the man came close, patted him down, and turned him around. He had a major's crown on his uniform, a granite-chiselled face, and Jack just knew his hair would be red. He peered into Jack's face.

"Are you McCrae?" he asked. "Jack McCrae?"

Jack nodded. "I am."

"Welcome to Guyana, Jack."

Jack's eyes took in the crumpled body of Torres lying lifeless on the ground behind the major. He tried to smile. "Thank you. Um, who the hell are you, exactly?"

"Aye, well, so...we're here on a joint mission with our Guyanese partners, that's all."

"But how–" Jack winced suddenly as something in his shoulder moved or twitched. He felt a new wave of light-headedness, and stumbled forward.

"Come on," said the Major, propping him up. "Let's get you seen to."

Jack shook his head. "No. These two... my people... wounded." His body felt so heavy. He tried to raise his left hand, but the effort was too much. He felt his knees buckle. Everything was coming at him from a crazy angle, and darkness was returning.

"Okay. Don't you worry yourself," the Major soothed. "We'll soon see to them." He called out in a voice loud enough to wake the dead. "Medic!"

More soldiers arrived. Jack realised he was kneeling on the ground again. Pitching forward. They were turning him, tearing his clothes. He recovered his vision. Felt better. He tried to get up and felt hands restraining him.

"Sorry laddie – you're not going anywhere," a voice boomed from beside him.

"Okay, okay," Jack said, feeling dizzy again. His eyes were closing. He forced them open again and saw the Major standing over him and someone fixing up a drip. "Just tell me..." He couldn't focus now, and had to close his eyes. "How the fu– how'd you know...?" he managed.

Sounds were fading, and his tongue felt strangely thick in his mouth. Someone was filling his head with expanding foam, and thoughts came slowly.

"A ruddy insistent journalist, that's how." The Major's trilled initial 'r' tunnelled its way through to him. "Turned up on ma' ruddy doorstep demanding to be heard. Wouldn't go away, cheeky bugger. Persuaded us you needed help. I wouldn't have believed a word of it, except we were at the airfield when your mayday came in, so we tracked you here. Simple."

"Simple," Jack mumbled, his mind spinning back over the past two months. "All so simple..."

80

He had reacted badly, and he regretted taking his anger out on Simon, but he could still feel those moments of burning frustration and resentment as he had recognised the truth of Simon's assessment. He was re-reading Simon's original article now, and even Jack could see that it was classy stuff. All the relevant details were there, with maps, photos, satellite images, data, quotes, the lot. The tone was measured, authoritative, challenging. It had rocked the world for one marvellous, hope-filled, brief weekend, but the story had already lost its way in a wasteland of lies, denials, misinformation, and a timely headline story that a bomb had been found on Air-force One. Simon dismissed the bomb story as complete nonsense, but was unable to give Jack anything else.

"You've got to be kidding me, right?" Jack had blurted out when Simon gave him the latest news.

Simon spread his arms in a gesture of hopelessness. "Sorry, Jack."

"Salinas?"

"Desalination plant."

"The ships?"

"One arrived, but with no cargo."

"Torres? The Manager?"

"Dead, missing, denied."

"The dams, then – the pumping stations – the *fucking big holes through the Andes!*"

"All on sovereign Peruvian territory," said Simon. "All legitimate infrastructure projects aimed at limited irrigation on the eastern slopes of the Andes." He sighed. "Look, the article has been well received–"

"Oh sure – and I hope it makes you all a fortune," snapped Jack.

"– and has also created a lot of international interest," Simon continued, ignoring the sarcasm. "Everyone is asking questions: NATO, the Russians, the Chinese. Brazil is ablaze with it–"

"So?" Jack cut in.

"So, the bastards have been stopped in their tracks. Permanently. People will be sniffing around this for years. American imperialism, Latin American rivalry, Russian and Chinese interests, not to mention kicking off the whole 'water wars' debate again. You won't be able scratch your arse in the Andes without a spy plane or satellite taking a photograph of it. You've won, Jack. They're screwed."

"Maybe. But they're all still out there – all the people who planned it, and all the people who took part in it. Life just goes on as normal for them, right?" Jack snorted in disgust. "The bastards are all probably still coining it in from the drugs running. What's happened about that?"

"In the U.S.? Not a lot, really. They're all still patting themselves on the back over the big bust in Tabatinga."

"Yeah. And that was a setup if ever there was one."

Simon shrugged. "No evidence."

"And the Peruvians – the Brazilians – what about the army base that Carla suspected?"

"Again, sovereign territory. The Peruvians and the Brazilians have clammed up."

"So the plot of the century – the millennium, probably – is uncovered at the eleventh hour by sheer dumb luck, and everyone just goes on as if nothing ever happened. What was the headline this morning - The World Remembers Princess Diana? Jesus, it doesn't say much for you lot, does it?"

Simon had been right to walk calmly away at the point, leaving Jack to fume on his own for a while before Elena came to his rescue with scampi and chips, a bottle of wine, a black dress and a mischievous grin. That night they booked a flight, and ran away to Ireland the next day.

Now, nearly three weeks later, Jack was seated in a comfortable old armchair in the lounge of their comfortable old seafront hotel in Donegal. It was sunny outside but blowing a gale, and he was staring out at the steely, white-topped waves of the North Atlantic rushing towards the unseen stony beach far below them. The wind shrieked at the edges of the bay window, and he could hear the rattle of cables along the side of the building. He turned his head to look at Elena, curled up on another chair, doing battle with an English-language edition of her favourite Vargas Llosa novel. She was wearing a white Aran sweater two sizes too big for her, she still had a support for her fractured arm, her black hair was tousled, and she had no make-up on. Jack smiled. She still managed to look like a diminutive super-model. He was still smiling when she suddenly closed her book and threw it at him.

"*Qué pasa,* Jack McCrae?" she cried. "Haven't you ever seen a woman reading a book?"

Jack laughed aloud as she jumped from her chair and sprang at him.

"Watch my bad arm," he chided her.

"'Watch my bad arm'," she mocked, as she shifted her position and sat in his lap with her legs over the side of the chair. "What about *my* bad arm?"

They sat in silence for a few moments, looking out the window.

"What were you thinking about?" Elena finally asked.

"You," said Jack, stroking her hair.

"No – I mean before."

"Oh. I was thinking about Simon. Trying to figure out why he wants to see me in person so urgently."

"Yes. It's strange," she sighed.

"Well, whatever the reason, it will be good to see him. I've been feeling bad about our last conversation."

"Good," said a voice behind them. "So you should!"

It startled them, and they both shot out of the chair, looking sheepish.

"Simon!" Elena beamed at him and ran over to give him a hug.

"Hi Simon," said Jack. He walked round the chair and extended his hand.

They shook hands firmly and Simon smiled.

"You're looking better now, Jack," he said.

"Thanks," said Jack. He hesitated. "Look, er, about–"

Simon held his hand up. "Don't worry about it," he said. "I'd feel the same way."

They were the only occupants of the lounge, and Jack was fairly certain they were the only guests in the hotel. They ordered coffee and sat down around a heavy oak dining table that looked like it might have been there long before the hotel was built. The waiter was back within a few short minutes to place their order on the table, and they watched him in silence. Dust specks swirled busily in the sunlight as the man retired, but the only sound was the moan of the wind and the grandfather clock's solemn counting of the passing seconds. The clouds that had been gathering out to sea, rolled in, and the room darkened.

"So," said Jack, breaking the spell. "Come on Simon – don't keep us in suspense. What have you rushed all the way from London in – Jack looked at his watch – six hours for?"

"Six hours of extreme discomfort, demanding at least a decent whisky once I've delivered my message."

"Message?"

"Yes. Well, messages plural, actually." He paused as the wind gusted again, whistling around the building and throwing the first few drops of rain against the big bay windows. "The newspaper received two identical emails late last night – identical apart from the fact that one was marked for Elena's attention, and one for yours, Jack. They were passed to me when I arrived this morning. I brought them straight here." He reached into an inside pocket and withdrew two pieces of paper, unfolding them and passing one to Jack and one to Elena.

Jack stared at his for a few seconds, and then turned it slightly so that Elena could see it. She looked at it, and held her own message up. They both said the same thing: É SUA RODADA.

A squall of rain hissed deafeningly around the windows before a sudden contrary gust sucked the noise away and pulled at the old building, threatening to tear everything out to sea.

"Carla," Jack and Elena said together.

Visit the Keir Farrell site

If you enjoyed the book, visit www.keirfarrell.com, where you can view other titles and register to receive an email when the next book is published.

Already published

On the Amazon - Diary of an Irish Emigrant
1: The Lean Years

It's Not My Canoe, Amigo

Work In Progress

A Run For Your Money

In the Planning

On the Amazon - Diary of an Irish Emigrant
2: The Mean Years

White Gloves

From the website, you can also view photos of some of the scenes and events in the On the Amazon books in the 'images' section.

Thanks for reading!

www.keirfarrell.com

About the Author

Keir Farrell was an accountant in his previous life in Ireland and England. He moved to the Brazilian Amazon in 2007, where he spends his time teaching, translating, writing, and showing people the wonders of the Amazon while trying to avoid an untimely death.

If he can sell enough books, he may someday make it back to civilisation with his wife and son.

Contact: via the website at keirfarrell.com
By email: *keir@keirfarrell.com*

www.ingramcontent.com/pod-product-compliance
Lightning Source LLC
Chambersburg PA
CBHW060340260626
47160CB00006B/2146